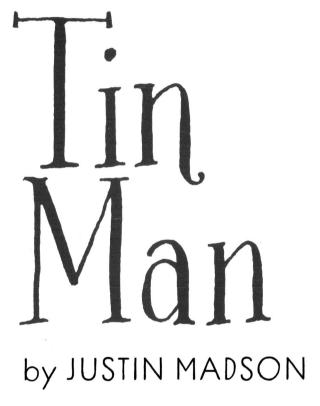

Tin Man

by JUSTIN MADSON

AMULET BOOKS · NEW YORK

CHAPTER 1: Finders Keepers

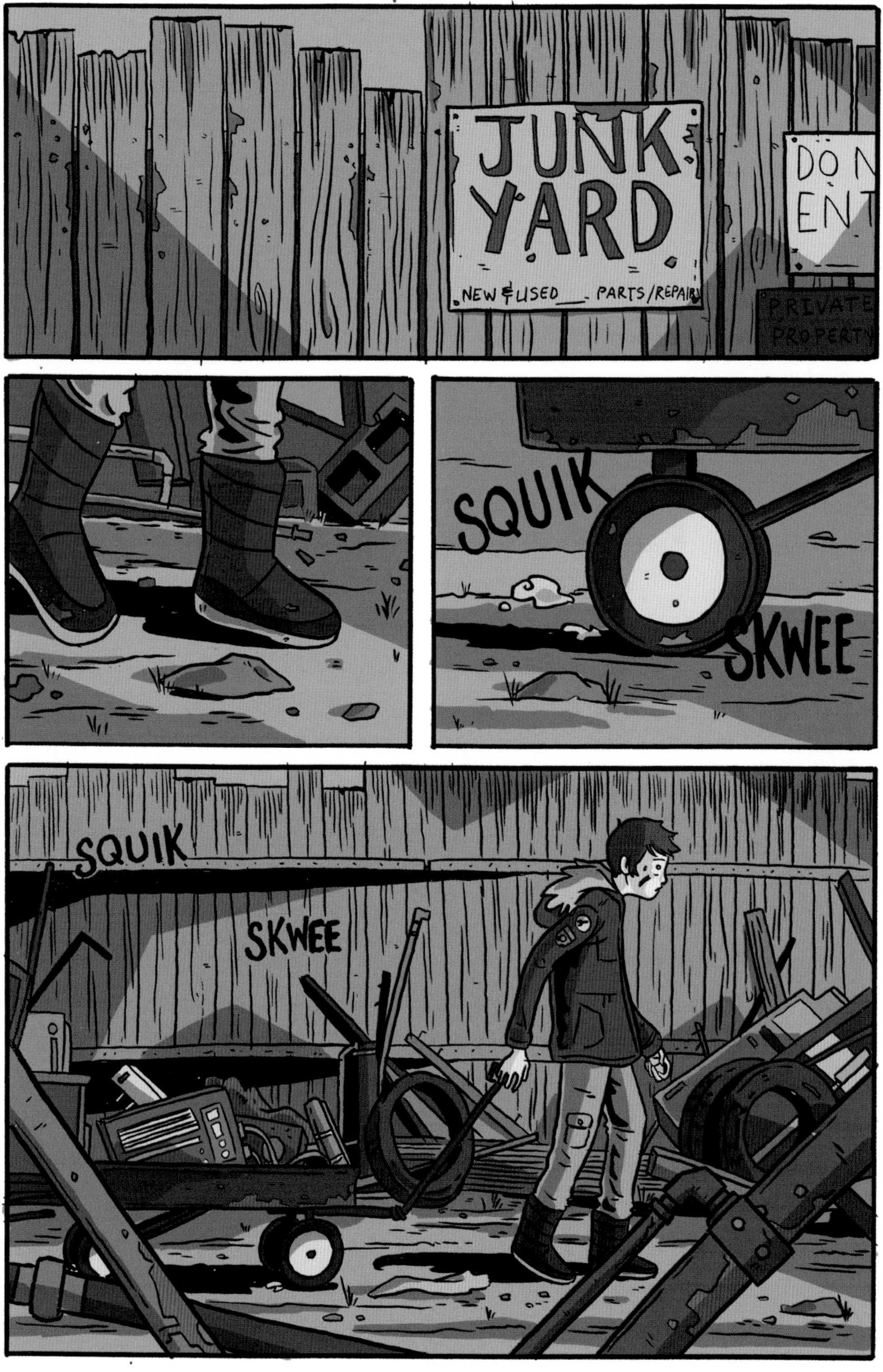
JUNK YARD
NEW & USED PARTS/REPAIR
DO N
ENT
PRIVATE PROPERTY
SQUIK
SKWEE
SQUIK
SKWEE

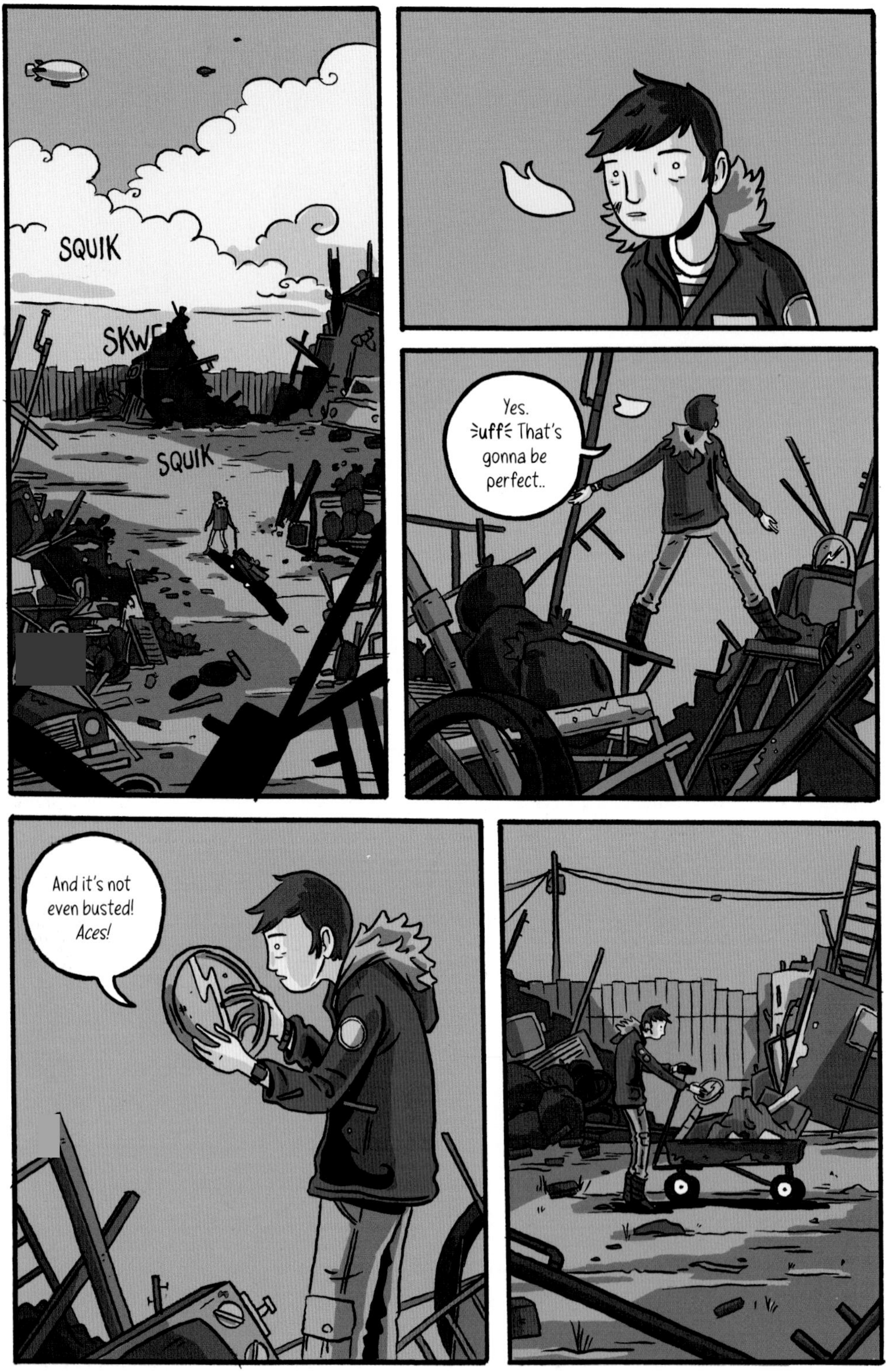
SQUIK
SKWE
SQUIK
Yes. ≶uff≷ That's gonna be perfect..
And it's not even busted! *Aces!*

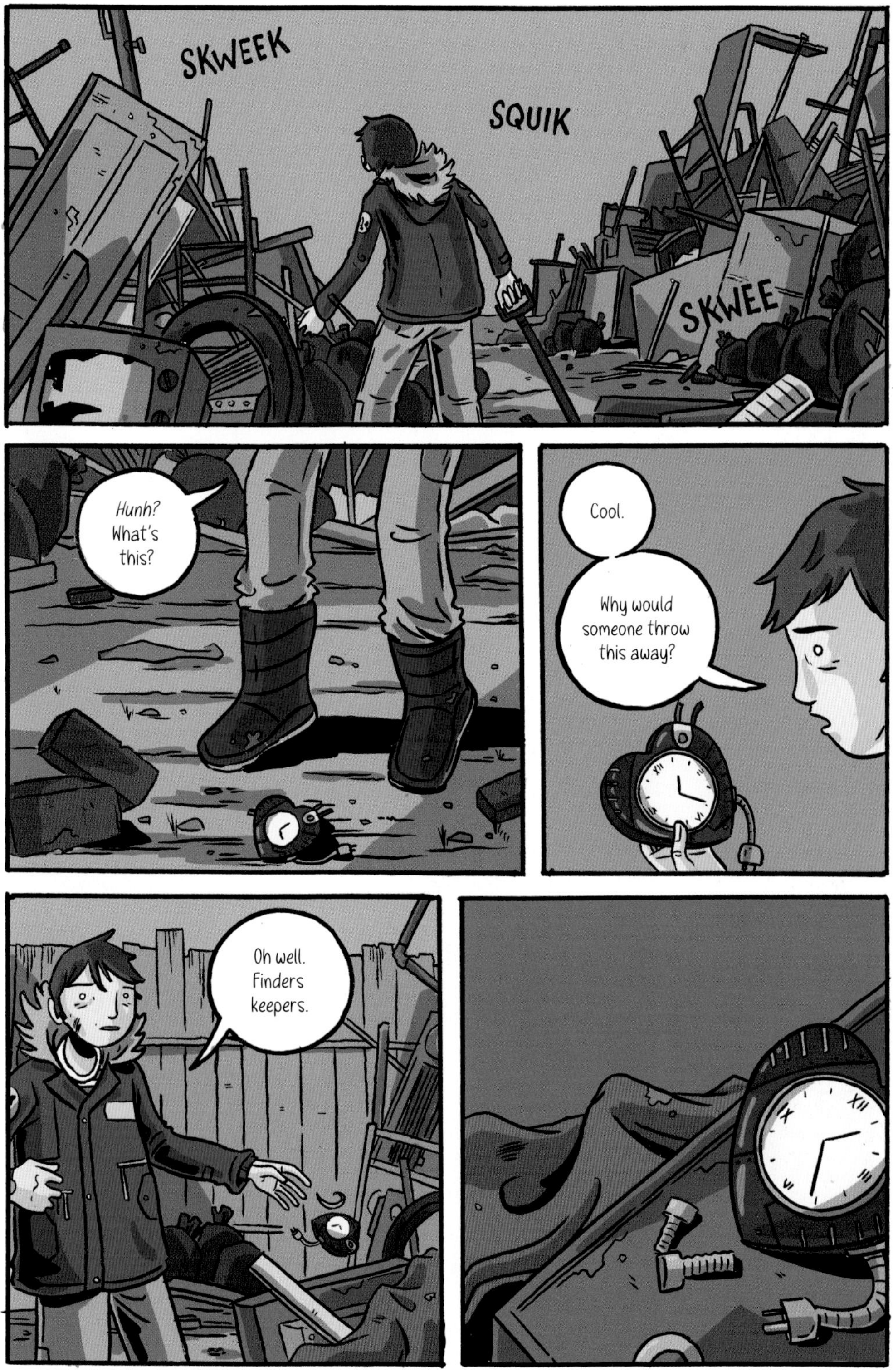
SKWEEK
SQUIK
SKWEE
Hunh? What's this?
Cool.
Why would someone throw this away?
Oh well. Finders keepers.

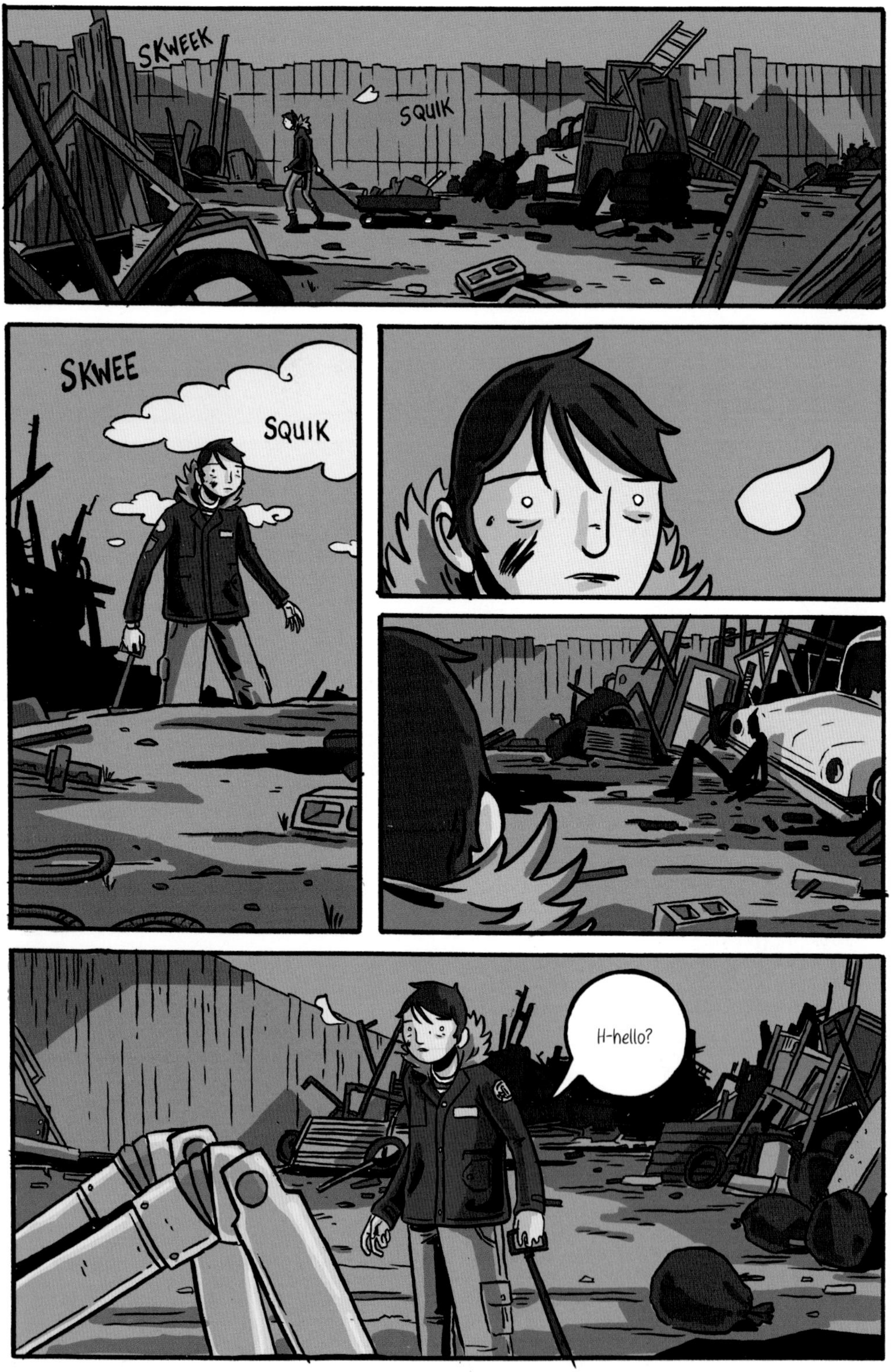
SKWEEK
SQUIK
SKWEE
SQUIK
H-hello?

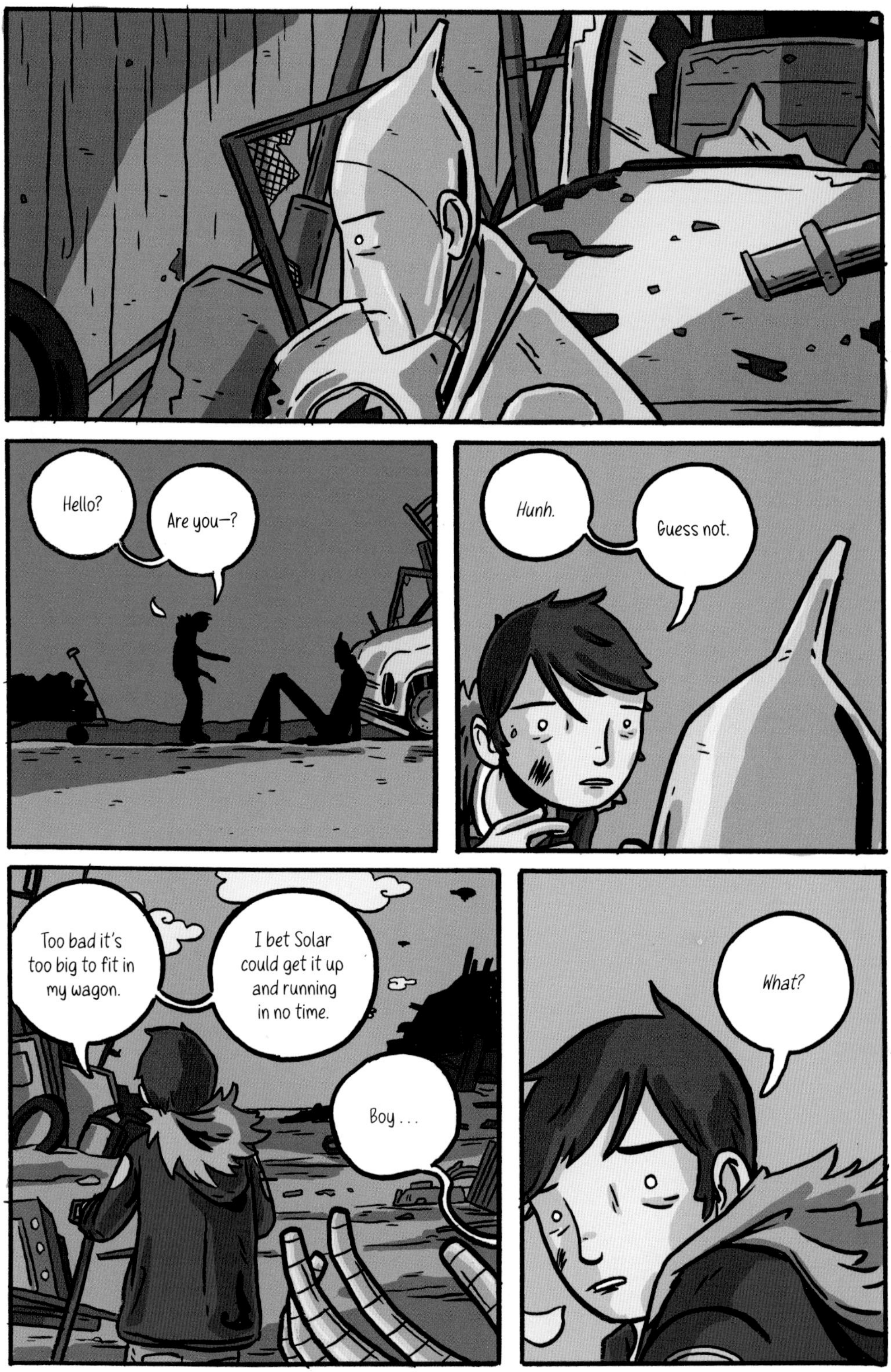
Hello?
Are you—?
Hunh.
Guess not.
Too bad it's too big to fit in my wagon.
I bet Solar could get it up and running in no time.
Boy . . .
What?

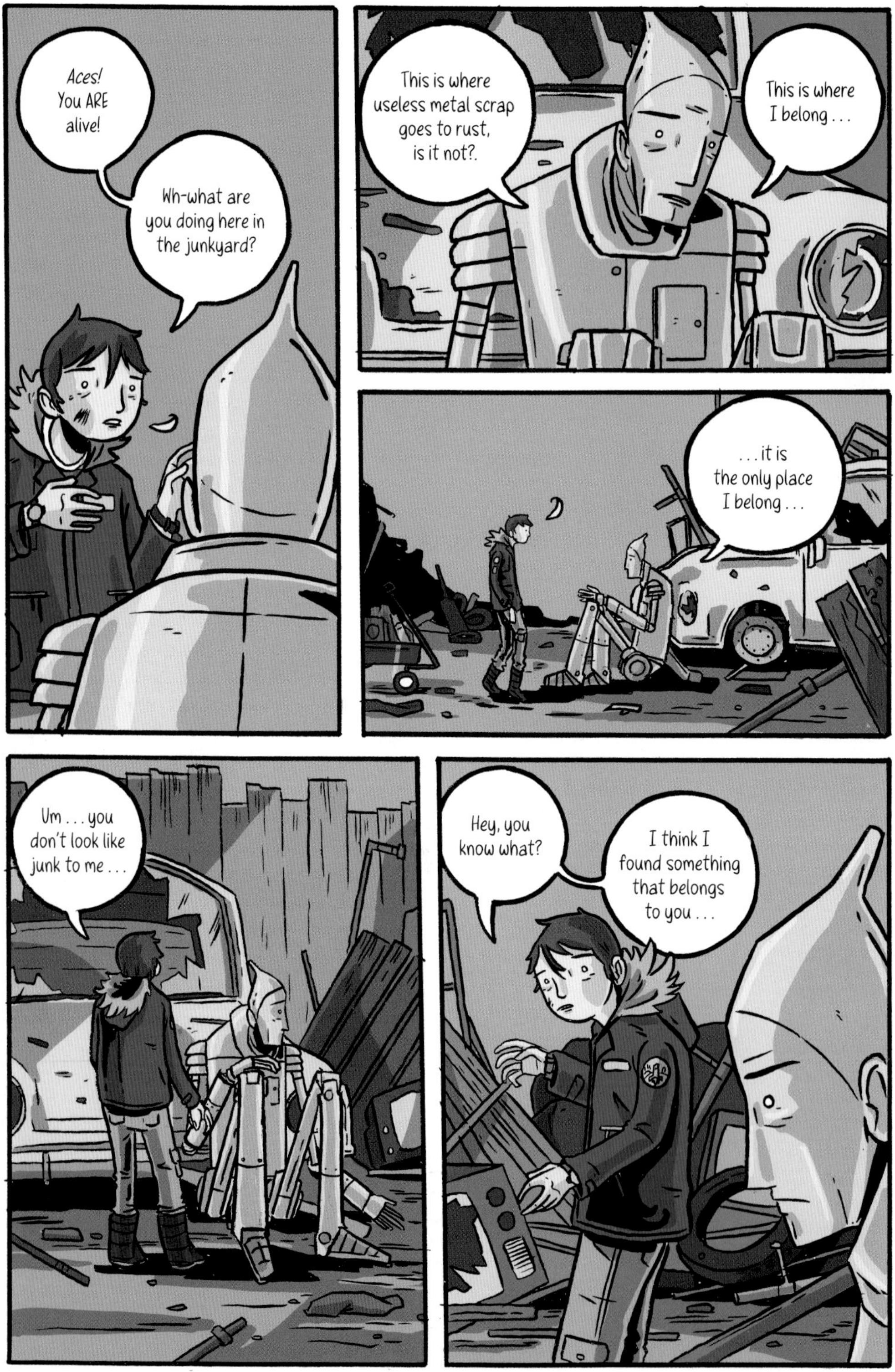
Aces! You ARE alive!
Wh-what are you doing here in the junkyard?
This is where useless metal scrap goes to rust, is it not?.
This is where I belong . . .
. . . it is the only place I belong . . .
Um . . . you don't look like junk to me . . .
Hey, you know what?
I think I found something that belongs to you . . .

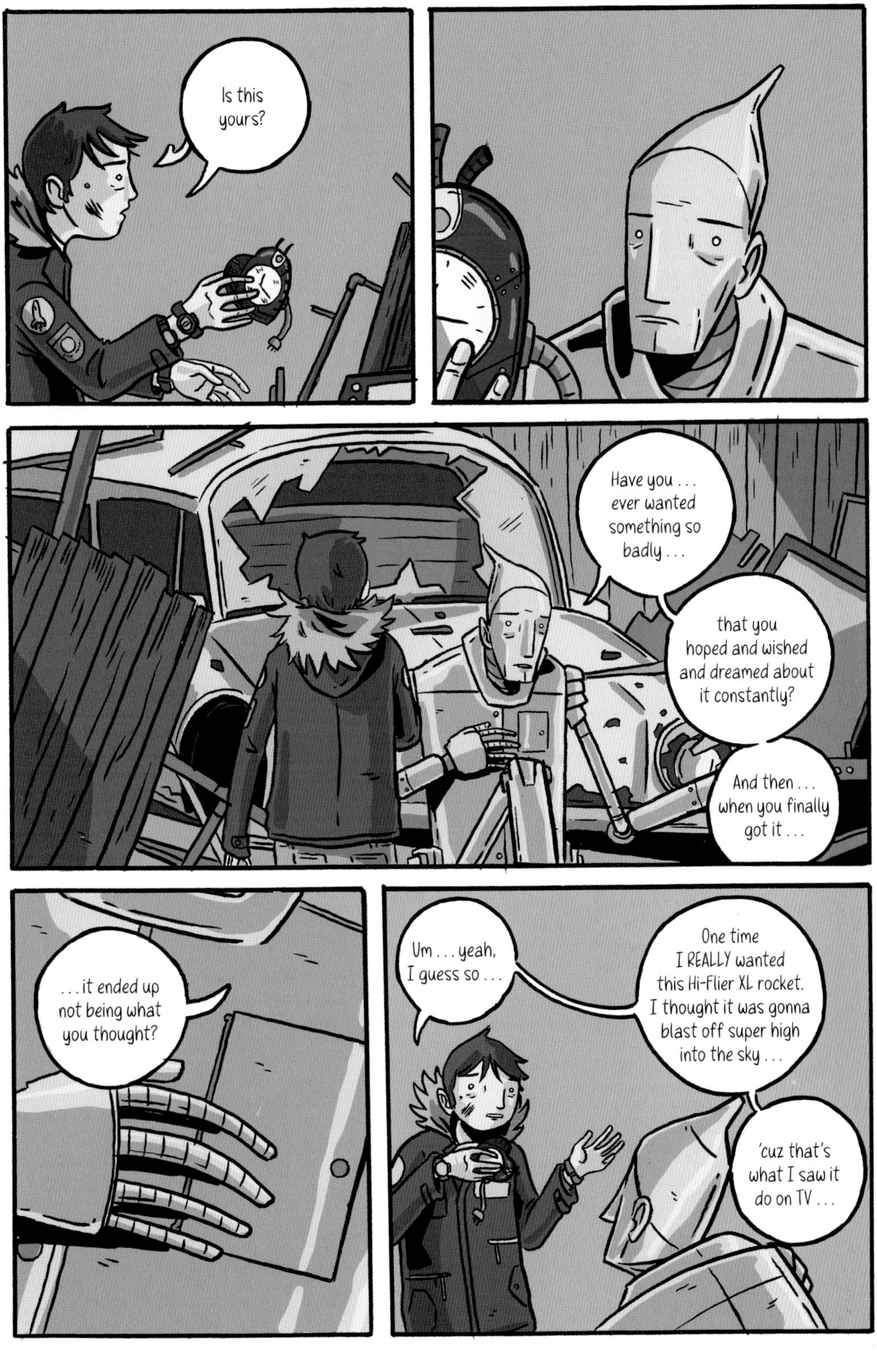
Is this yours?
Have you . . . ever wanted something so badly . . .
that you hoped and wished and dreamed about it constantly?
And then . . . when you finally got it . . .
. . . it ended up not being what you thought?
Um . . . yeah, I guess so . . .
One time I REALLY wanted this Hi-Flier XL rocket. I thought it was gonna blast off super high into the sky . . .
'cuz that's what I saw it do on TV . . .

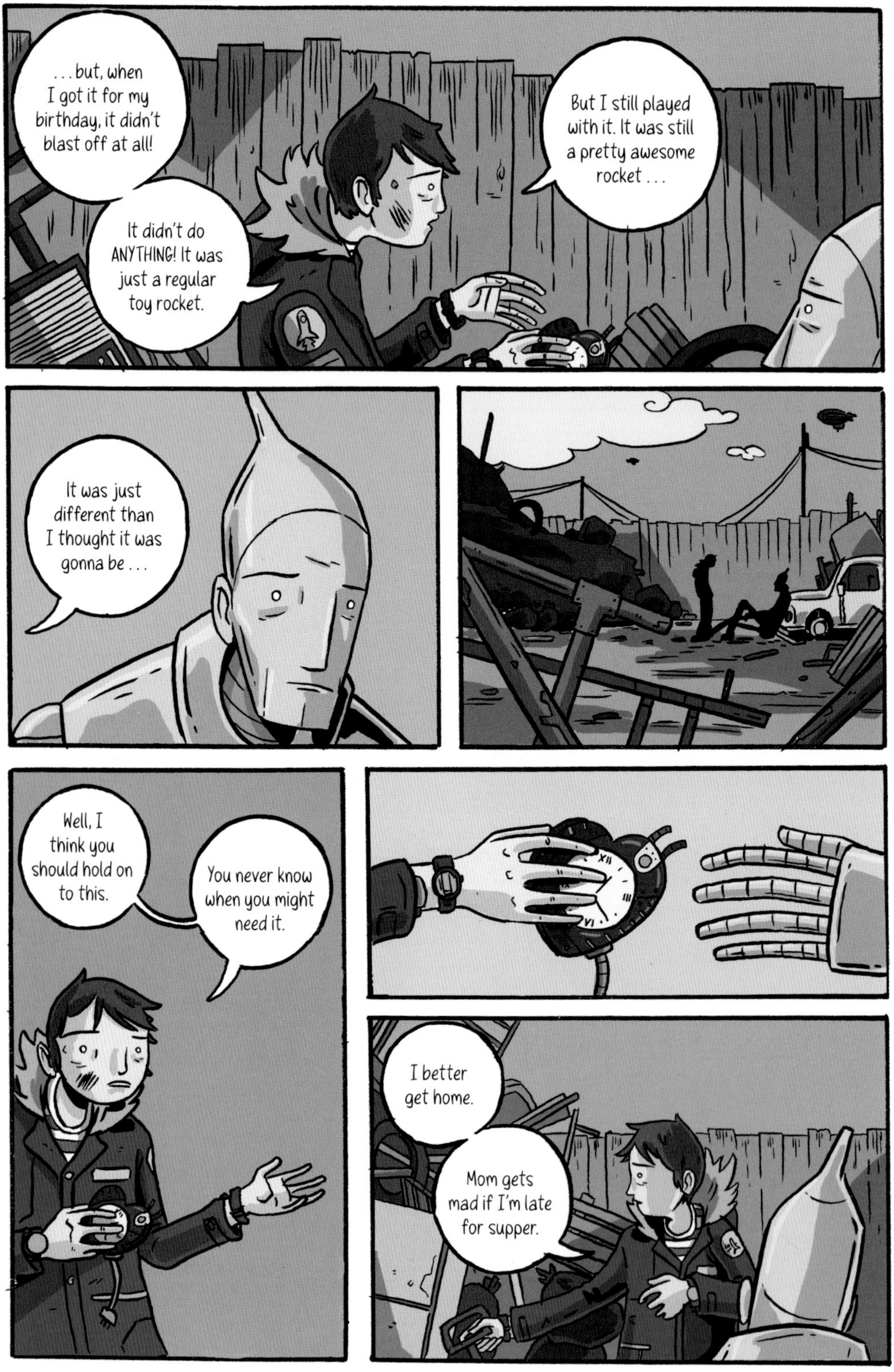
. . . but, when I got it for my birthday, it didn't blast off at all!
It didn't do ANYTHING! It was just a regular toy rocket.
But I still played with it. It was still a pretty awesome rocket . . .
It was just different than I thought it was gonna be . . .
Well, I think you should hold on to this.
You never know when you might need it.
I better get home.
Mom gets mad if I'm late for supper.

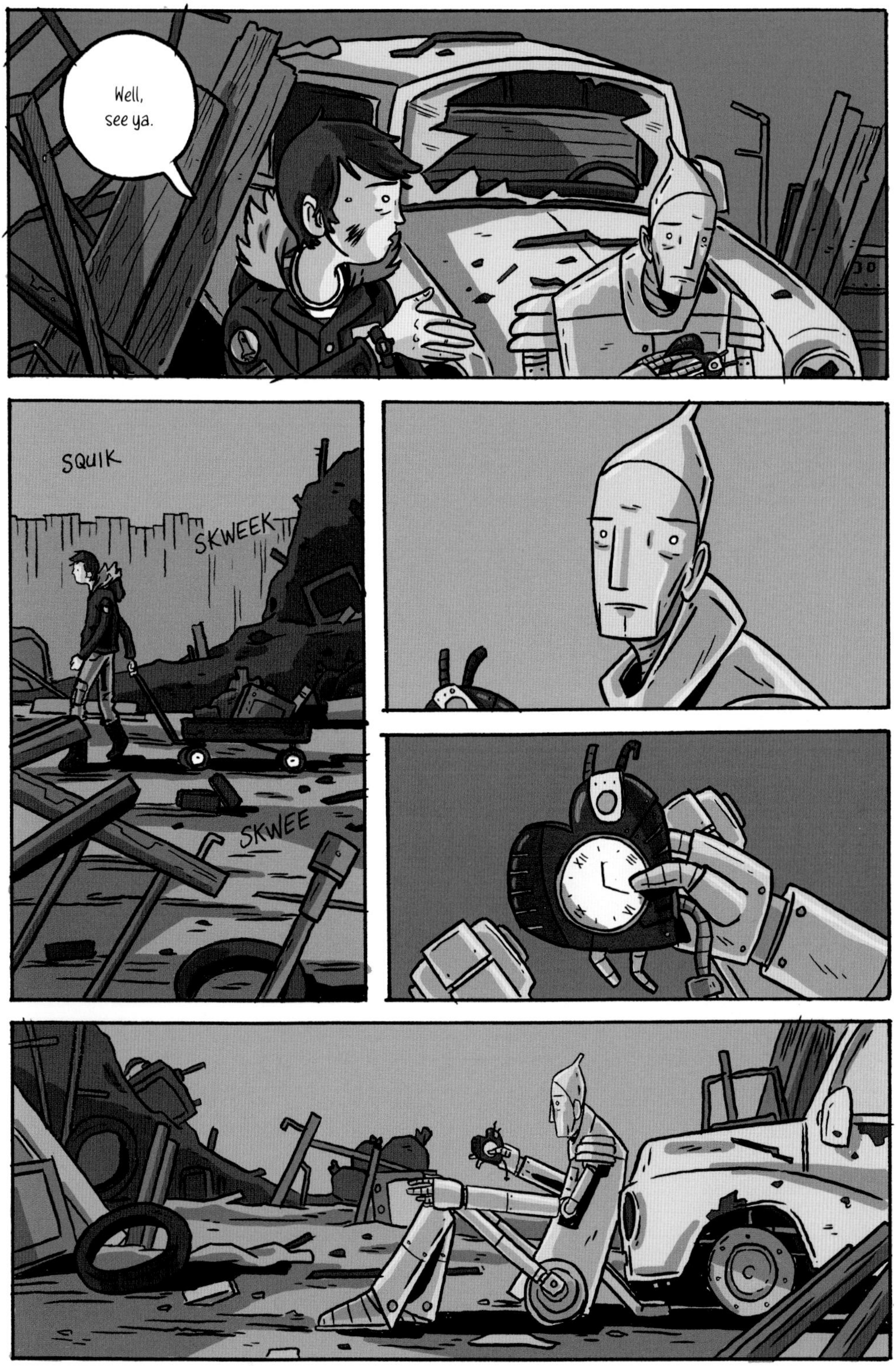
Well, see ya.
SQUIK
SKWEEK
SKWEE

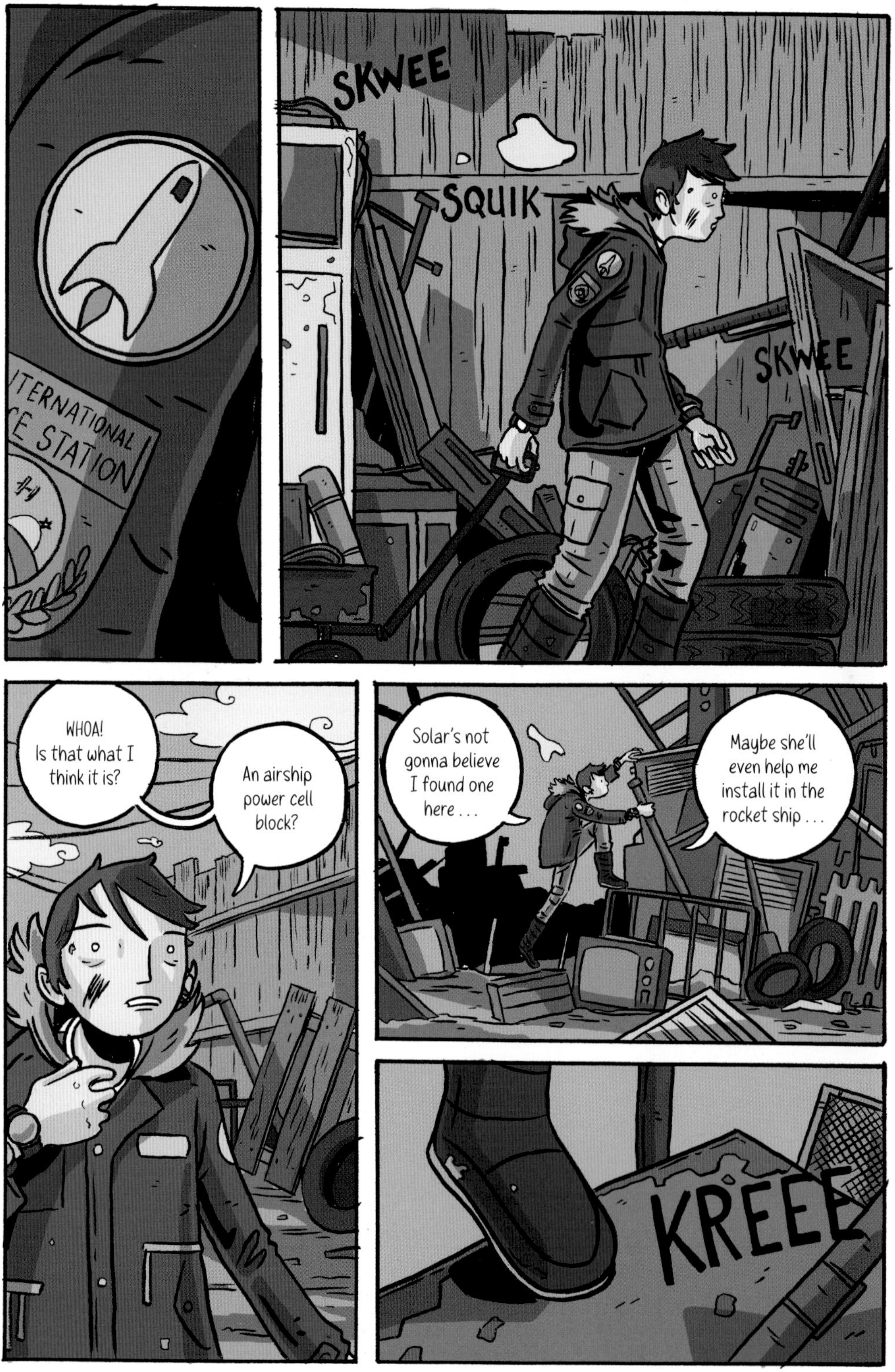
INTERNATIONAL
CE STATION
SKWEE
SQUIK
SKWEE
WHOA! Is that what I think it is?
An airship power cell block?
Solar's not gonna believe I found one here . . .
Maybe she'll even help me install it in the rocket ship . . .
KREEE

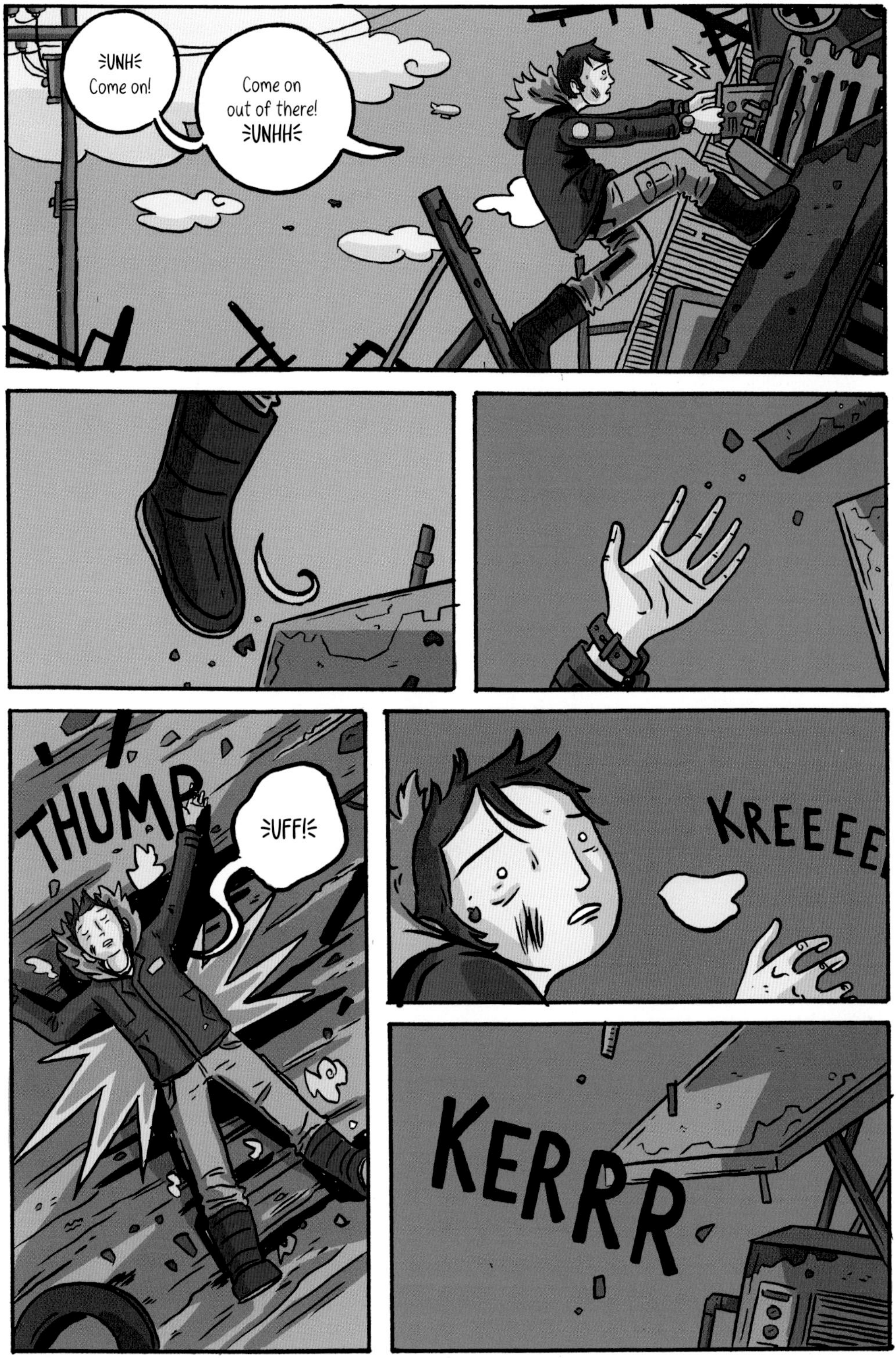

UNH Come on!
Come on out of there! UNHH
THUMP
UFF!
KREEEEE
KERRR

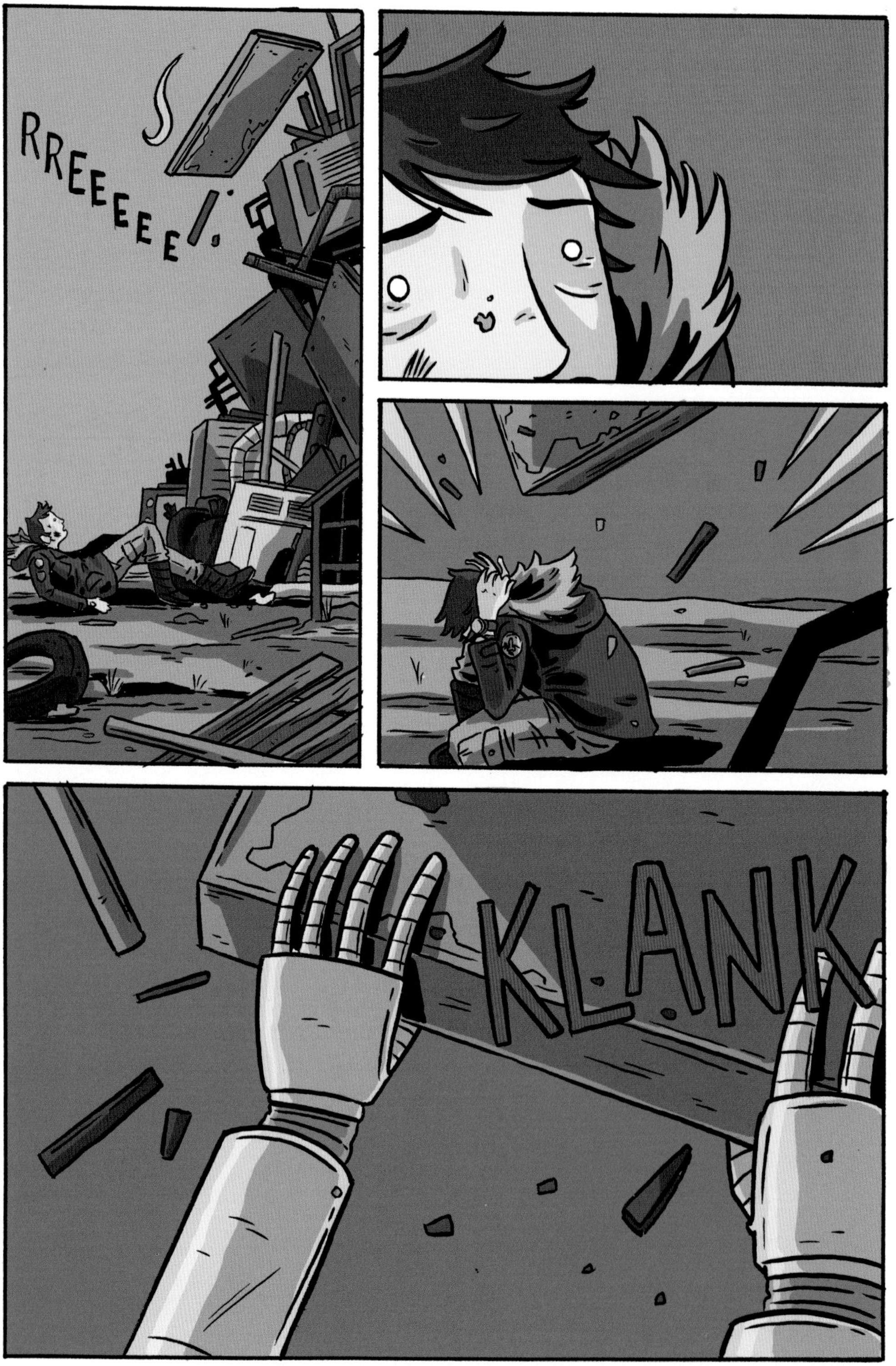
RREEEEEE
KLANK

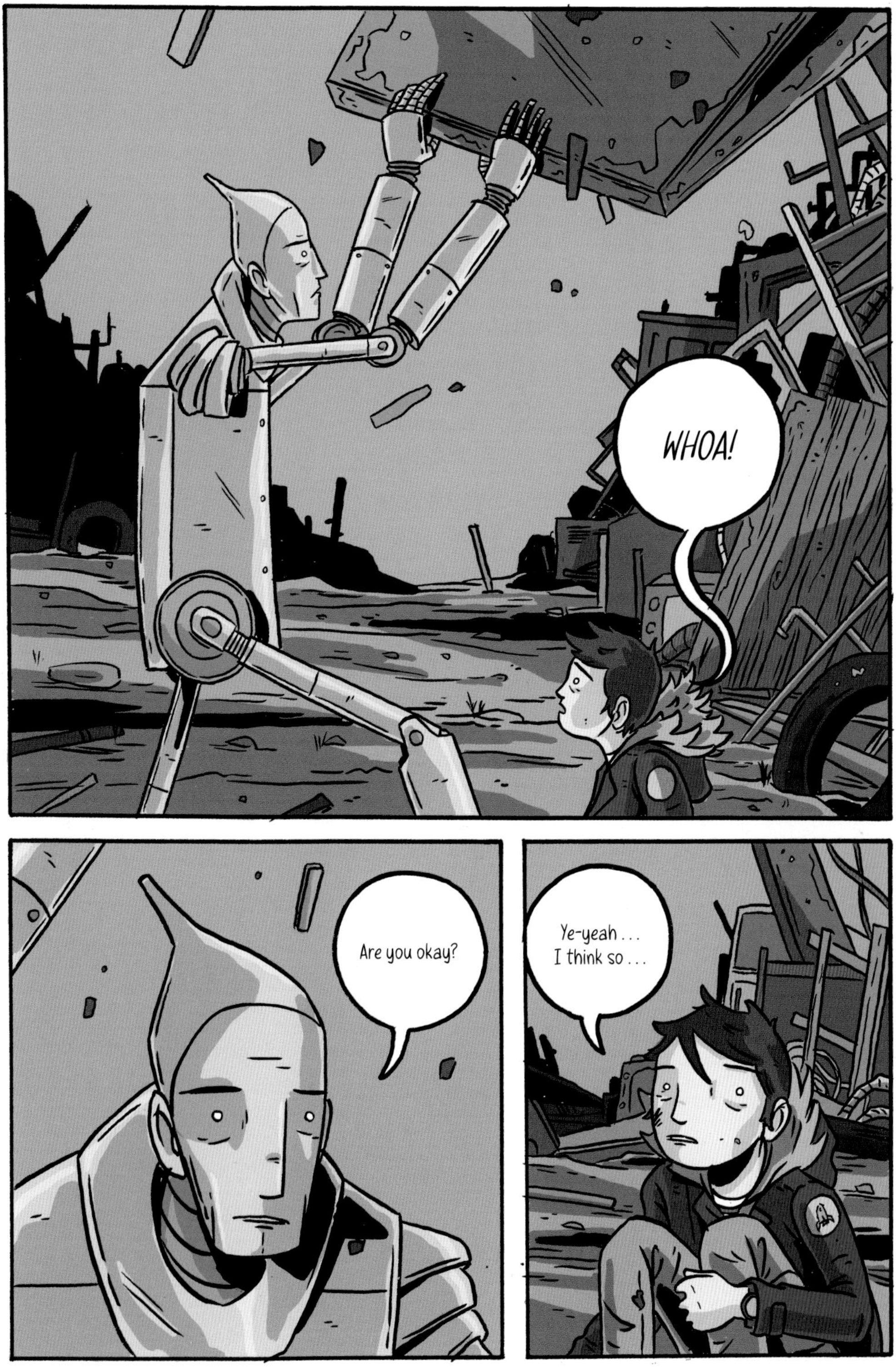
WHOA!
Are you okay?
Ye-yeah . . .
I think so . . .

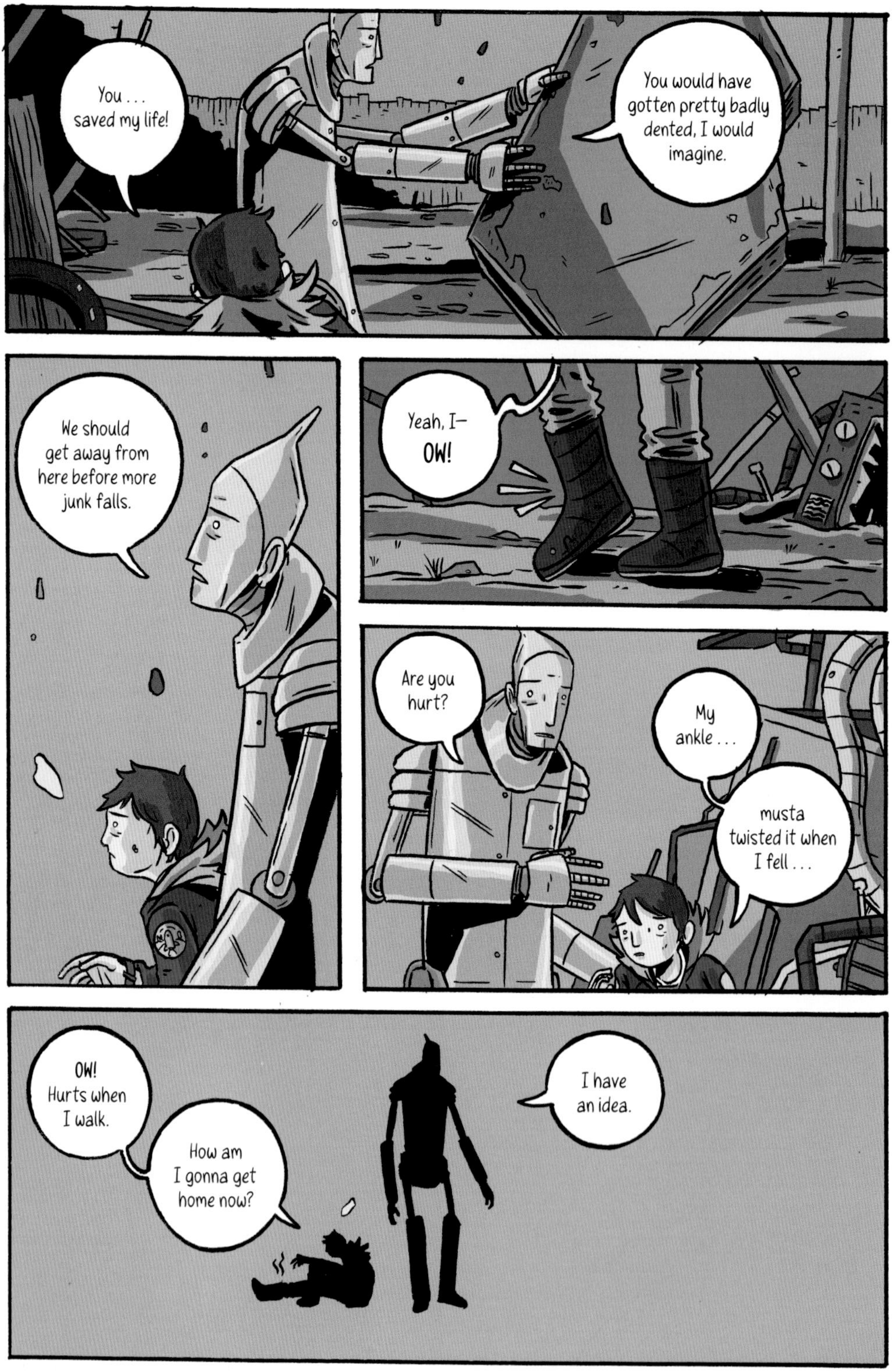
You . . . saved my life!
You would have gotten pretty badly dented, I would imagine.
We should get away from here before more junk falls.
Yeah, I— OW!
Are you hurt?
My ankle . . .
musta twisted it when I fell . . .
OW! Hurts when I walk.
How am I gonna get home now?
I have an idea.

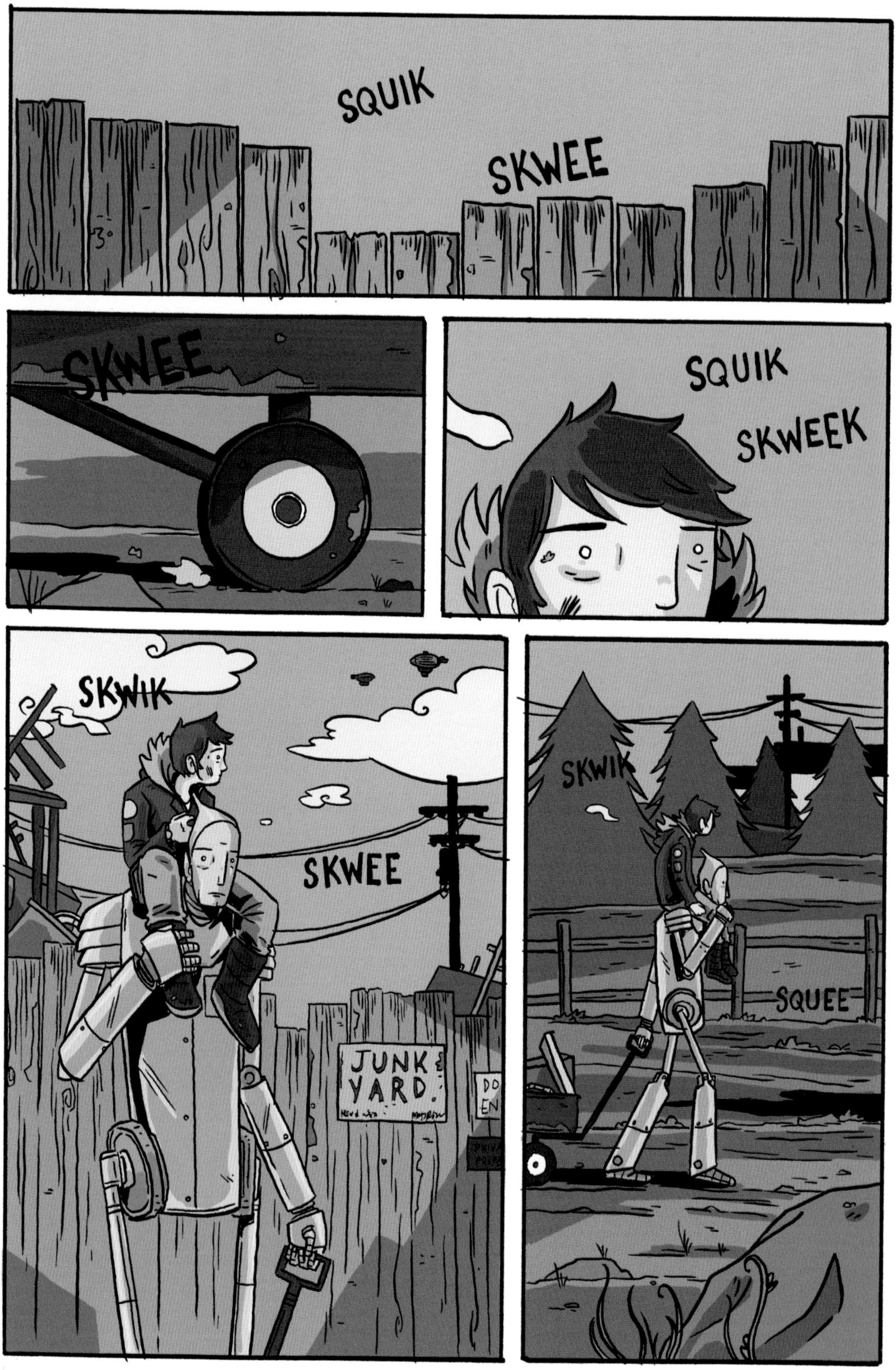
SQUIK
SKWEE
SKWEE
SQUIK
SKWEEK
SKWIK
SKWEE
JUNK YARD
SKWIK
SQUEE

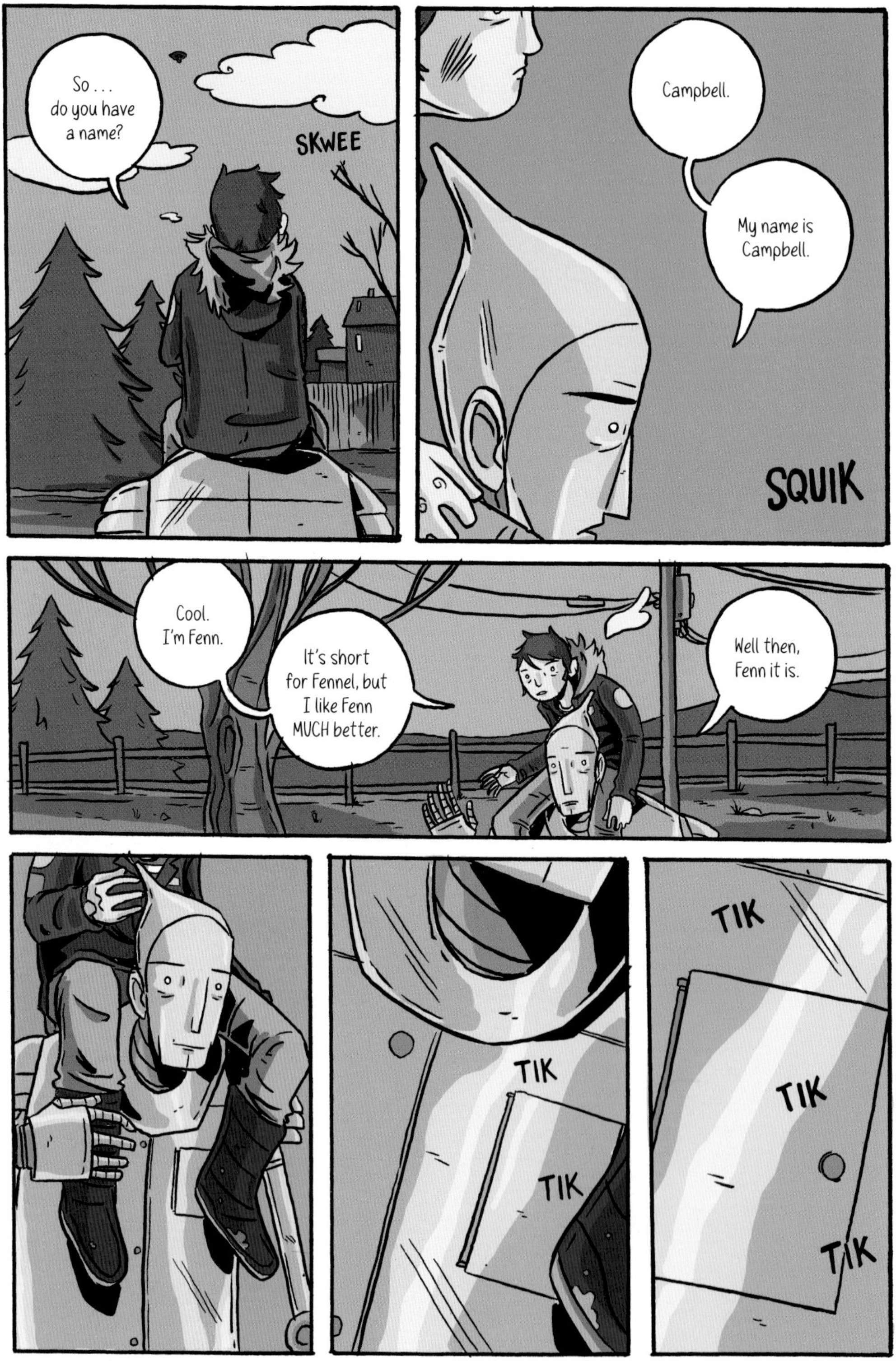
So . . .
do you have
a name?
SKWEE
Campbell.
My name is
Campbell.
SQUIK
Cool.
I'm Fenn.
It's short
for Fennel, but
I like Fenn
MUCH better.
Well then,
Fenn it is.
TIK
TIK
TIK
TIK
TIK

CHAPTER 2: Goody Two Shoes

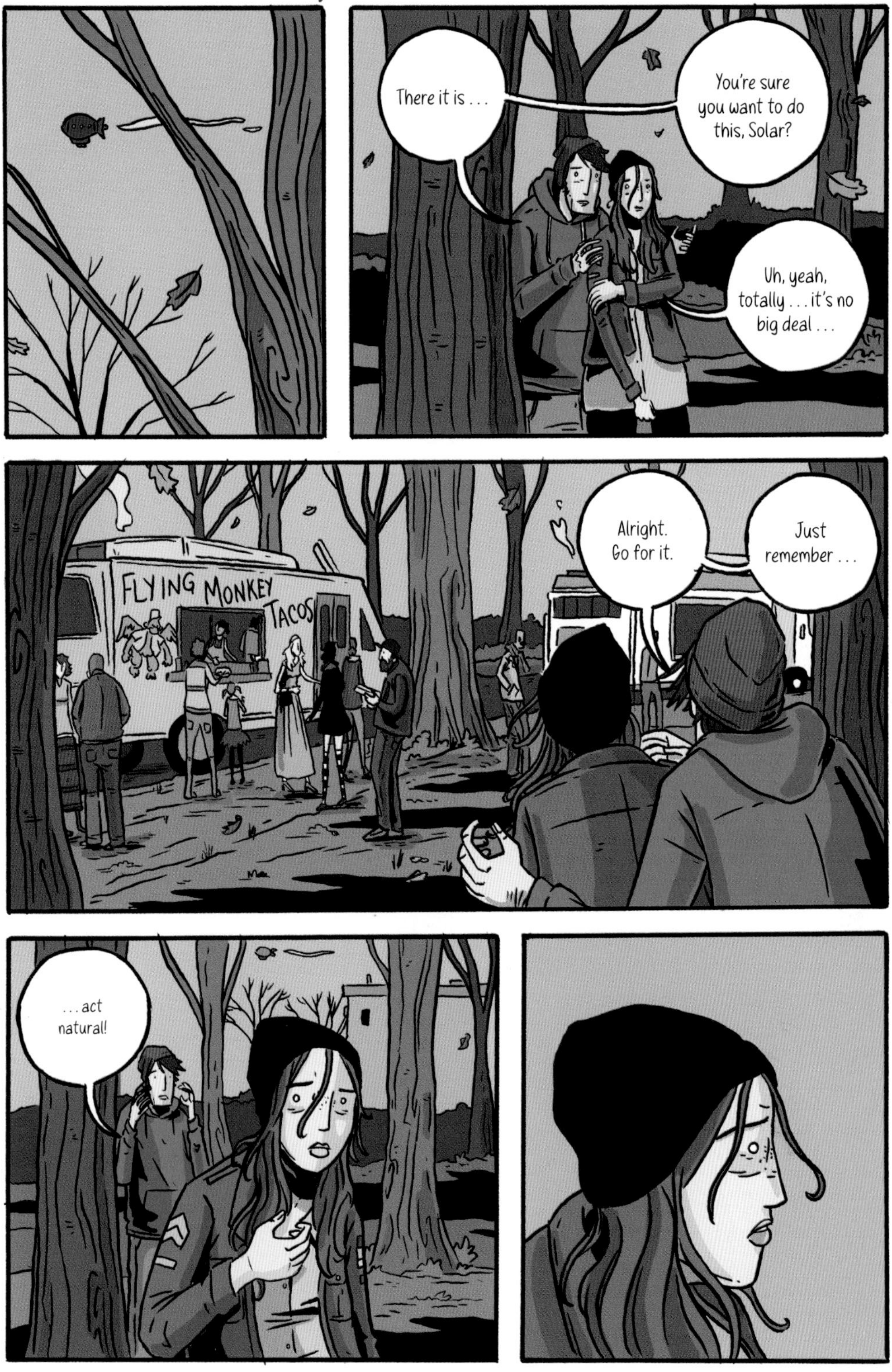
There it is . . .
You're sure you want to do this, Solar?
Uh, yeah, totally . . . it's no big deal . . .
FLYING MONKEY TACOS
Alright. Go for it.
Just remember . . .
. . . act natural!

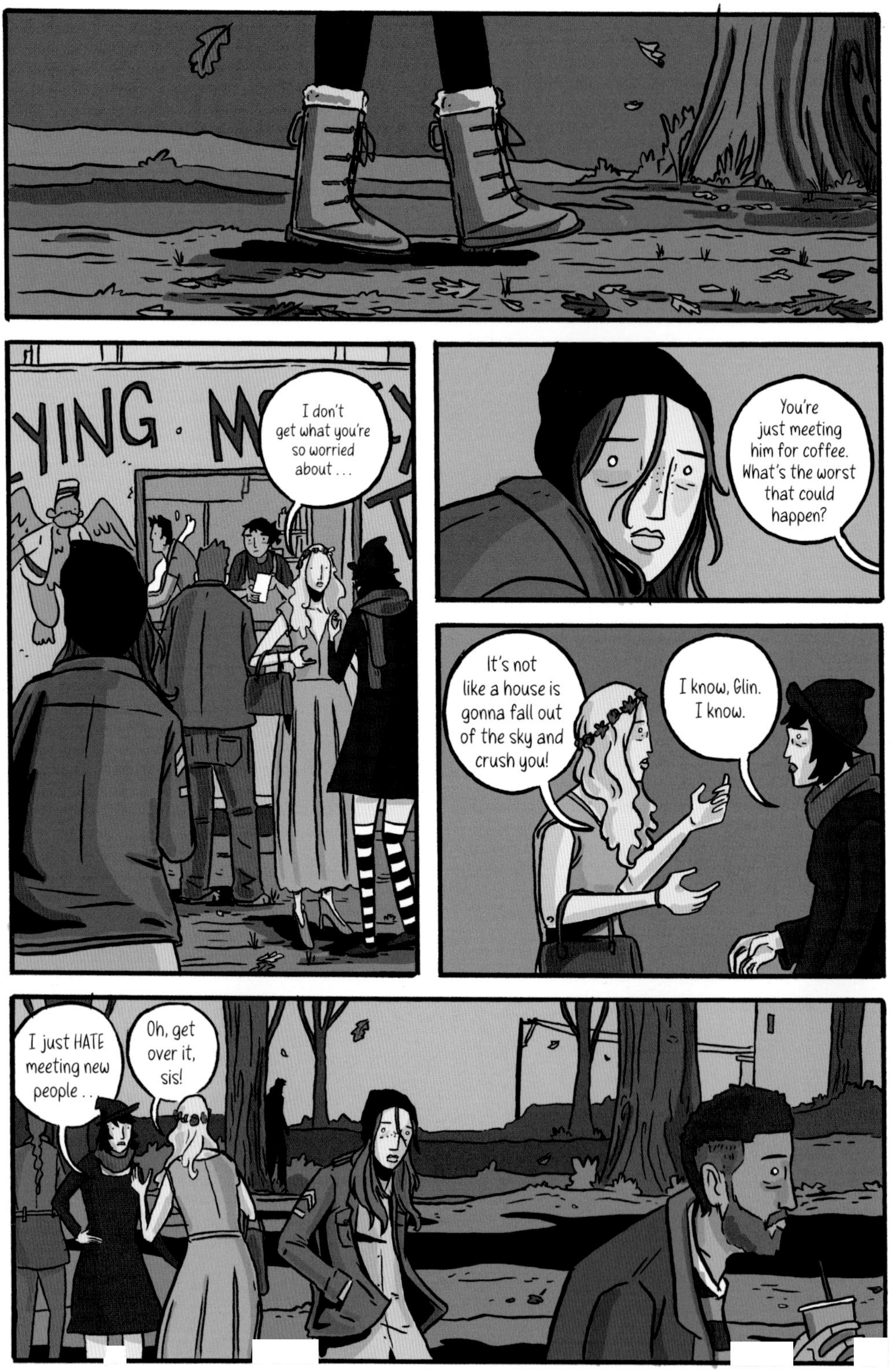

YING · M
I don't get what you're so worried about . . .
You're just meeting him for coffee. What's the worst that could happen?
It's not like a house is gonna fall out of the sky and crush you!
I know, Glin. I know.
I just HATE meeting new people . . .
Oh, get over it, sis!

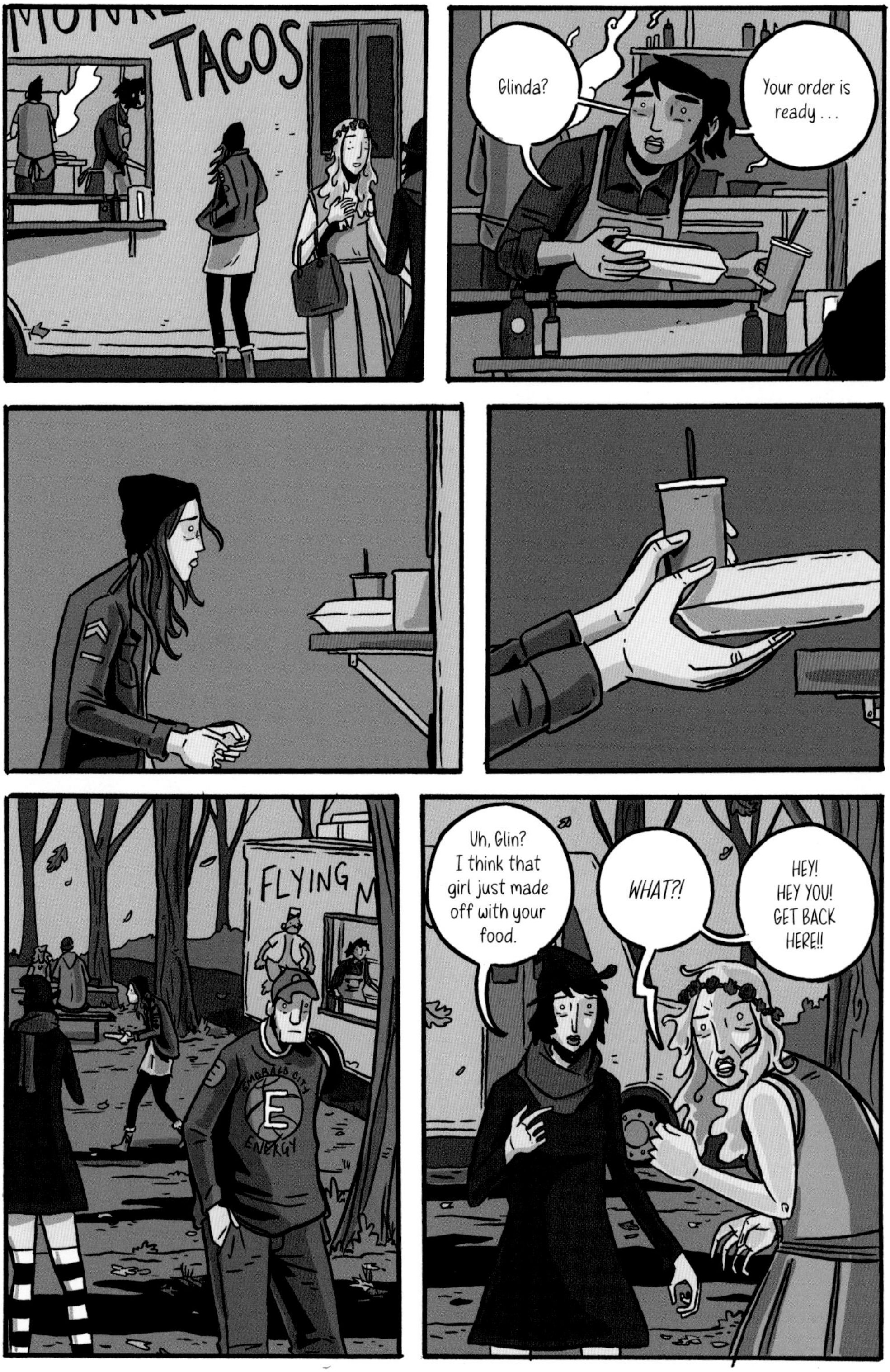
MONKE
TACOS
Glinda?
Your order is ready . . .
FLYING
EMERALD CITY
E
ENERGY
Uh, Glin? I think that girl just made off with your food.
WHAT?!
HEY! HEY YOU! GET BACK HERE!!

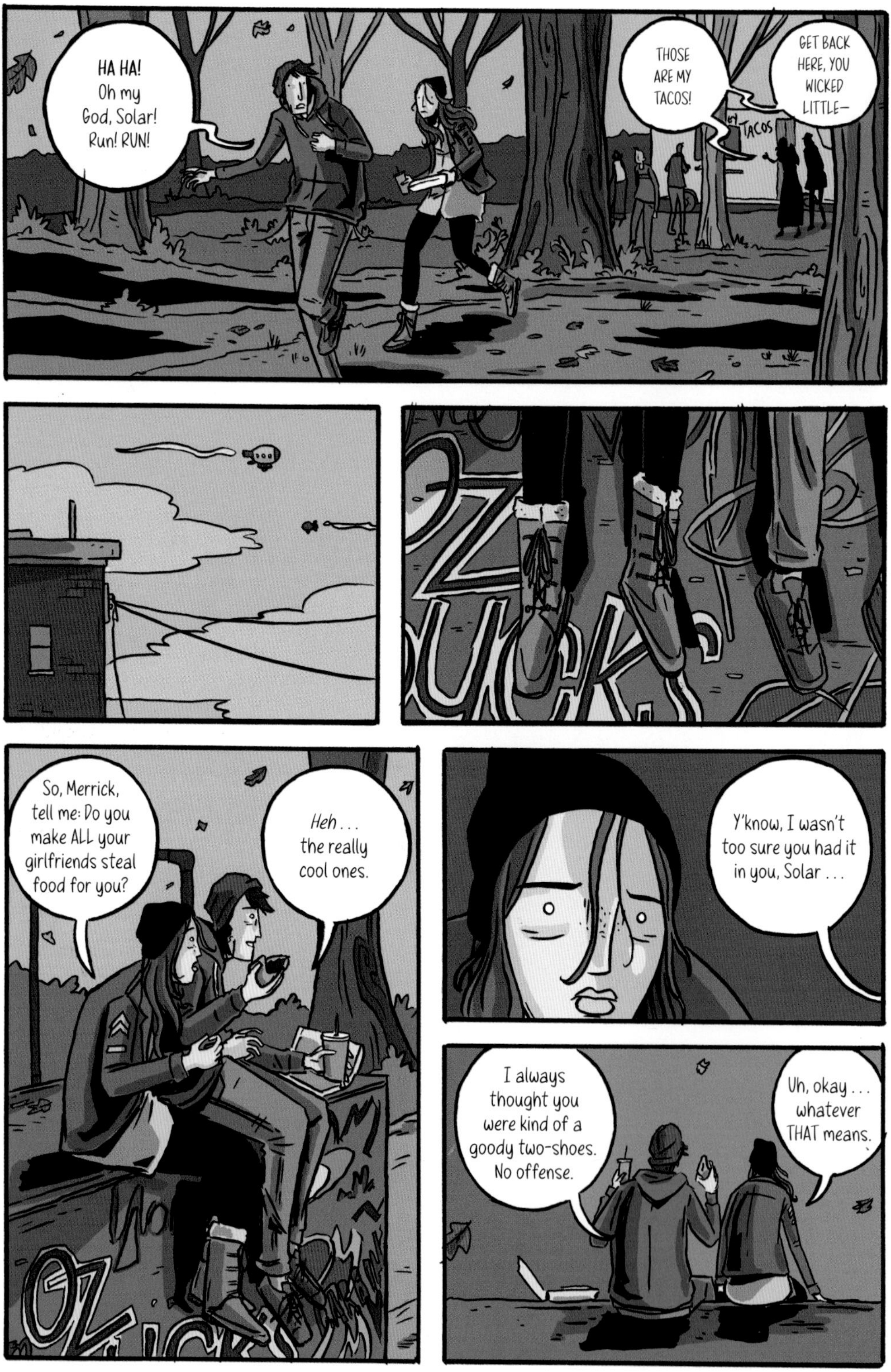
HA HA! Oh my God, Solar! Run! RUN!
THOSE ARE MY TACOS!
GET BACK HERE, YOU WICKED LITTLE—
TACOS
So, Merrick, tell me: Do you make ALL your girlfriends steal food for you?
Heh . . . the really cool ones.
Y'know, I wasn't too sure you had it in you, Solar . . .
I always thought you were kind of a goody two-shoes. No offense.
Uh, okay . . . whatever THAT means.

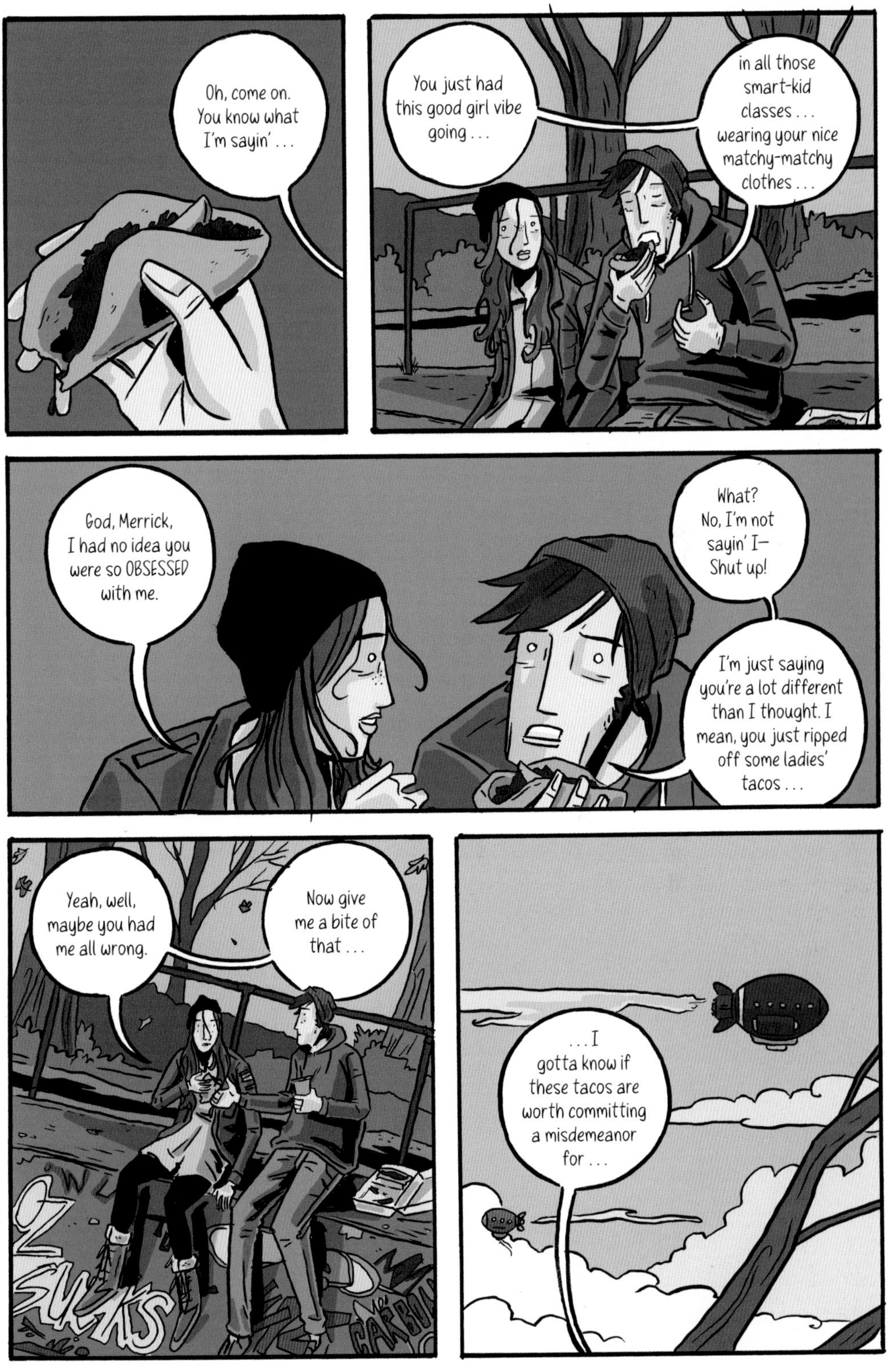
Oh, come on. You know what I'm sayin' . . .
You just had this good girl vibe going . . .
in all those smart-kid classes . . . wearing your nice matchy-matchy clothes . . .
God, Merrick, I had no idea you were so OBSESSED with me.
What? No, I'm not sayin' I— Shut up!
I'm just saying you're a lot different than I thought. I mean, you just ripped off some ladies' tacos . . .
Yeah, well, maybe you had me all wrong.
Now give me a bite of that . . .
. . . I gotta know if these tacos are worth committing a misdemeanor for . . .

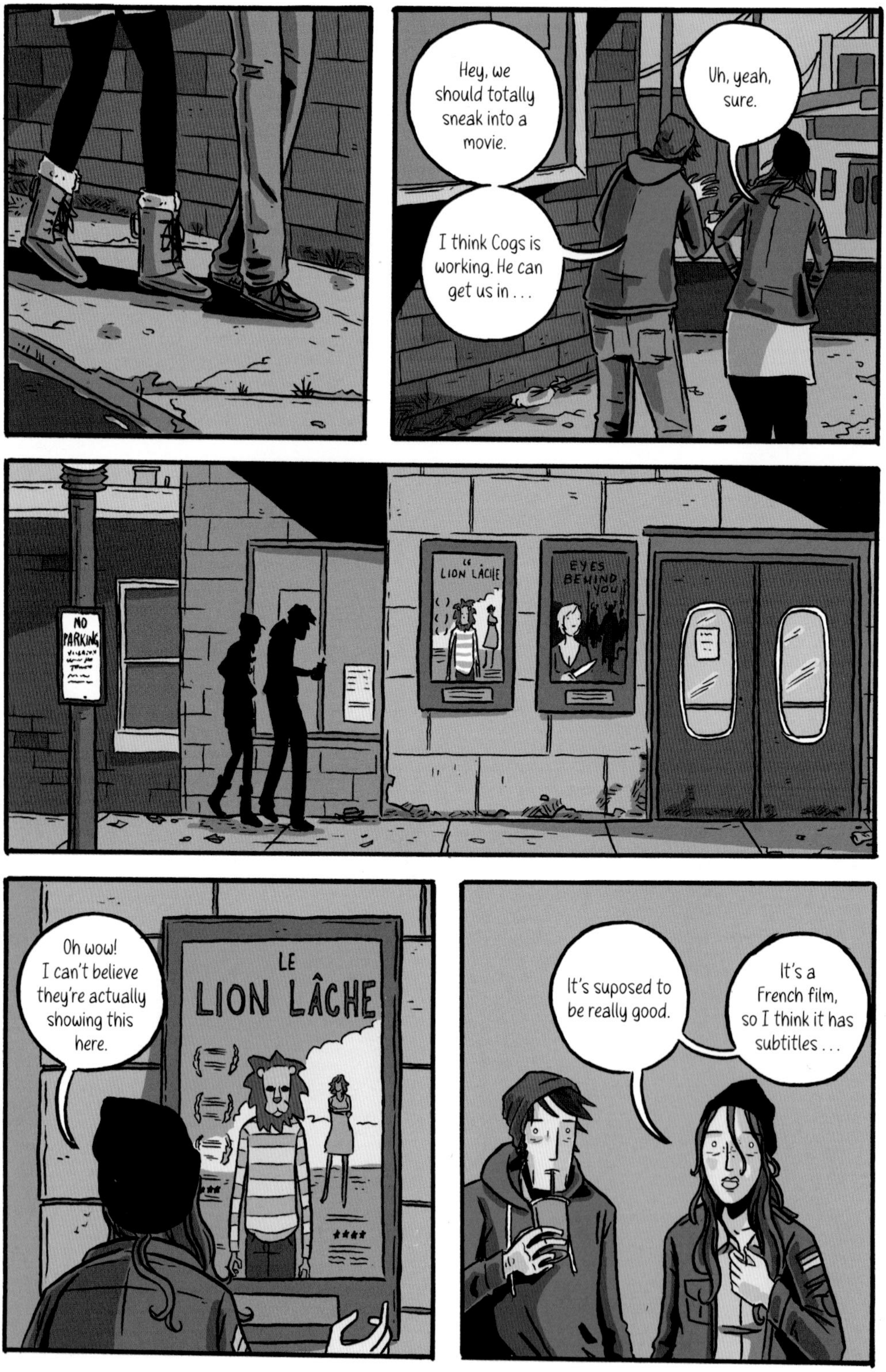

Hey, we should totally sneak into a movie.
Uh, yeah, sure.
I think Cogs is working. He can get us in . . .
NO PARKING
LE LION LÂCHE
Oh wow! I can't believe they're actually showing this here.
It's suposed to be really good.
It's a French film, so I think it has subtitles . . .

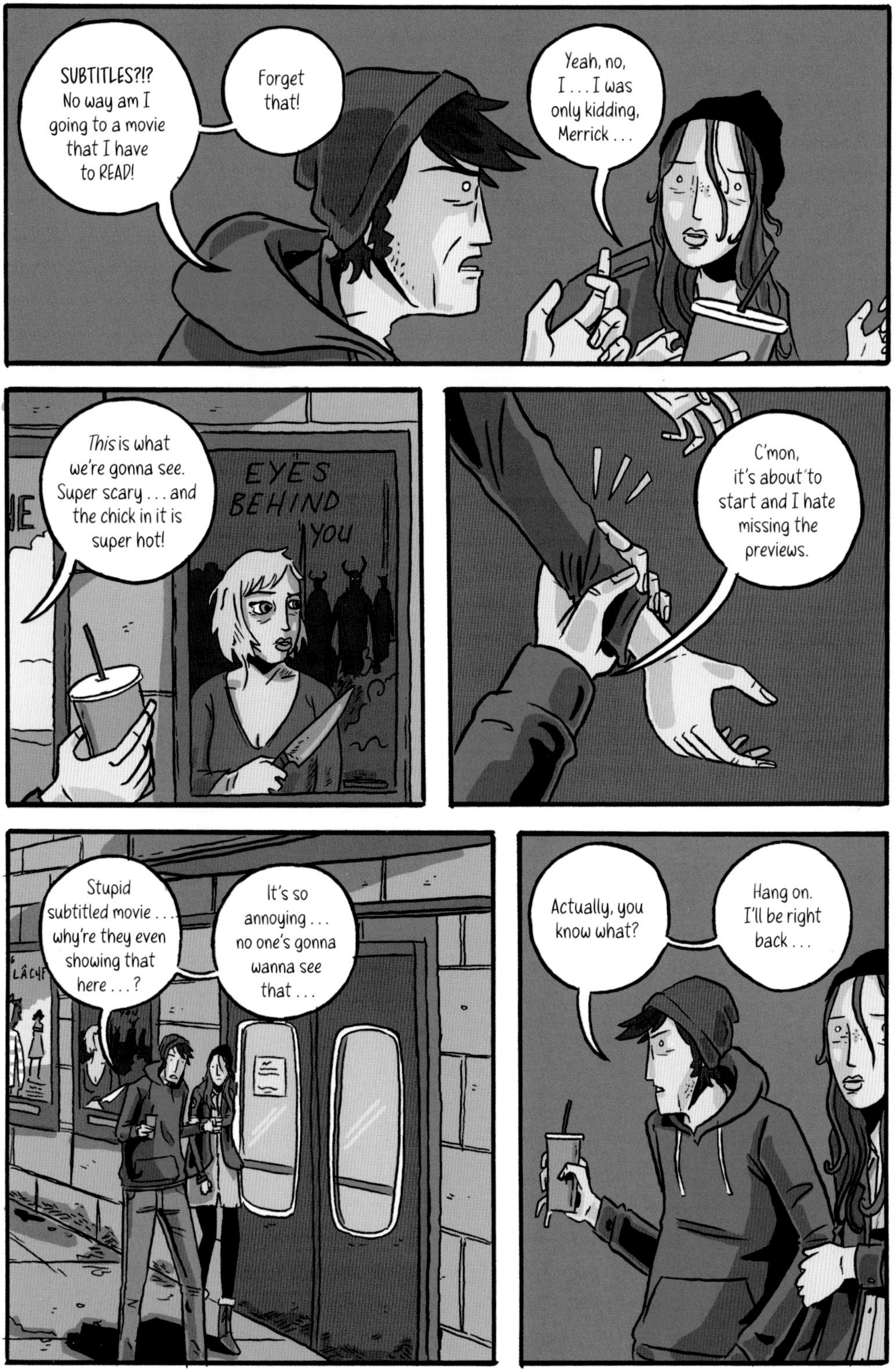
SUBTITLES?!? No way am I going to a movie that I have to READ!
Forget that!
Yeah, no, I . . . I was only kidding, Merrick . . .
This is what we're gonna see. Super scary . . . and the chick in it is super hot!
EYES BEHIND YOU
C'mon, it's about to start and I hate missing the previews.
Stupid subtitled movie . . . why're they even showing that here . . . ?
It's so annoying . . . no one's gonna wanna see that . . .
Actually, you know what?
Hang on. I'll be right back . . .

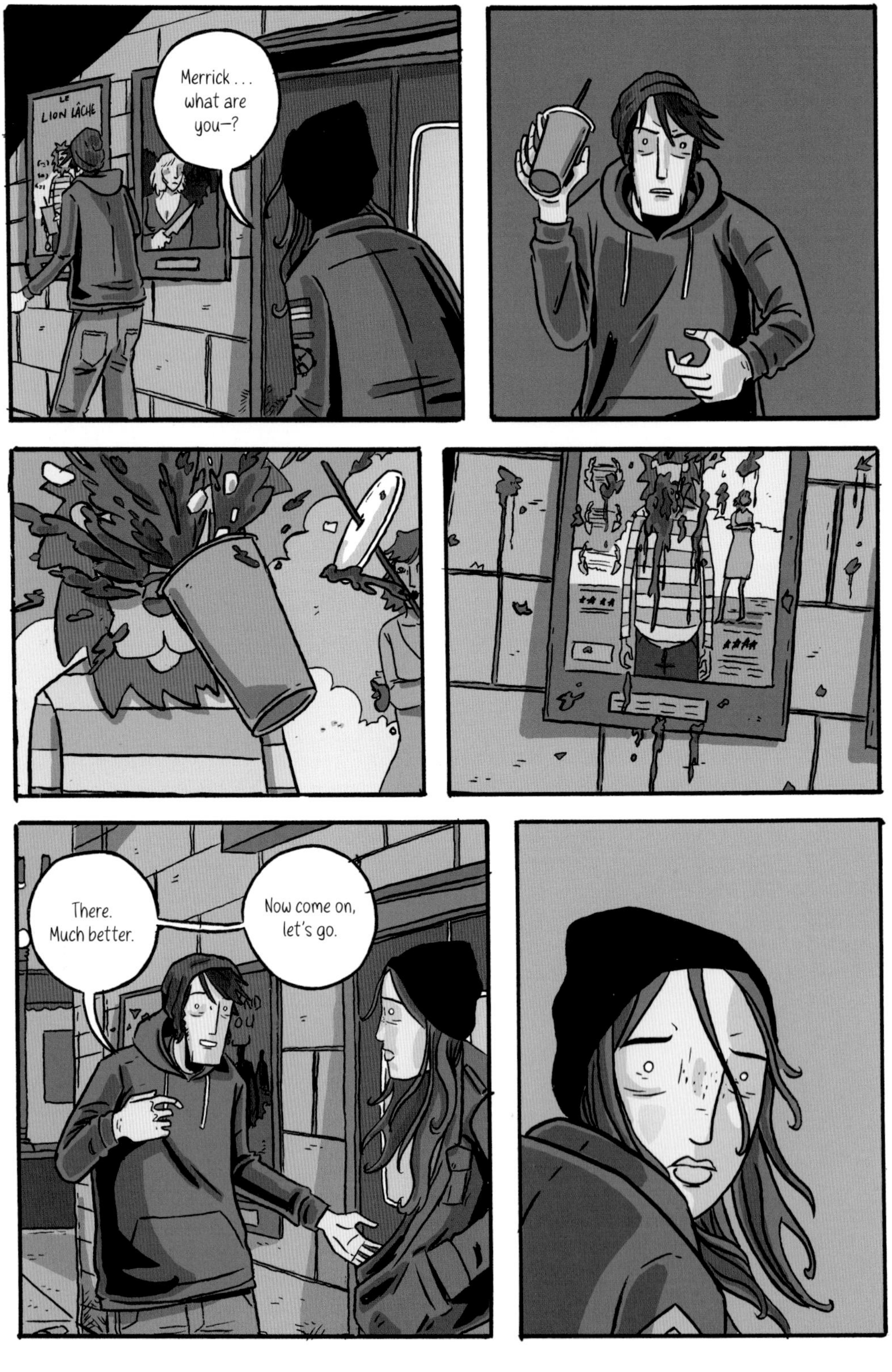
LE LION LÂCHE
Merrick . . . what are you—?
There. Much better.
Now come on, let's go.

CHAPTER 3: Hollow

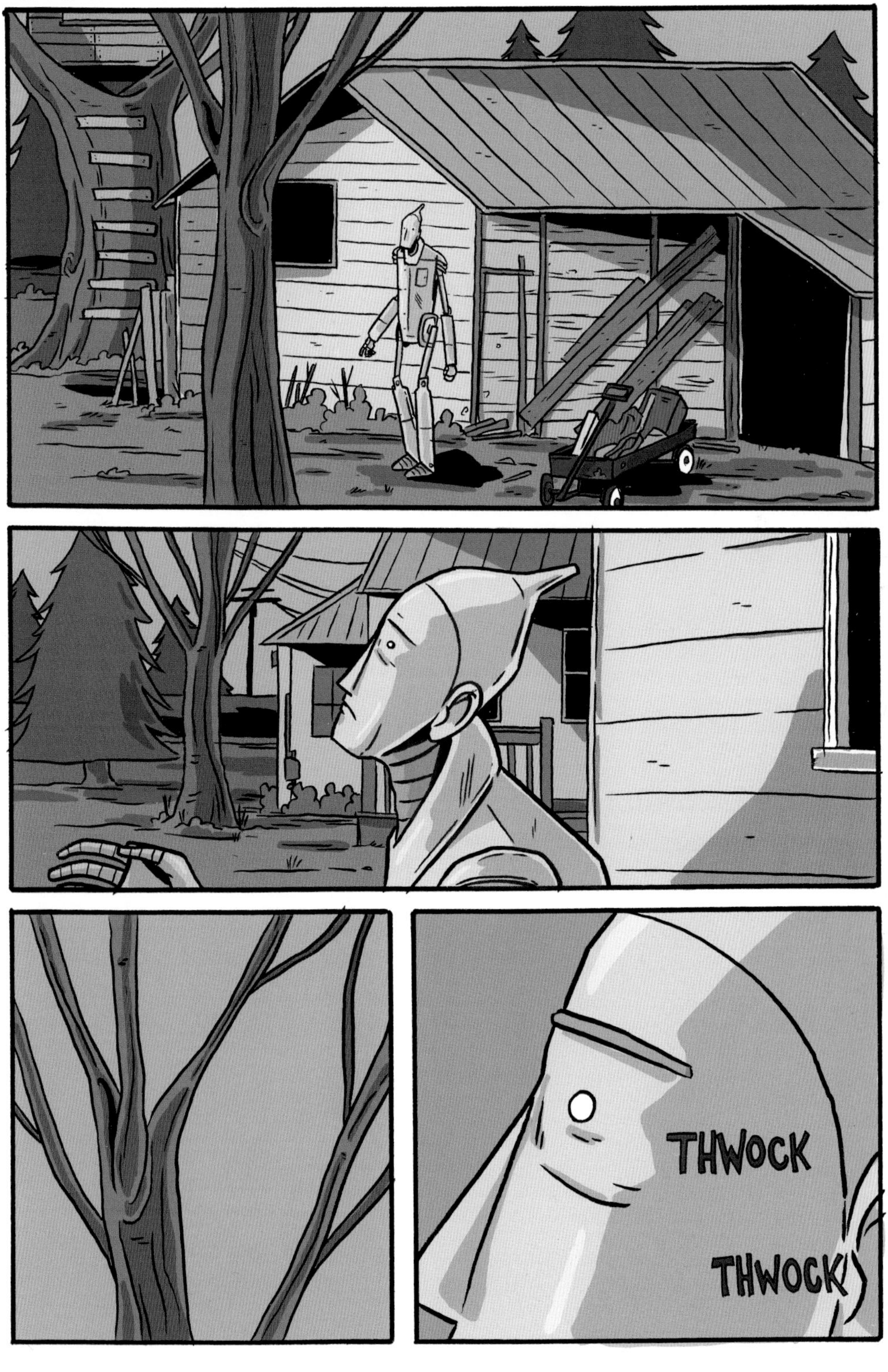
THWOCK
THWOCK

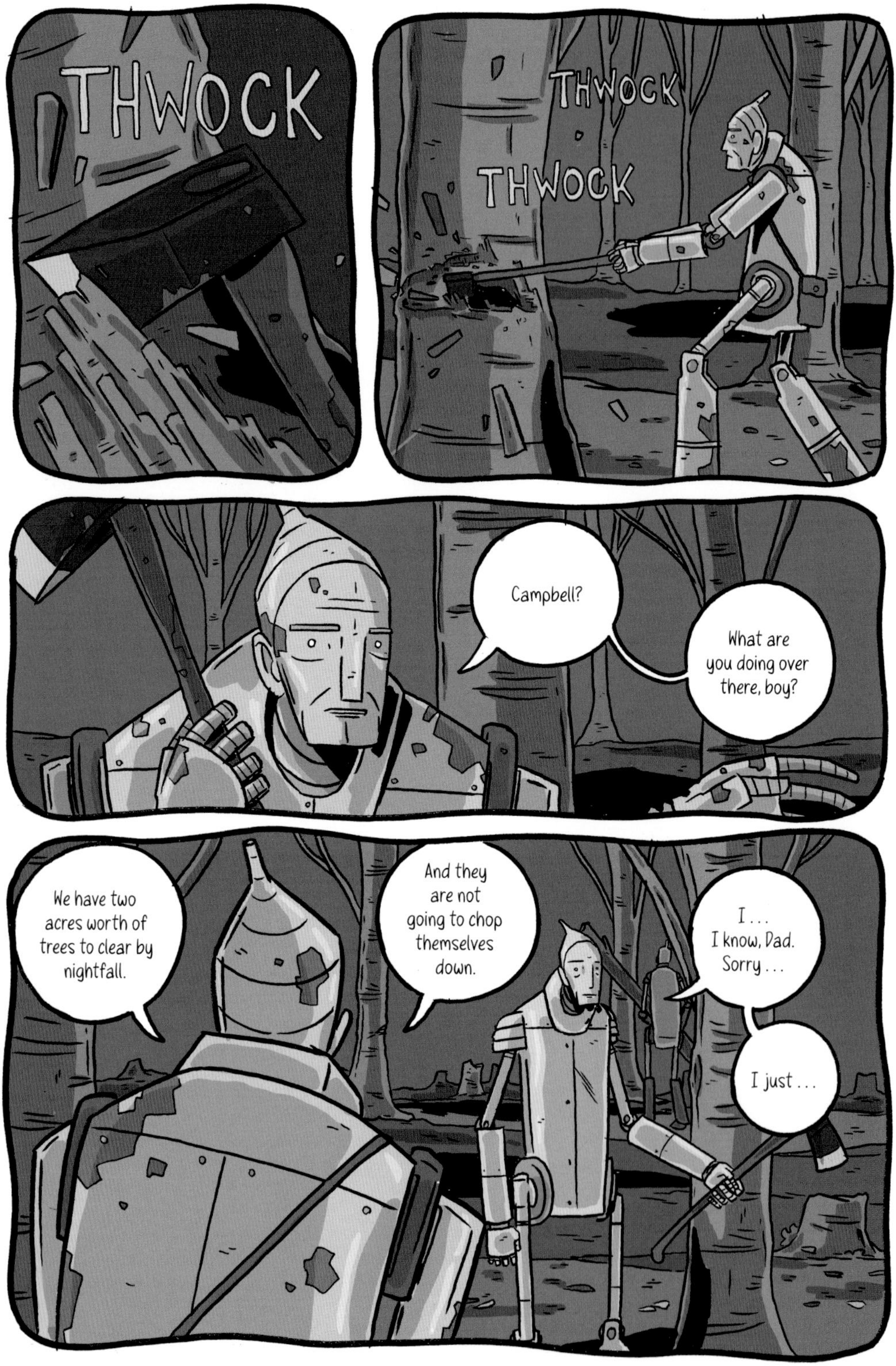
THWOCK
THWOCK
THWOCK
Campbell?
What are you doing over there, boy?
We have two acres worth of trees to clear by nightfall.
And they are not going to chop themselves down.
I . . . I know, Dad. Sorry . . .
I just . . .

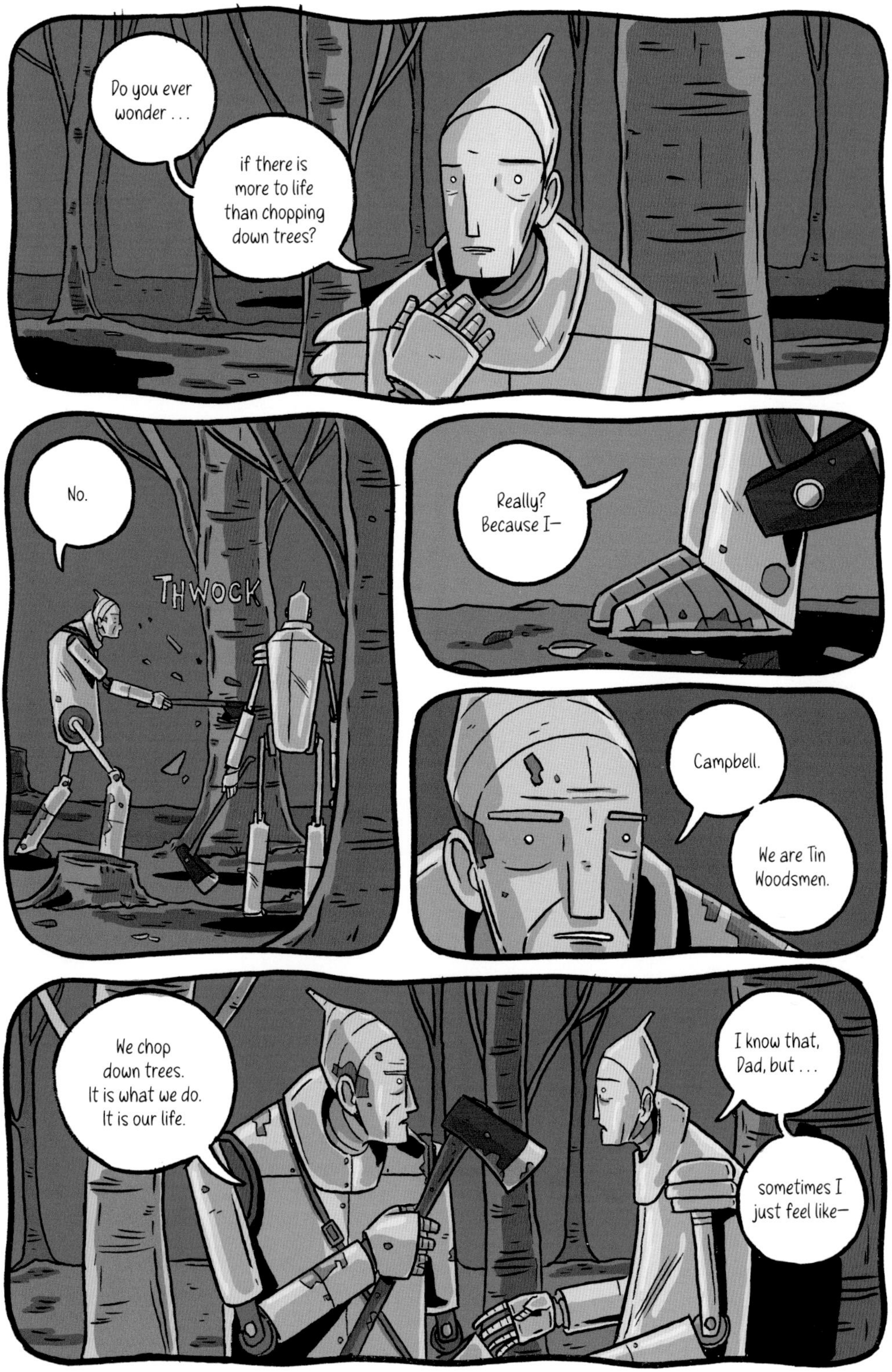
Do you ever wonder . . .
if there is more to life than chopping down trees?
No.
THWOCK
Really? Because I—
Campbell.
We are Tin Woodsmen.
We chop down trees. It is what we do. It is our life.
I know that, Dad, but . . .
sometimes I just feel like—

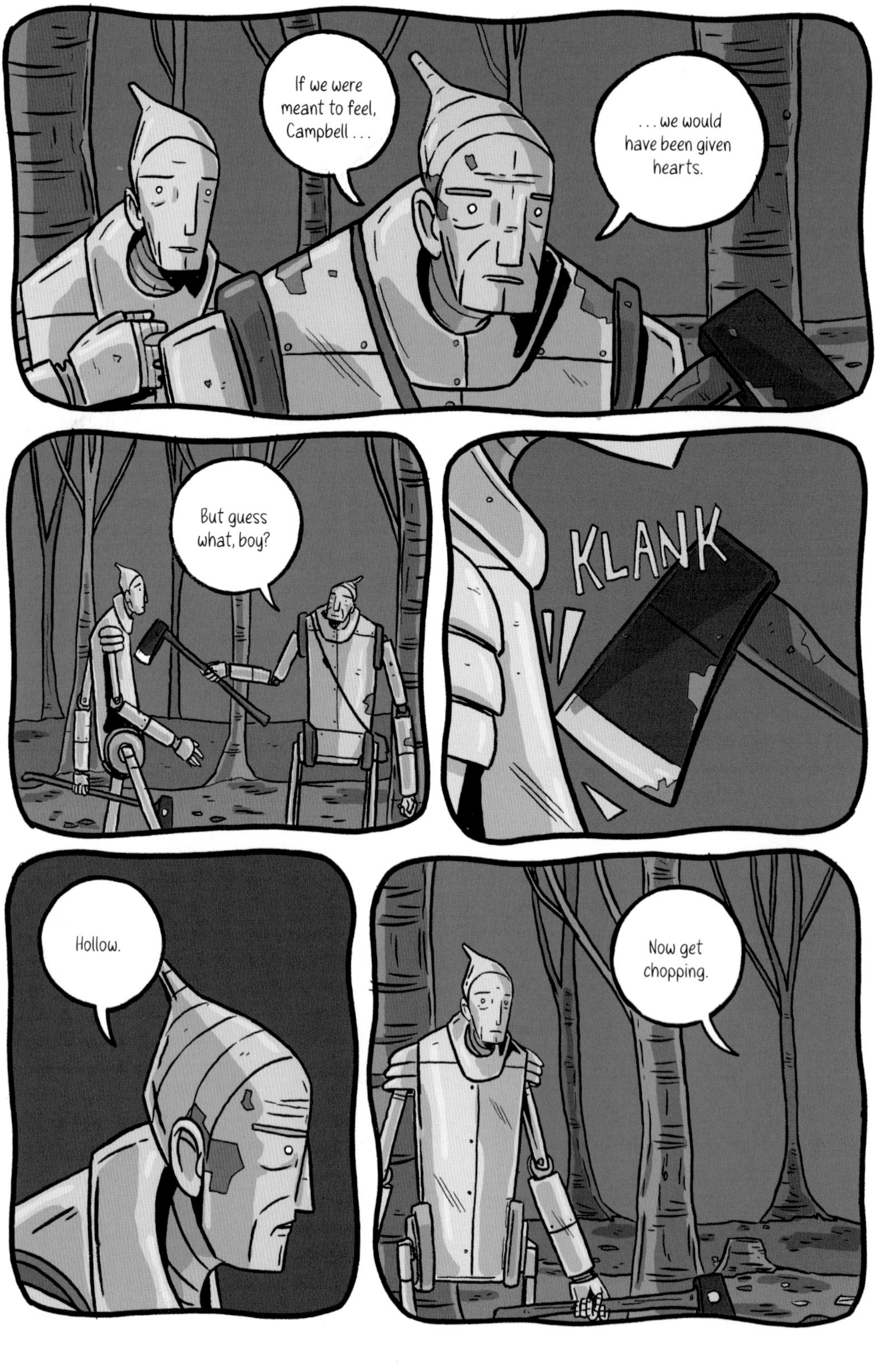
If we were meant to feel, Campbell . . .
. . . we would have been given hearts.
But guess what, boy?
KLANK
Hollow.
Now get chopping.

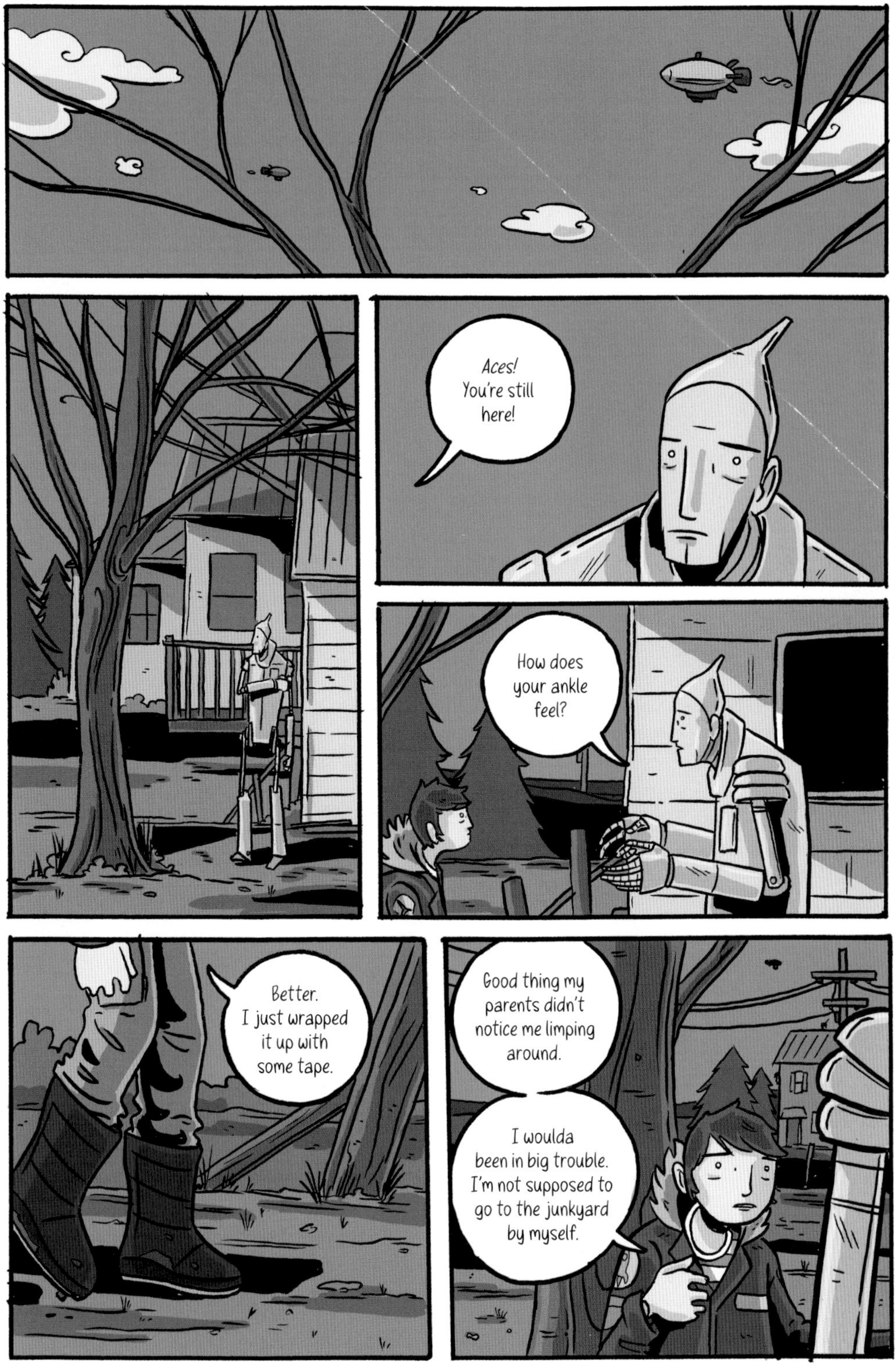
Aces! You're still here!
How does your ankle feel?
Better. I just wrapped it up with some tape.
Good thing my parents didn't notice me limping around.
I woulda been in big trouble. I'm not supposed to go to the junkyard by myself.

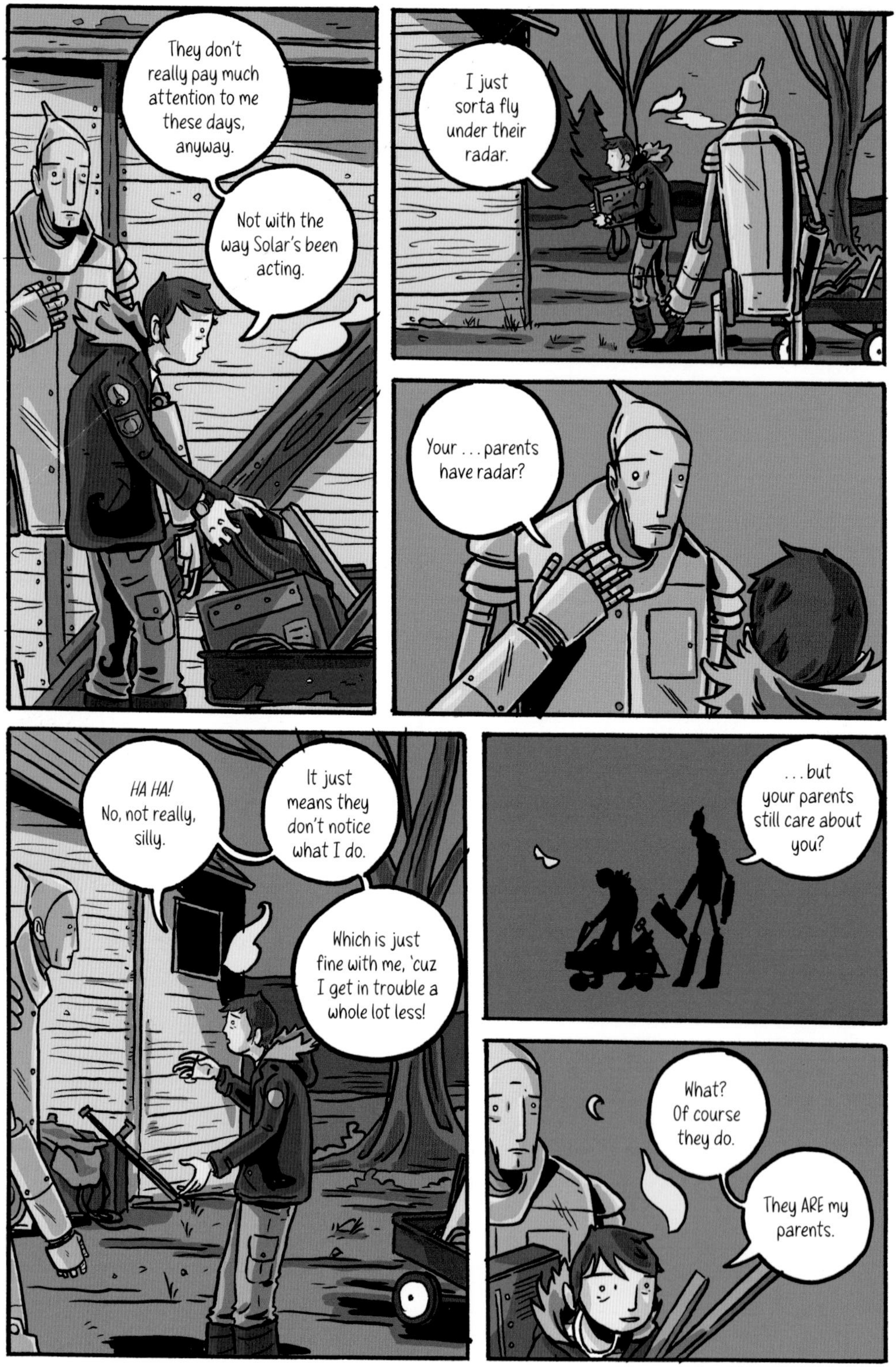

They don't really pay much attention to me these days, anyway.
Not with the way Solar's been acting.
I just sorta fly under their radar.
Your . . . parents have radar?
HA HA! No, not really, silly.
It just means they don't notice what I do.
Which is just fine with me, 'cuz I get in trouble a whole lot less!
. . . but your parents still care about you?
What? Of course they do.
They ARE my parents.

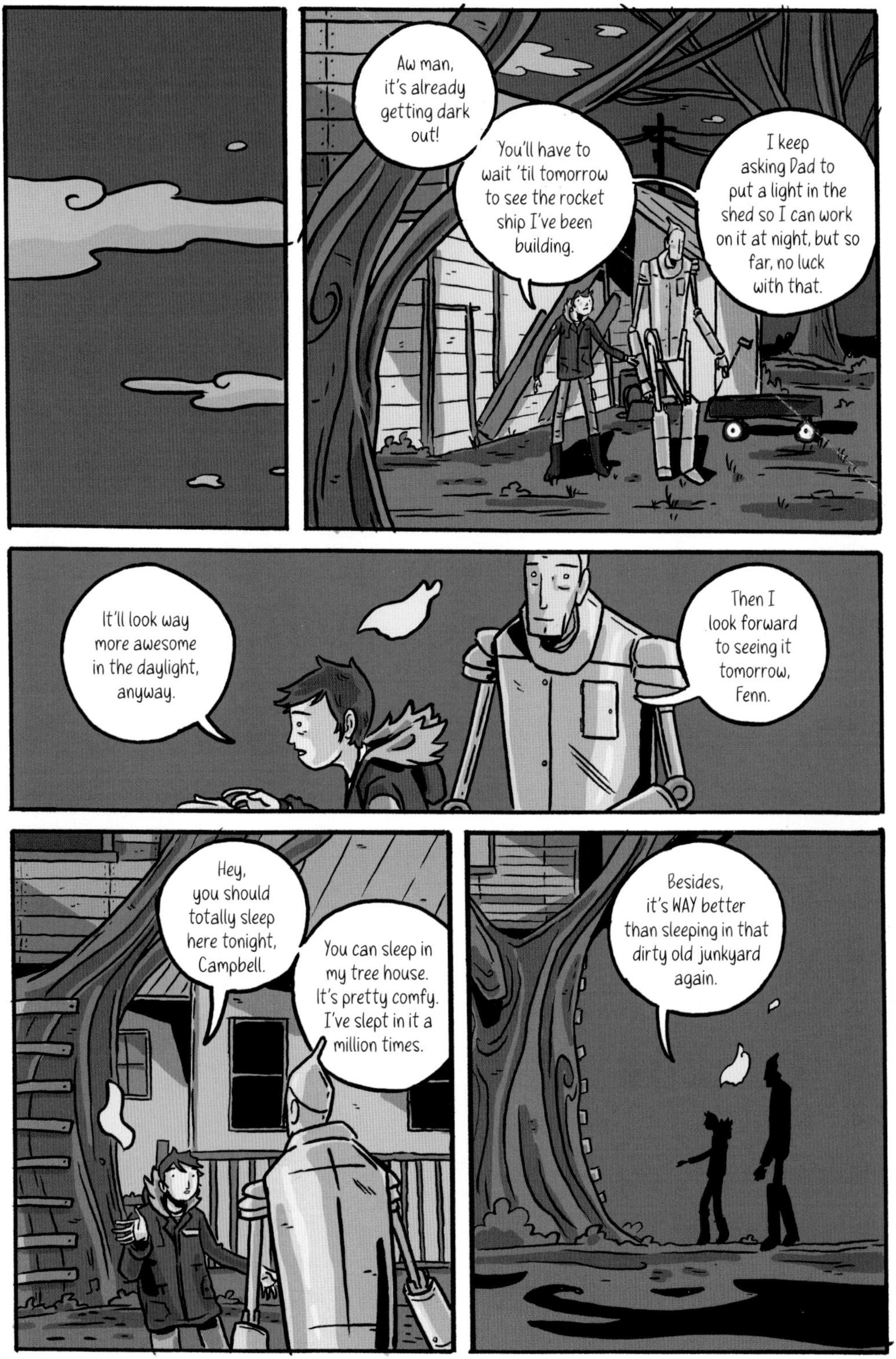
Aw man, it's already getting dark out!
You'll have to wait 'til tomorrow to see the rocket ship I've been building.
I keep asking Dad to put a light in the shed so I can work on it at night, but so far, no luck with that.
It'll look way more awesome in the daylight, anyway.
Then I look forward to seeing it tomorrow, Fenn.
Hey, you should totally sleep here tonight, Campbell.
You can sleep in my tree house. It's pretty comfy. I've slept in it a million times.
Besides, it's WAY better than sleeping in that dirty old junkyard again.

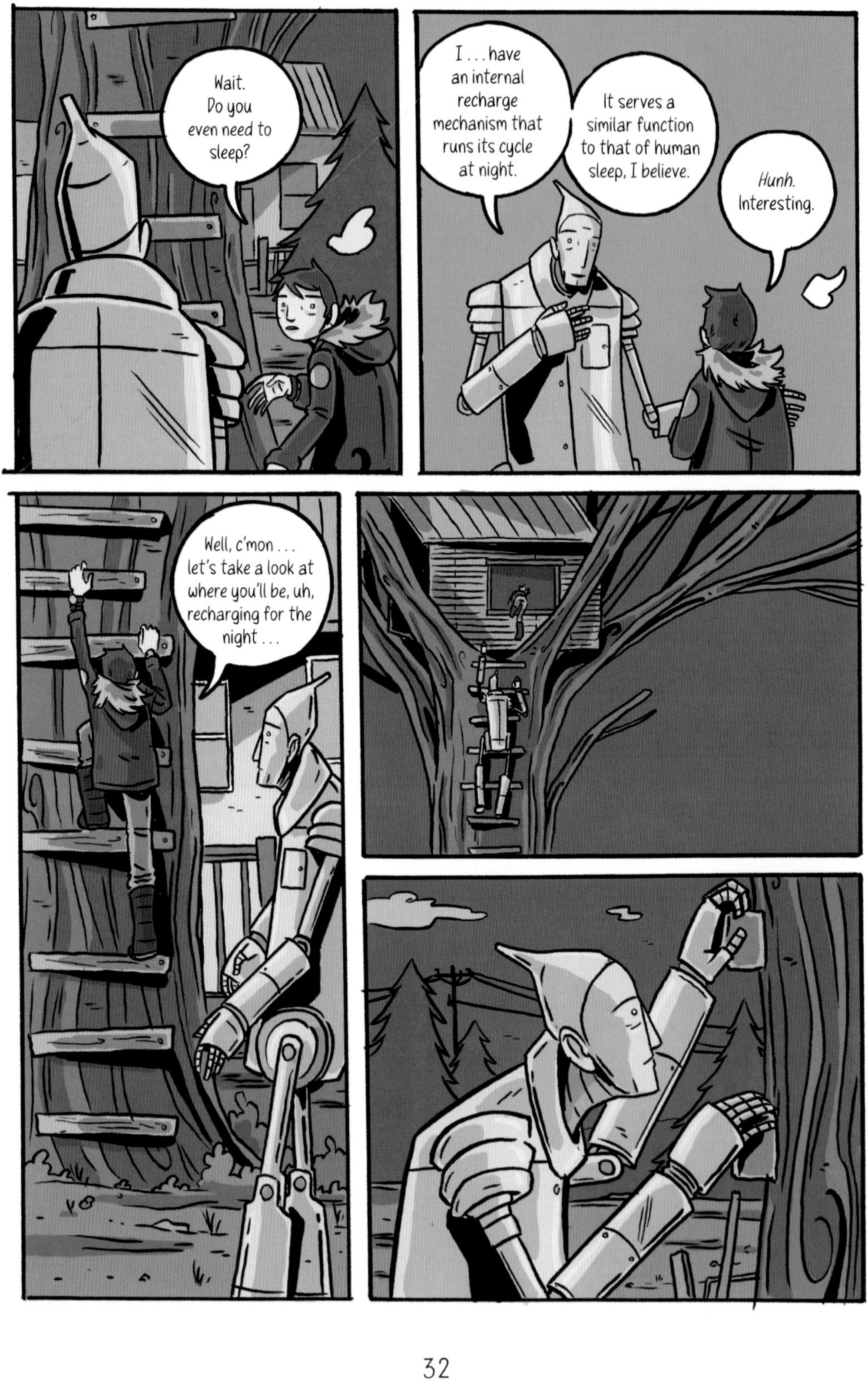
Wait.
Do you even need to sleep?
I . . . have an internal recharge mechanism that runs its cycle at night.
It serves a similar function to that of human sleep, I believe.
Hunh. Interesting.
Well, c'mon . . . let's take a look at where you'll be, uh, recharging for the night . . .

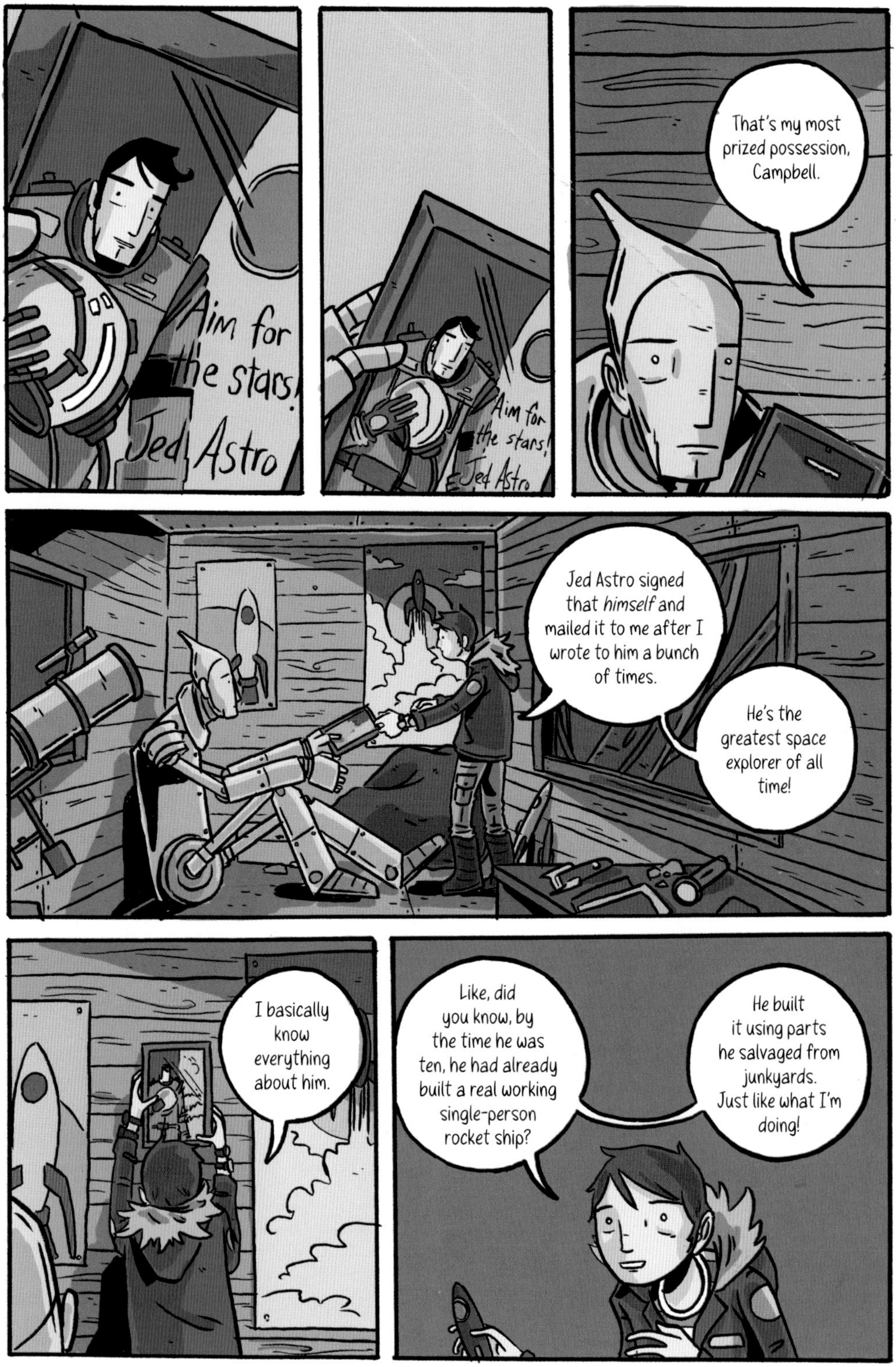
Aim for the stars!
Jed Astro
Aim for the stars!
Jed Astro
That's my most prized possession, Campbell.
Jed Astro signed that *himself* and mailed it to me after I wrote to him a bunch of times.
He's the greatest space explorer of all time!
I basically know everything about him.
Like, did you know, by the time he was ten, he had already built a real working single-person rocket ship?
He built it using parts he salvaged from junkyards. Just like what I'm doing!

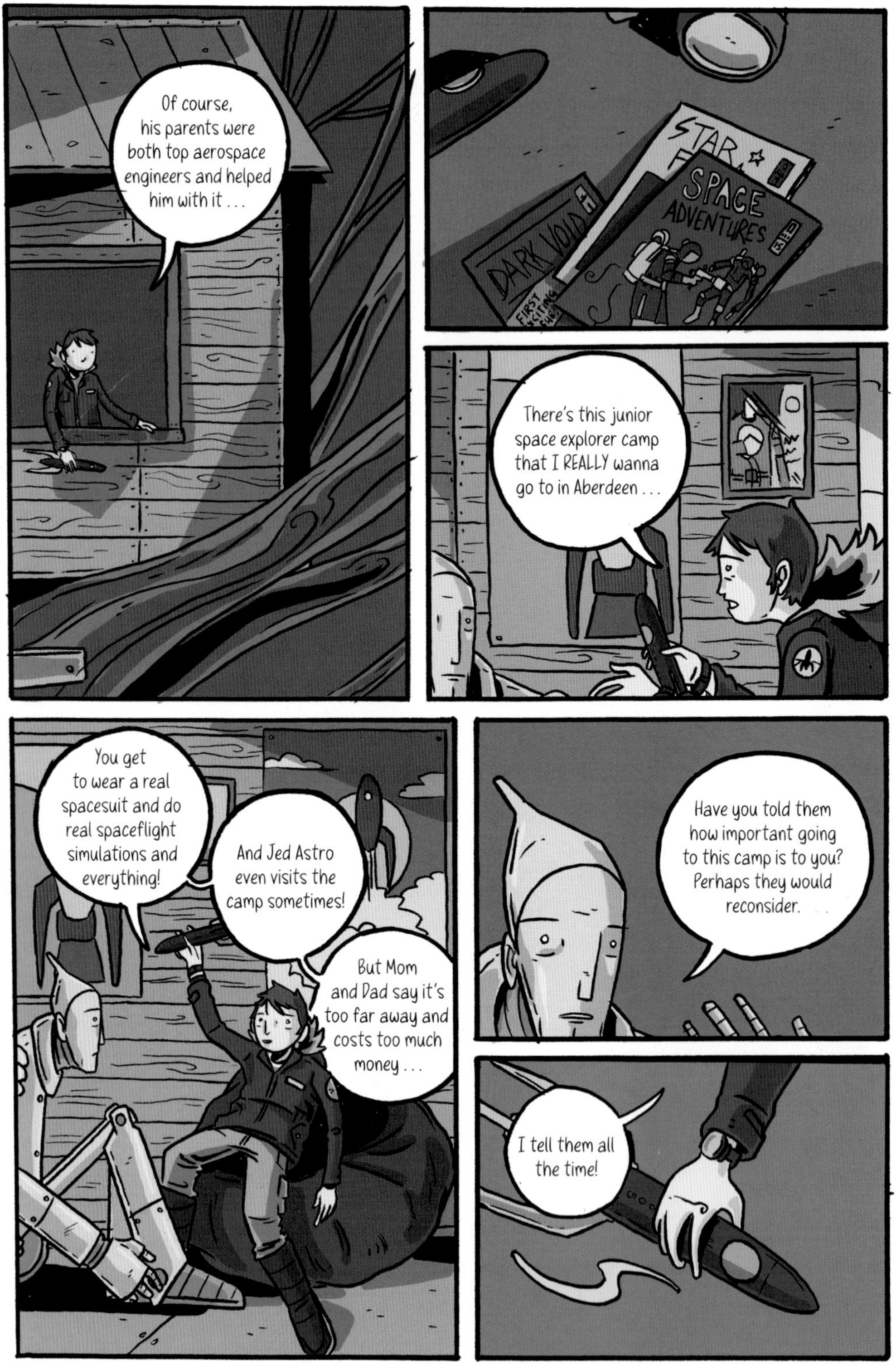
Of course, his parents were both top aerospace engineers and helped him with it . . .
STAR
SPACE ADVENTURES
DARK VOID
There's this junior space explorer camp that I REALLY wanna go to in Aberdeen . . .
You get to wear a real spacesuit and do real spaceflight simulations and everything!
And Jed Astro even visits the camp sometimes!
But Mom and Dad say it's too far away and costs too much money . . .
Have you told them how important going to this camp is to you? Perhaps they would reconsider.
I tell them all the time!

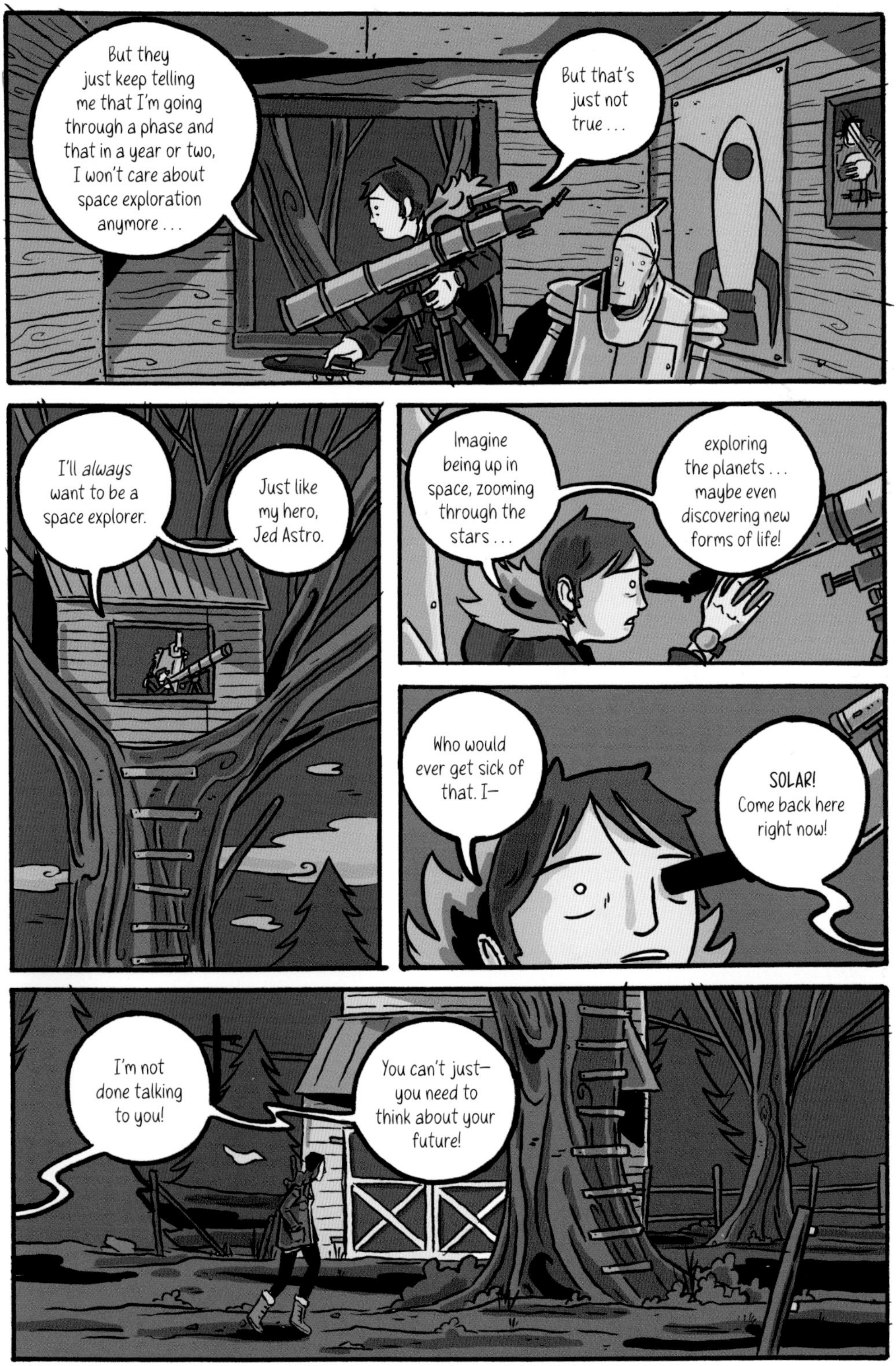
But they just keep telling me that I'm going through a phase and that in a year or two, I won't care about space exploration anymore . . .
But that's just not true . . .
I'll *always* want to be a space explorer.
Just like my hero, Jed Astro.
Imagine being up in space, zooming through the stars . . .
exploring the planets . . . maybe even discovering new forms of life!
Who would ever get sick of that. I—
SOLAR! Come back here right now!
I'm not done talking to you!
You can't just— you need to think about your future!

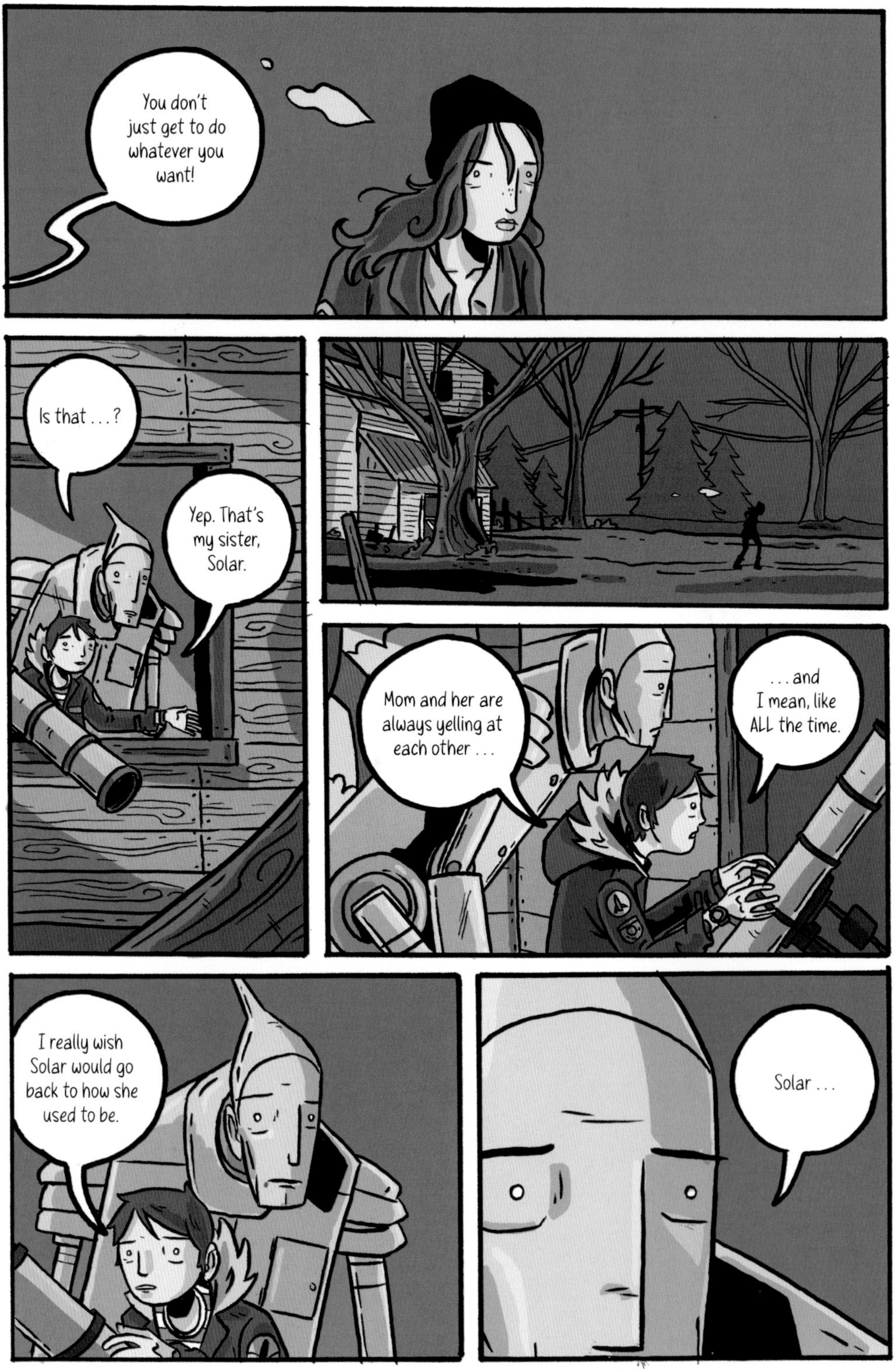
You don't just get to do whatever you want!
Is that . . . ?
Yep. That's my sister, Solar.
Mom and her are always yelling at each other . . .
. . . and I mean, like ALL the time.
I really wish Solar would go back to how she used to be.
Solar . . .

CHAPTER 4: Sky's the Limit

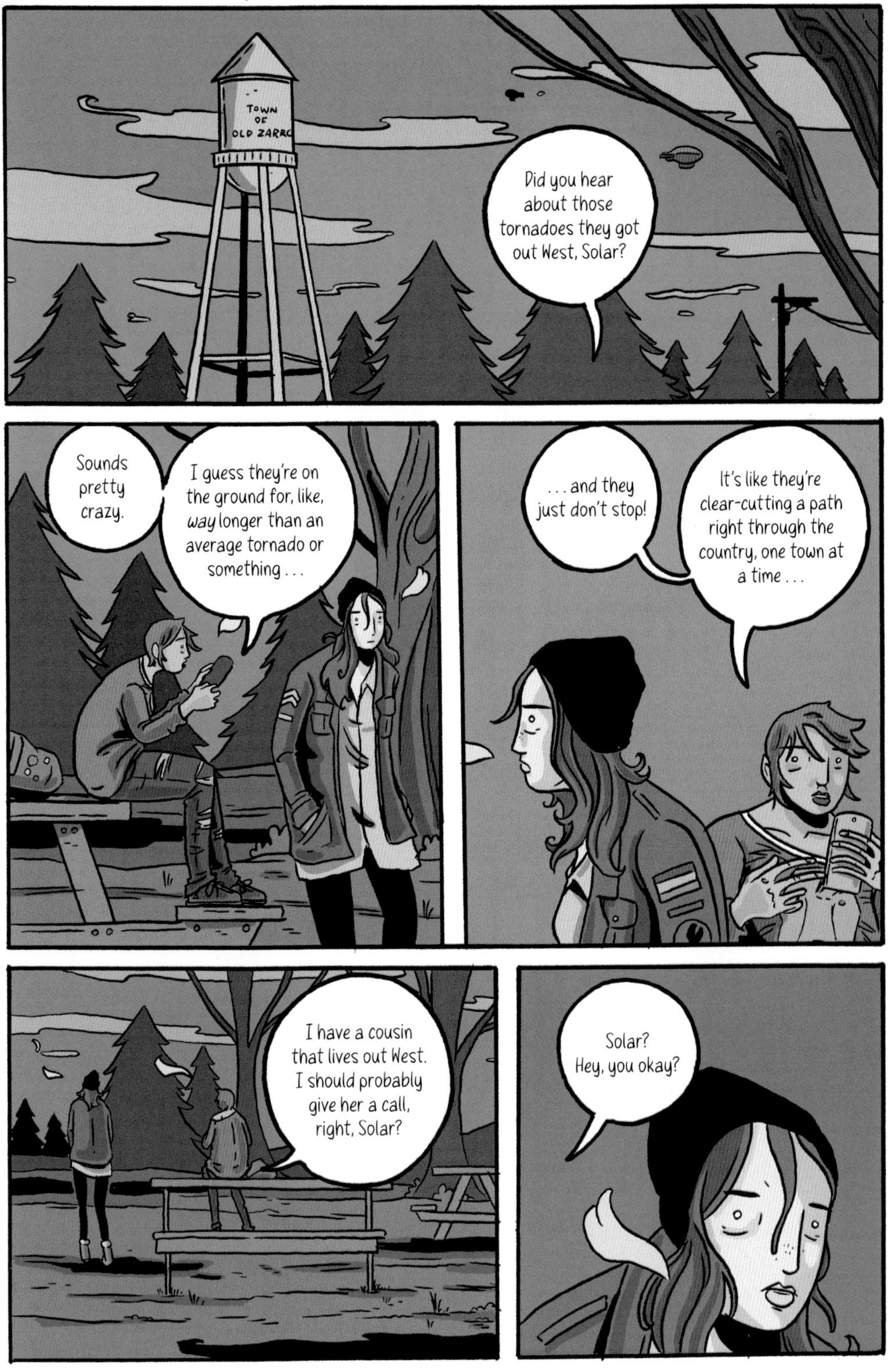
TOWN OF OLD ZARRO
Did you hear about those tornadoes they got out West, Solar?
Sounds pretty crazy.
I guess they're on the ground for, like, *way* longer than an average tornado or something . . .
. . . and they just don't stop!
It's like they're clear-cutting a path right through the country, one town at a time . . .
I have a cousin that lives out West. I should probably give her a call, right, Solar?
Solar? Hey, you okay?

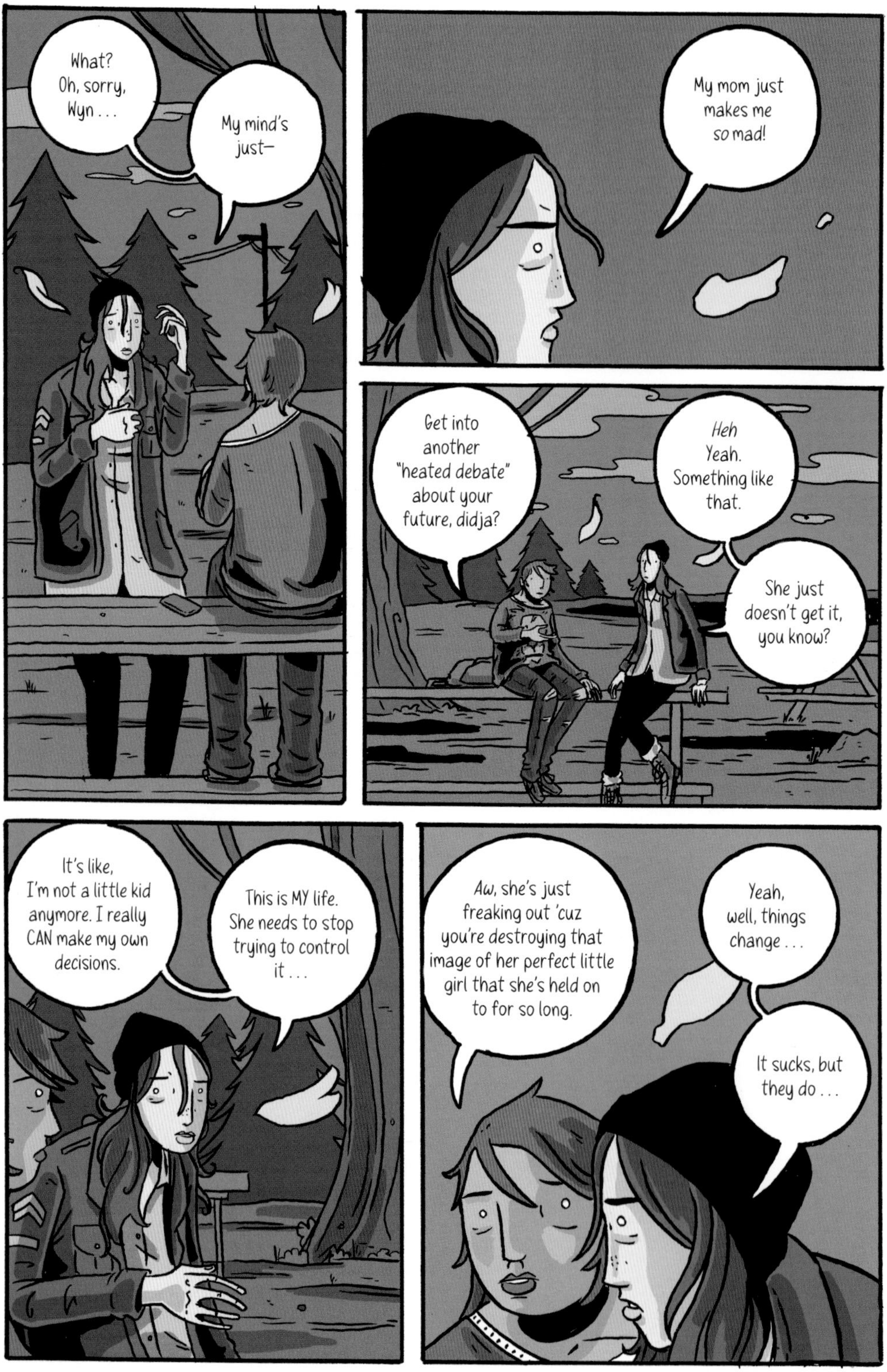
What? Oh, sorry, Wyn . . .
My mind's just—
My mom just makes me so mad!
Get into another "heated debate" about your future, didja?
Heh Yeah. Something like that.
She just doesn't get it, you know?
It's like, I'm not a little kid anymore. I really CAN make my own decisions.
This is MY life. She needs to stop trying to control it . . .
Aw, she's just freaking out 'cuz you're destroying that image of her perfect little girl that she's held on to for so long.
Yeah, well, things change . . .
It sucks, but they do . . .

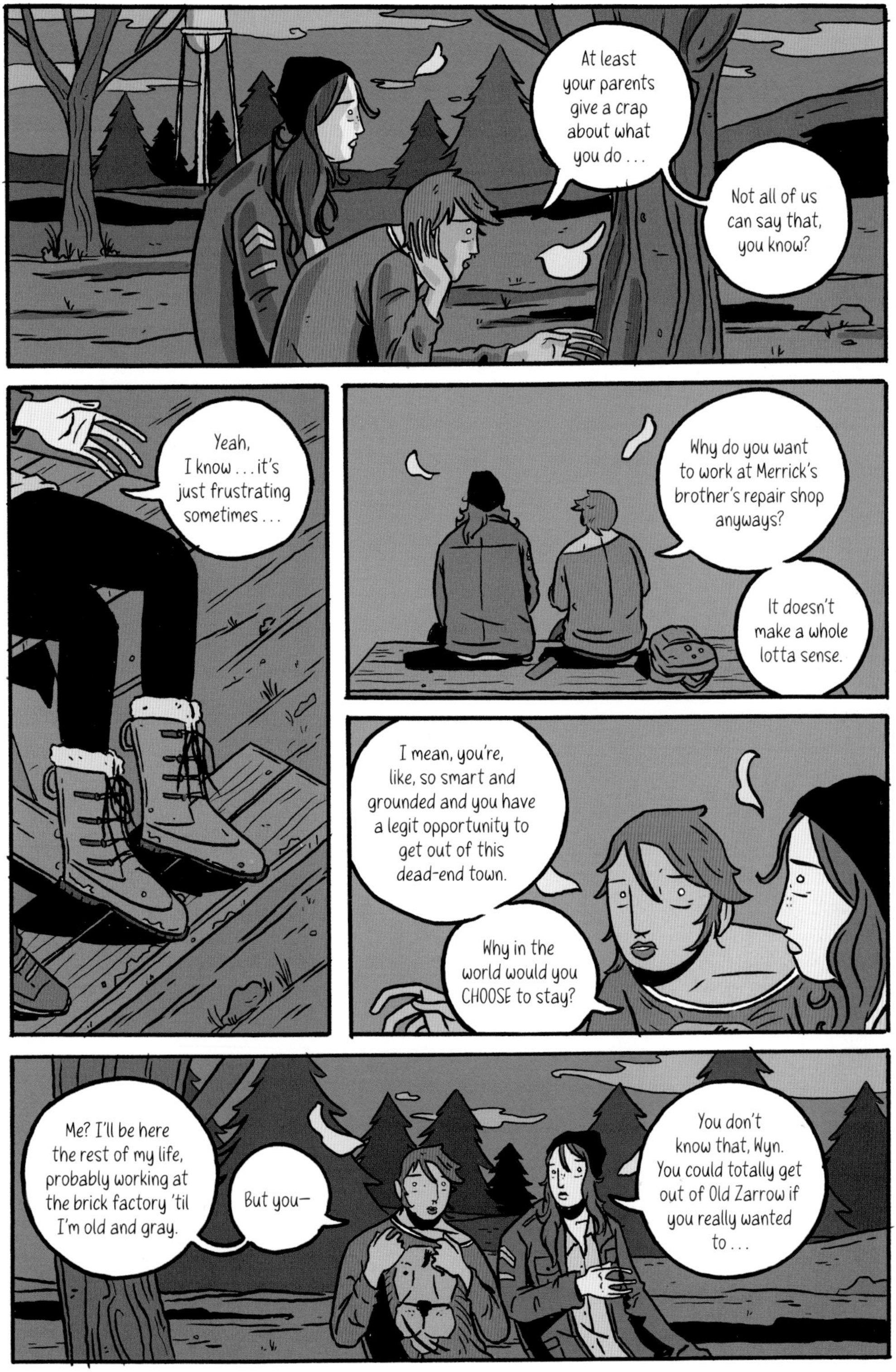
At least your parents give a crap about what you do . . .
Not all of us can say that, you know?
Yeah, I know . . . it's just frustrating sometimes . . .
Why do you want to work at Merrick's brother's repair shop anyways?
It doesn't make a whole lotta sense.
I mean, you're, like, so smart and grounded and you have a legit opportunity to get out of this dead-end town.
Why in the world would you CHOOSE to stay?
Me? I'll be here the rest of my life, probably working at the brick factory 'til I'm old and gray.
But you—
You don't know that, Wyn. You could totally get out of Old Zarrow if you really wanted to . . .

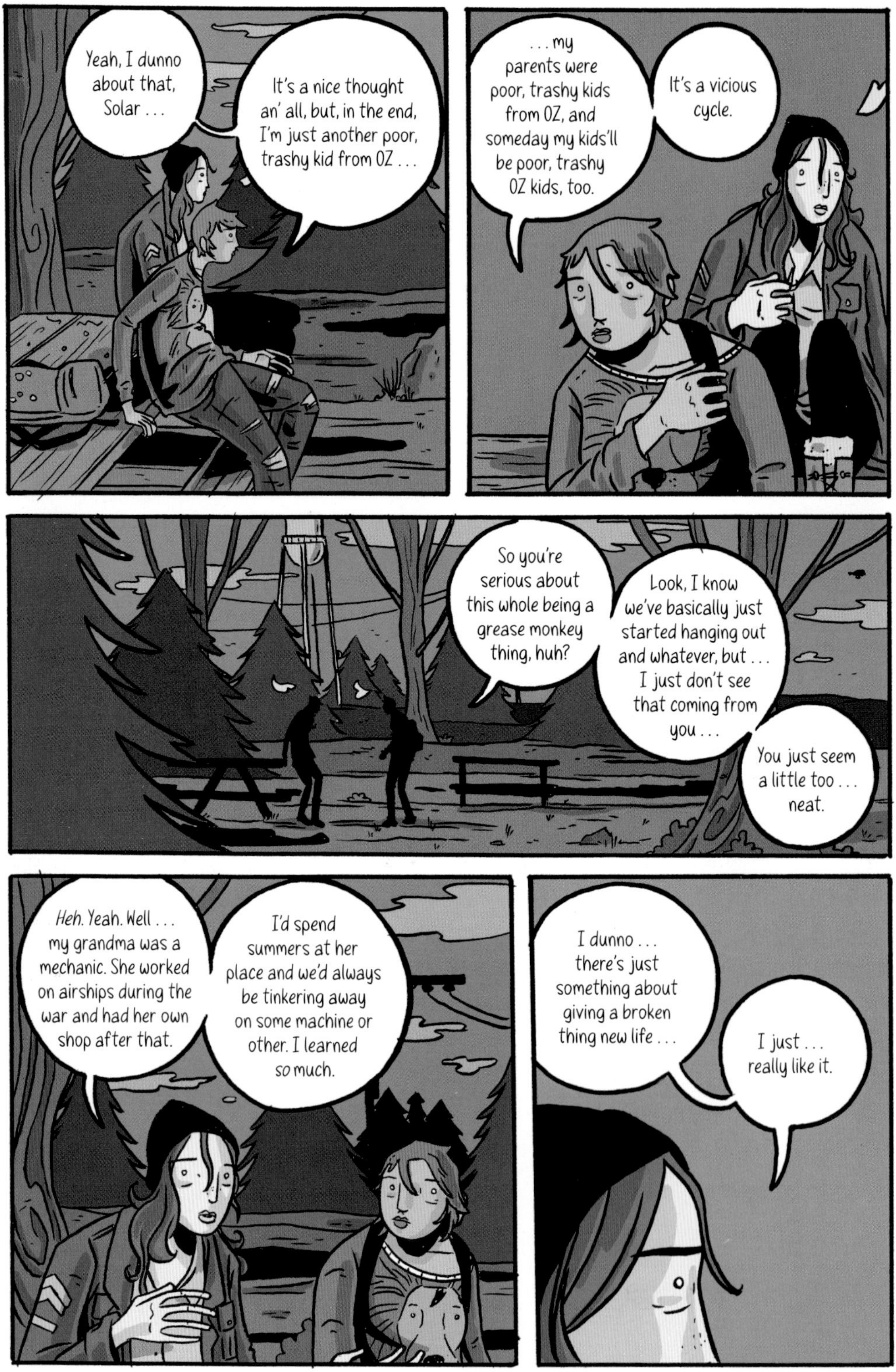
Yeah, I dunno about that, Solar . . .
It's a nice thought an' all, but, in the end, I'm just another poor, trashy kid from OZ . . .
. . . my parents were poor, trashy kids from OZ, and someday my kids'll be poor, trashy OZ kids, too.
It's a vicious cycle.
So you're serious about this whole being a grease monkey thing, huh?
Look, I know we've basically just started hanging out and whatever, but . . . I just don't see that coming from you . . .
You just seem a little too . . . neat.
Heh. Yeah. Well . . . my grandma was a mechanic. She worked on airships during the war and had her own shop after that.
I'd spend summers at her place and we'd always be tinkering away on some machine or other. I learned *so* much.
I dunno . . . there's just something about giving a broken thing new life . . .
I just . . . really like it.

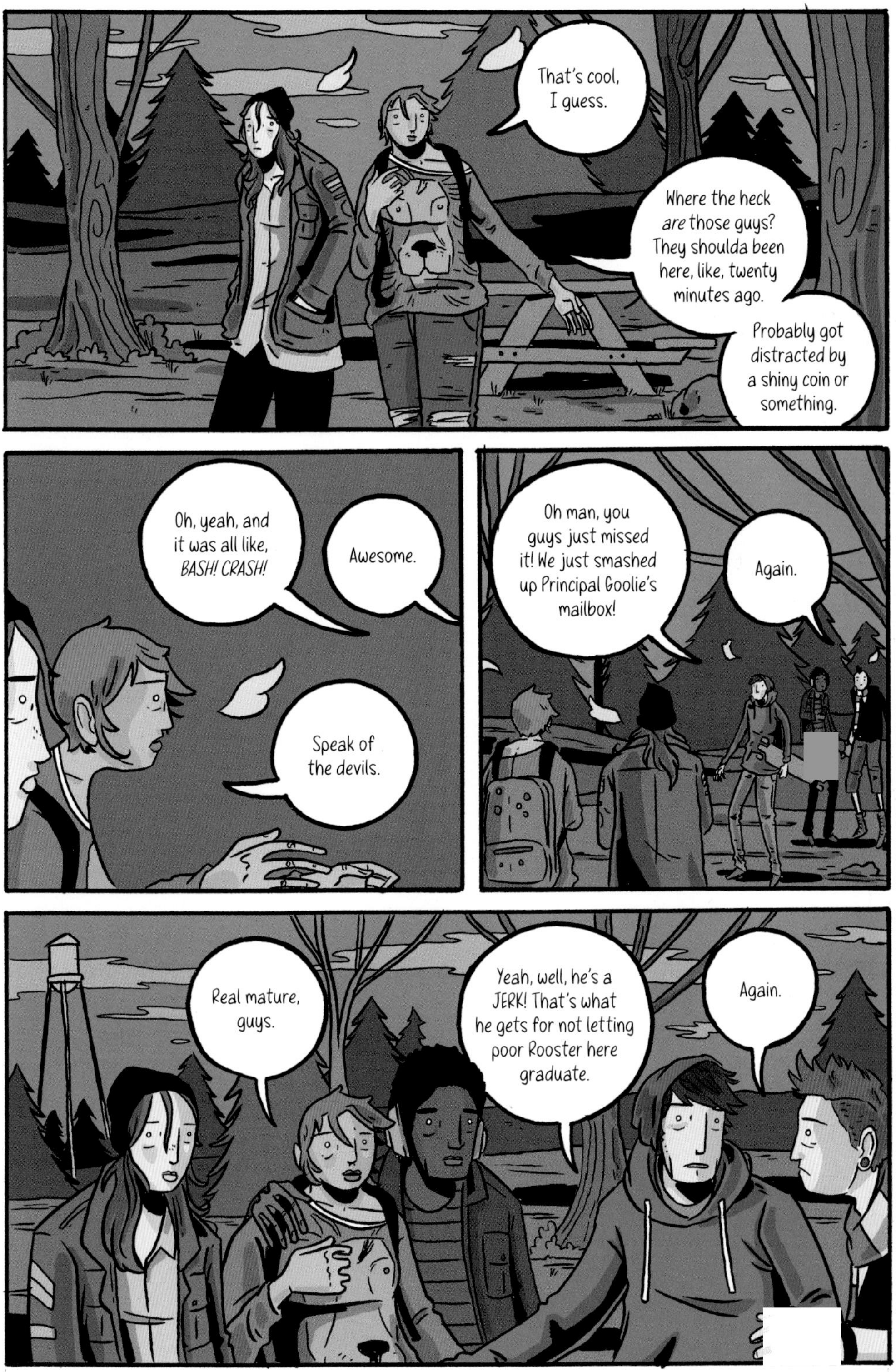
That's cool, I guess.
Where the heck *are* those guys? They shoulda been here, like, twenty minutes ago.
Probably got distracted by a shiny coin or something.
Oh, yeah, and it was all like, *BASH! CRASH!*
Awesome.
Speak of the devils.
Oh man, you guys just missed it! We just smashed up Principal Goolie's mailbox!
Again.
Real mature, guys.
Yeah, well, he's a JERK! That's what he gets for not letting poor Rooster here graduate.
Again.

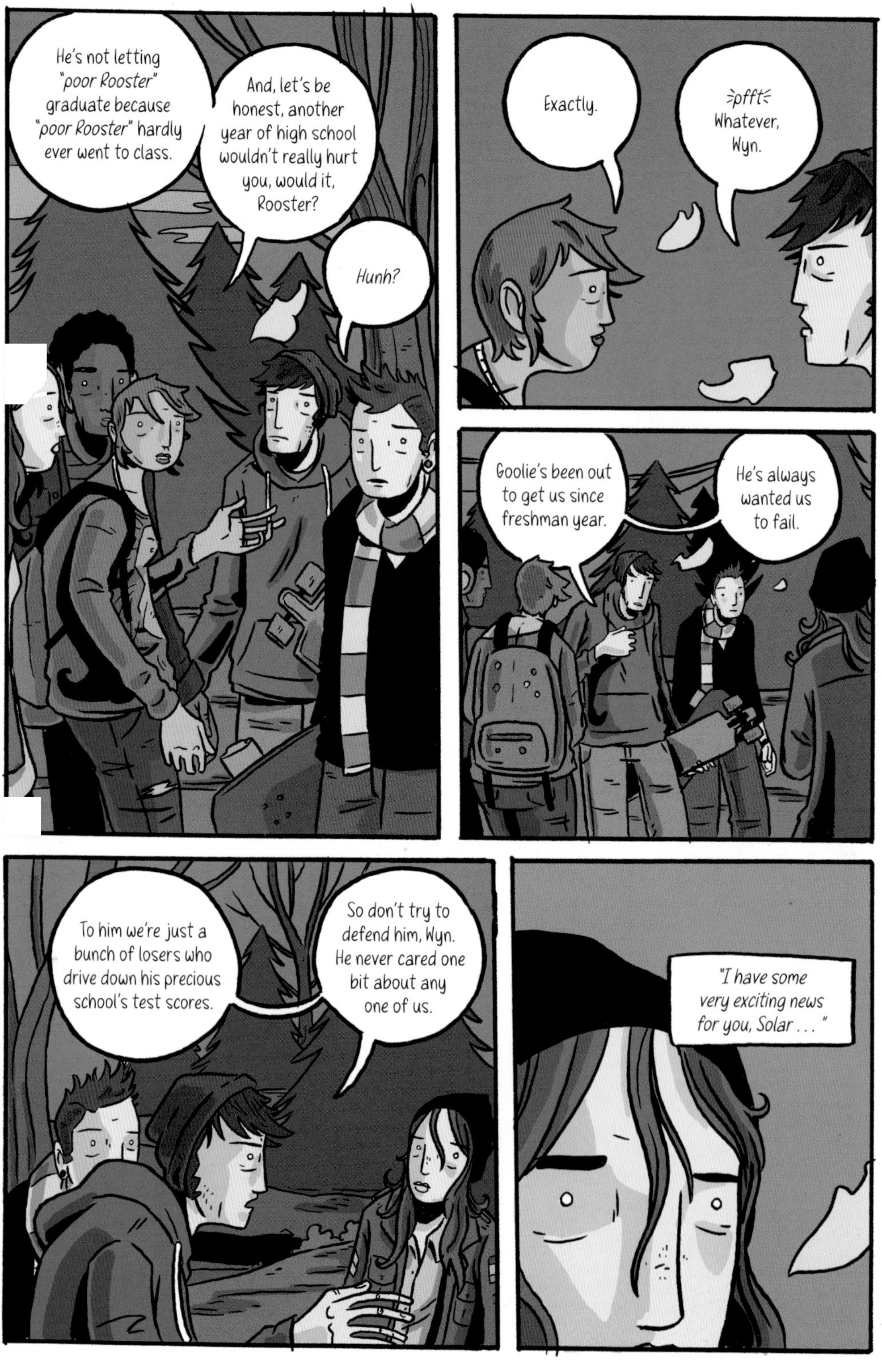
He's not letting "poor Rooster" graduate because "poor Rooster" hardly ever went to class.
And, let's be honest, another year of high school wouldn't really hurt you, would it, Rooster?
Hunh?
Exactly.
≠pfft≠ Whatever, Wyn.
Goolie's been out to get us since freshman year.
He's always wanted us to fail.
To him we're just a bunch of losers who drive down his precious school's test scores.
So don't try to defend him, Wyn. He never cared one bit about any one of us.
"I have some very exciting news for you, Solar . . ."

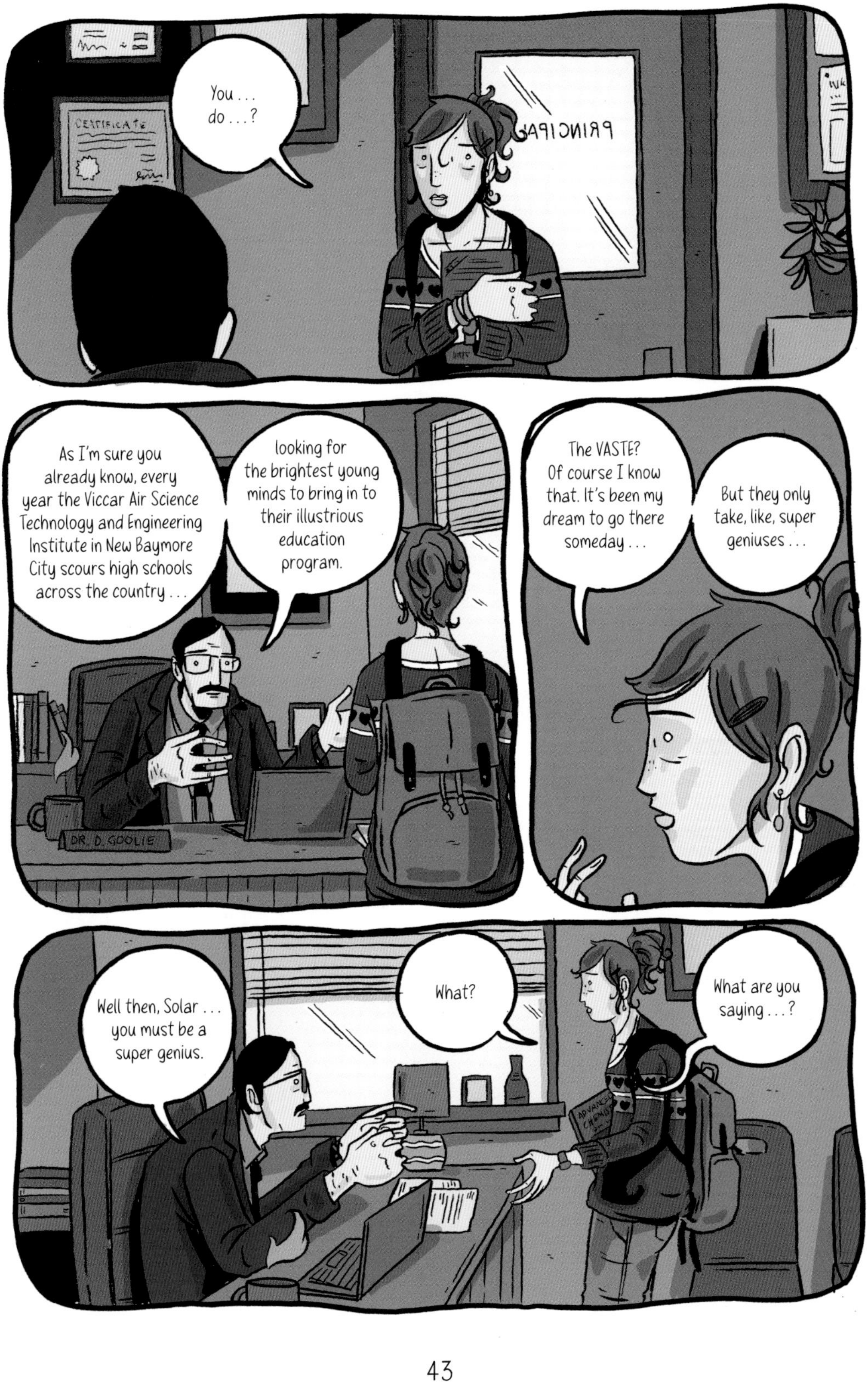
You . . . do . . . ?
PRINCIPAL
CERTIFICATE
As I'm sure you already know, every year the Viccar Air Science Technology and Engineering Institute in New Baymore City scours high schools across the country . . .
looking for the brightest young minds to bring in to their illustrious education program.
DR. D. GOOLIE
The VASTE? Of course I know that. It's been my dream to go there someday . . .
But they only take, like, super geniuses . . .
Well then, Solar . . . you must be a super genius.
What?
What are you saying . . . ?

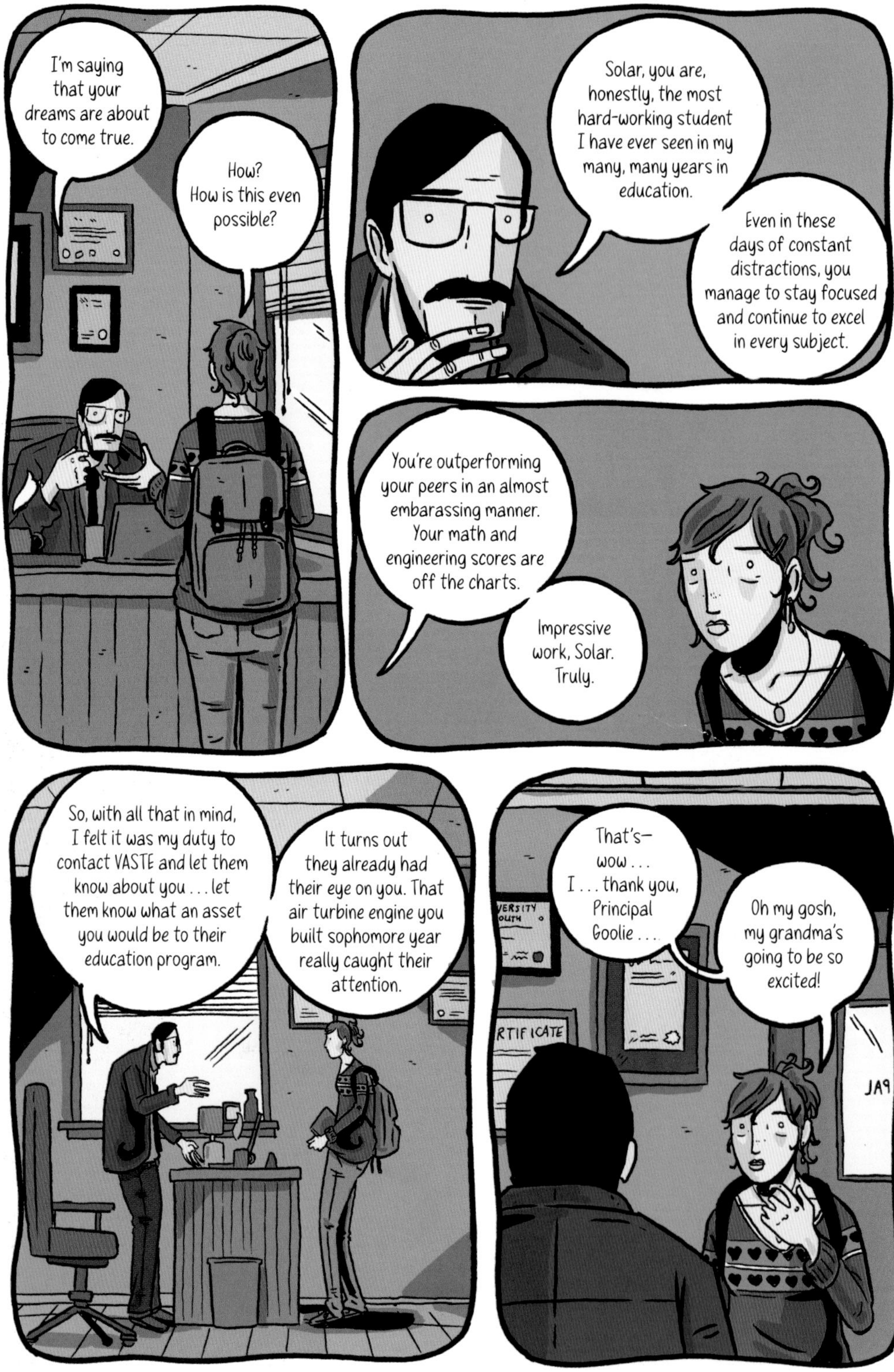
I'm saying that your dreams are about to come true.
How? How is this even possible?
Solar, you are, honestly, the most hard-working student I have ever seen in my many, many years in education.
Even in these days of constant distractions, you manage to stay focused and continue to excel in every subject.
You're outperforming your peers in an almost embarassing manner. Your math and engineering scores are off the charts.
Impressive work, Solar. Truly.
So, with all that in mind, I felt it was my duty to contact VASTE and let them know about you . . . let them know what an asset you would be to their education program.
It turns out they already had their eye on you. That air turbine engine you built sophomore year really caught their attention.
That's— wow . . . I . . . thank you, Principal Goolie . . .
Oh my gosh, my grandma's going to be so excited!

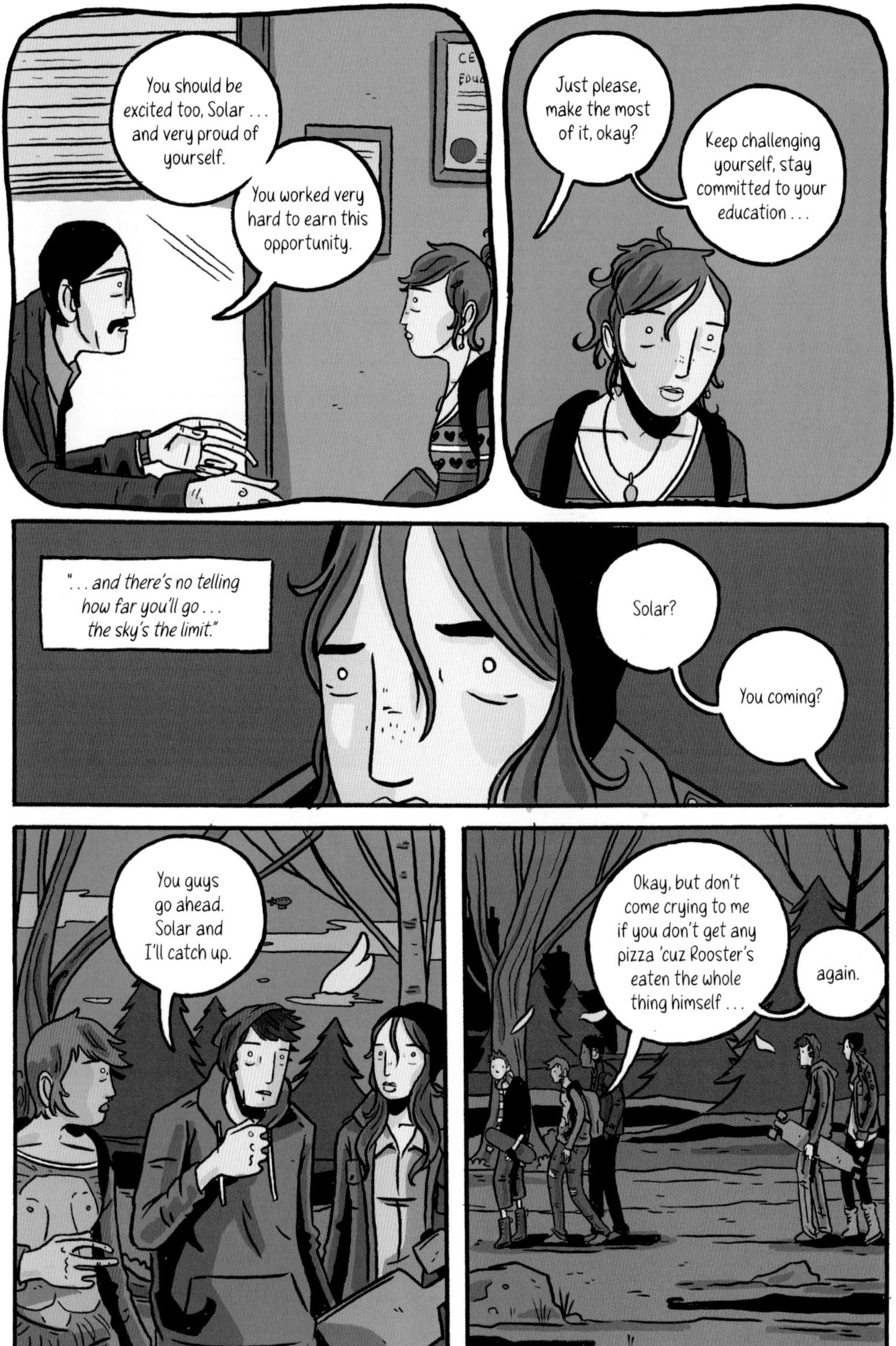
You should be excited too, Solar . . . and very proud of yourself.
You worked very hard to earn this opportunity.
Just please, make the most of it, okay?
Keep challenging yourself, stay committed to your education . . .
". . . and there's no telling how far you'll go . . . the sky's the limit."
Solar?
You coming?
You guys go ahead. Solar and I'll catch up.
Okay, but don't come crying to me if you don't get any pizza 'cuz Rooster's eaten the whole thing himself . . .
again.

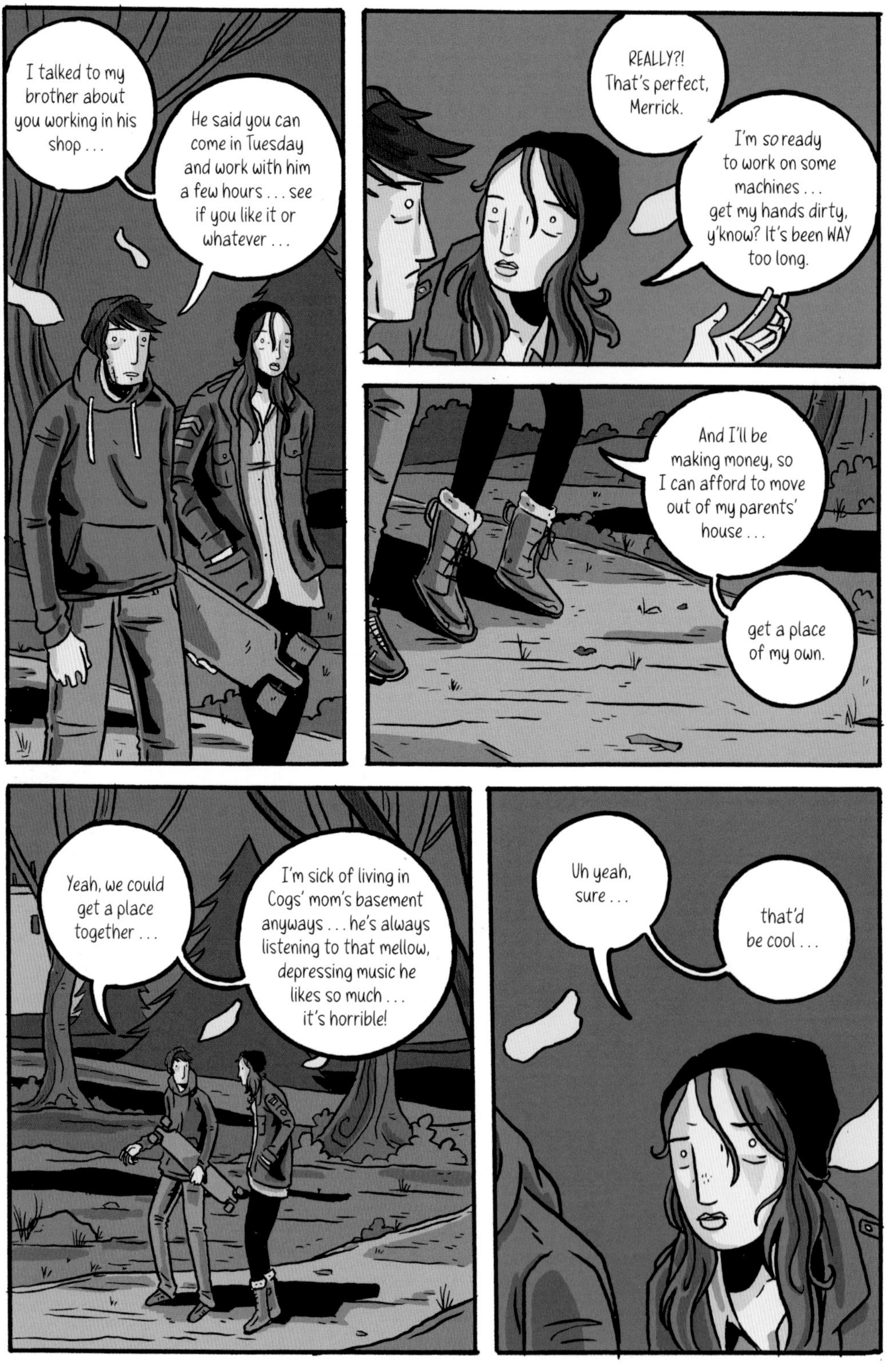
I talked to my brother about you working in his shop . . .
He said you can come in Tuesday and work with him a few hours . . . see if you like it or whatever . . .
REALLY?! That's perfect, Merrick.
I'm so ready to work on some machines . . . get my hands dirty, y'know? It's been WAY too long.
And I'll be making money, so I can afford to move out of my parents' house . . .
get a place of my own.
Yeah, we could get a place together . . .
I'm sick of living in Cogs' mom's basement anyways . . . he's always listening to that mellow, depressing music he likes so much . . . it's horrible!
Uh yeah, sure . . .
that'd be cool . . .

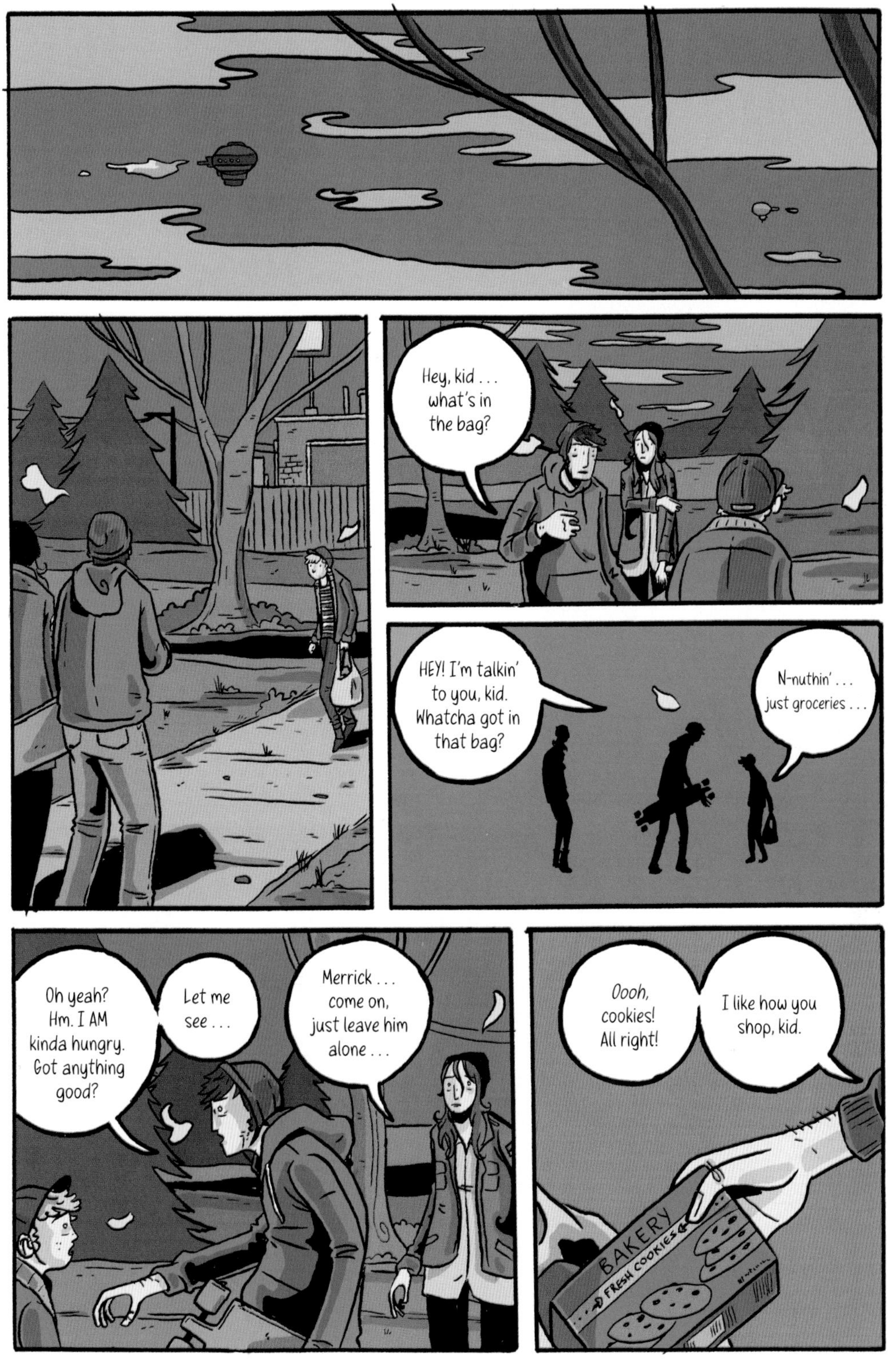
Hey, kid . . . what's in the bag?
HEY! I'm talkin' to you, kid. Whatcha got in that bag?
N-nuthin' . . . just groceries . . .
Oh yeah? Hm. I AM kinda hungry. Got anything good?
Let me see . . .
Merrick . . . come on, just leave him alone . . .
Oooh, cookies! All right!
I like how you shop, kid.
BAKERY
FRESH COOKIES

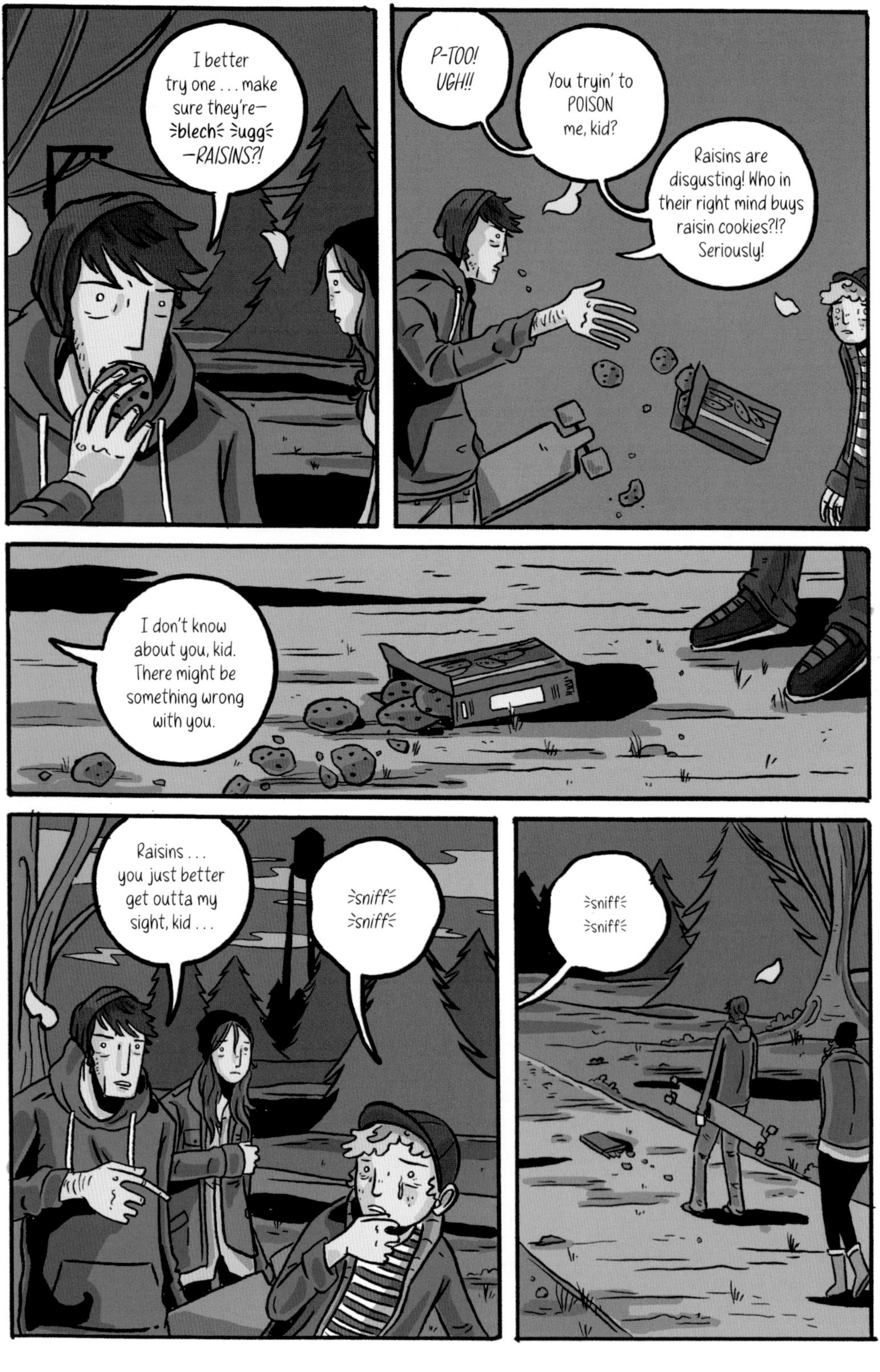
I better try one . . . make sure they're— ⋛blech⋚ ⋛ugg⋚ —RAISINS?!
P-TOO! UGH!!
You tryin' to POISON me, kid?
Raisins are disgusting! Who in their right mind buys raisin cookies?!? Seriously!
I don't know about you, kid. There might be something wrong with you.
Raisins . . . you just better get outta my sight, kid . . .
⋛sniff⋚ ⋛sniff⋚
⋛sniff⋚ ⋛sniff⋚

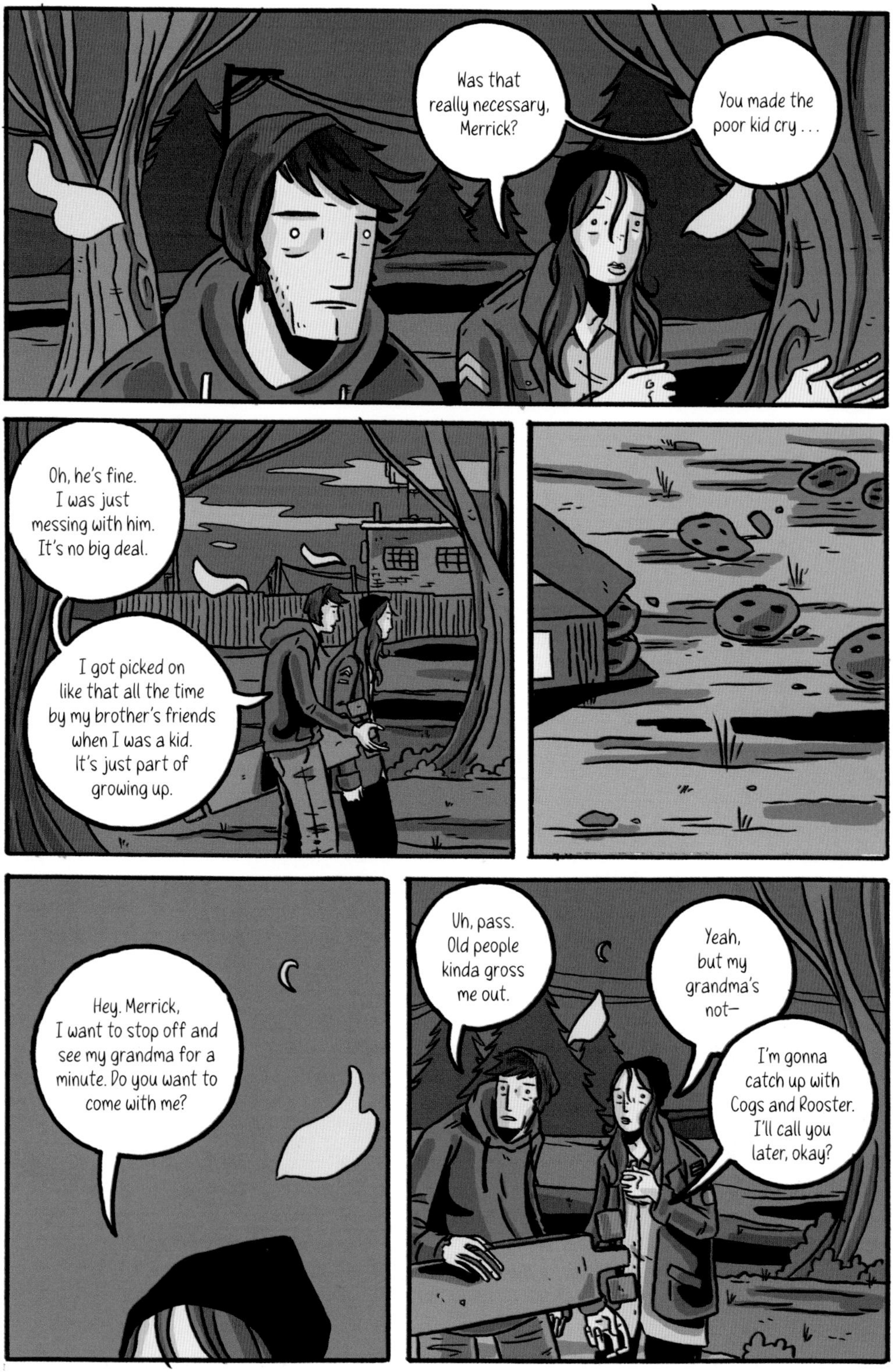
Was that really necessary, Merrick?
You made the poor kid cry . . .
Oh, he's fine. I was just messing with him. It's no big deal.
I got picked on like that all the time by my brother's friends when I was a kid. It's just part of growing up.
Hey. Merrick, I want to stop off and see my grandma for a minute. Do you want to come with me?
Uh, pass. Old people kinda gross me out.
Yeah, but my grandma's not—
I'm gonna catch up with Cogs and Rooster. I'll call you later, okay?

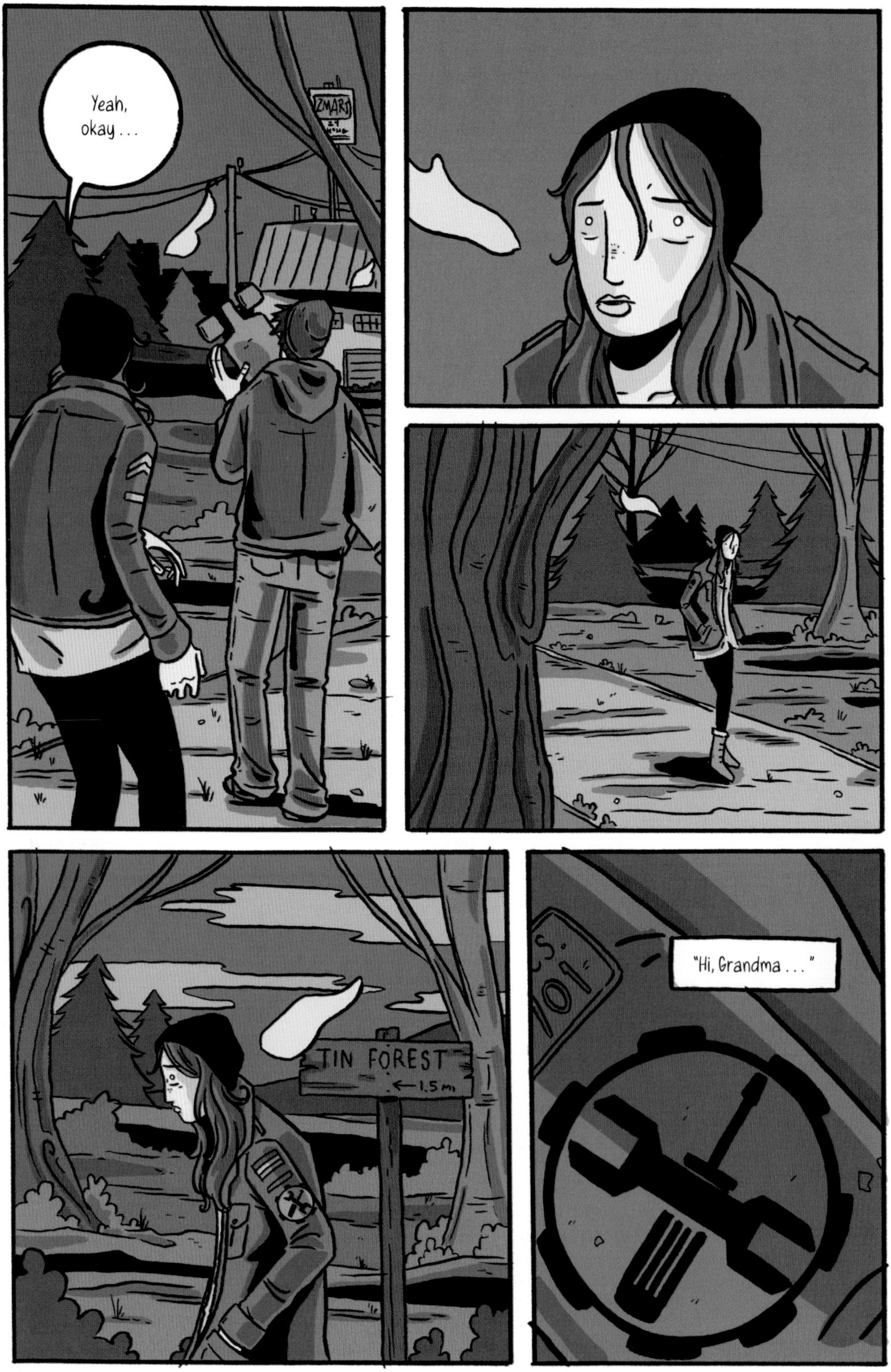
Yeah, okay . . .
"Hi, Grandma . . ."
TIN FOREST
←1.5 mi

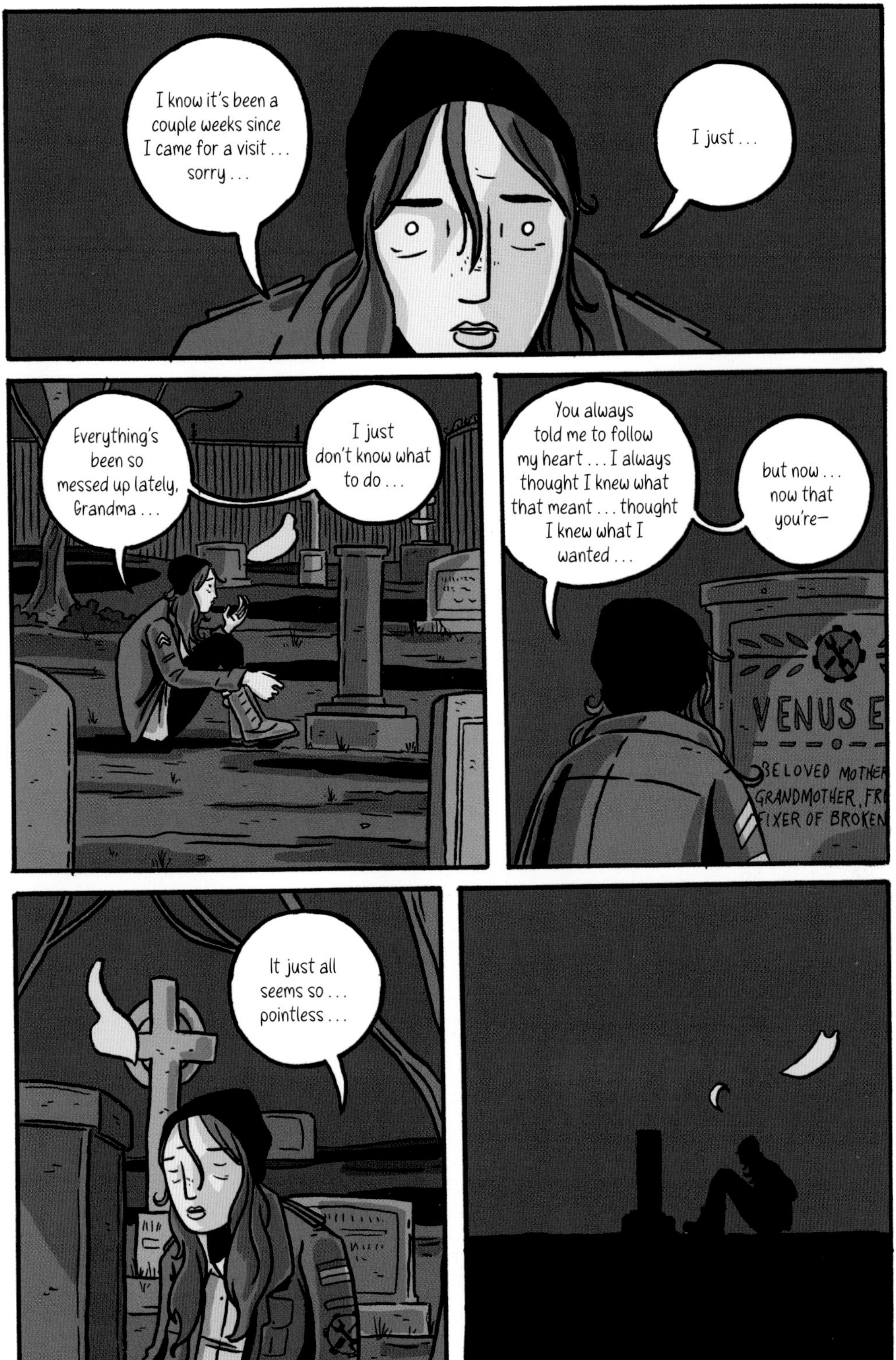
I know it's been a couple weeks since I came for a visit... sorry...
I just...
Everything's been so messed up lately, Grandma...
I just don't know what to do...
You always told me to follow my heart... I always thought I knew what that meant... thought I knew what I wanted...
but now... now that you're—
VENUS E
BELOVED MOTHER
GRANDMOTHER, FR
FIXER OF BROKEN
It just all seems so... pointless...

CHAPTER 5: Stuck

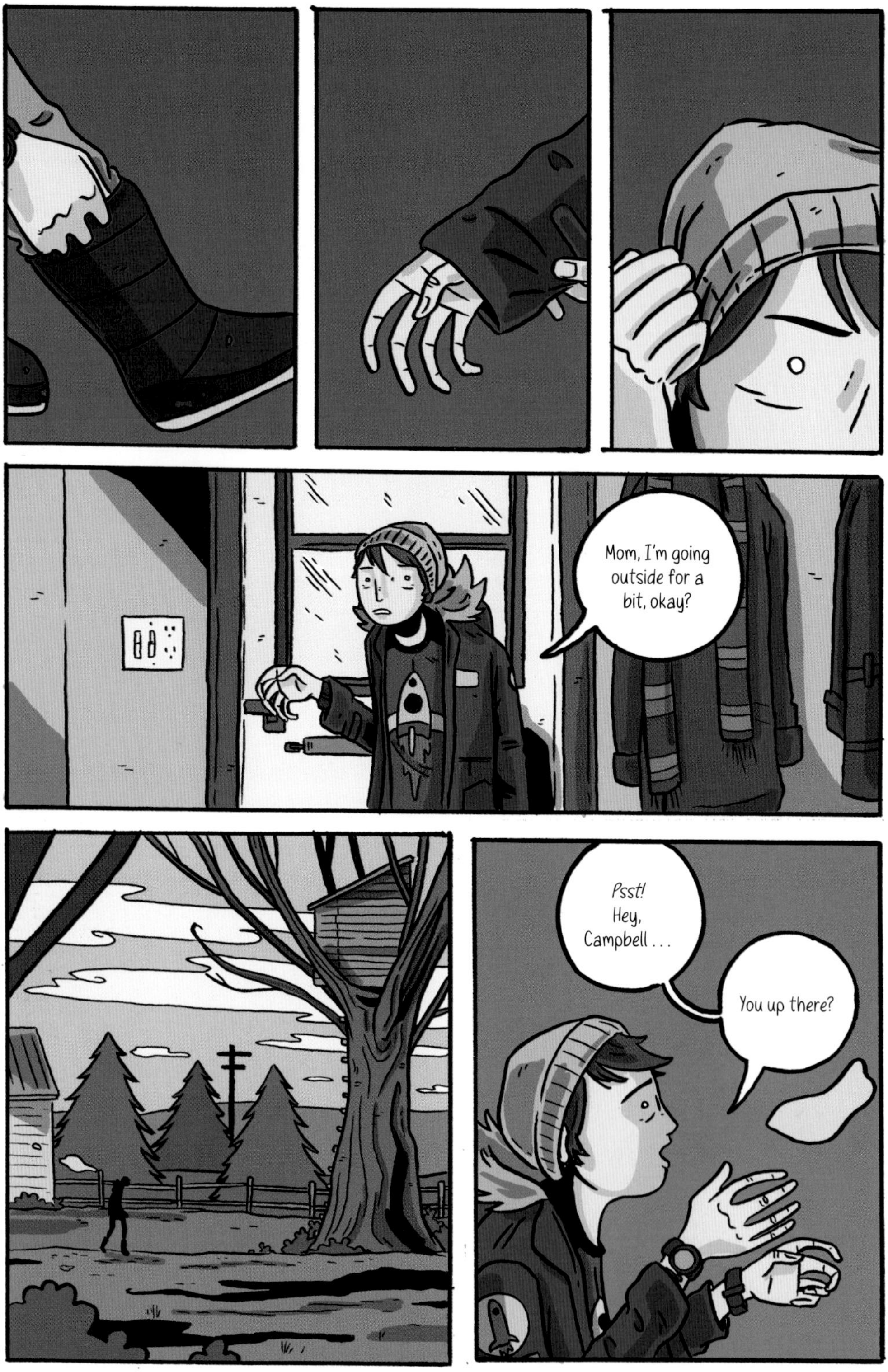
Mom, I'm going outside for a bit, okay?
Psst! Hey, Campbell . . .
You up there?

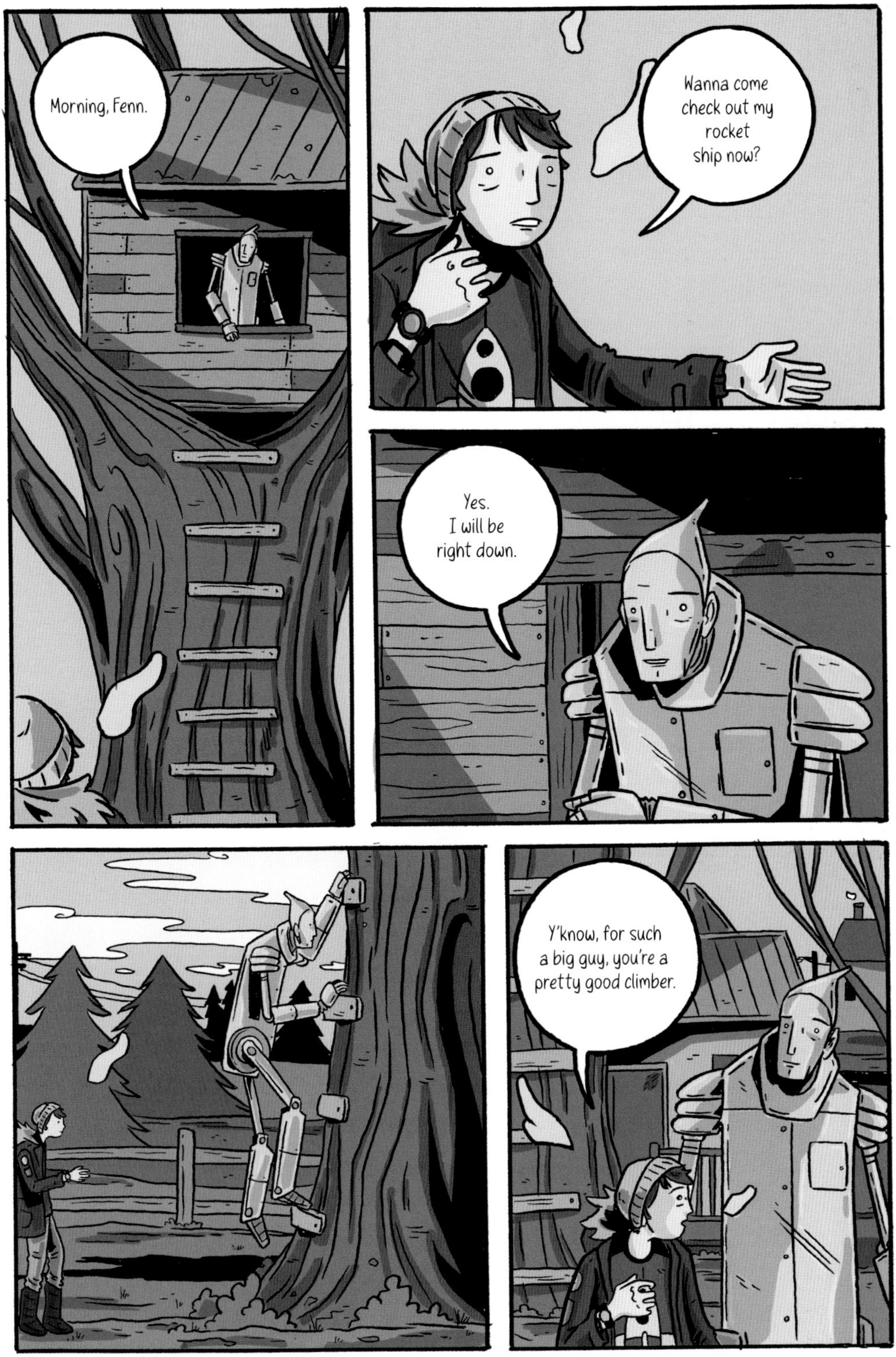
Morning, Fenn.
Wanna come check out my rocket ship now?
Yes. I will be right down.
Y'know, for such a big guy, you're a pretty good climber.

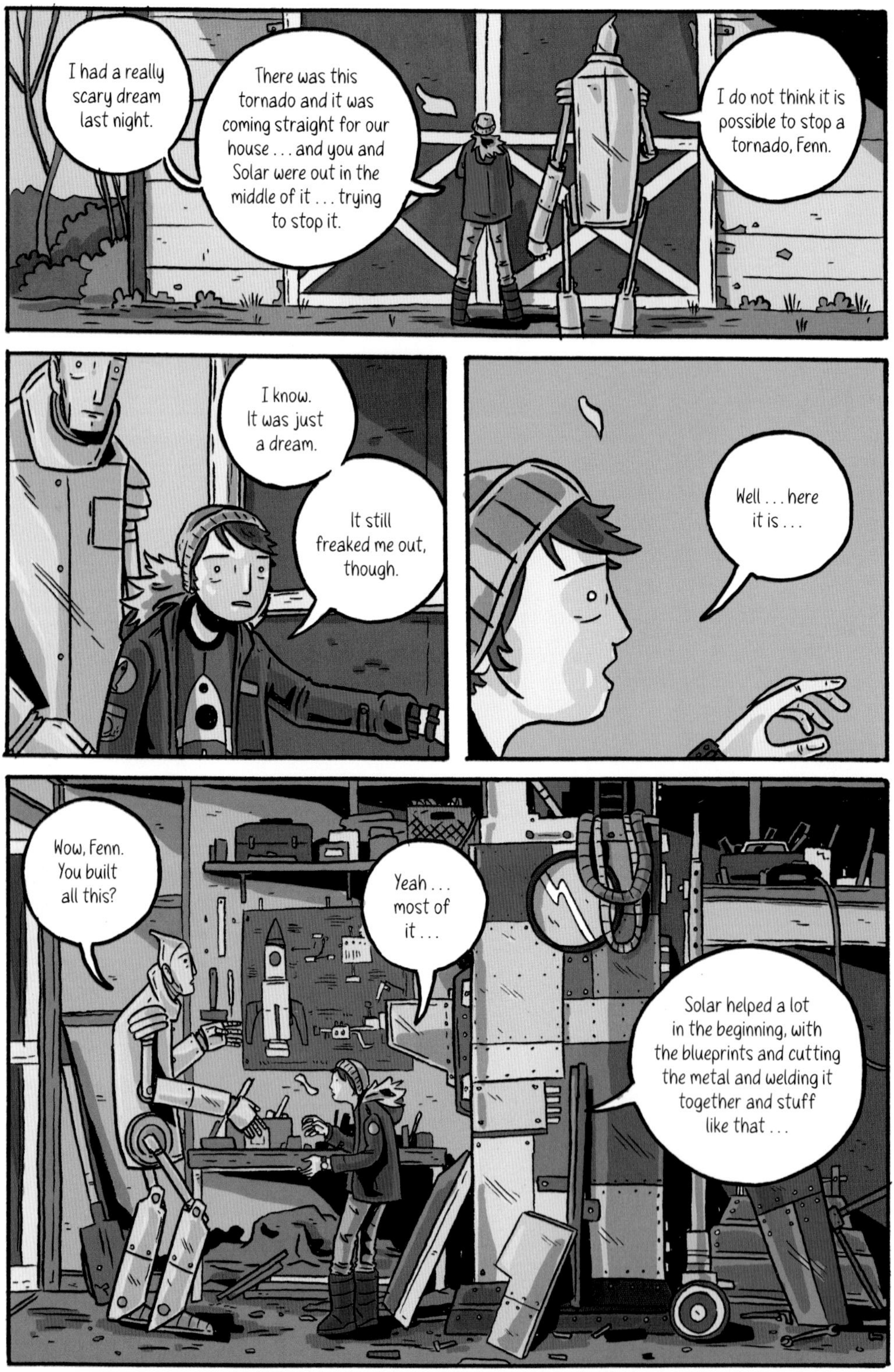
I had a really scary dream last night.
There was this tornado and it was coming straight for our house . . . and you and Solar were out in the middle of it . . . trying to stop it.
I do not think it is possible to stop a tornado, Fenn.
I know. It was just a dream.
It still freaked me out, though.
Well . . . here it is . . .
Wow, Fenn. You built all this?
Yeah . . . most of it . . .
Solar helped a lot in the beginning, with the blueprints and cutting the metal and welding it together and stuff like that . . .

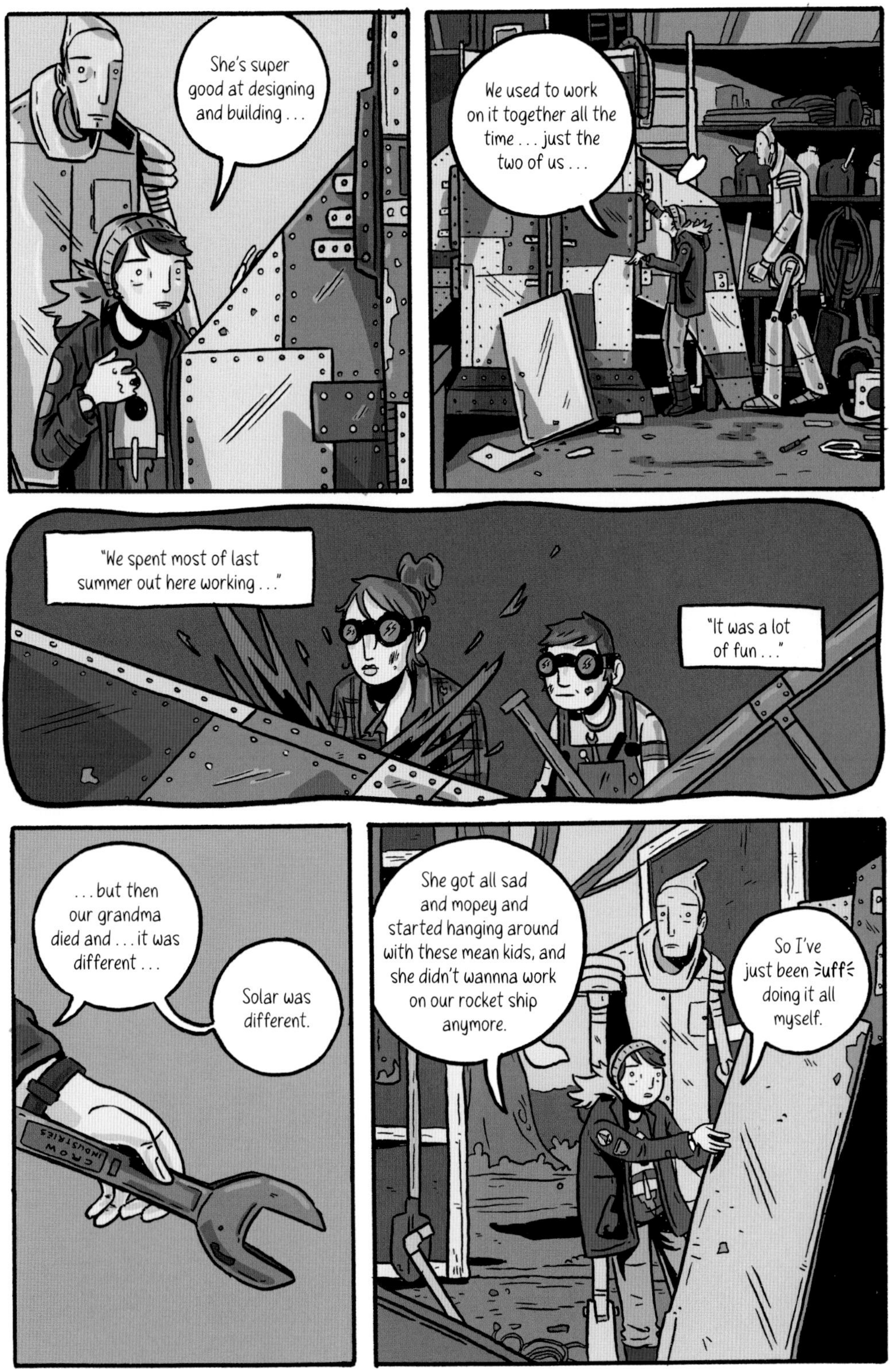
She's super good at designing and building . . .
We used to work on it together all the time . . . just the two of us . . .
"We spent most of last summer out here working . . ."
"It was a lot of fun . . ."
. . . but then our grandma died and . . . it was different . . .
Solar was different.
CROW INDUSTRIES
She got all sad and mopey and started hanging around with these mean kids, and she didn't wanna work on our rocket ship anymore.
So I've just been uff doing it all myself.

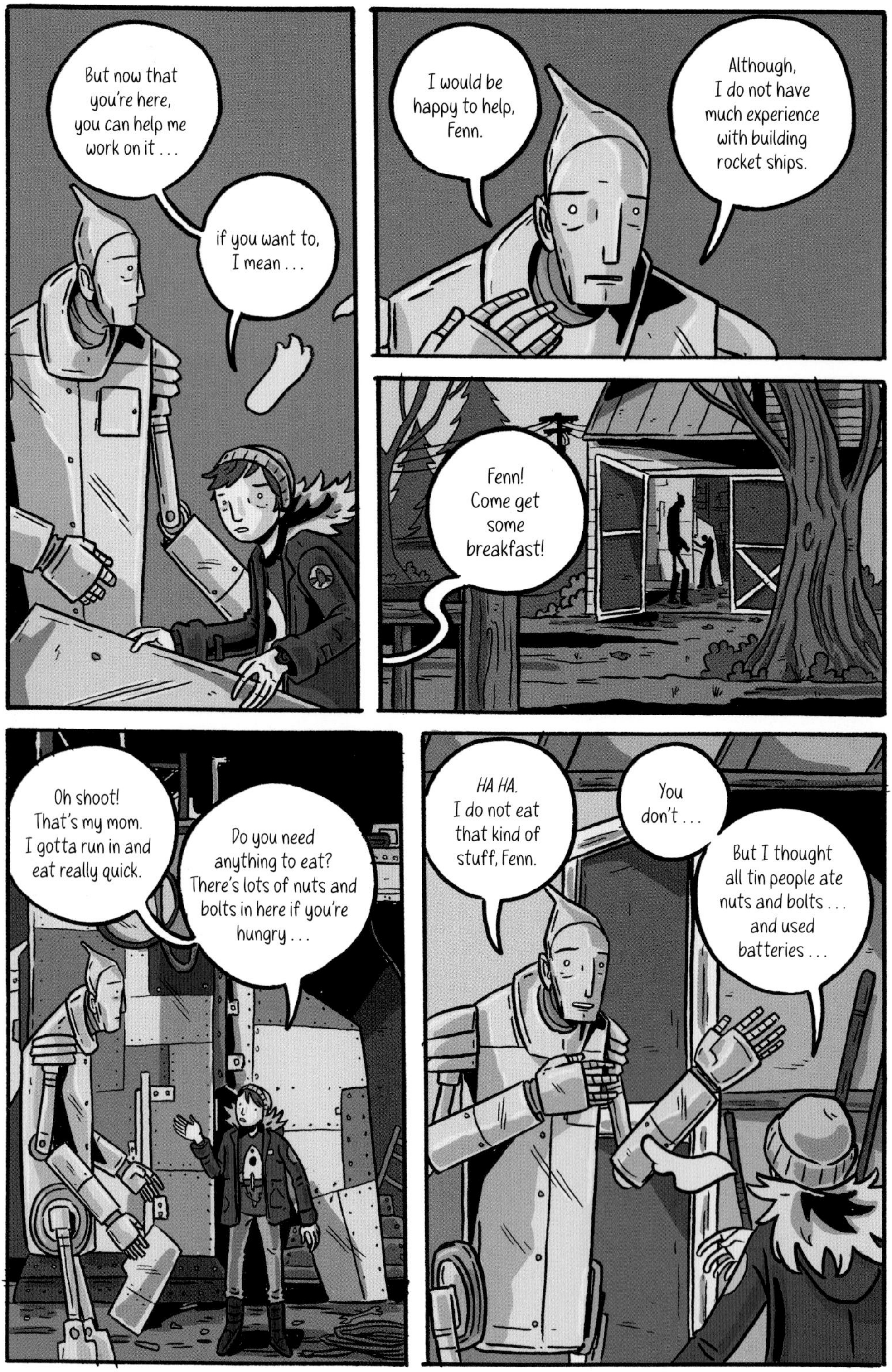
But now that you're here, you can help me work on it . . .
if you want to, I mean . . .
I would be happy to help, Fenn.
Although, I do not have much experience with building rocket ships.
Fenn! Come get some breakfast!
Oh shoot! That's my mom. I gotta run in and eat really quick.
Do you need anything to eat? There's lots of nuts and bolts in here if you're hungry . . .
HA HA. I do not eat that kind of stuff, Fenn.
You don't . . .
But I thought all tin people ate nuts and bolts . . . and used batteries . . .

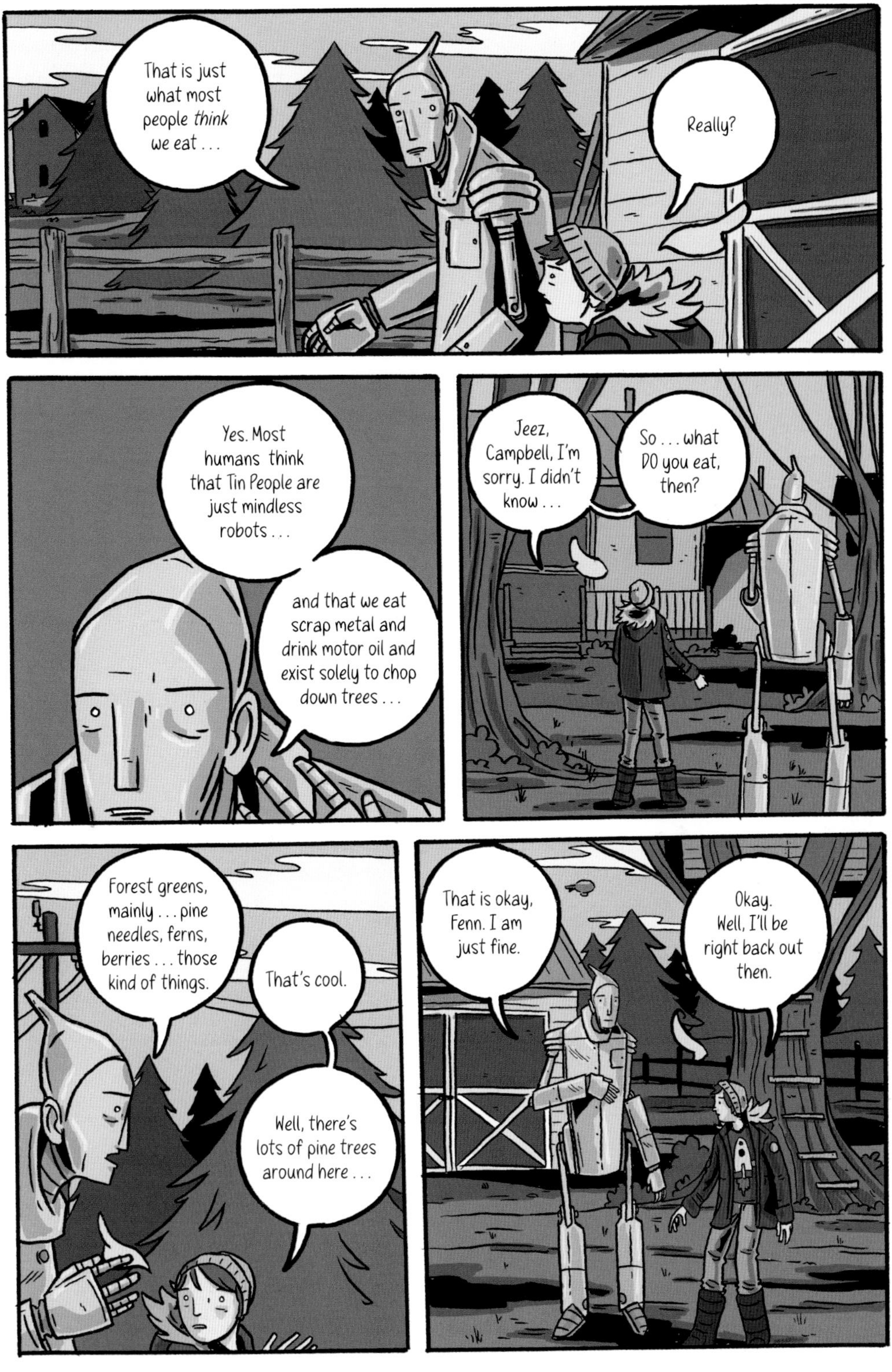
That is just what most people *think* we eat . . .
Really?
Yes. Most humans think that Tin People are just mindless robots . . .
and that we eat scrap metal and drink motor oil and exist solely to chop down trees . . .
Jeez, Campbell, I'm sorry. I didn't know . . .
So . . . what DO you eat, then?
Forest greens, mainly . . . pine needles, ferns, berries . . . those kind of things.
That's cool.
Well, there's lots of pine trees around here . . .
That is okay, Fenn. I am just fine.
Okay. Well, I'll be right back out then.

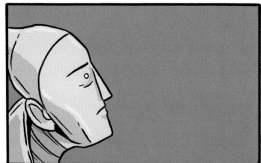

"Dad! Dad . . . you are *not* going to believe this . . ."

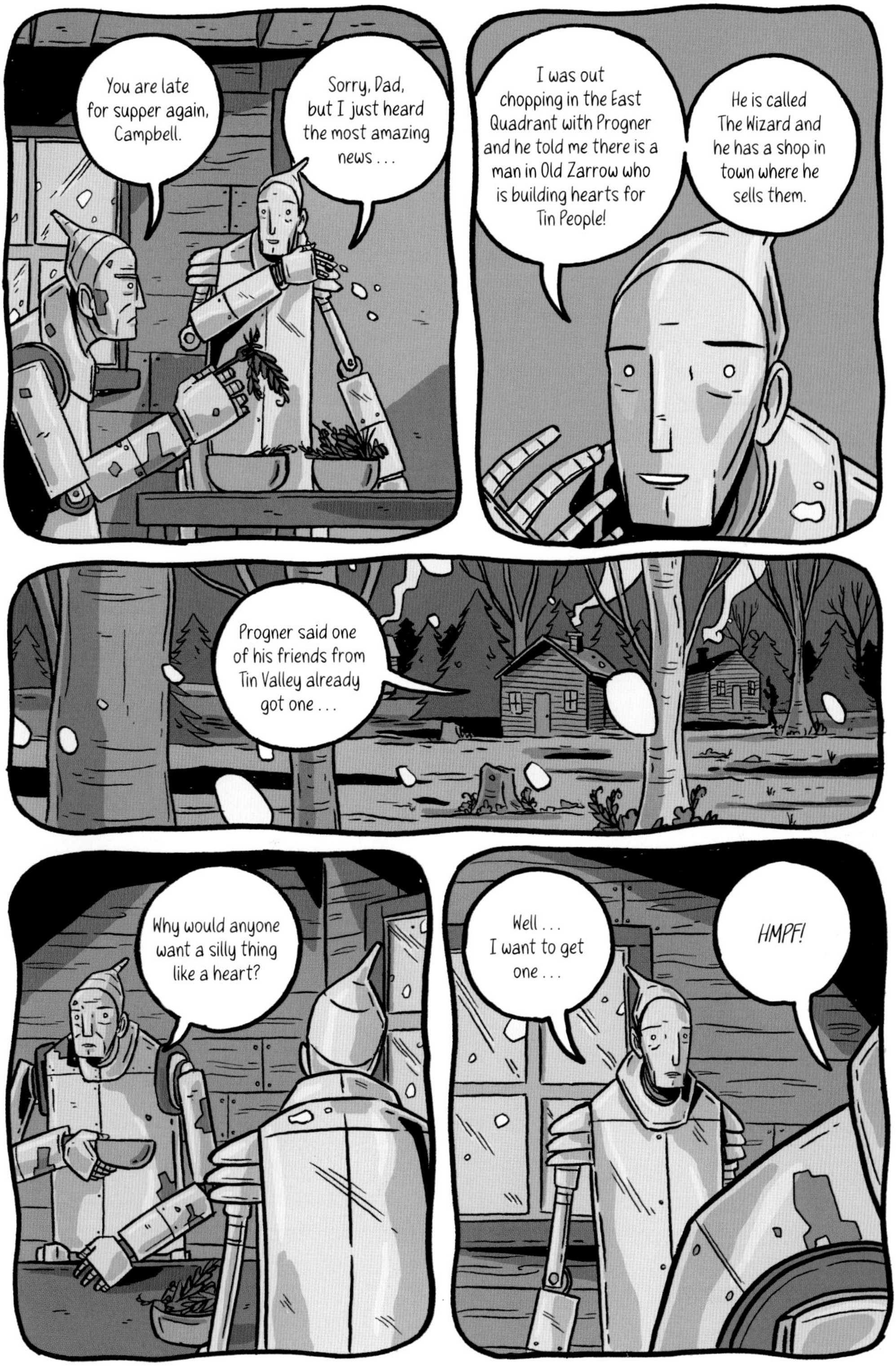
You are late for supper again, Campbell.
Sorry, Dad, but I just heard the most amazing news . . .
I was out chopping in the East Quadrant with Progner and he told me there is a man in Old Zarrow who is building hearts for Tin People!
He is called The Wizard and he has a shop in town where he sells them.
Progner said one of his friends from Tin Valley already got one . . .
Why would anyone want a silly thing like a heart?
Well . . . I want to get one . . .
HMPF!

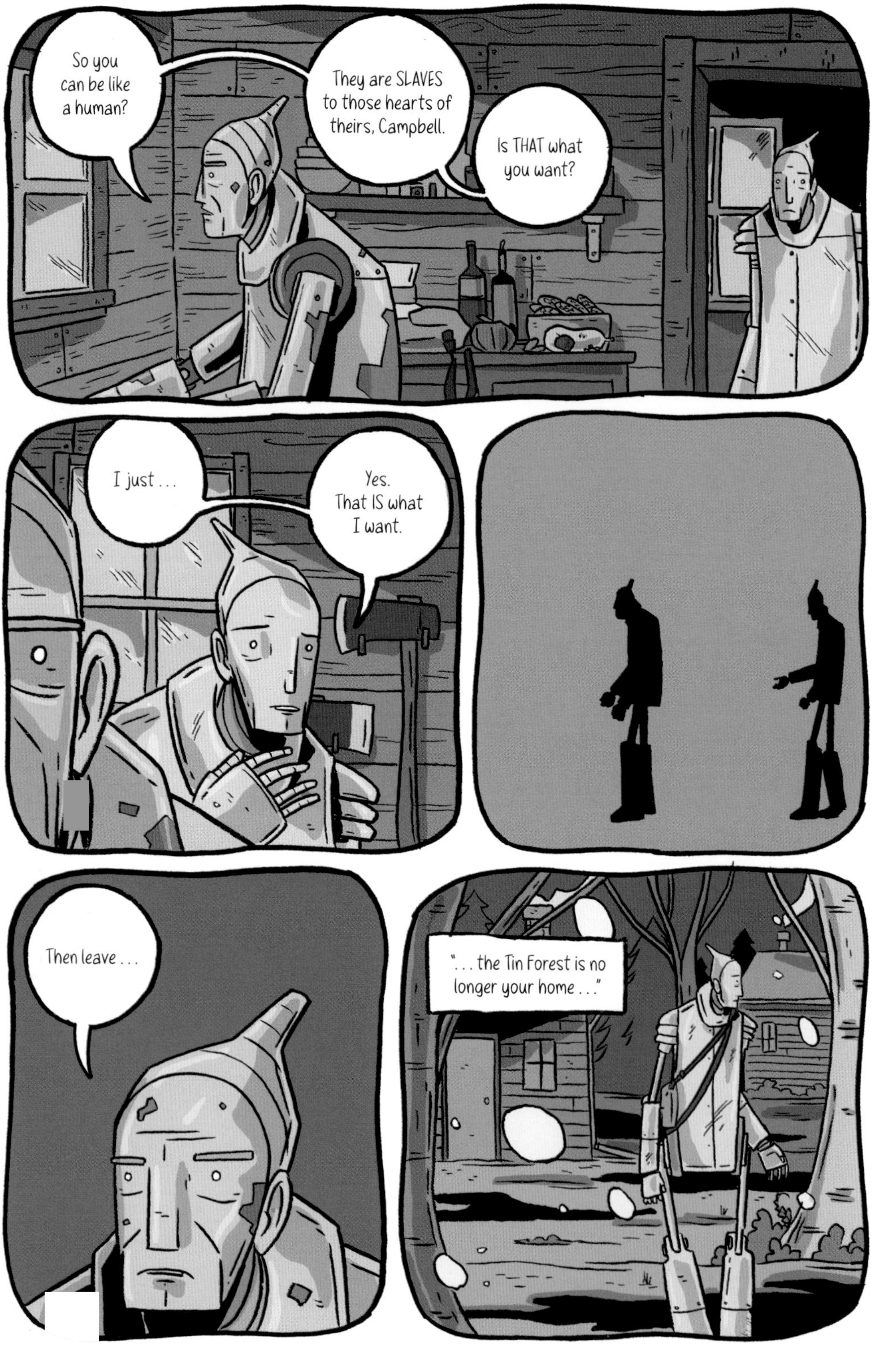
So you can be like a human?
They are SLAVES to those hearts of theirs, Campbell.
Is THAT what you want?
I just . . .
Yes. That IS what I want.
Then leave . . .
". . . the Tin Forest is no longer your home . . ."

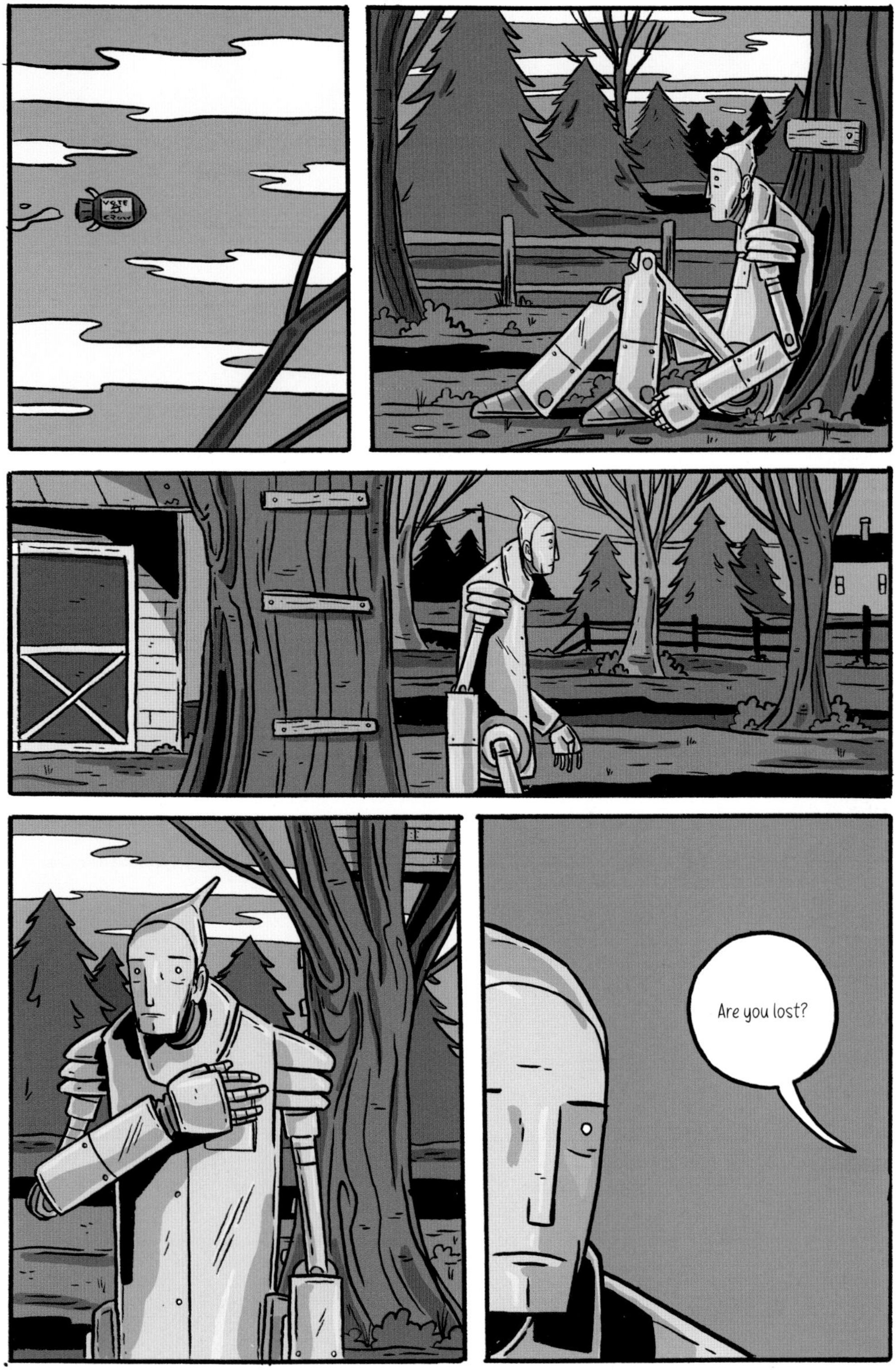
Are you lost?

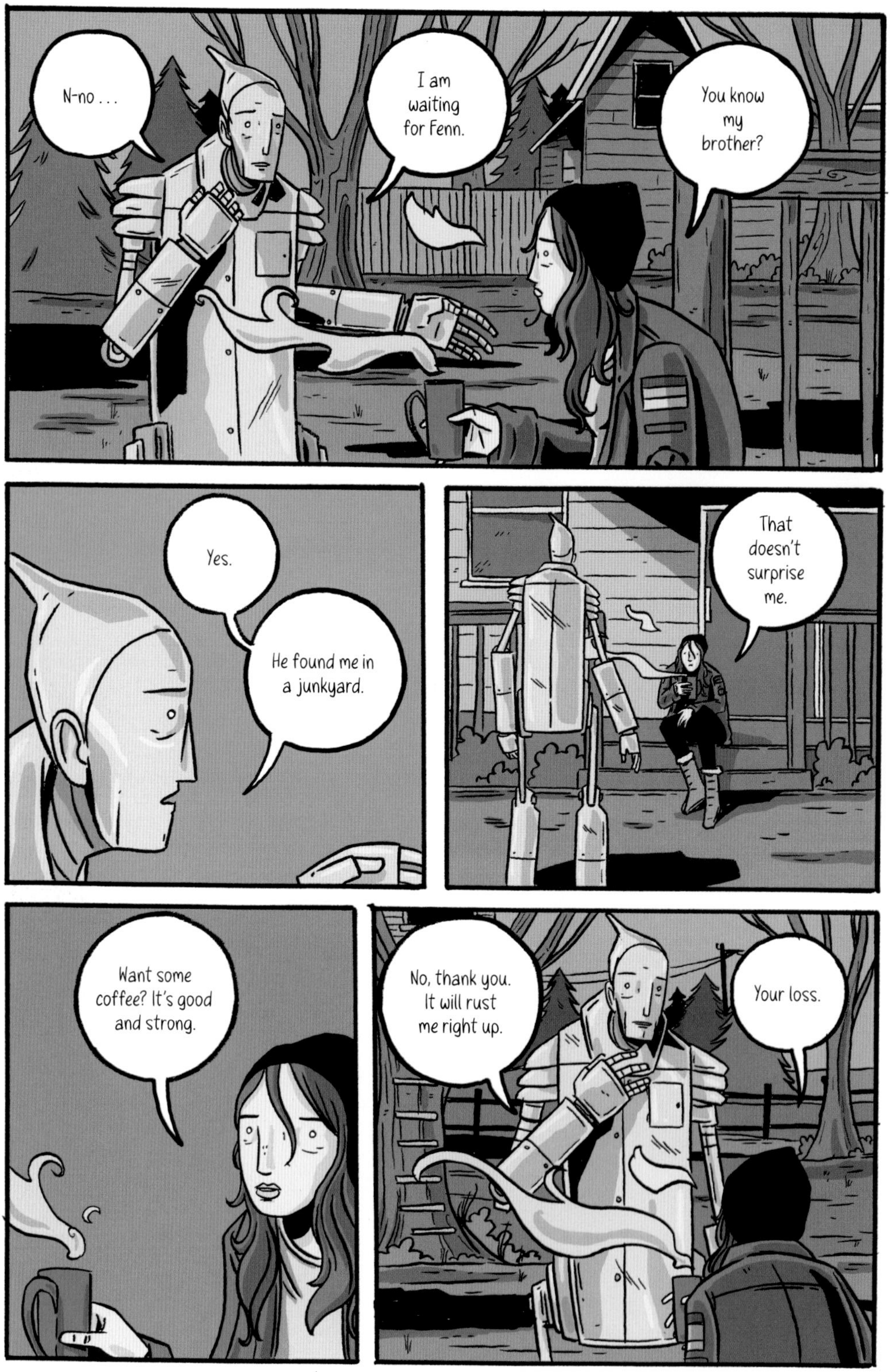
N-no . . .
I am waiting for Fenn.
You know my brother?
Yes.
He found me in a junkyard.
That doesn't surprise me.
Want some coffee? It's good and strong.
No, thank you. It will rust me right up.
Your loss.

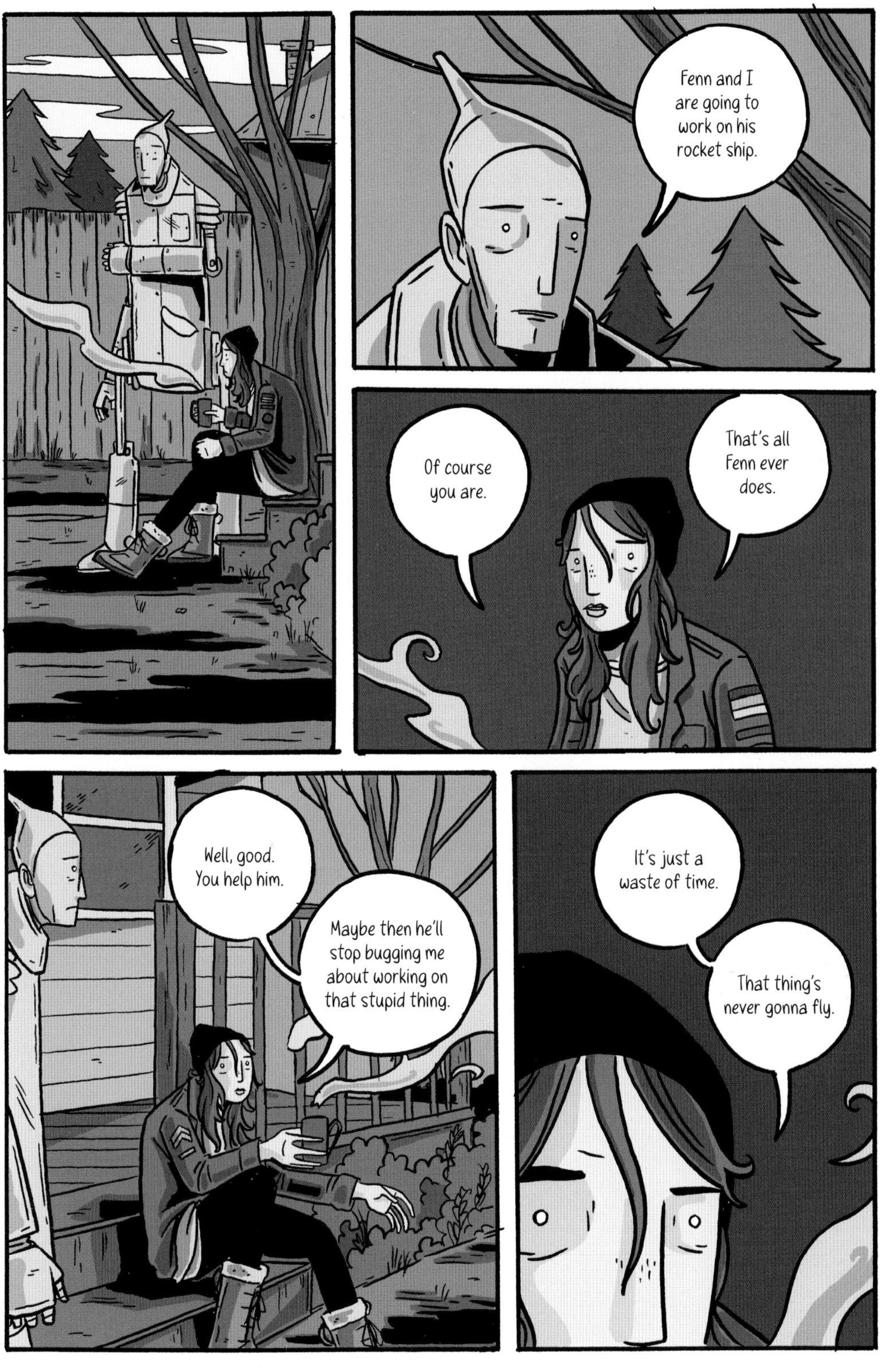

Fenn and I are going to work on his rocket ship.
Of course you are.
That's all Fenn ever does.
Well, good. You help him.
Maybe then he'll stop bugging me about working on that stupid thing.
It's just a waste of time.
That thing's never gonna fly.

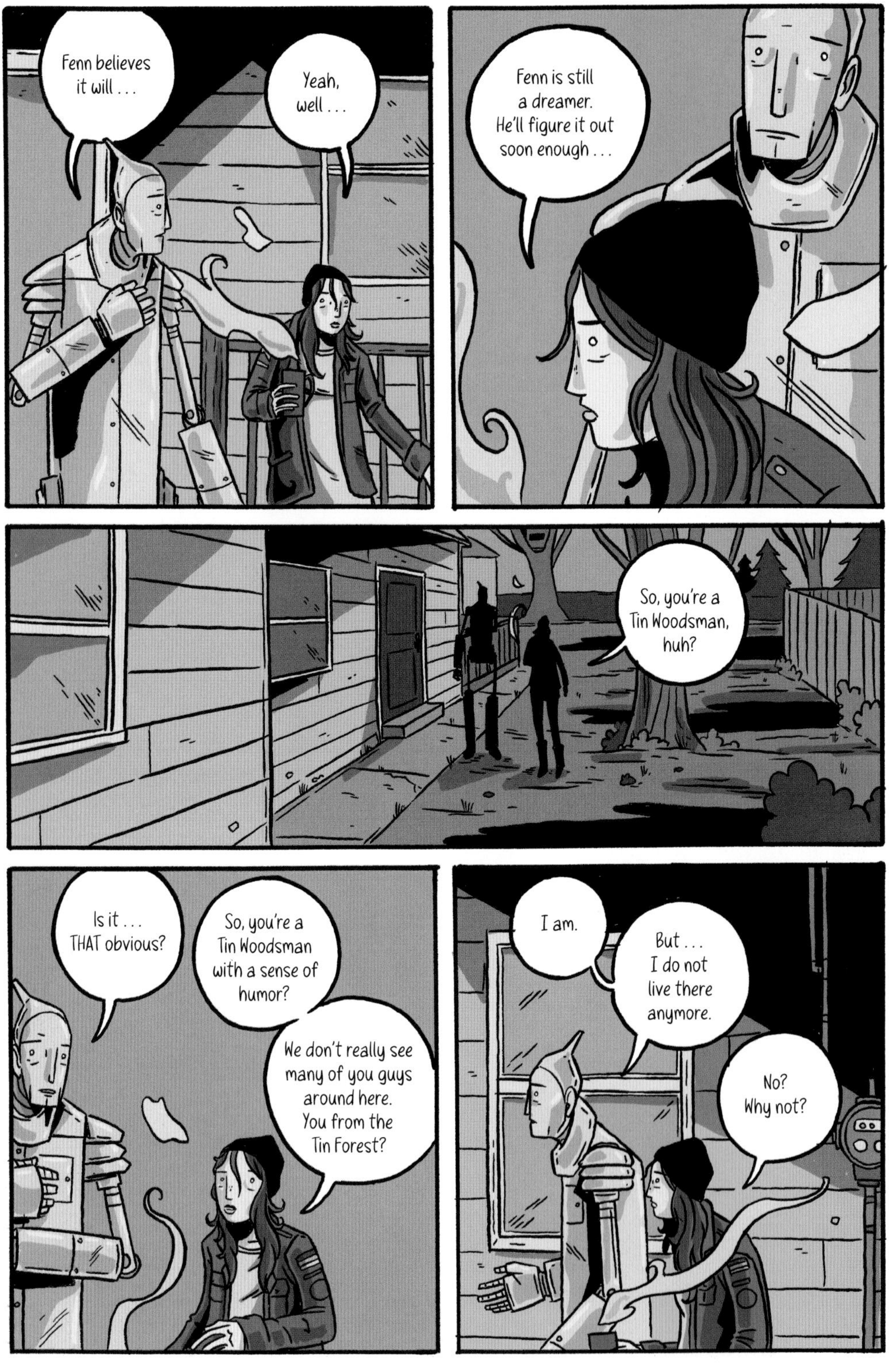
Fenn believes it will . . .
Yeah, well . . .
Fenn is still a dreamer. He'll figure it out soon enough . . .
So, you're a Tin Woodsman, huh?
Is it . . . THAT obvious?
So, you're a Tin Woodsman with a sense of humor?
We don't really see many of you guys around here. You from the Tin Forest?
I am.
But . . . I do not live there anymore.
No? Why not?

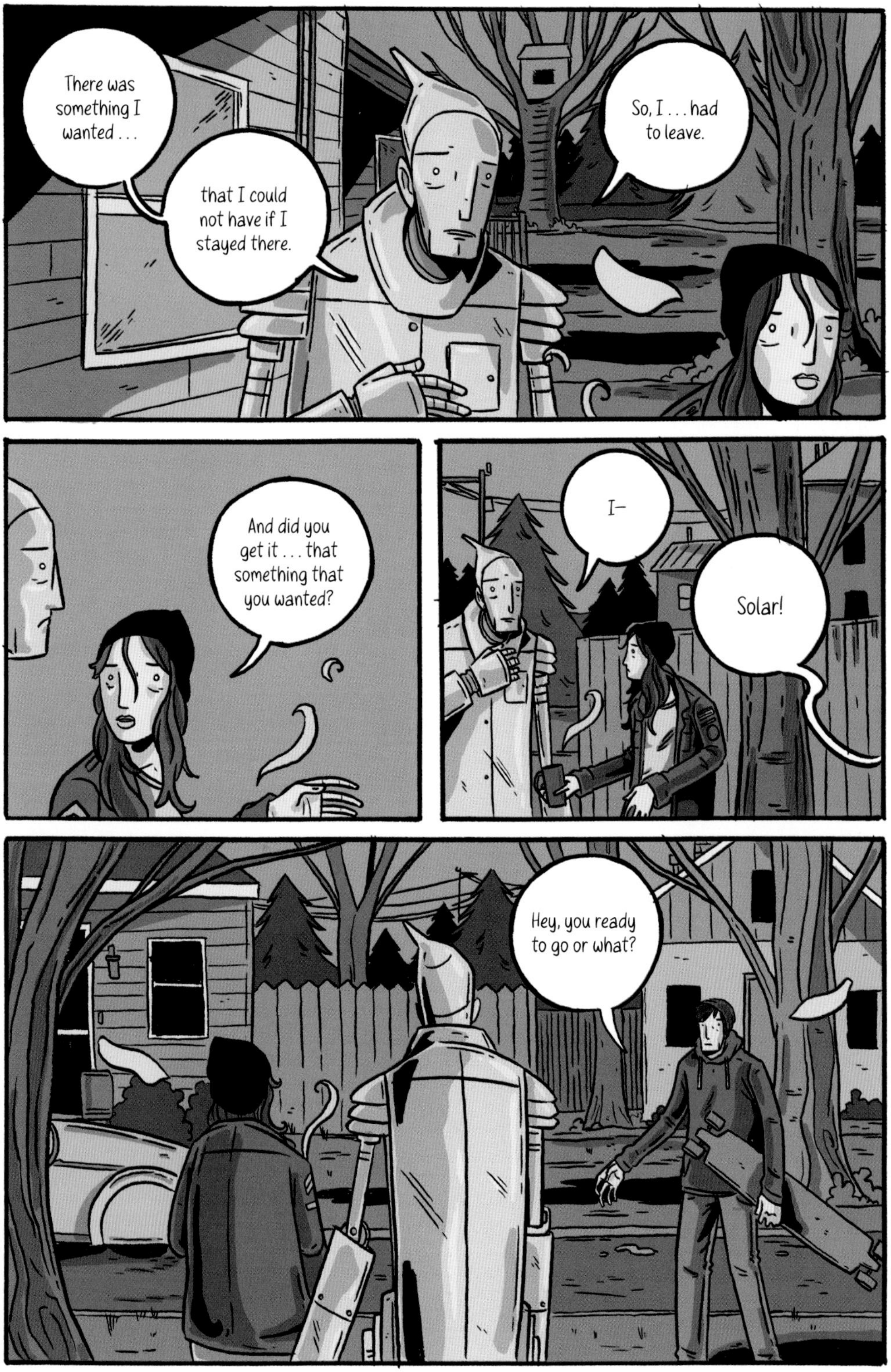
There was something I wanted . . .
that I could not have if I stayed there.
So, I . . . had to leave.
And did you get it . . . that something that you wanted?
I–
Solar!
Hey, you ready to go or what?

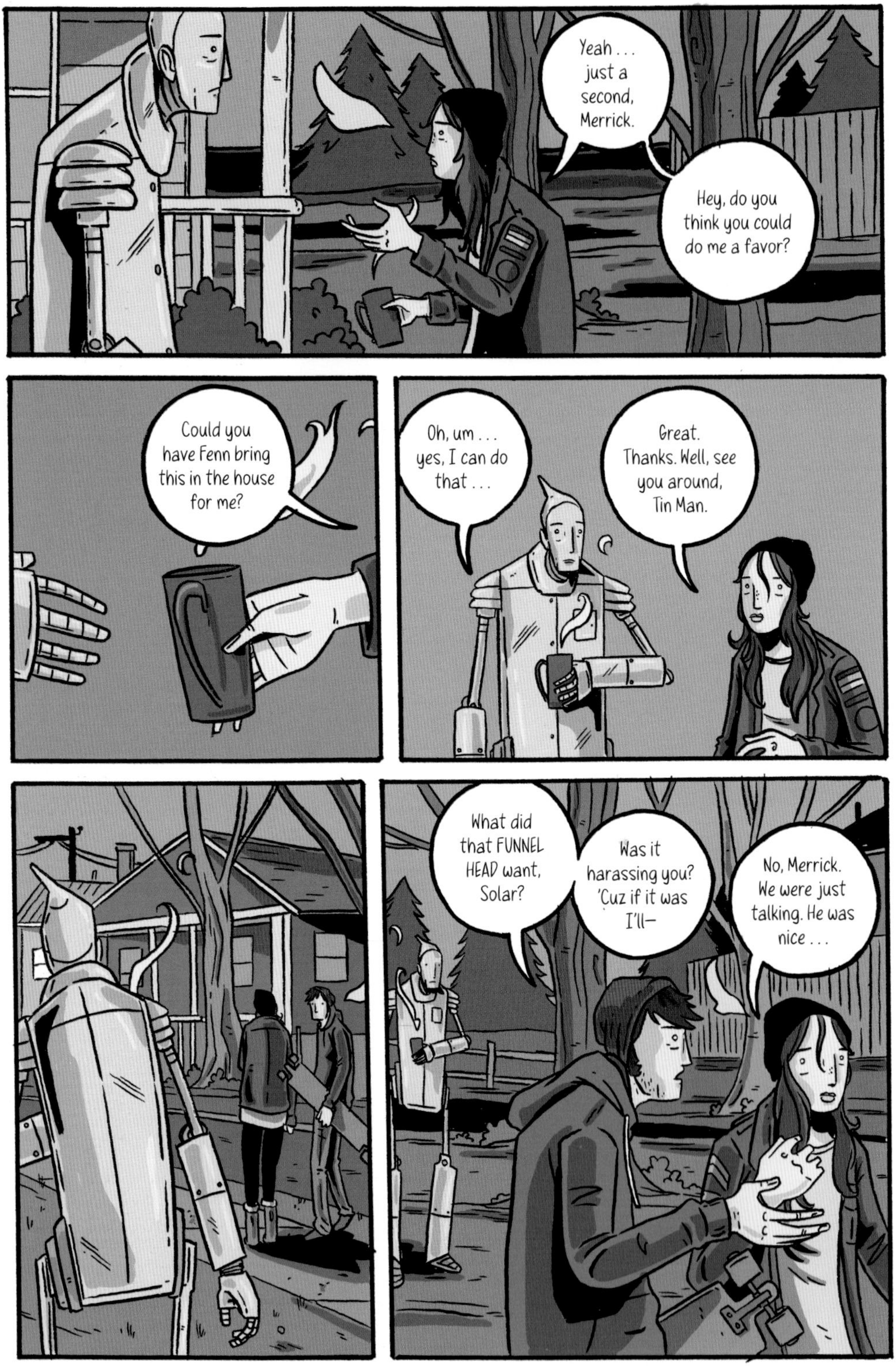
Yeah . . . just a second, Merrick.
Hey, do you think you could do me a favor?
Could you have Fenn bring this in the house for me?
Oh, um . . . yes, I can do that . . .
Great. Thanks. Well, see you around, Tin Man.
What did that FUNNEL HEAD want, Solar?
Was it harassing you? 'Cuz if it was I'll—
No, Merrick. We were just talking. He was nice . . .

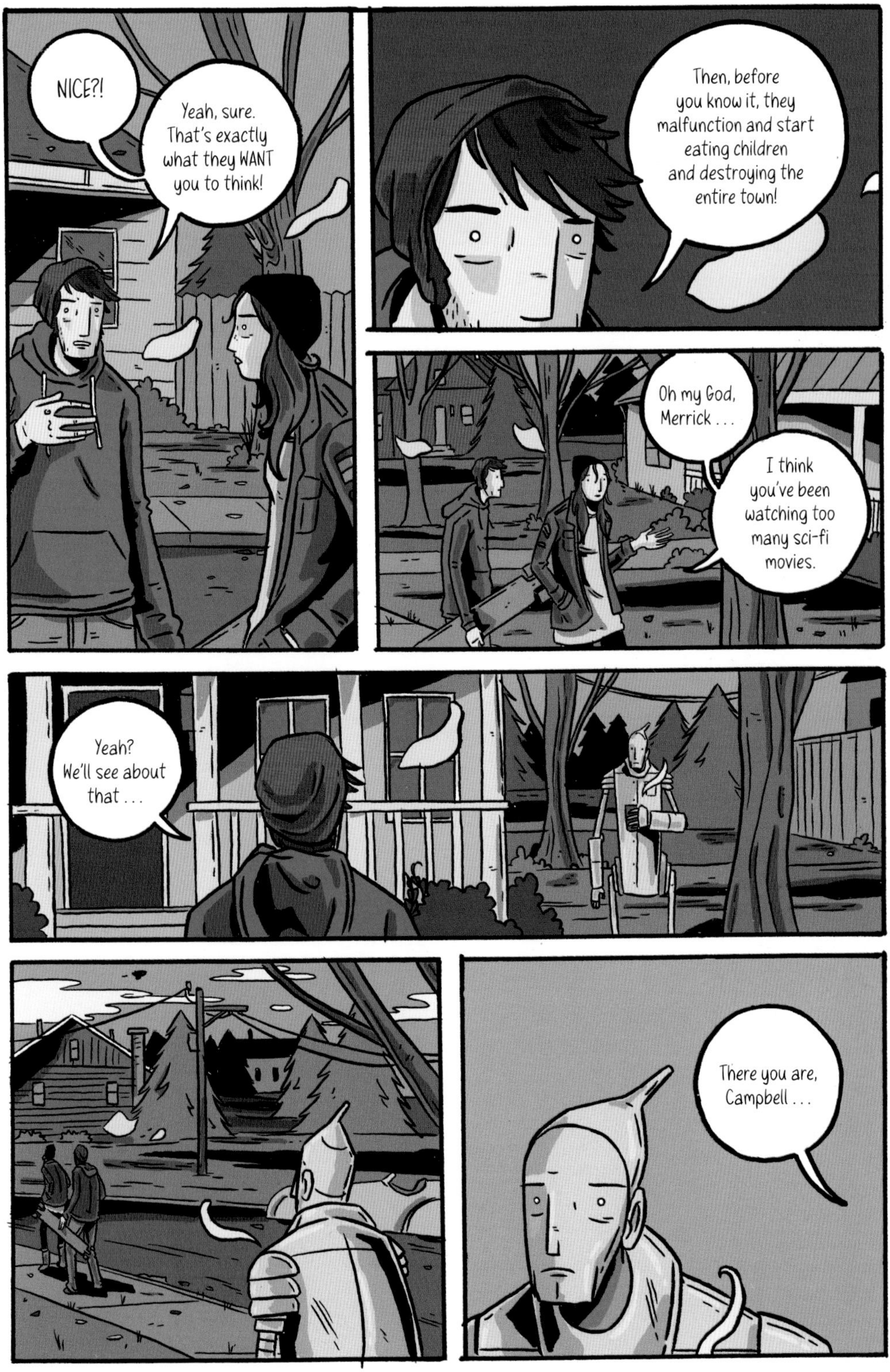
NICE?!
Yeah, sure. That's exactly what they WANT you to think!
Then, before you know it, they malfunction and start eating children and destroying the entire town!
Oh my God, Merrick . . .
I think you've been watching too many sci-fi movies.
Yeah? We'll see about that . . .
There you are, Campbell . . .

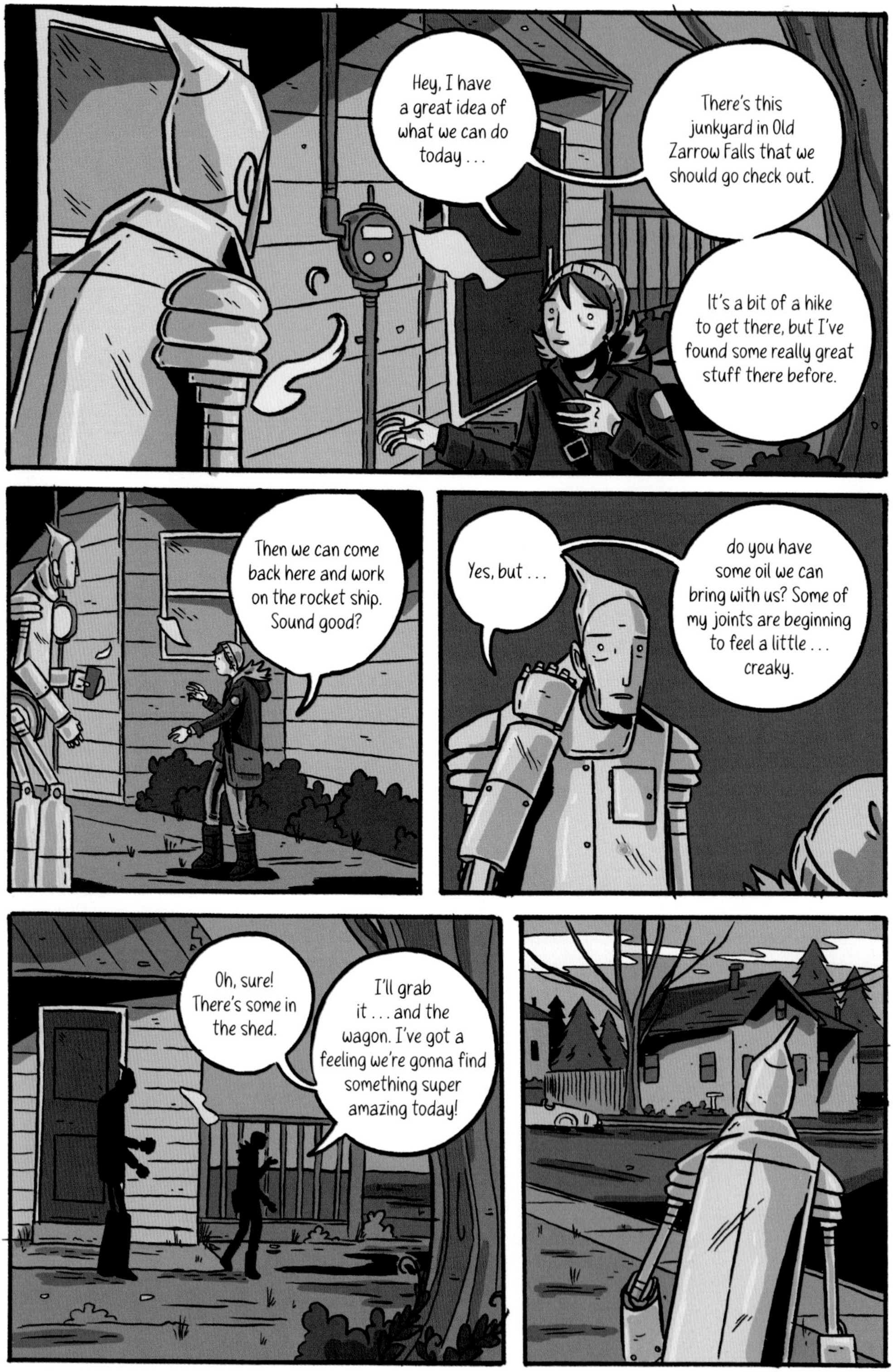
Hey, I have a great idea of what we can do today . . .
There's this junkyard in Old Zarrow Falls that we should go check out.
It's a bit of a hike to get there, but I've found some really great stuff there before.
Then we can come back here and work on the rocket ship. Sound good?
Yes, but . . .
do you have some oil we can bring with us? Some of my joints are beginning to feel a little . . . creaky.
Oh, sure! There's some in the shed.
I'll grab it . . . and the wagon. I've got a feeling we're gonna find something super amazing today!

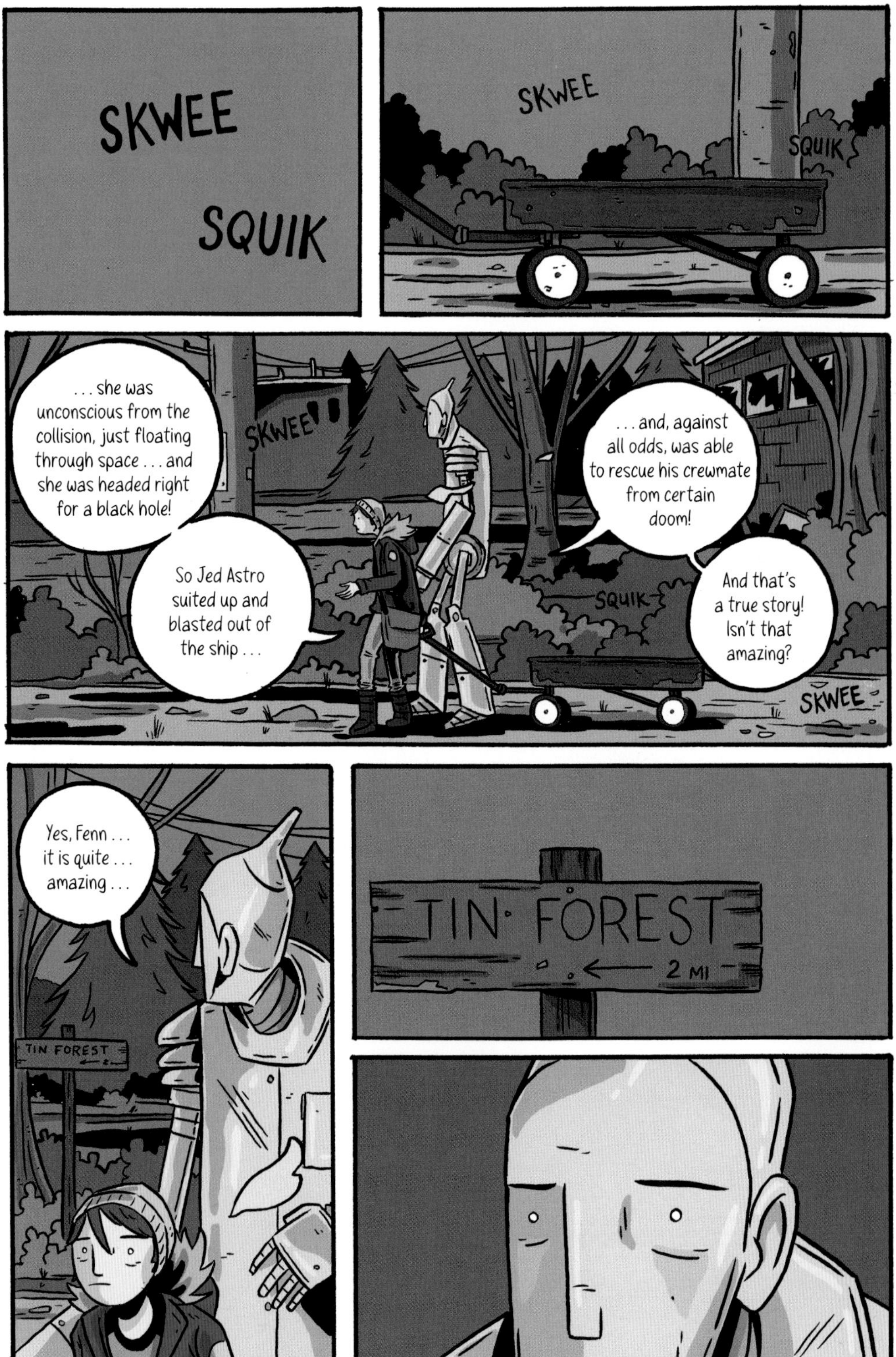
SKWEE
SQUIK
SKWEE
SQUIK
. . . she was unconscious from the collision, just floating through space . . . and she was headed right for a black hole!
SKWEE
So Jed Astro suited up and blasted out of the ship . . .
. . . and, against all odds, was able to rescue his crewmate from certain doom!
SQUIK
And that's a true story! Isn't that amazing?
SKWEE
Yes, Fenn . . . it is quite . . . amazing . . .
TIN FOREST
TIN FOREST 2 MI

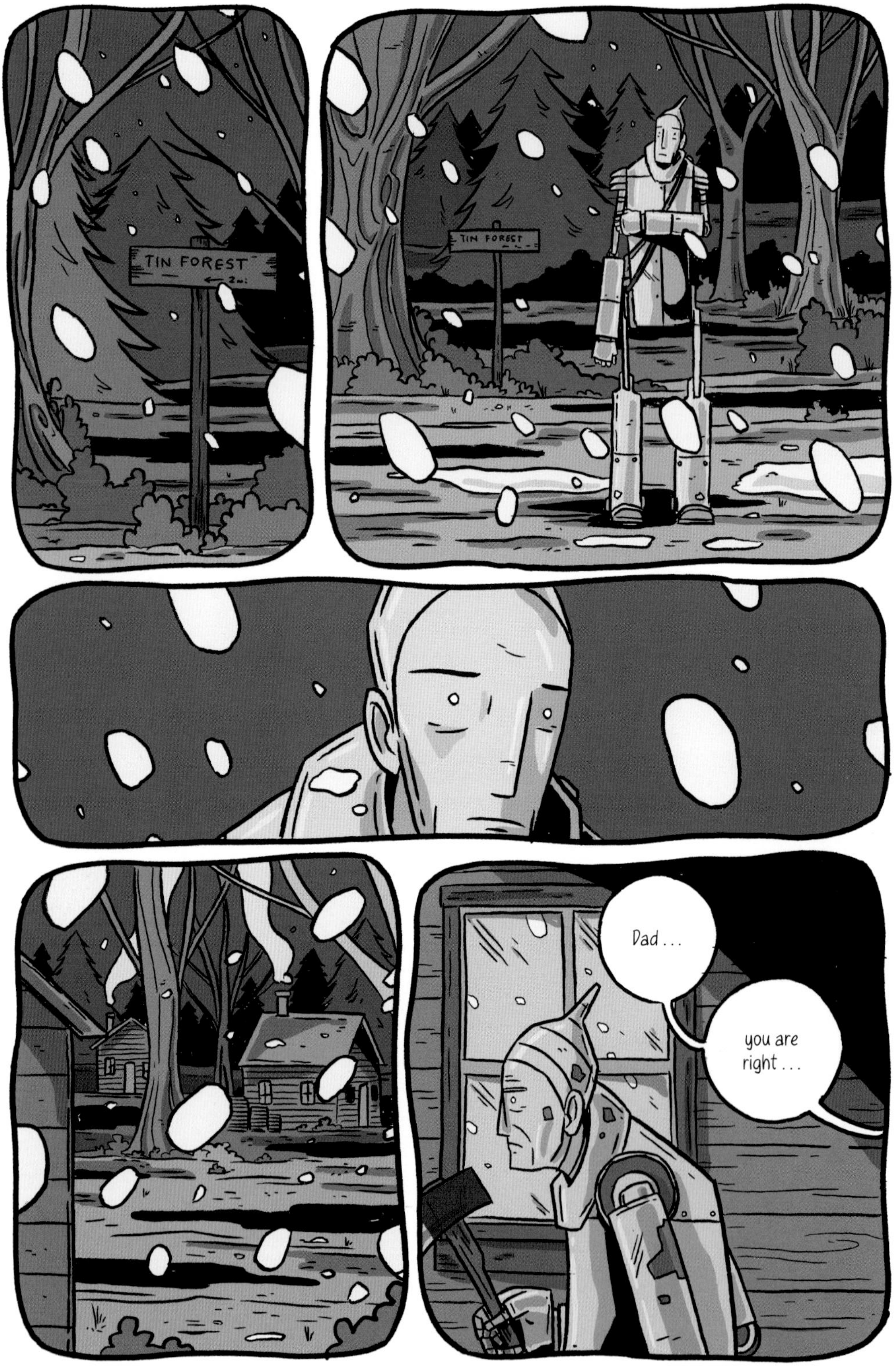
TIN FOREST
2 mi
TIN FOREST
Dad . . .
you are right . . .

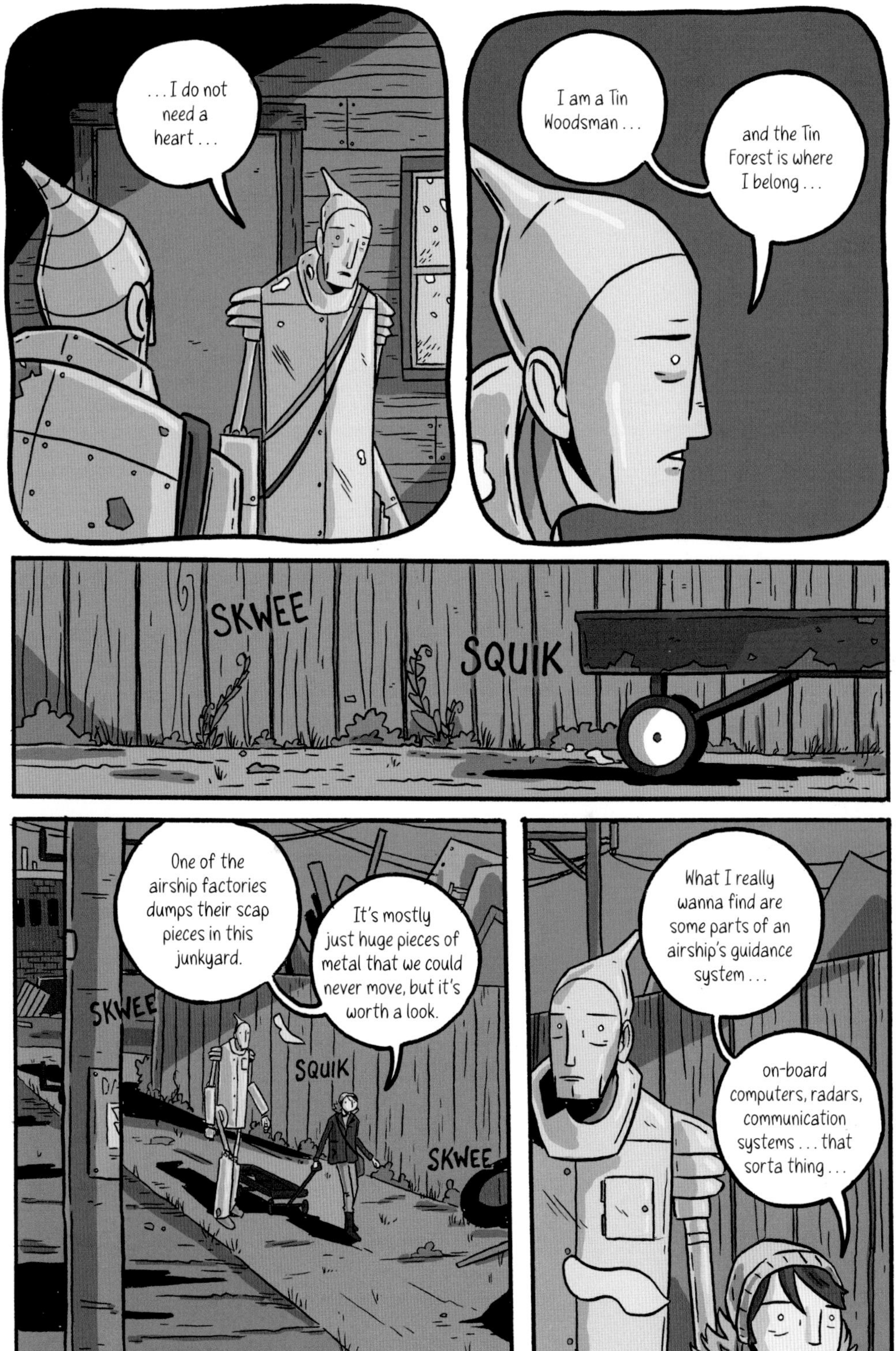

...I do not need a heart...
I am a Tin Woodsman...
and the Tin Forest is where I belong...
SKWEE
SQUIK
One of the airship factories dumps their scap pieces in this junkyard.
It's mostly just huge pieces of metal that we could never move, but it's worth a look.
SKWEE
SQUIK
SKWEE
What I really wanna find are some parts of an airship's guidance system...
on-board computers, radars, communication systems... that sorta thing...

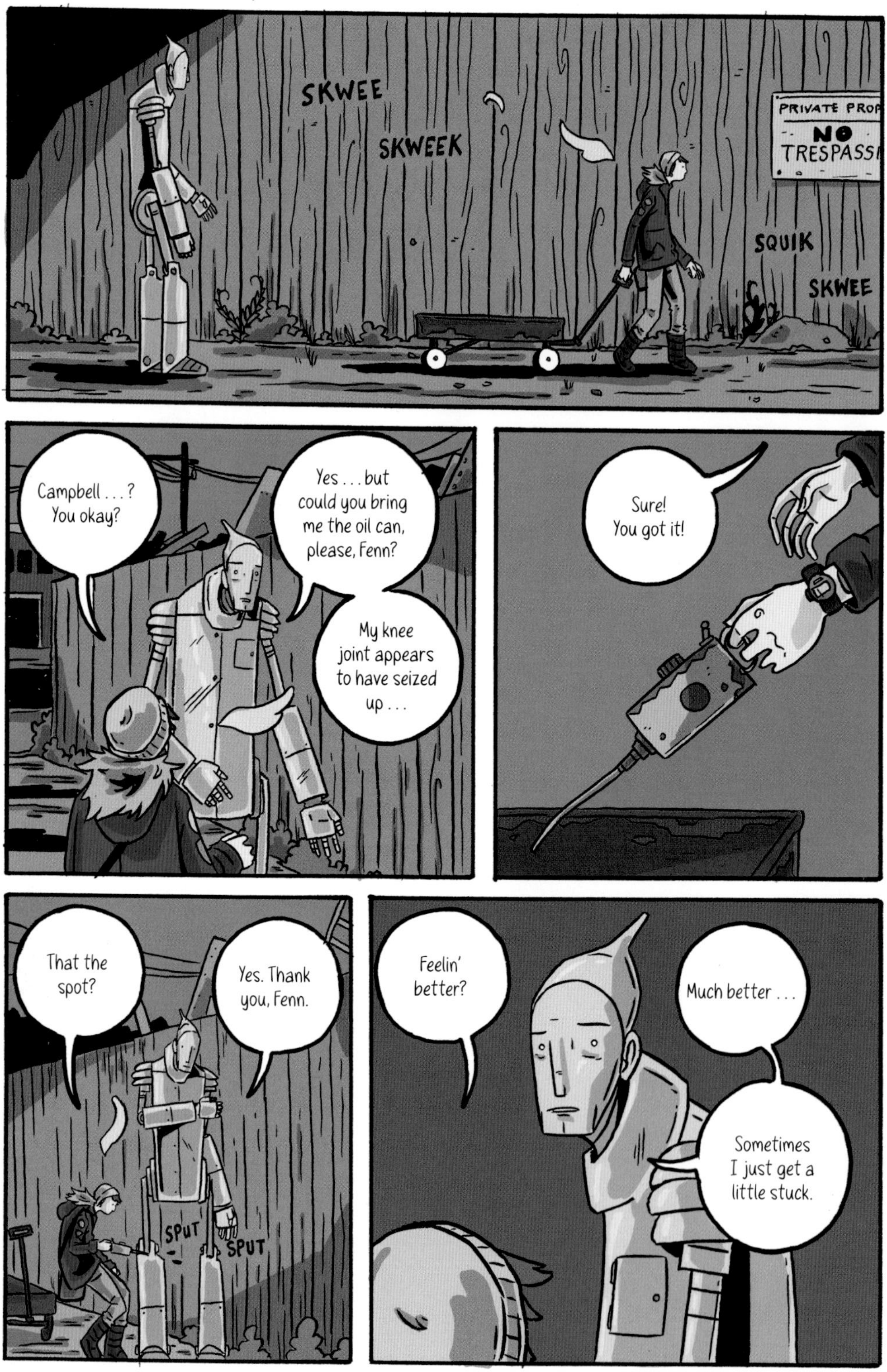
SKWEE
SKWEEK
PRIVATE PROP
NO
TRESPASS
SQUIK
SKWEE
Campbell . . . ? You okay?
Yes . . . but could you bring me the oil can, please, Fenn?
My knee joint appears to have seized up . . .
Sure! You got it!
That the spot?
Yes. Thank you, Fenn.
SPUT
SPUT
Feelin' better?
Much better . . .
Sometimes I just get a little stuck.

CHAPTER 6: Bullies

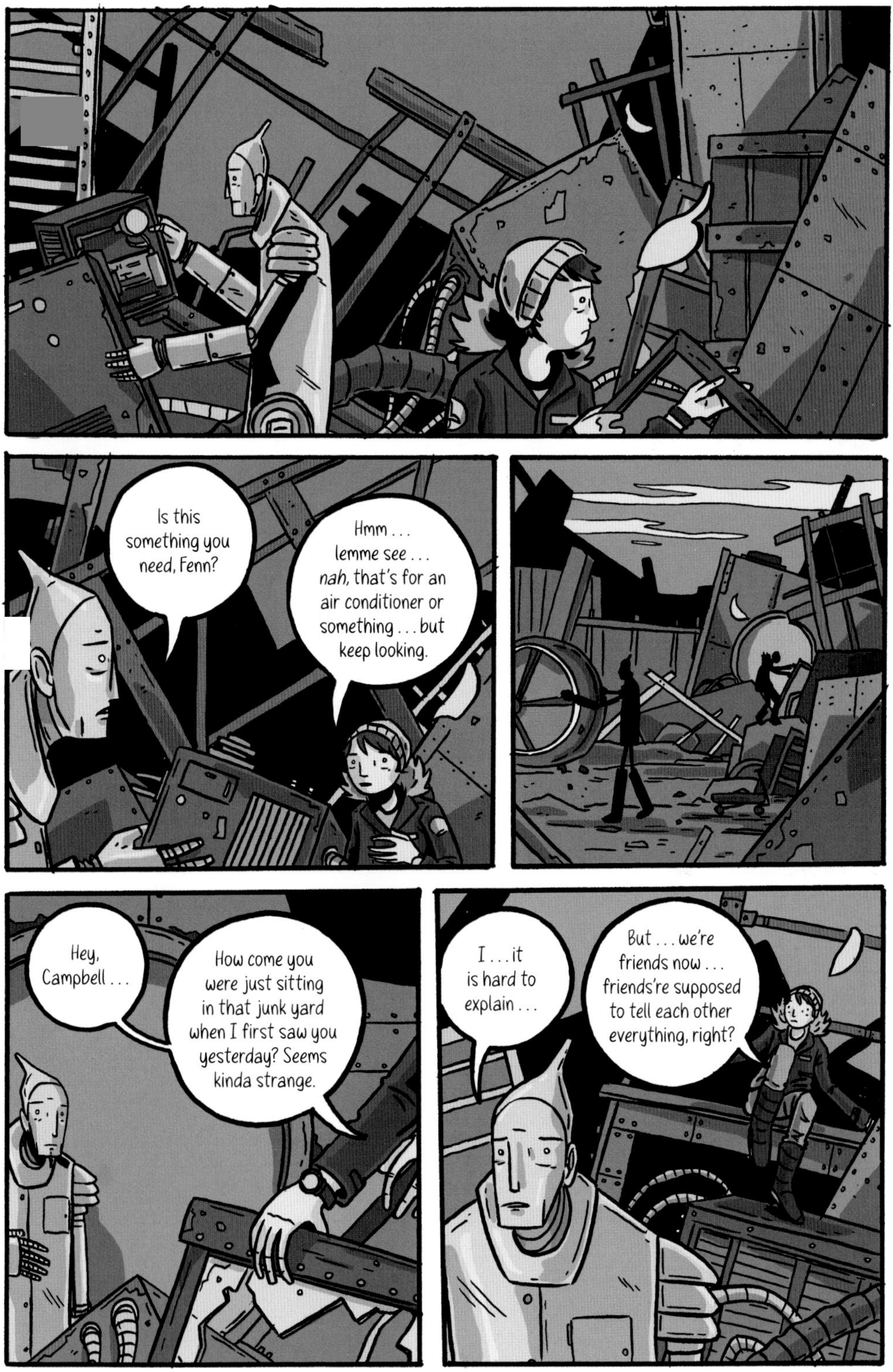

Is this something you need, Fenn?
Hmm . . . lemme see . . . *nah,* that's for an air conditioner or something . . . but keep looking.
Hey, Campbell . . .
How come you were just sitting in that junk yard when I first saw you yesterday? Seems kinda strange.
I . . . it is hard to explain . . .
But . . . we're friends now . . . friends're supposed to tell each other everything, right?

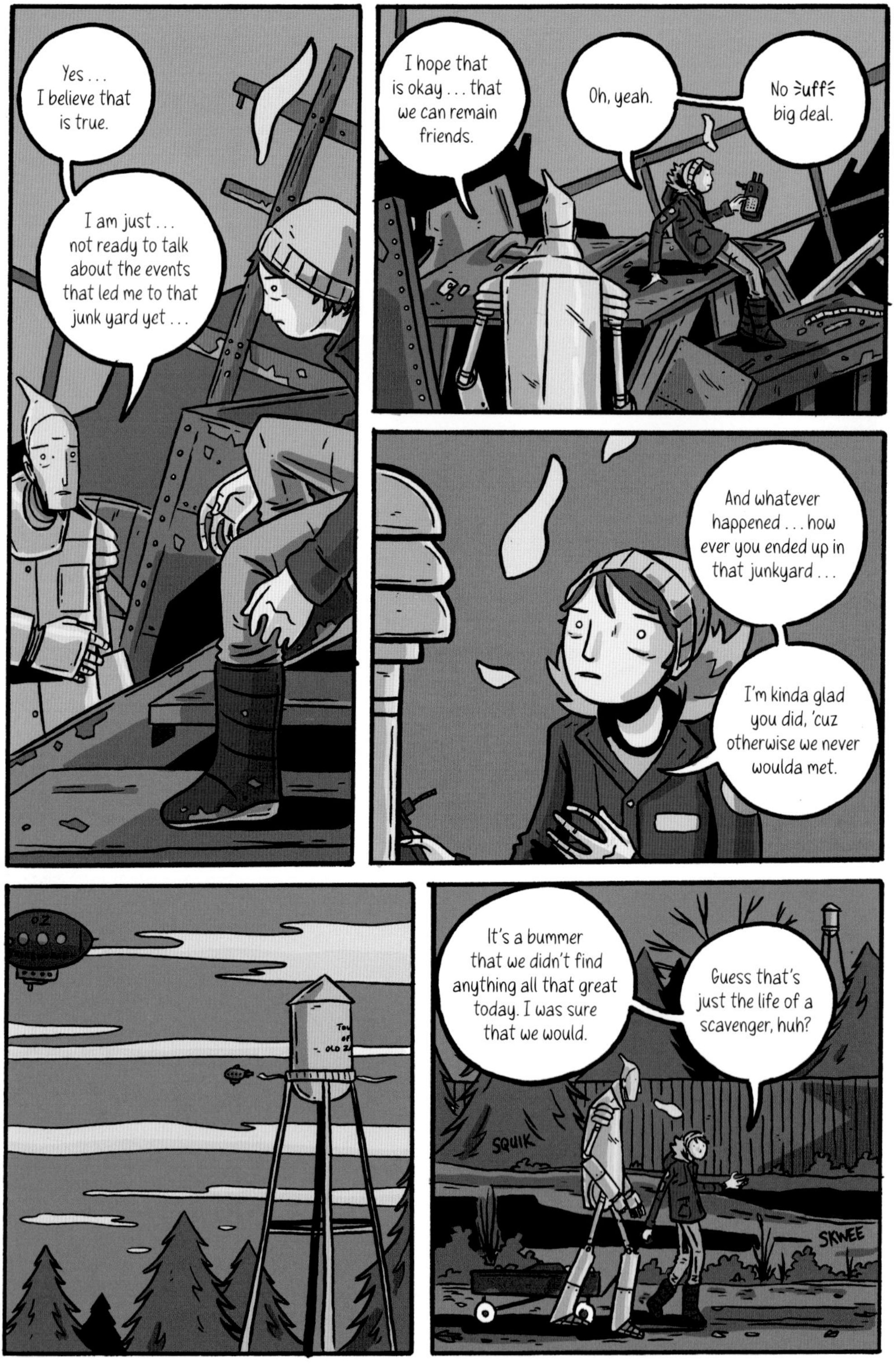
Yes . . . I believe that is true.
I am just . . . not ready to talk about the events that led me to that junk yard yet . . .
I hope that is okay . . . that we can remain friends.
Oh, yeah.
No uff big deal.
And whatever happened . . . how ever you ended up in that junkyard . . .
I'm kinda glad you did, 'cuz otherwise we never woulda met.
It's a bummer that we didn't find anything all that great today. I was sure that we would.
Guess that's just the life of a scavenger, huh?
SQUIK
SKWEE

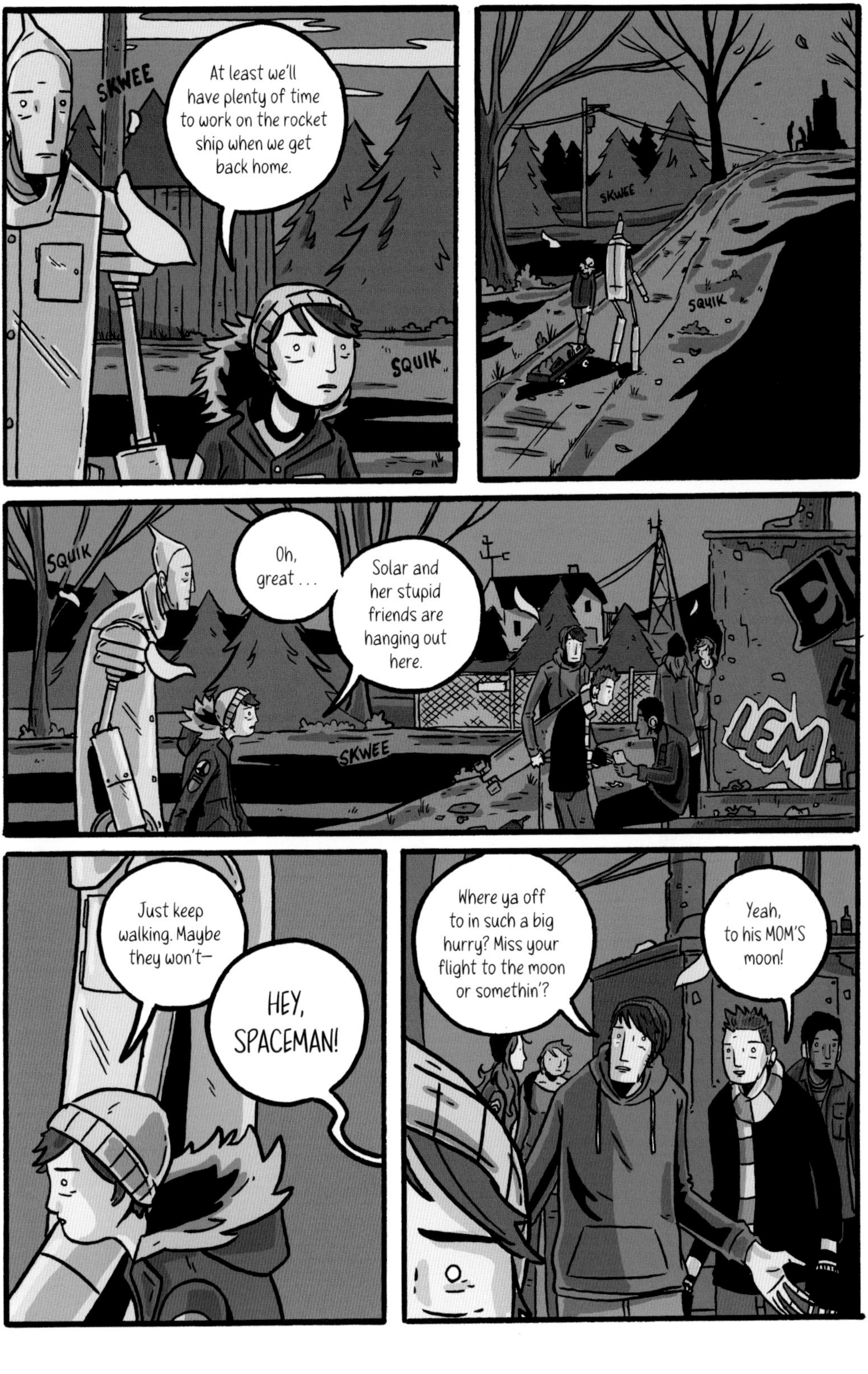
At least we'll have plenty of time to work on the rocket ship when we get back home.
SKWEE
SQUIK
SKWEE
SQUIK
SQUIK
Oh, great . . .
Solar and her stupid friends are hanging out here.
SKWEE
LEM
Just keep walking. Maybe they won't—
HEY, SPACEMAN!
Where ya off to in such a big hurry? Miss your flight to the moon or somethin'?
Yeah, to his MOM'S moon!

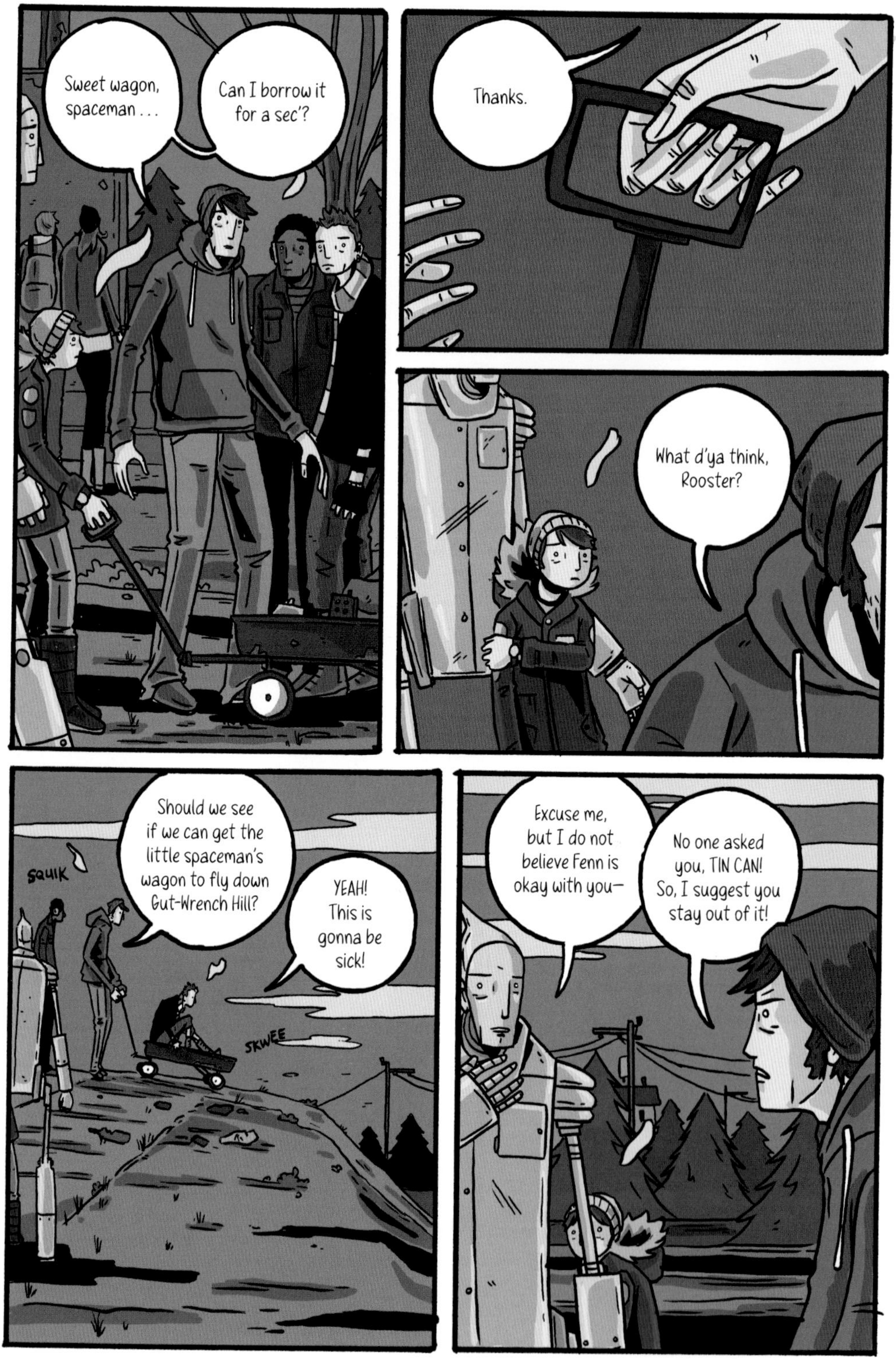
Sweet wagon, spaceman . . .
Can I borrow it for a sec'?
Thanks.
What d'ya think, Rooster?
Should we see if we can get the little spaceman's wagon to fly down Gut-Wrench Hill?
SQUIK
YEAH! This is gonna be sick!
SKWEE
Excuse me, but I do not believe Fenn is okay with you—
No one asked you, TIN CAN! So, I suggest you stay out of it!

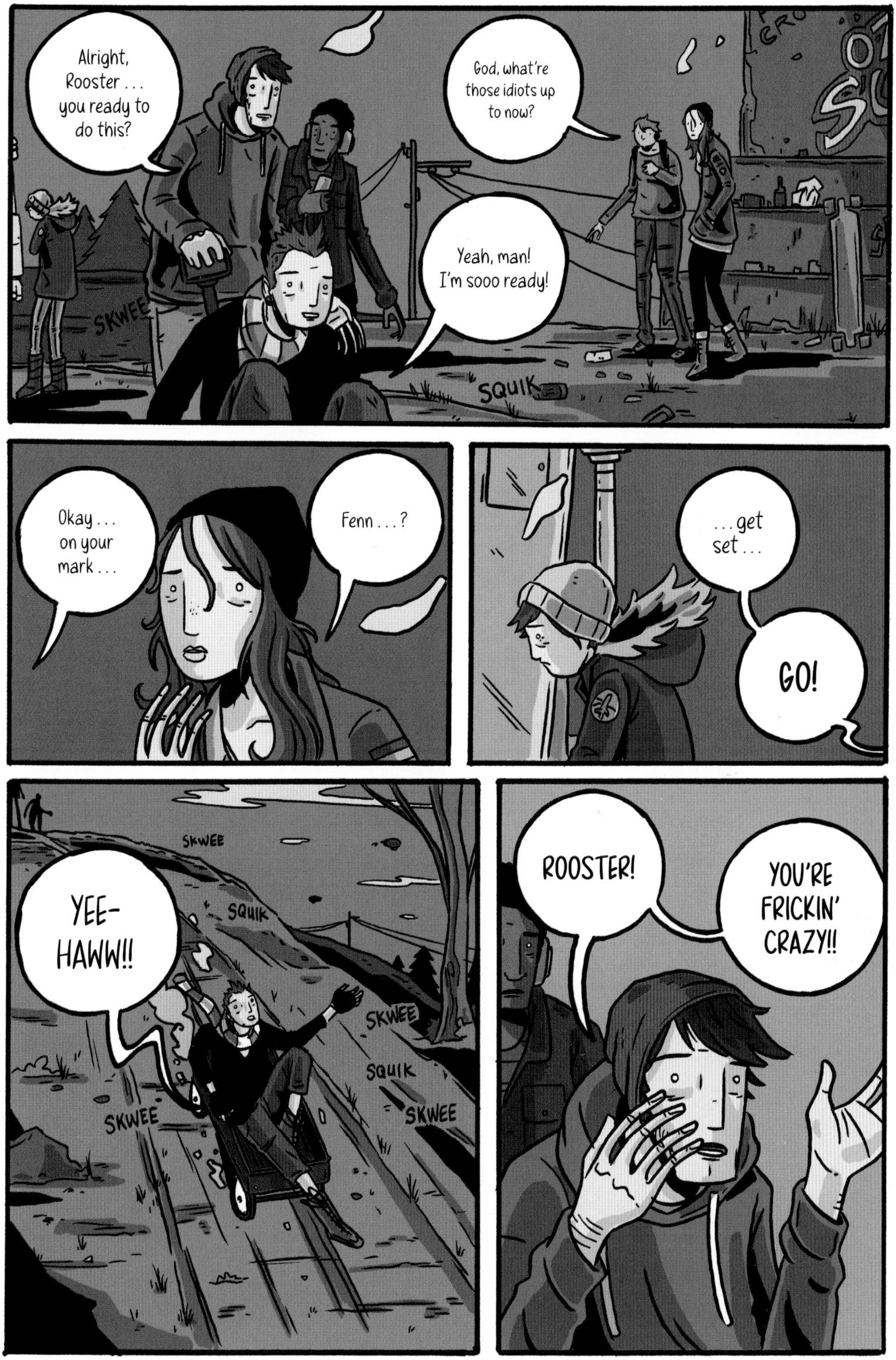
Alright, Rooster . . . you ready to do this?
God, what're those idiots up to now?
Yeah, man! I'm sooo ready!
SKWEE
SQUIK
Okay . . . on your mark . . .
Fenn . . . ?
. . . get set . . .
GO!
SKWEE
SQUIK
YEE-HAWW!!
SKWEE
SQUIK
SKWEE
SKWEE
ROOSTER!
YOU'RE FRICKIN' CRAZY!!

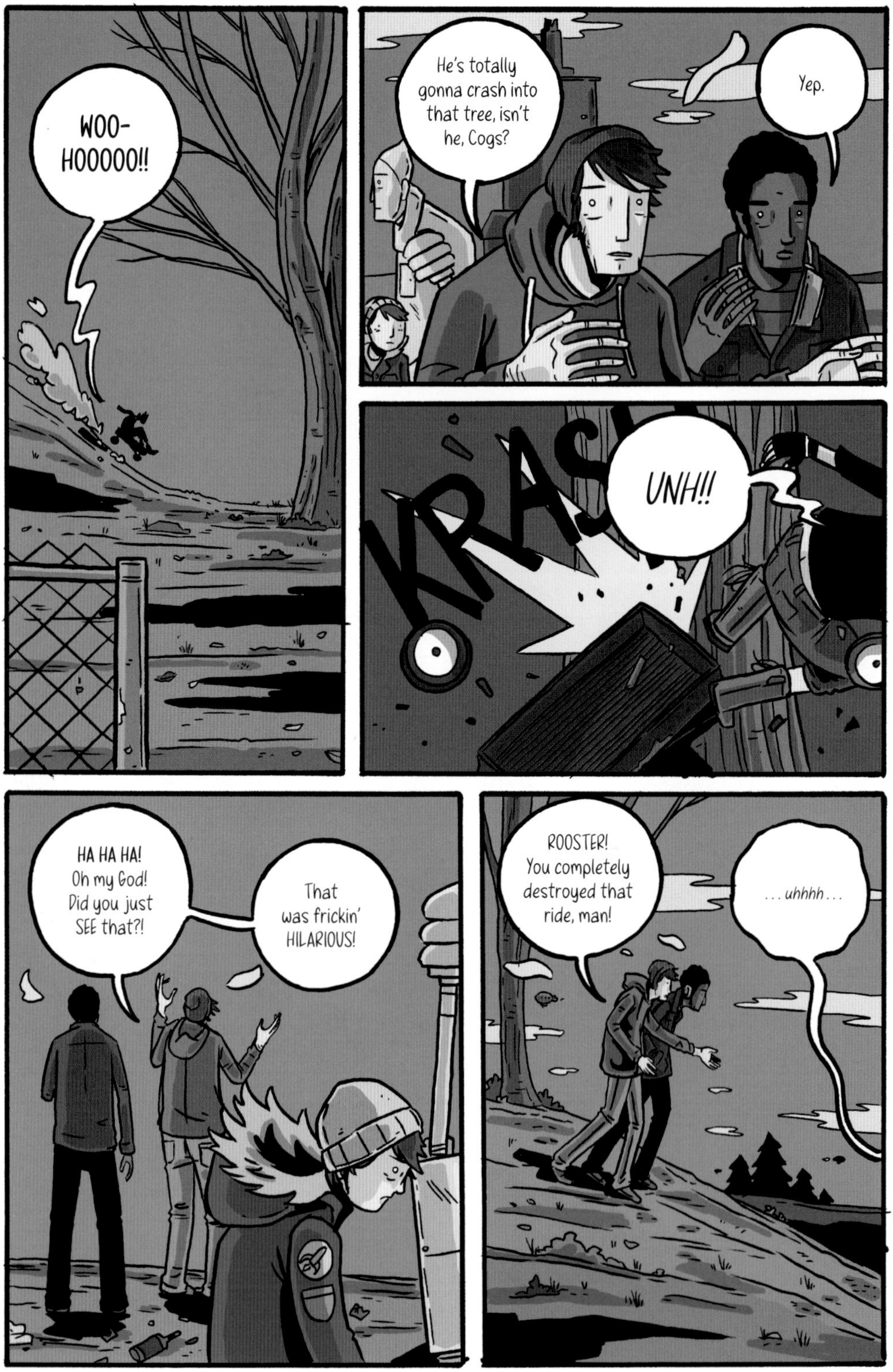
WOO-HOOOOO!!
He's totally gonna crash into that tree, isn't he, Cogs?
Yep.
KRASH
UNH!!
HA HA HA! Oh my God! Did you just SEE that?!
That was frickin' HILARIOUS!
ROOSTER! You completely destroyed that ride, man!
. . . uhhhh . . .

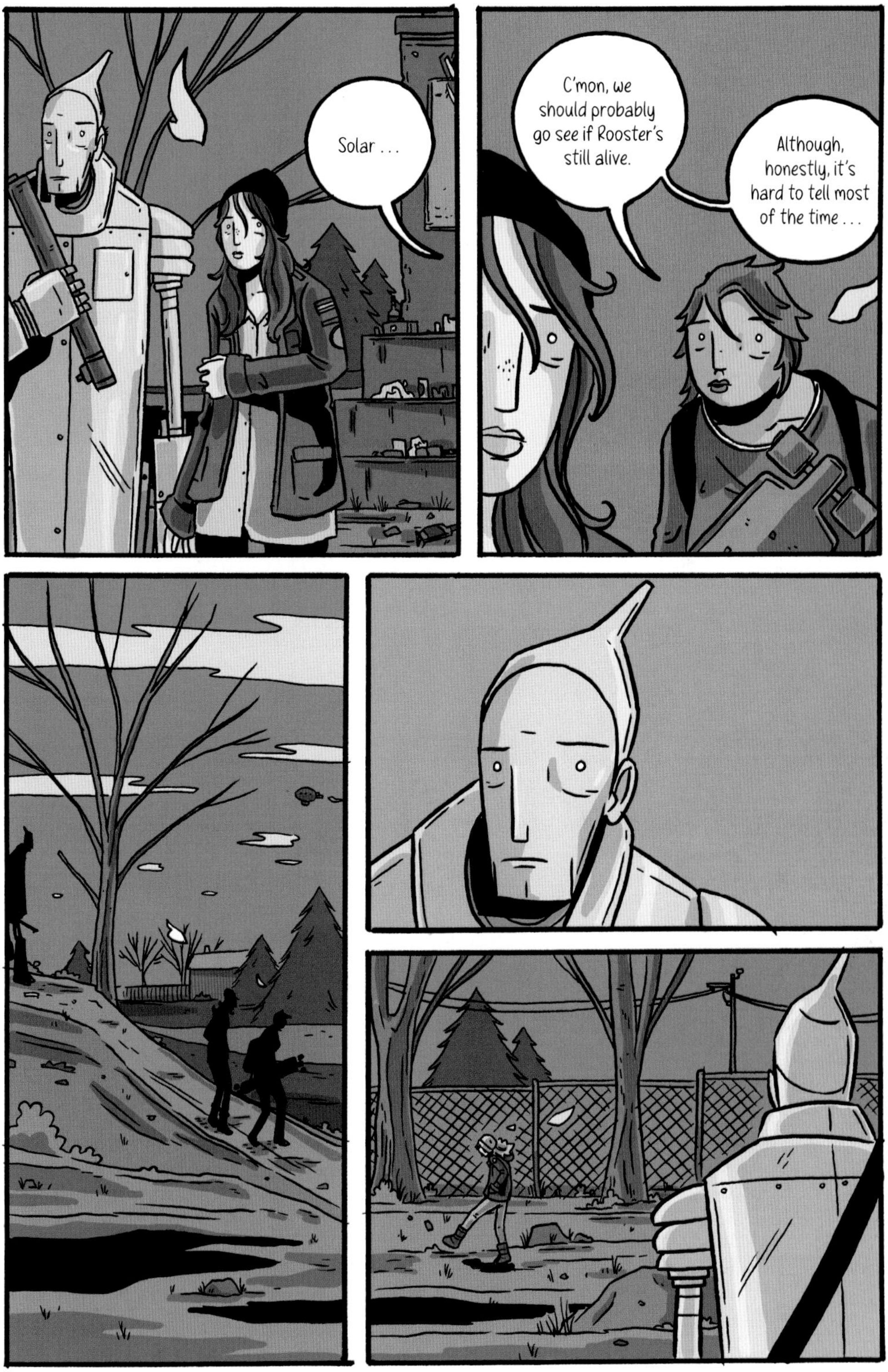
Solar . . .
C'mon, we should probably go see if Rooster's still alive.
Although, honestly, it's hard to tell most of the time . . .

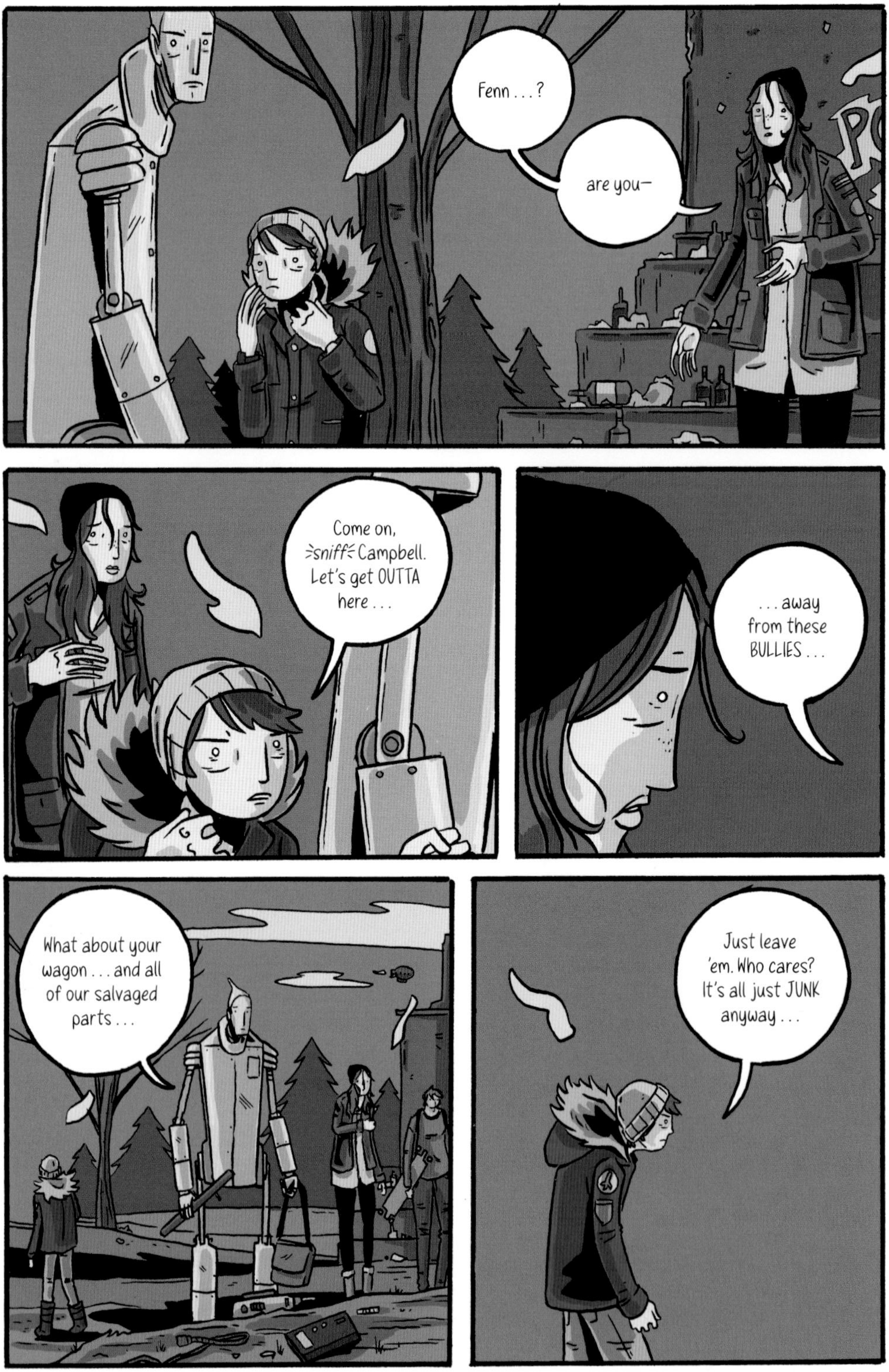
Fenn . . . ?
are you—
Come on, ≶sniff≶ Campbell. Let's get OUTTA here . . .
. . . away from these BULLIES . . .
What about your wagon . . . and all of our salvaged parts . . .
Just leave 'em. Who cares? It's all just JUNK anyway . . .

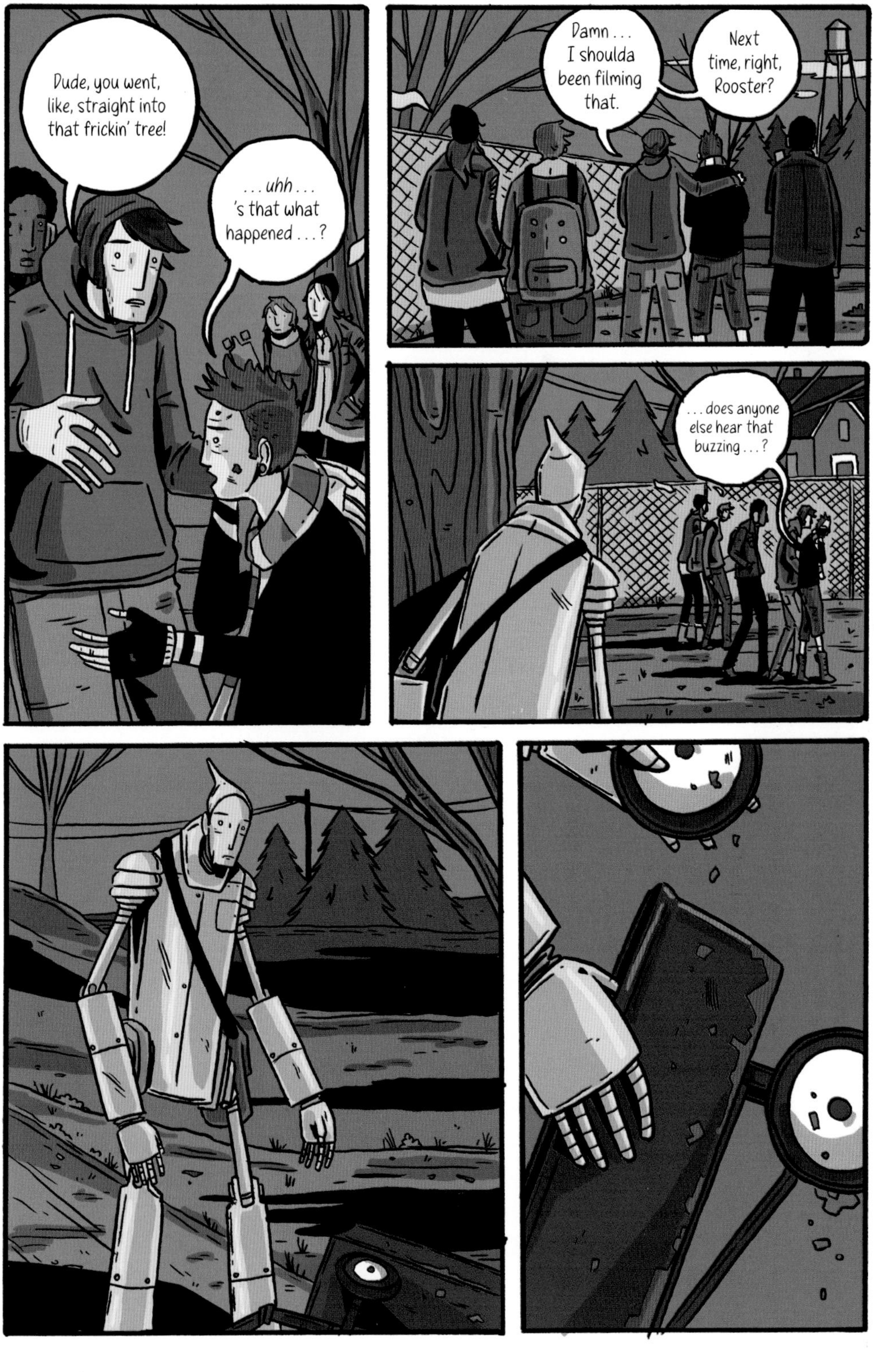
Dude, you went, like, straight into that frickin' tree!
. . . uhh . . . 's that what happened . . . ?
Damn . . . I shoulda been filming that.
Next time, right, Rooster?
. . . does anyone else hear that buzzing . . . ?

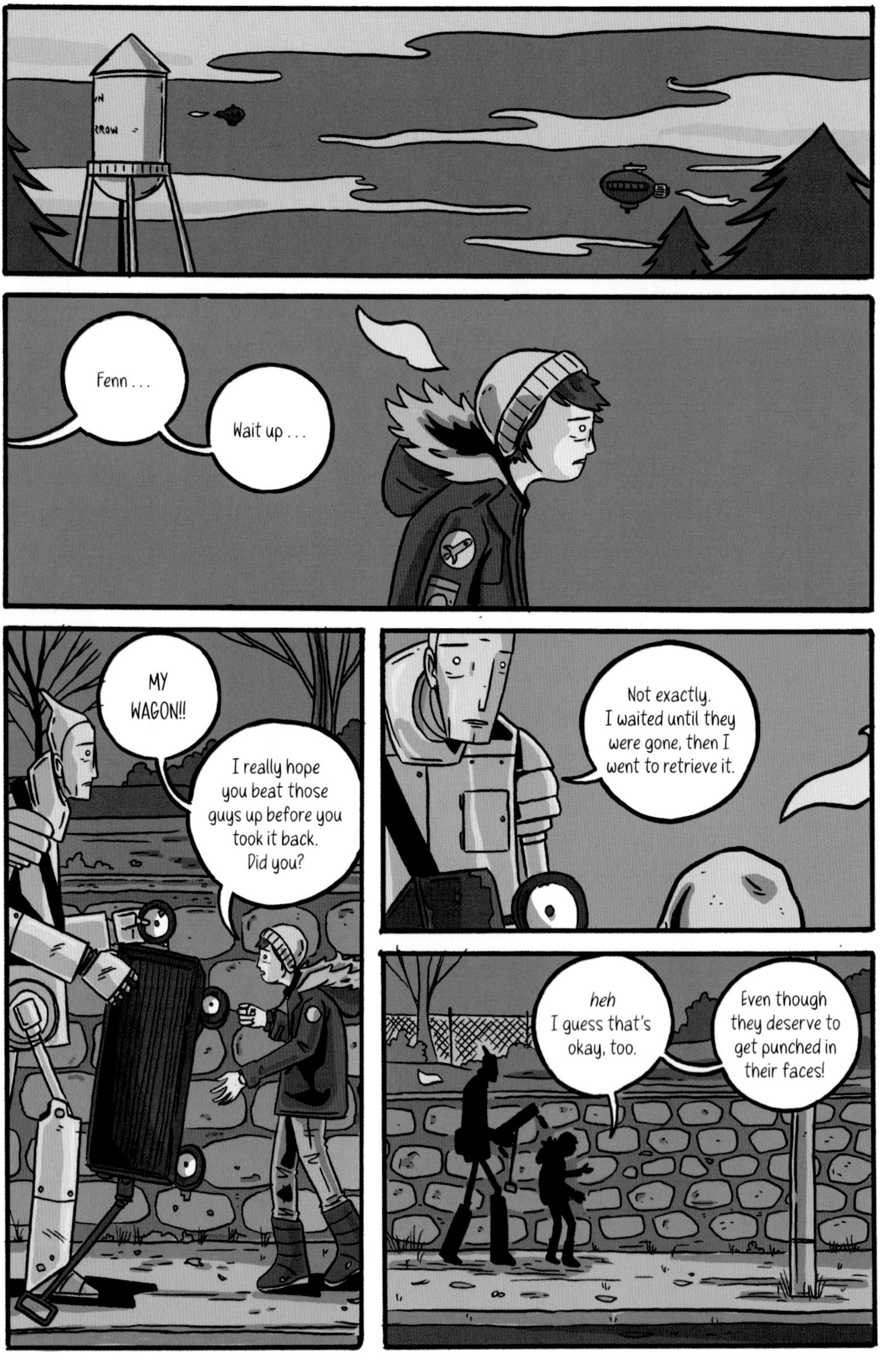
Fenn . . .
Wait up . . .
MY WAGON!!
I really hope you beat those guys up before you took it back. Did you?
Not exactly. I waited until they were gone, then I went to retrieve it.
heh I guess that's okay, too.
Even though they deserve to get punched in their faces!

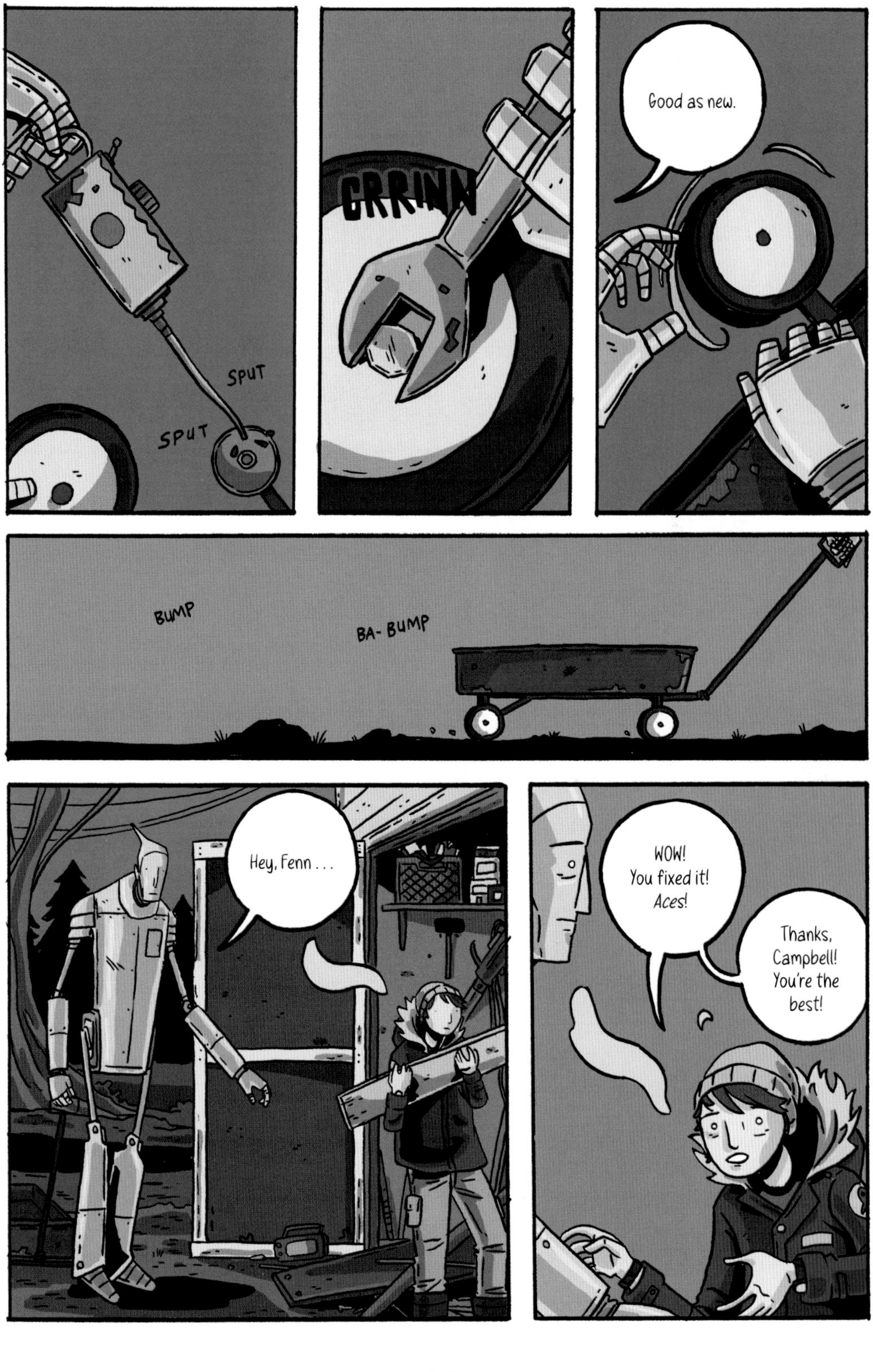
SPUT
SPUT
GRRINN
Good as new.
BUMP
BA-BUMP
Hey, Fenn . . .
WOW! You fixed it! *Aces!*
Thanks, Campbell! You're the best!

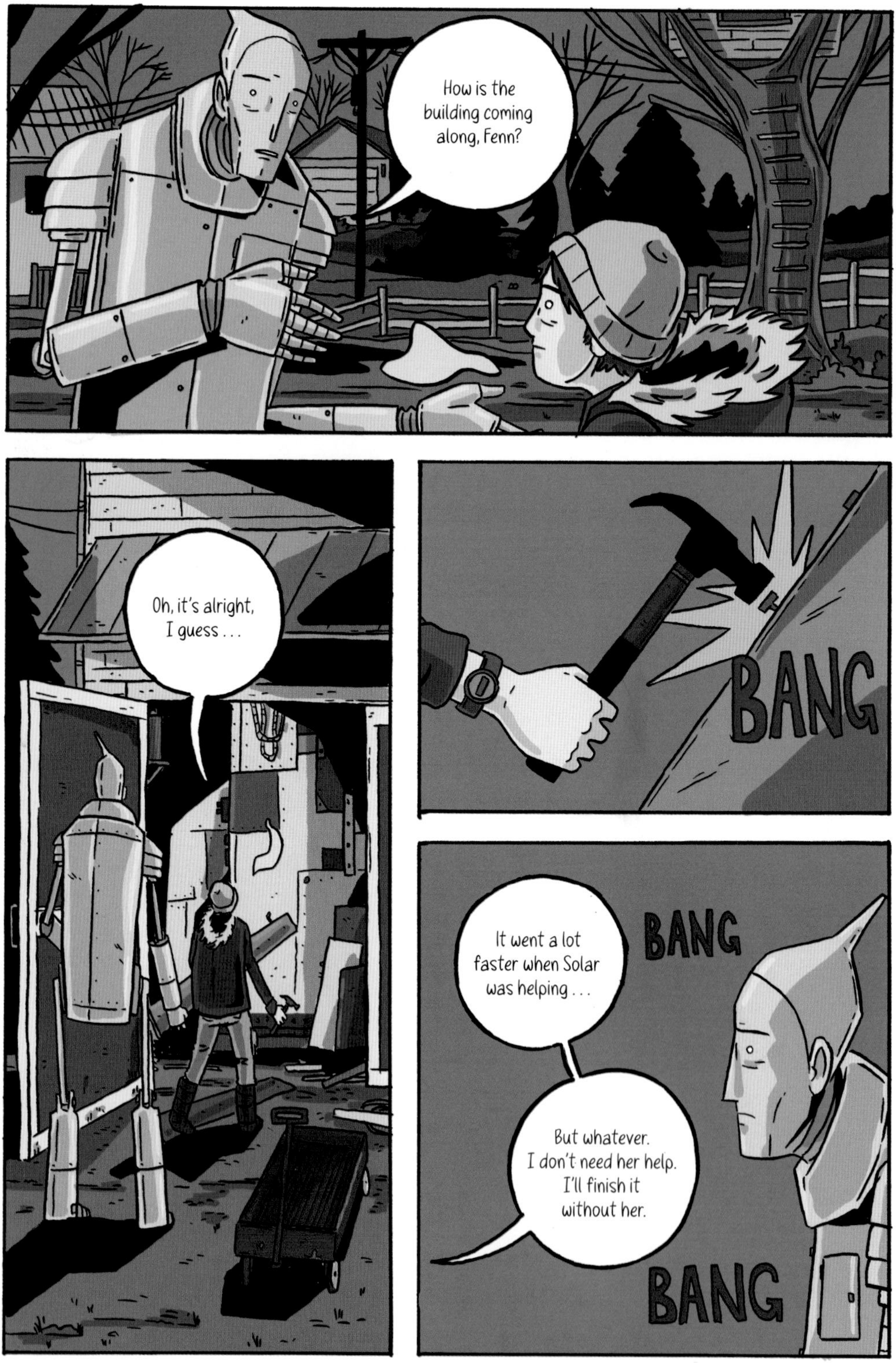
How is the building coming along, Fenn?
Oh, it's alright, I guess . . .
BANG
It went a lot faster when Solar was helping . . .
BANG
But whatever. I don't need her help. I'll finish it without her.
BANG

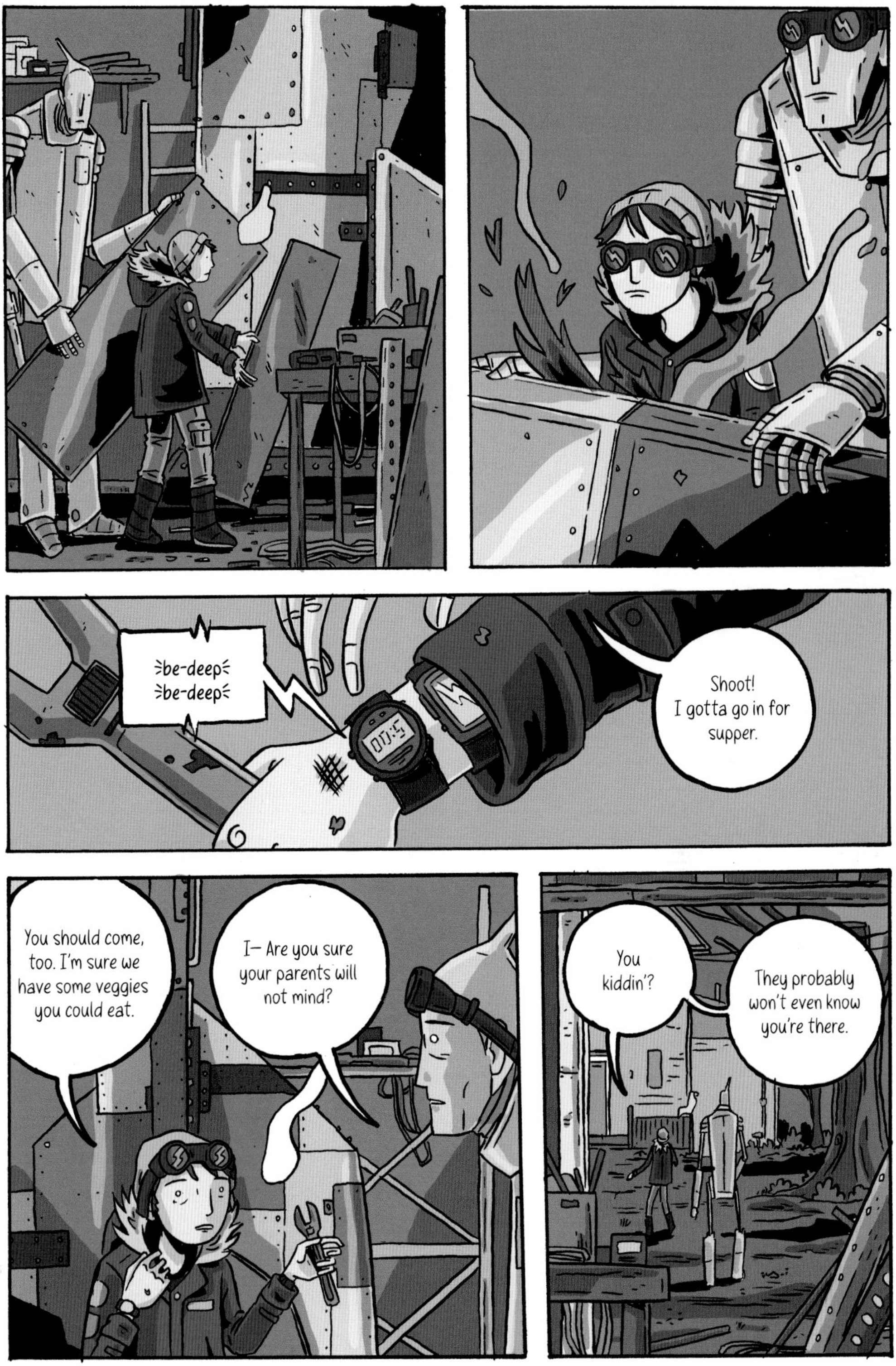
be-deep
be-deep
Shoot! I gotta go in for supper.
You should come, too. I'm sure we have some veggies you could eat.
I— Are you sure your parents will not mind?
You kiddin'?
They probably won't even know you're there.

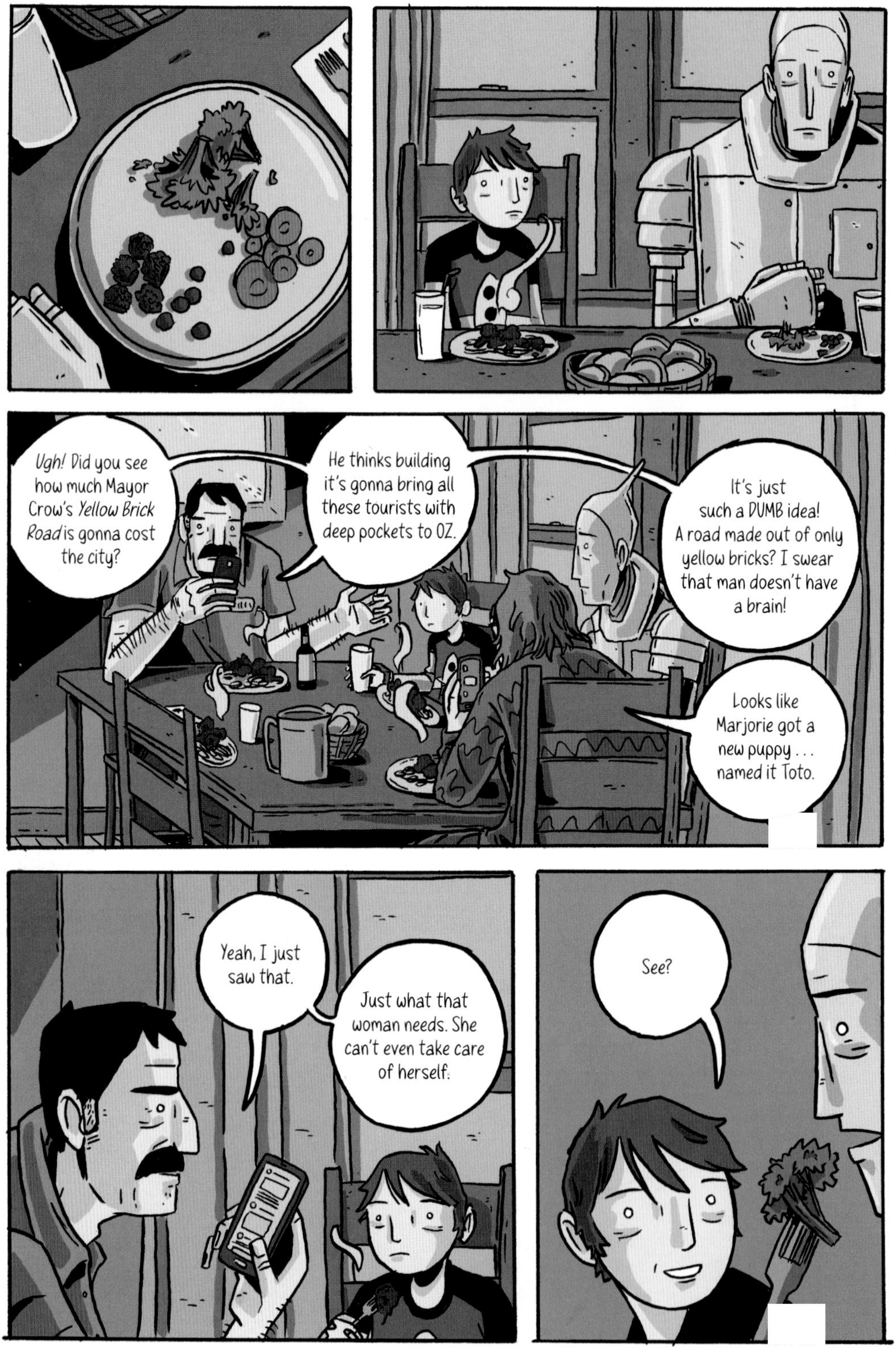
Ugh! Did you see how much Mayor Crow's *Yellow Brick Road* is gonna cost the city?
He thinks building it's gonna bring all these tourists with deep pockets to OZ.
It's just such a DUMB idea! A road made out of only yellow bricks? I swear that man doesn't have a brain!
Looks like Marjorie got a new puppy . . . named it Toto.
Yeah, I just saw that.
Just what that woman needs. She can't even take care of herself.
See?

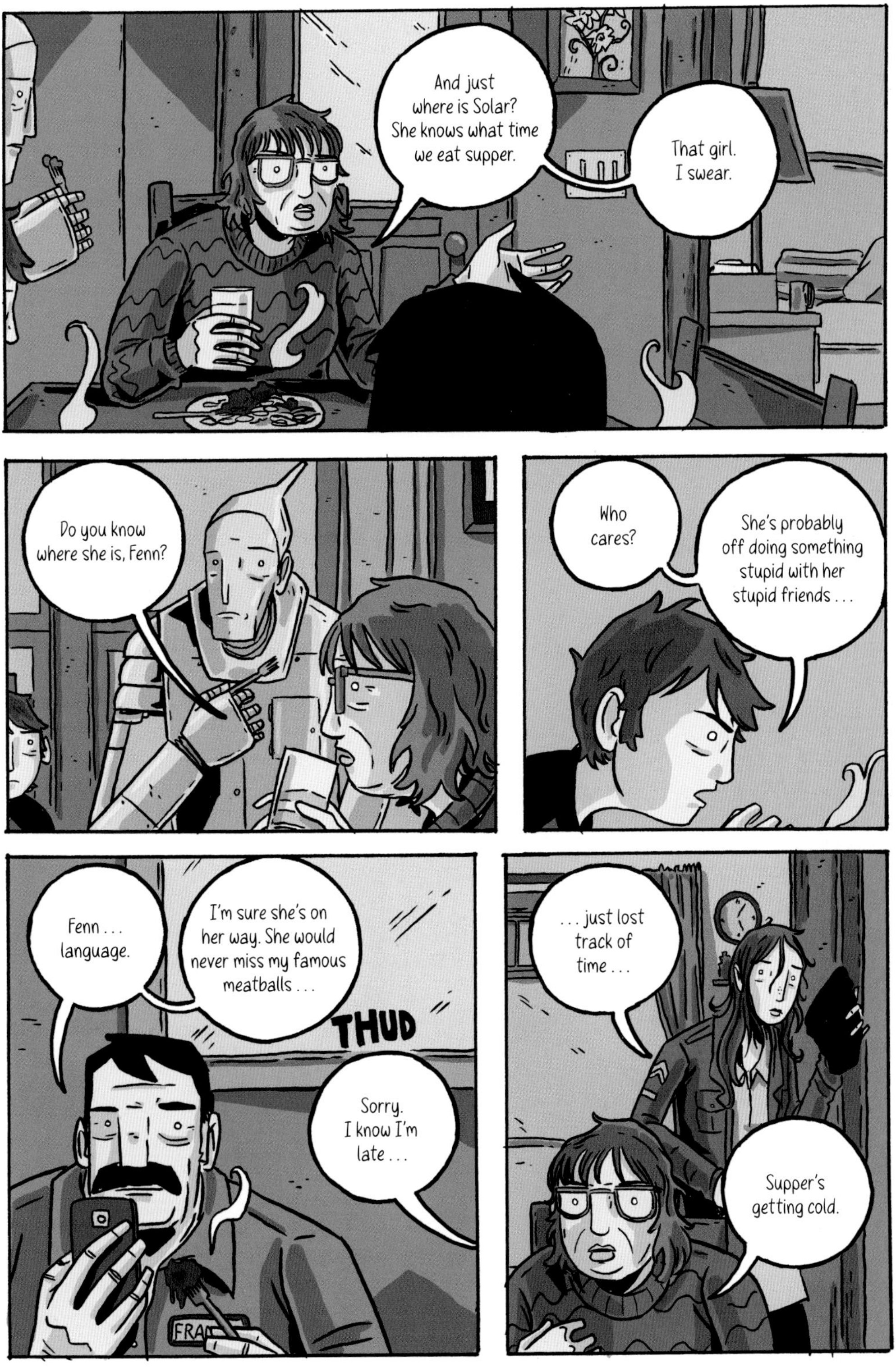
And just where is Solar? She knows what time we eat supper.
That girl. I swear.
Do you know where she is, Fenn?
Who cares?
She's probably off doing something stupid with her stupid friends . . .
Fenn . . . language.
I'm sure she's on her way. She would never miss my famous meatballs . . .
THUD
Sorry. I know I'm late . . .
. . . just lost track of time . . .
Supper's getting cold.

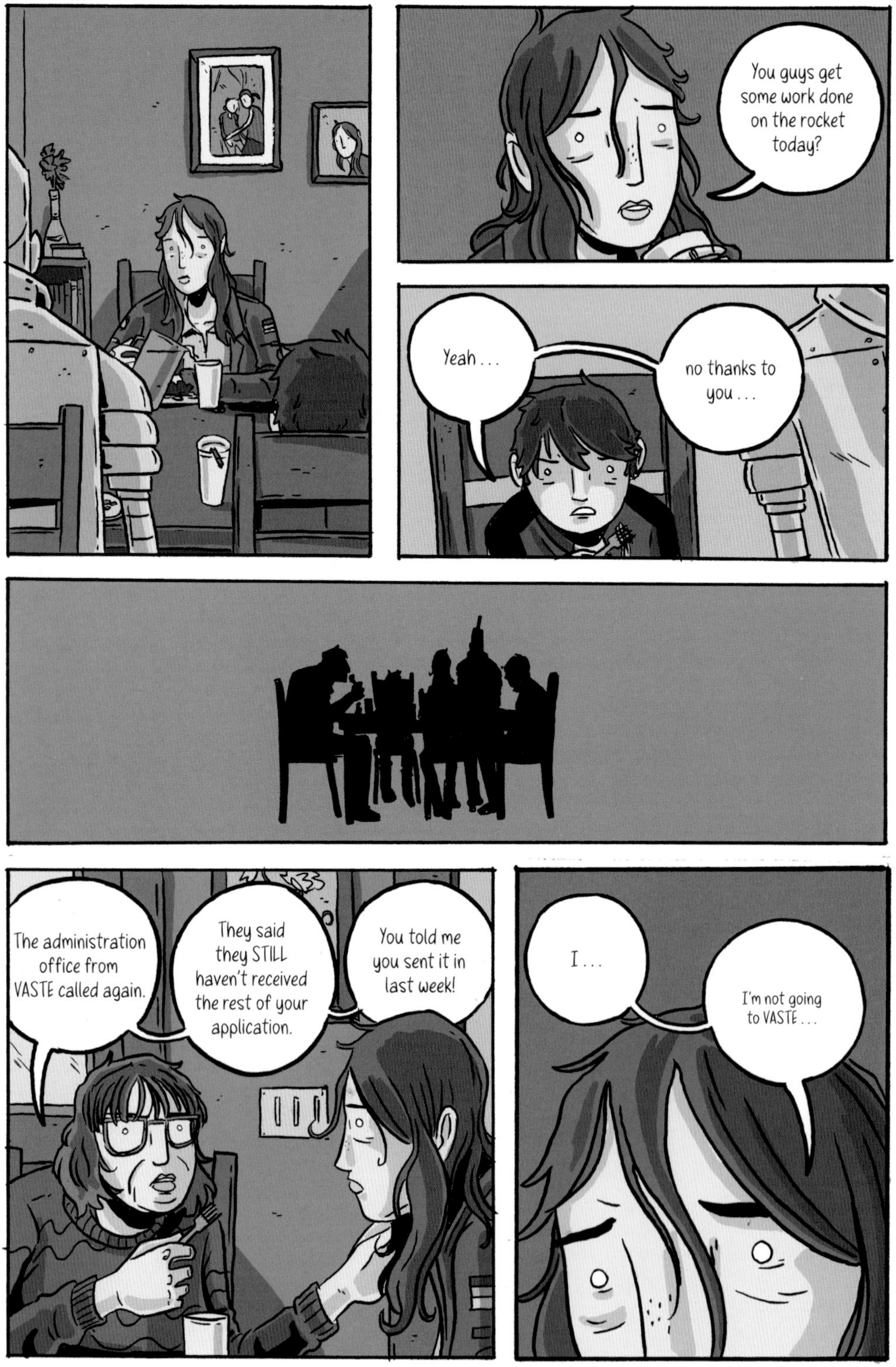
You guys get some work done on the rocket today?
Yeah . . .
no thanks to you . . .
The administration office from VASTE called again.
They said they STILL haven't received the rest of your application.
You told me you sent it in last week!
I . . .
I'm not going to VASTE . . .

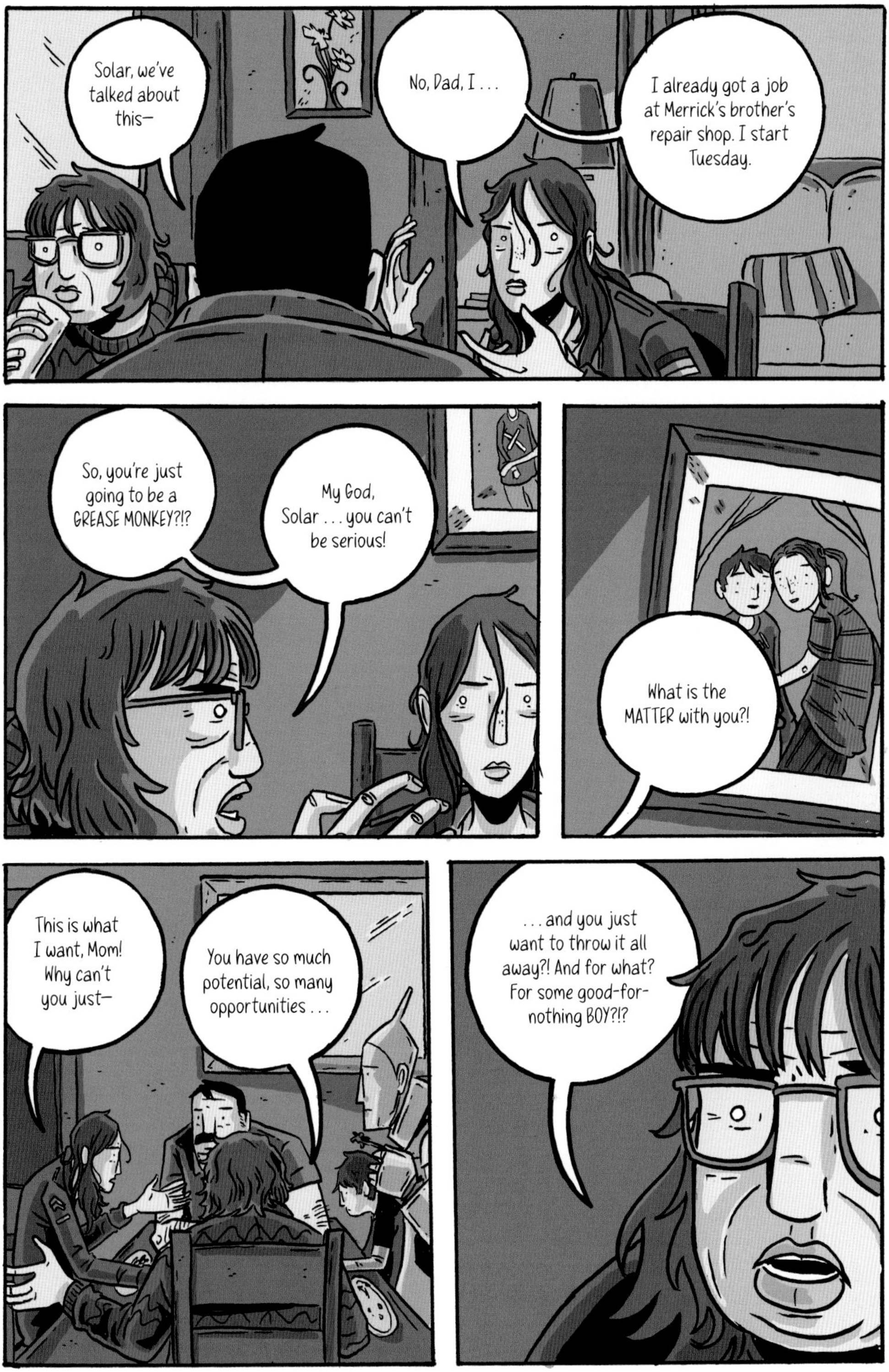
Solar, we've talked about this—
No, Dad, I . . .
I already got a job at Merrick's brother's repair shop. I start Tuesday.
So, you're just going to be a GREASE MONKEY?!?
My God, Solar . . . you can't be serious!
What is the MATTER with you?!
This is what I want, Mom! Why can't you just—
You have so much potential, so many opportunities . . .
. . . and you just want to throw it all away?! And for what? For some good-for-nothing BOY?!?

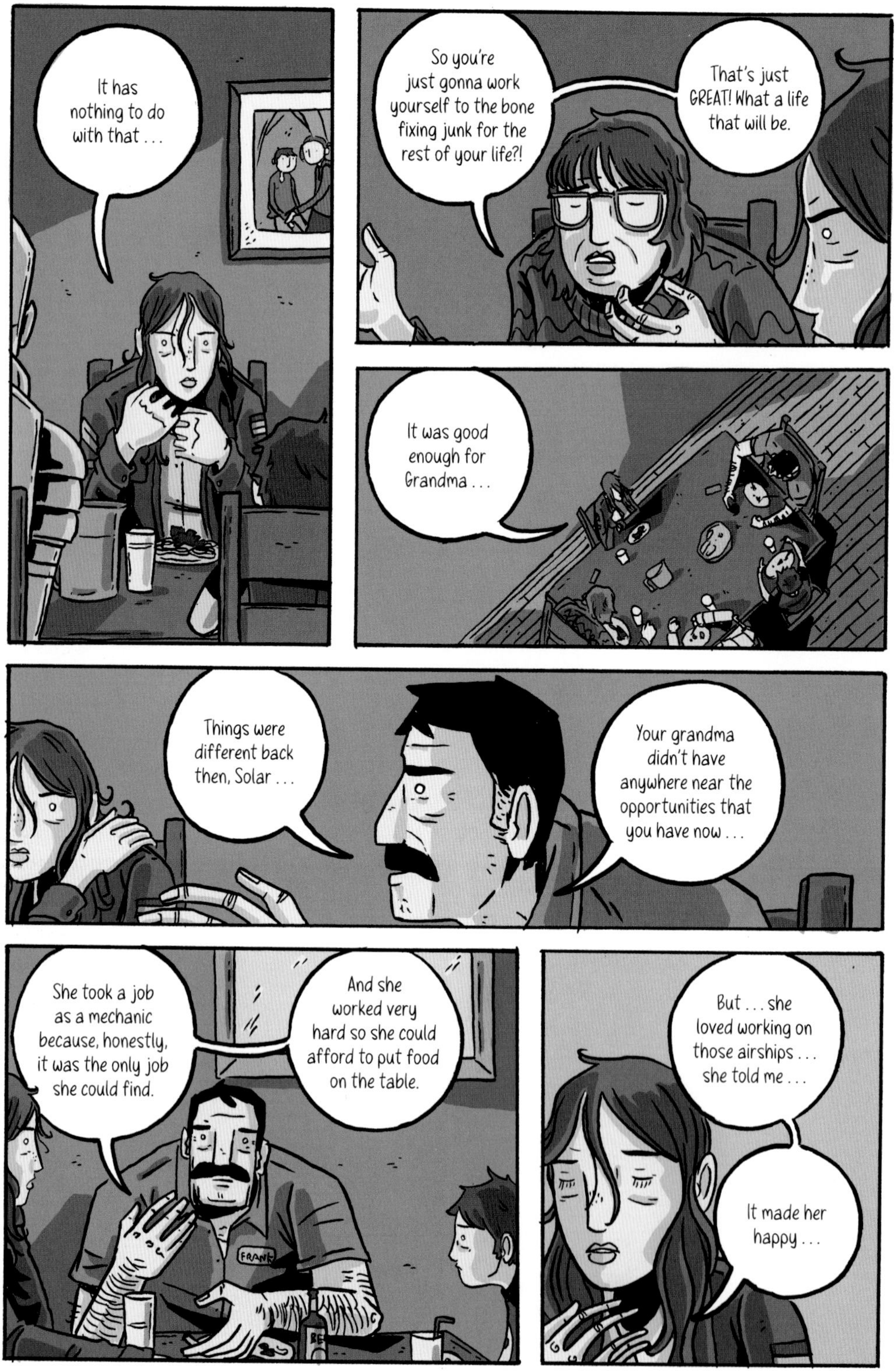
It has nothing to do with that . . .
So you're just gonna work yourself to the bone fixing junk for the rest of your life?!
That's just GREAT! What a life that will be.
It was good enough for Grandma . . .
Things were different back then, Solar . . .
Your grandma didn't have anywhere near the opportunities that you have now . . .
She took a job as a mechanic because, honestly, it was the only job she could find.
And she worked very hard so she could afford to put food on the table.
FRANK
But . . . she loved working on those airships . . . she told me . . .
It made her happy . . .

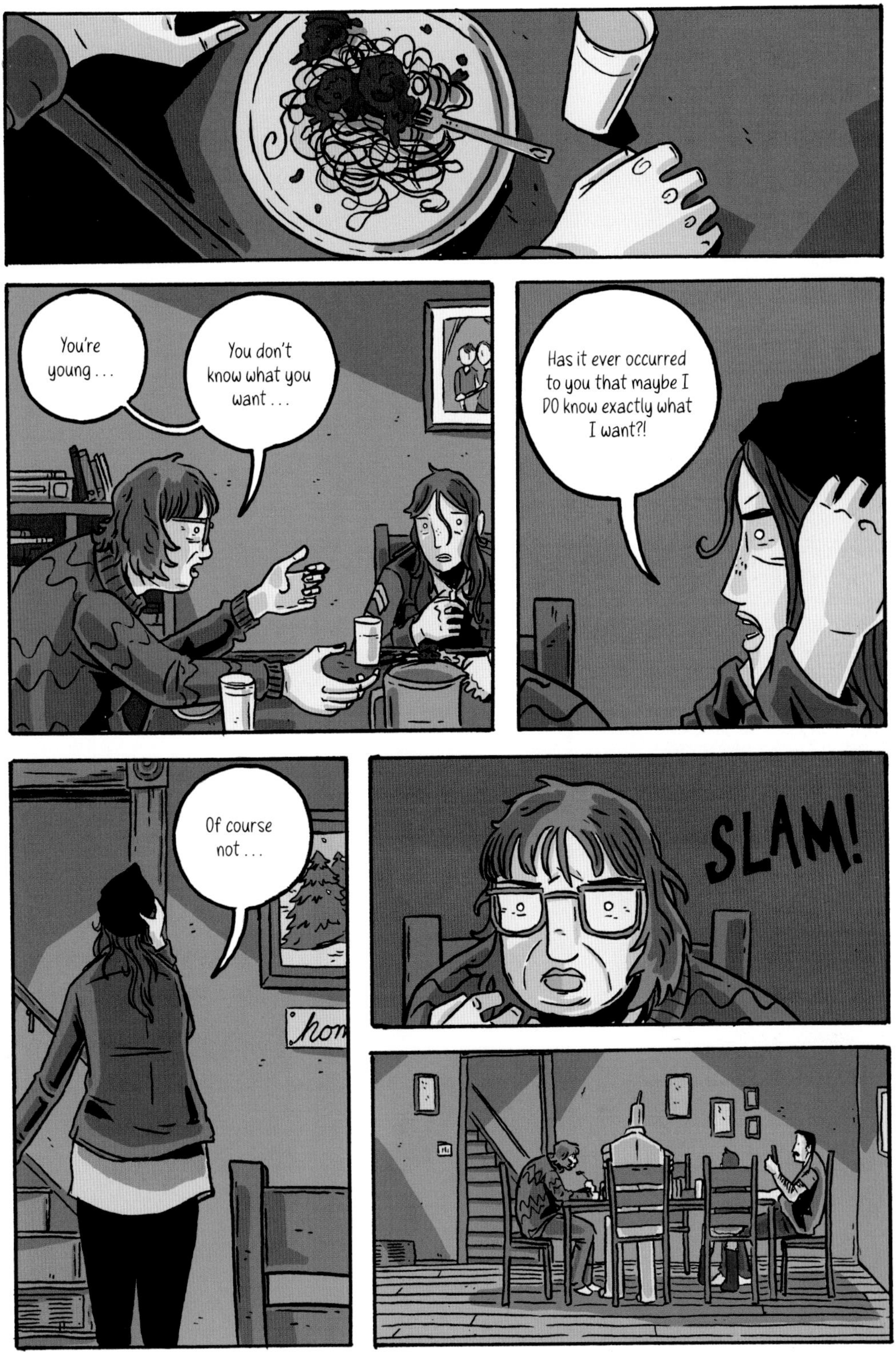
You're young . . .
You don't know what you want . . .
Has it ever occurred to you that maybe I DO know exactly what I want?!
Of course not . . .
SLAM!

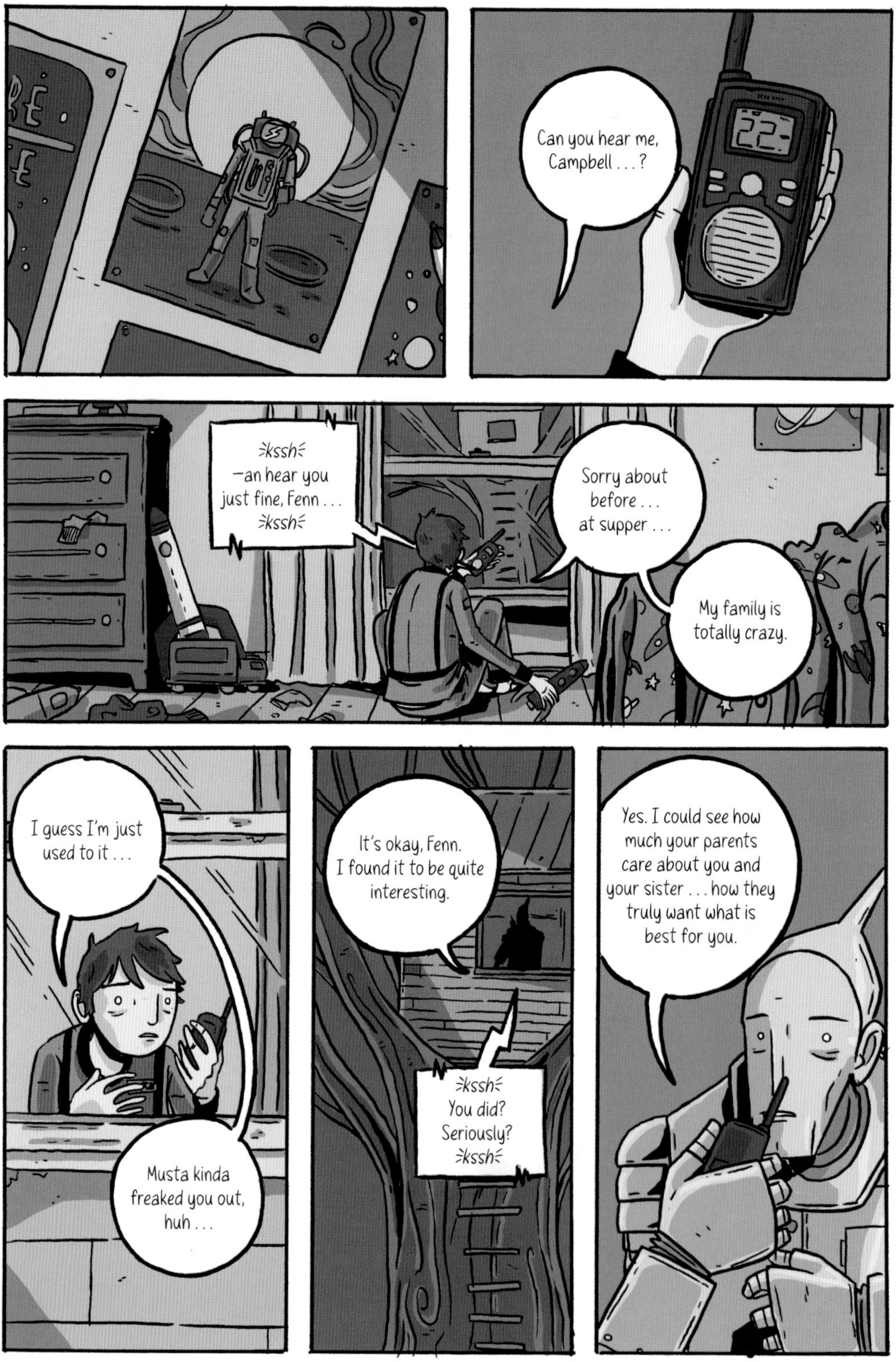
Can you hear me, Campbell . . . ?
⪢kssh⪡ —an hear you just fine, Fenn . . . ⪢kssh⪡
Sorry about before . . . at supper . . .
My family is totally crazy.
I guess I'm just used to it . . .
Musta kinda freaked you out, huh . . .
It's okay, Fenn. I found it to be quite interesting.
⪢kssh⪡ You did? Seriously? ⪢kssh⪡
Yes. I could see how much your parents care about you and your sister . . . how they truly want what is best for you.

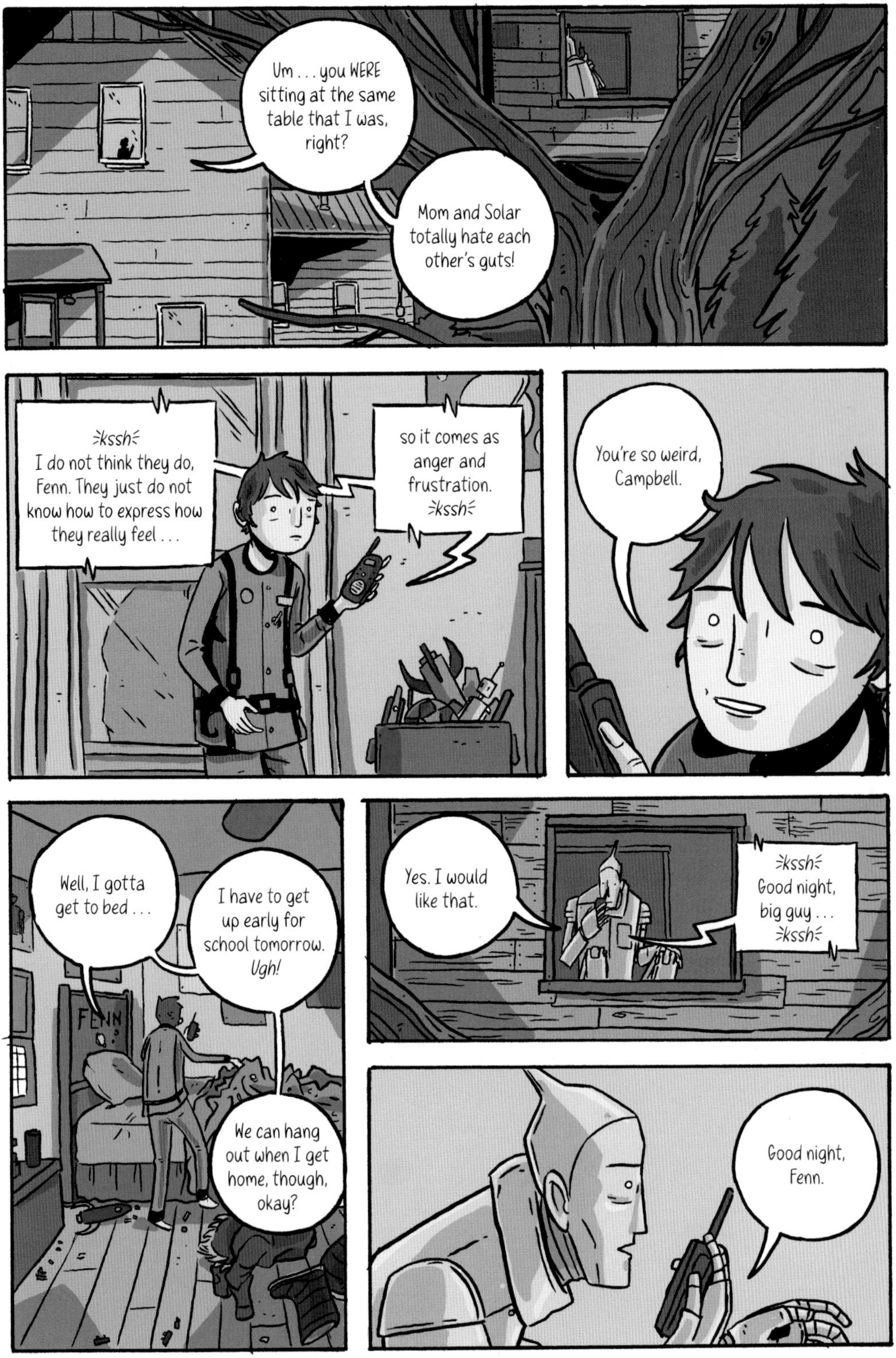
Um . . . you WERE sitting at the same table that I was, right?
Mom and Solar totally hate each other's guts!
≷kssh≶ I do not think they do, Fenn. They just do not know how to express how they really feel . . .
so it comes as anger and frustration. ≷kssh≶
You're so weird, Campbell.
Well, I gotta get to bed . . .
I have to get up early for school tomorrow. *Ugh!*
We can hang out when I get home, though, okay?
Yes. I would like that.
≷kssh≶ Good night, big guy . . . ≷kssh≶
Good night, Fenn.

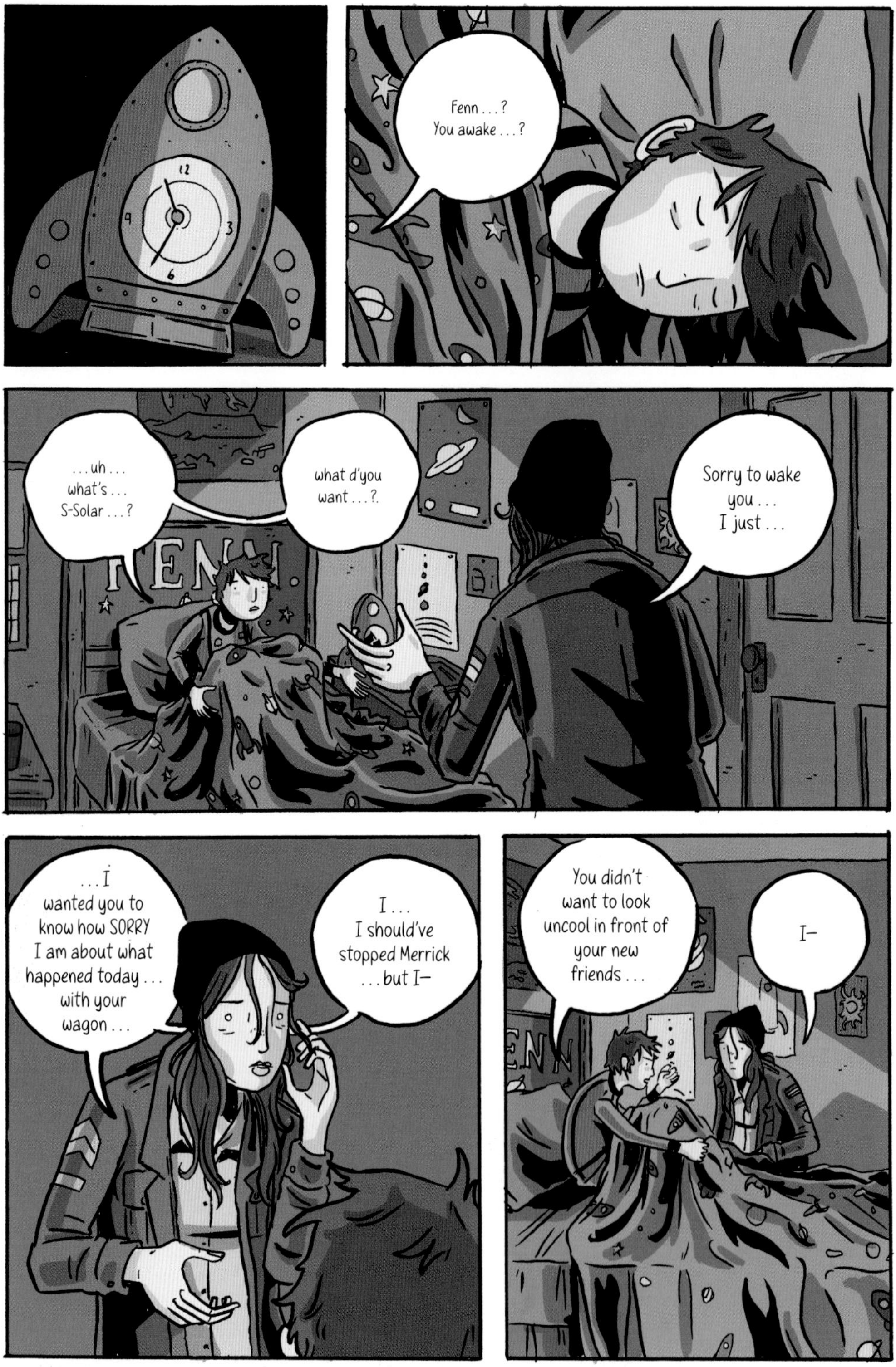
Fenn . . . ?
You awake . . . ?
. . . uh . . .
what's . . .
S-Solar . . . ?
what d'you want . . . ?.
Sorry to wake you . . .
I just . . .
. . . I wanted you to know how SORRY I am about what happened today . . . with your wagon . . .
I . . .
I should've stopped Merrick . . . but I–
You didn't want to look uncool in front of your new friends . . .
I–

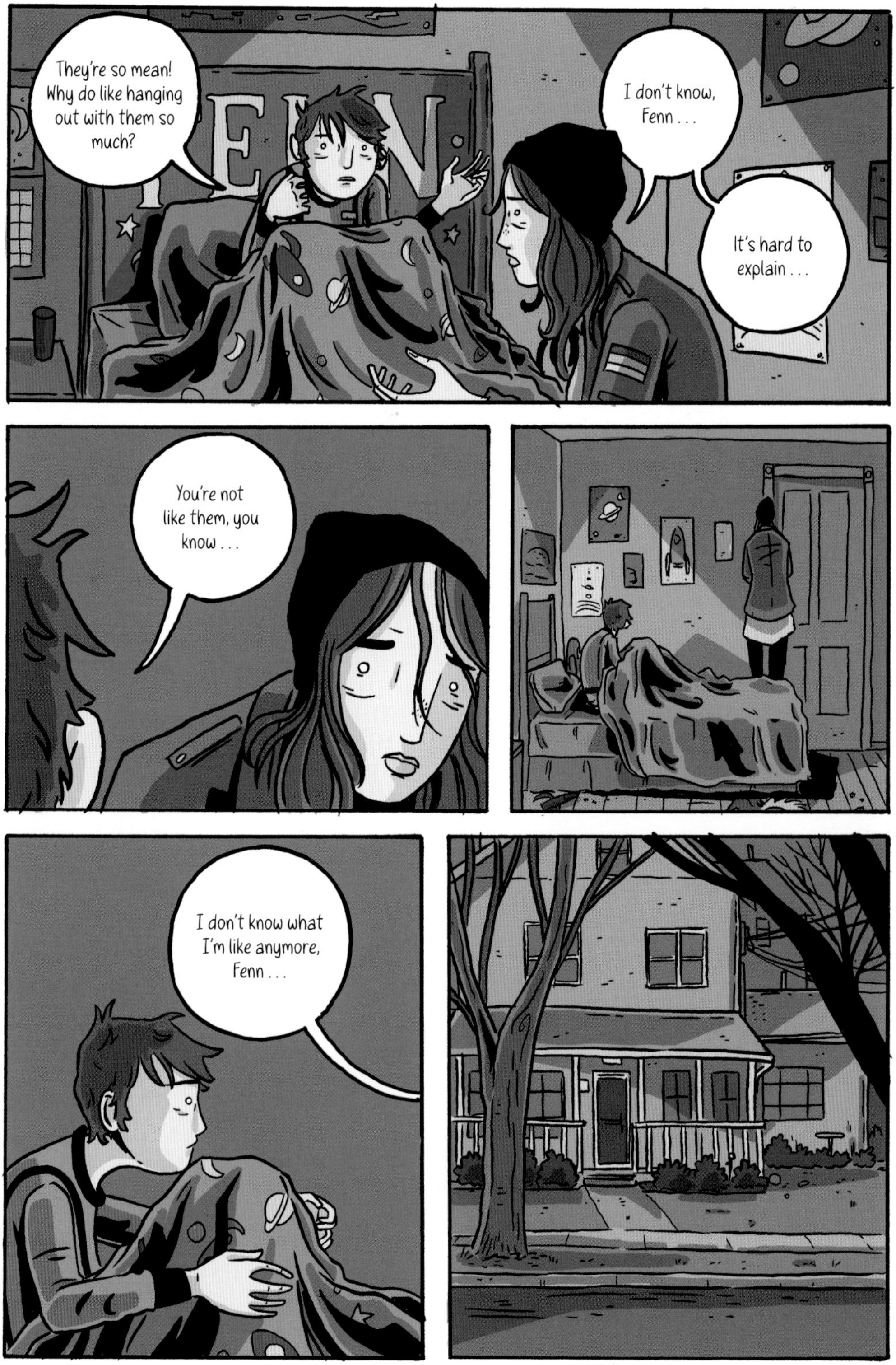
They're so mean! Why do like hanging out with them so much?
I don't know, Fenn . . .
It's hard to explain . . .
You're not like them, you know . . .
I don't know what I'm like anymore, Fenn . . .

CHAPTER 7: Hero

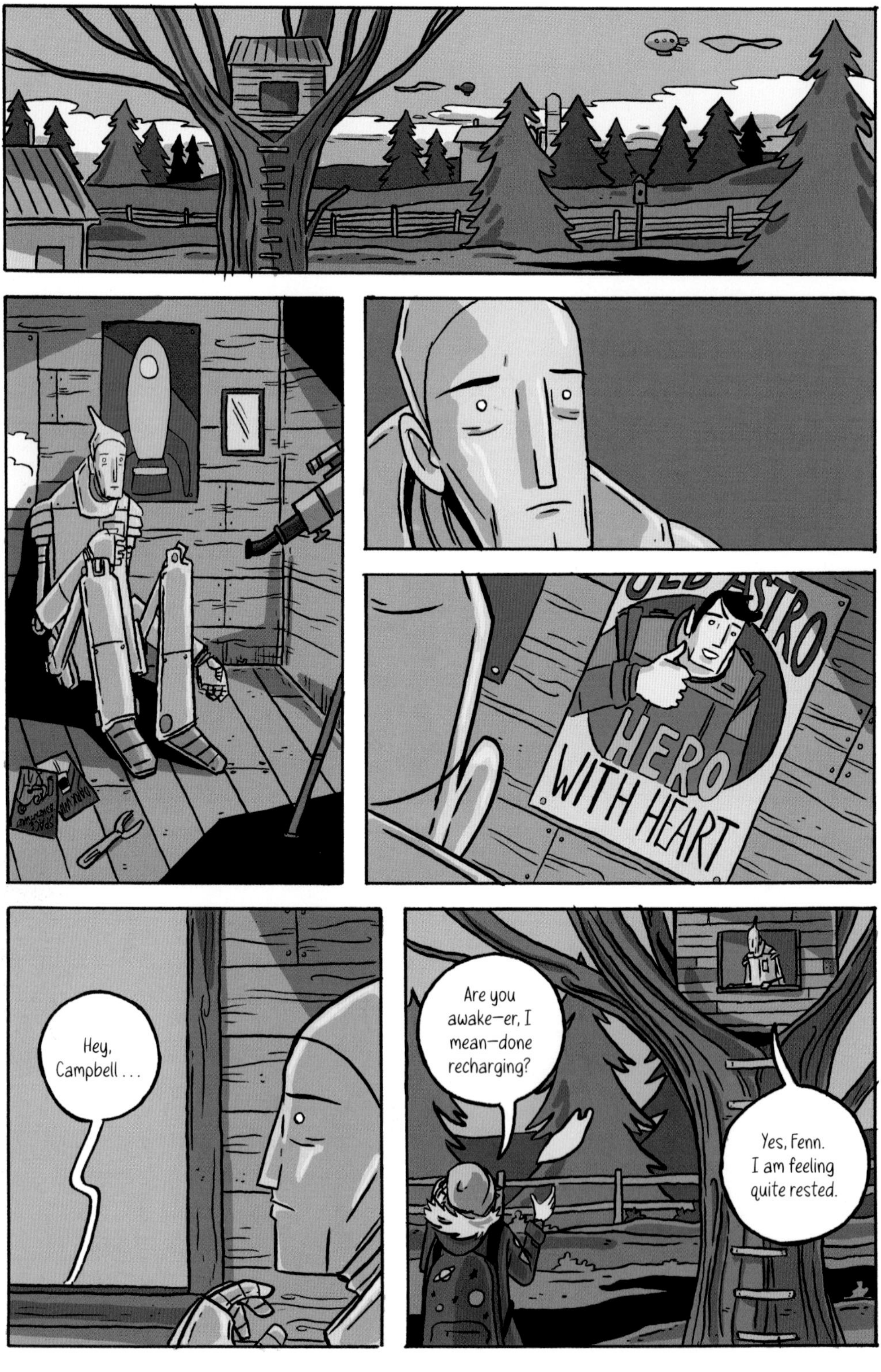
HERO
WITH HEART
Hey, Campbell . . .
Are you awake—er, I mean—done recharging?
Yes, Fenn. I am feeling quite rested.

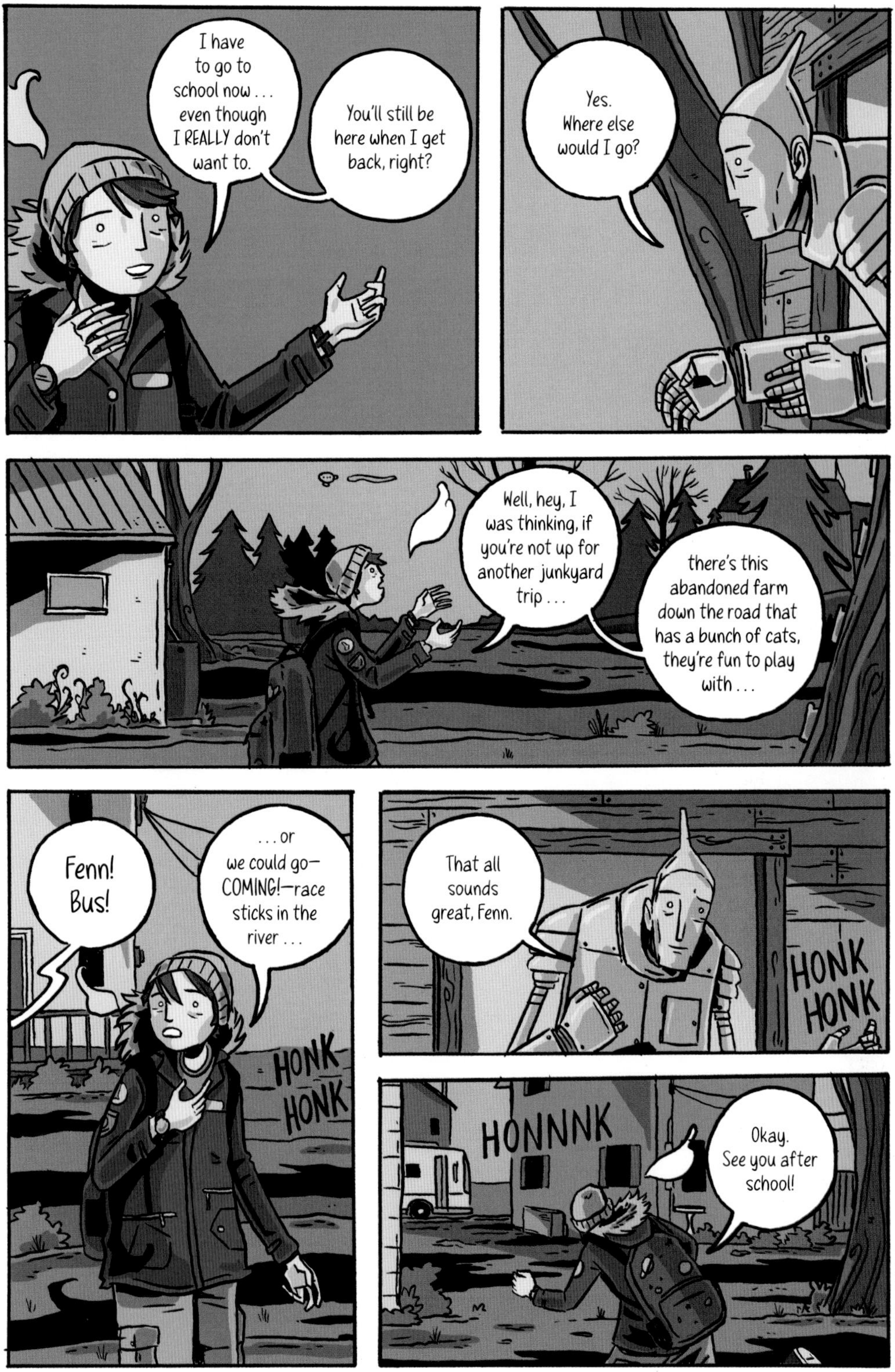
I have to go to school now . . . even though I REALLY don't want to.
You'll still be here when I get back, right?
Yes. Where else would I go?
Well, hey, I was thinking, if you're not up for another junkyard trip . . .
there's this abandoned farm down the road that has a bunch of cats, they're fun to play with . . .
Fenn! Bus!
. . . or we could go—COMING!—race sticks in the river . . .
HONK HONK
That all sounds great, Fenn.
HONK HONK
HONNNK
Okay. See you after school!

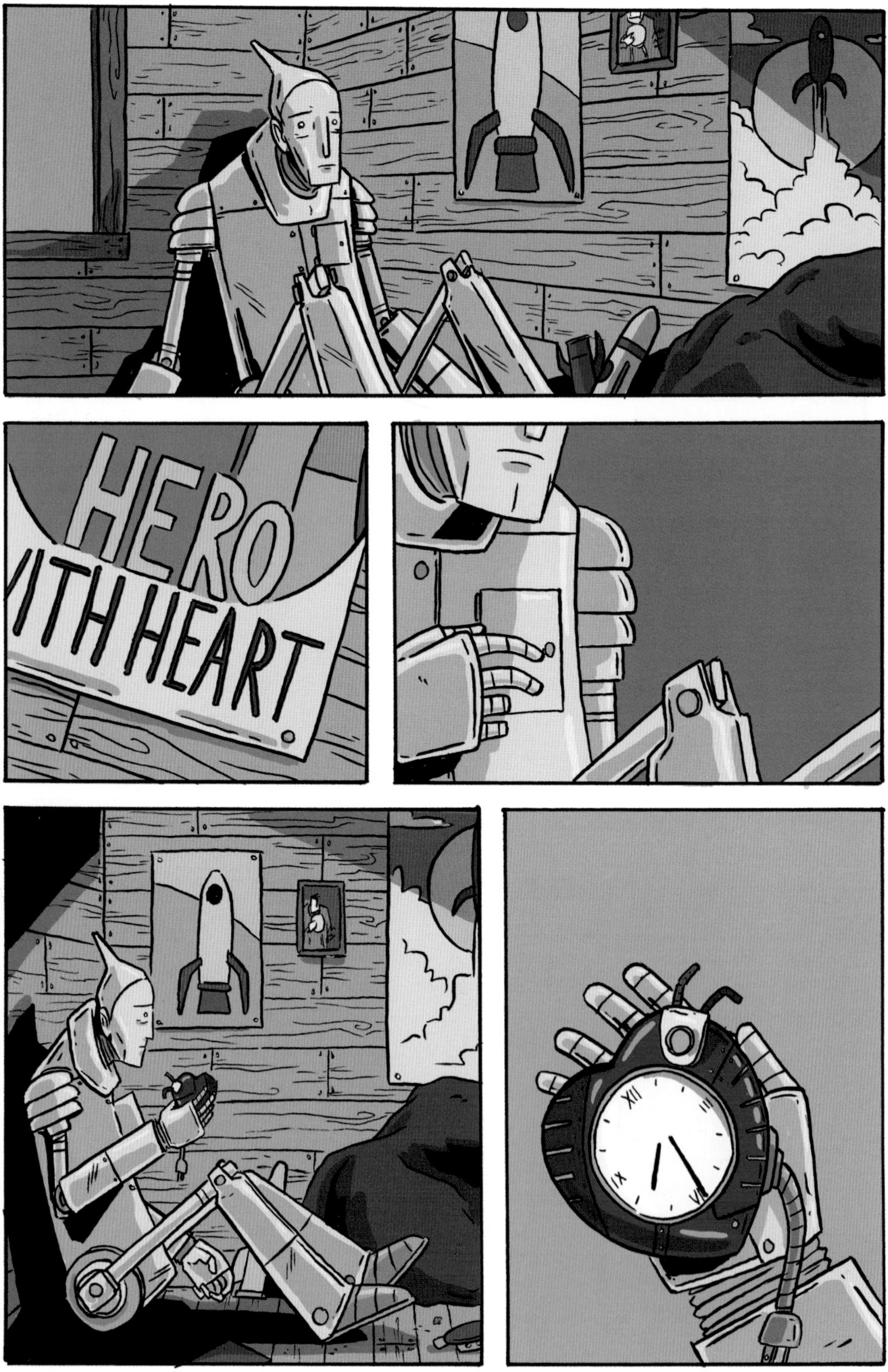
HERO
ITH HEART

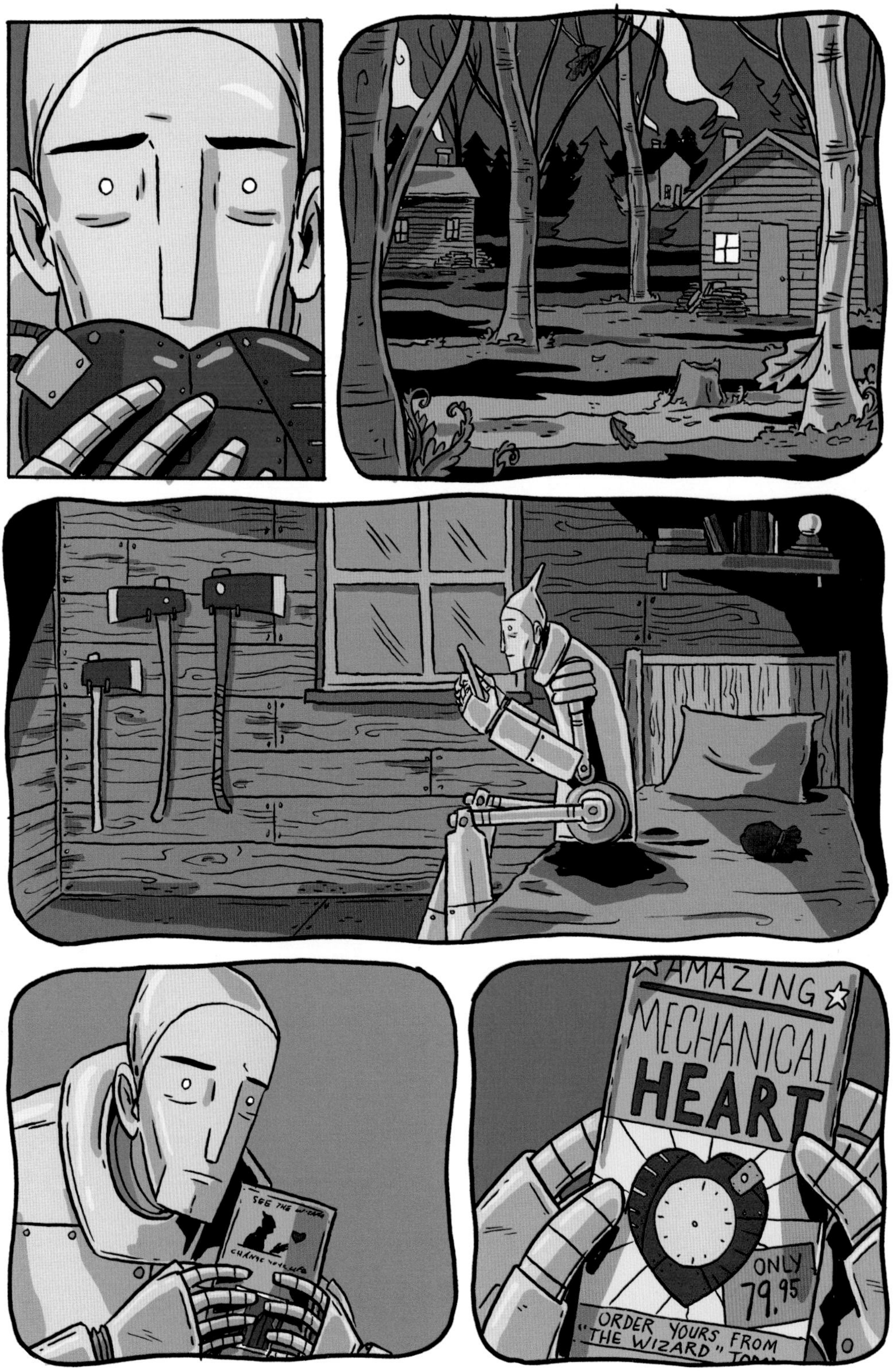
AMAZING
MECHANICAL
HEART
ONLY
79.95
ORDER YOURS FROM
"THE WIZARD"

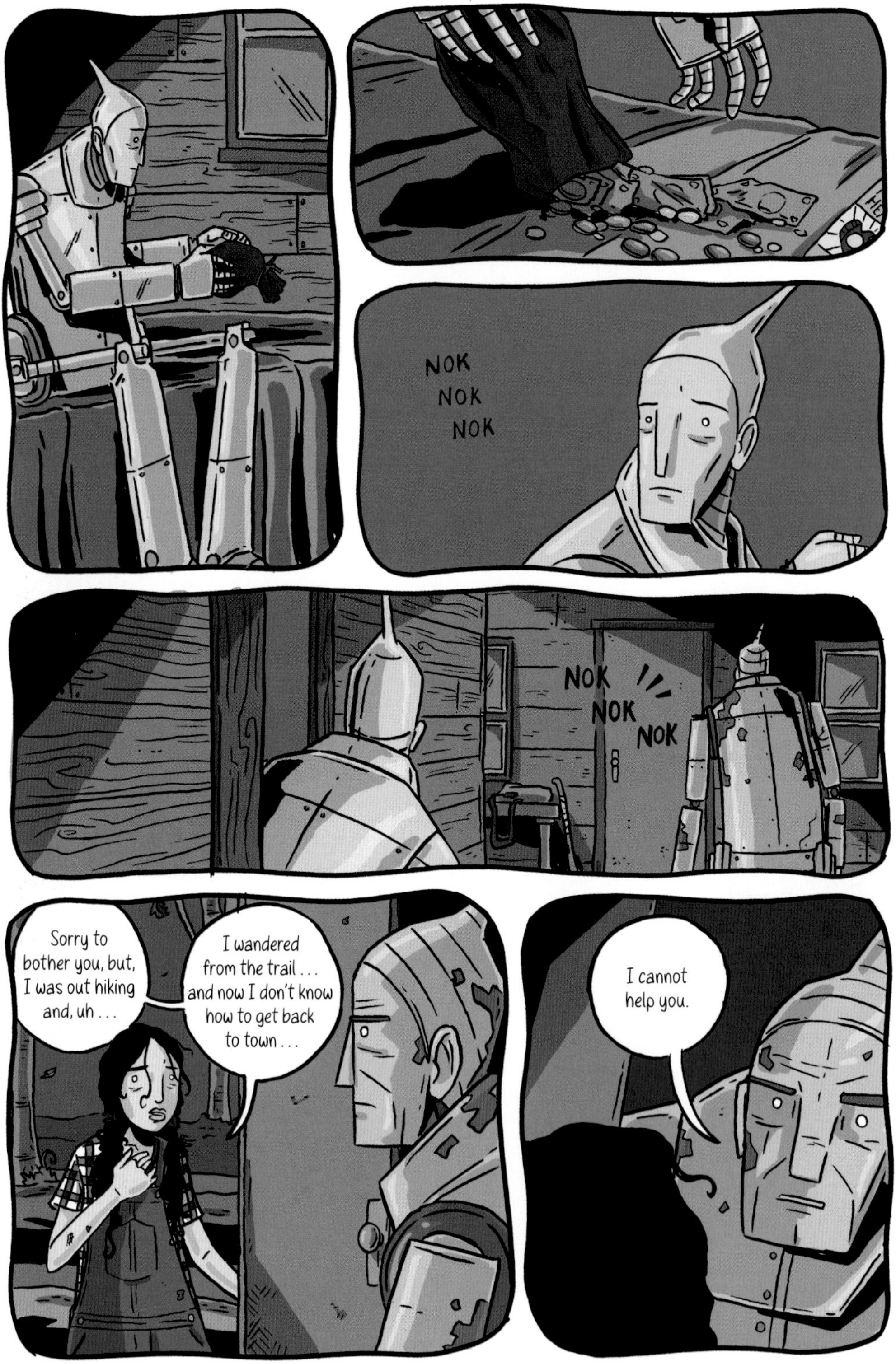
NOK
NOK
NOK
NOK
NOK
NOK
Sorry to bother you, but, I was out hiking and, uh . . .
I wandered from the trail . . . and now I don't know how to get back to town . . .
I cannot help you.

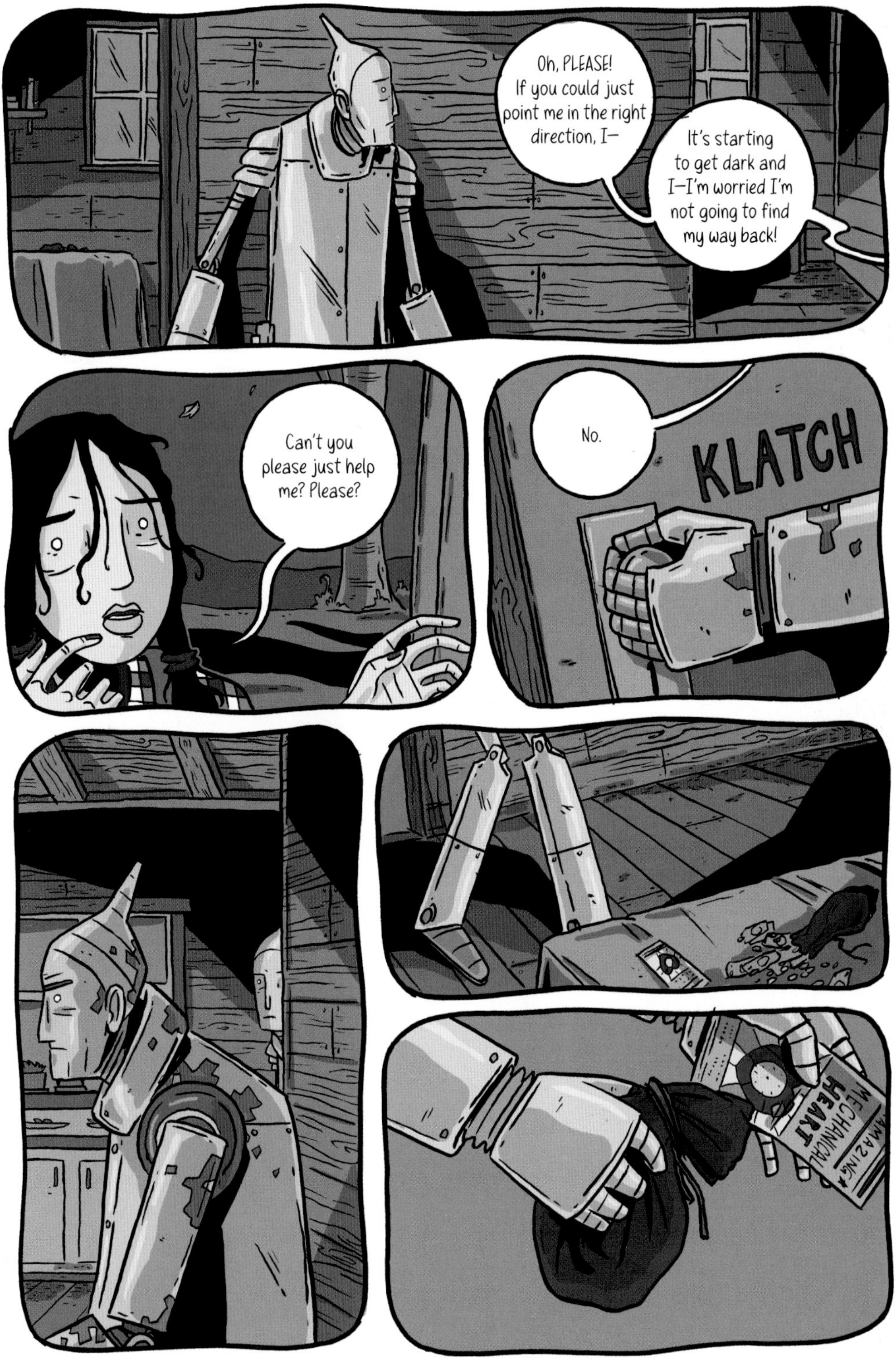
Oh, PLEASE! If you could just point me in the right direction, I—
It's starting to get dark and I—I'm worried I'm not going to find my way back!
Can't you please just help me? Please?
No.
KLATCH
AMAZING★ MECHANICAL HEART

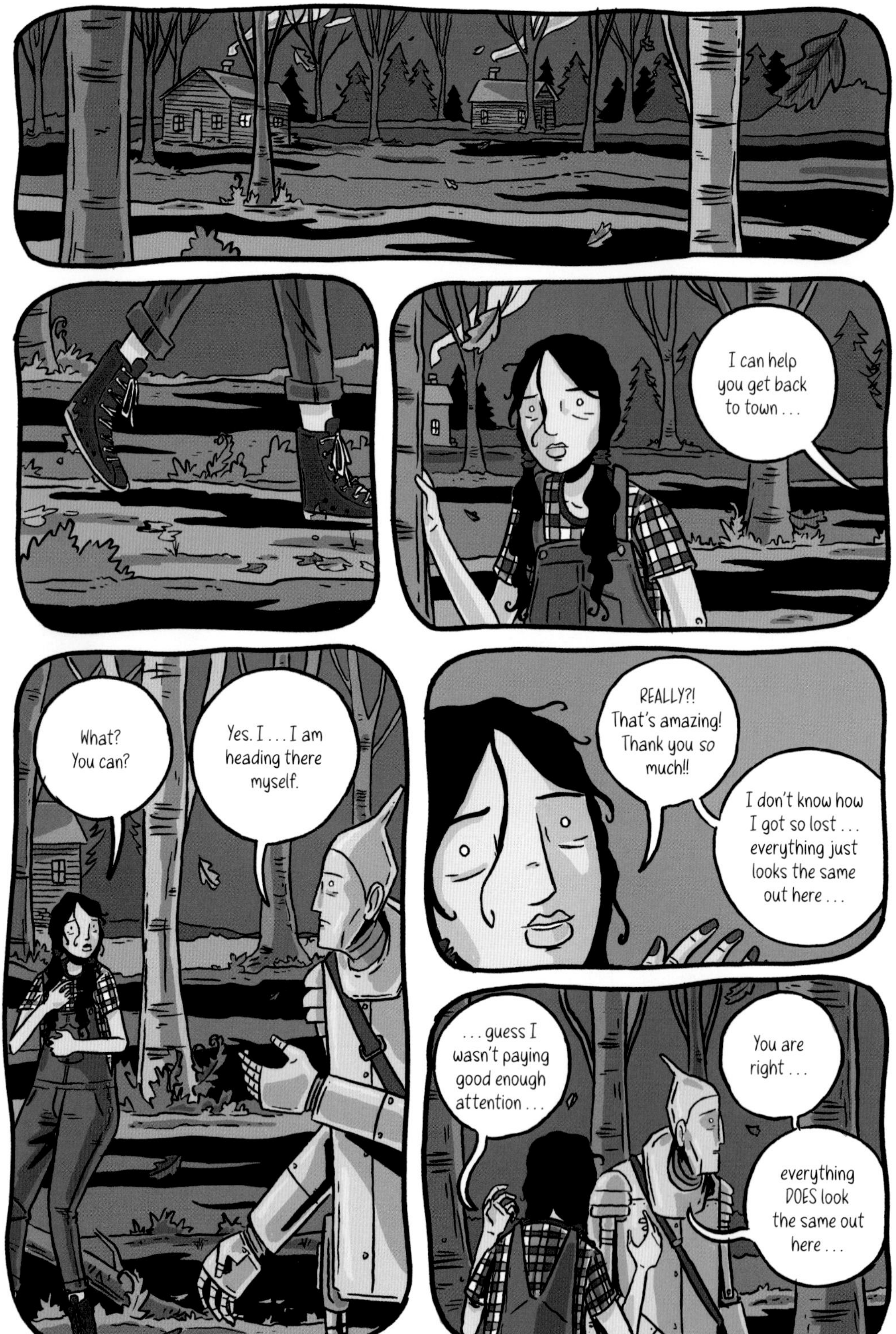
I can help you get back to town . . .
What? You can?
Yes. I . . . I am heading there myself.
REALLY?! That's amazing! Thank you so much!!
I don't know how I got so lost . . . everything just looks the same out here . . .
. . . guess I wasn't paying good enough attention . . .
You are right . . .
everything DOES look the same out here . . .

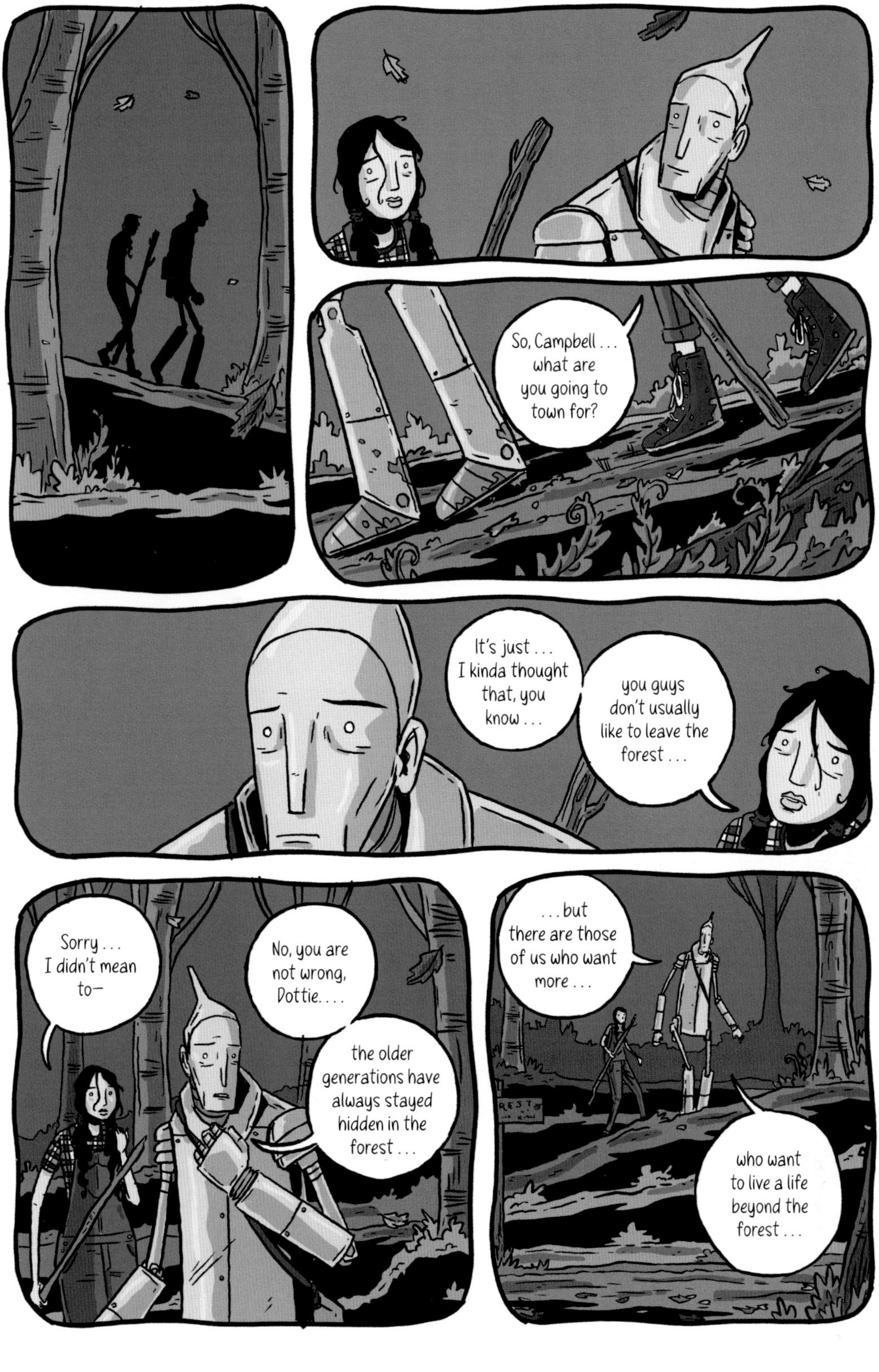
So, Campbell . . . what are you going to town for?
It's just . . . I kinda thought that, you know . . .
you guys don't usually like to leave the forest . . .
Sorry . . . I didn't mean to—
No, you are not wrong, Dottie. . . .
the older generations have always stayed hidden in the forest . . .
. . . but there are those of us who want more . . .
who want to live a life beyond the forest . . .

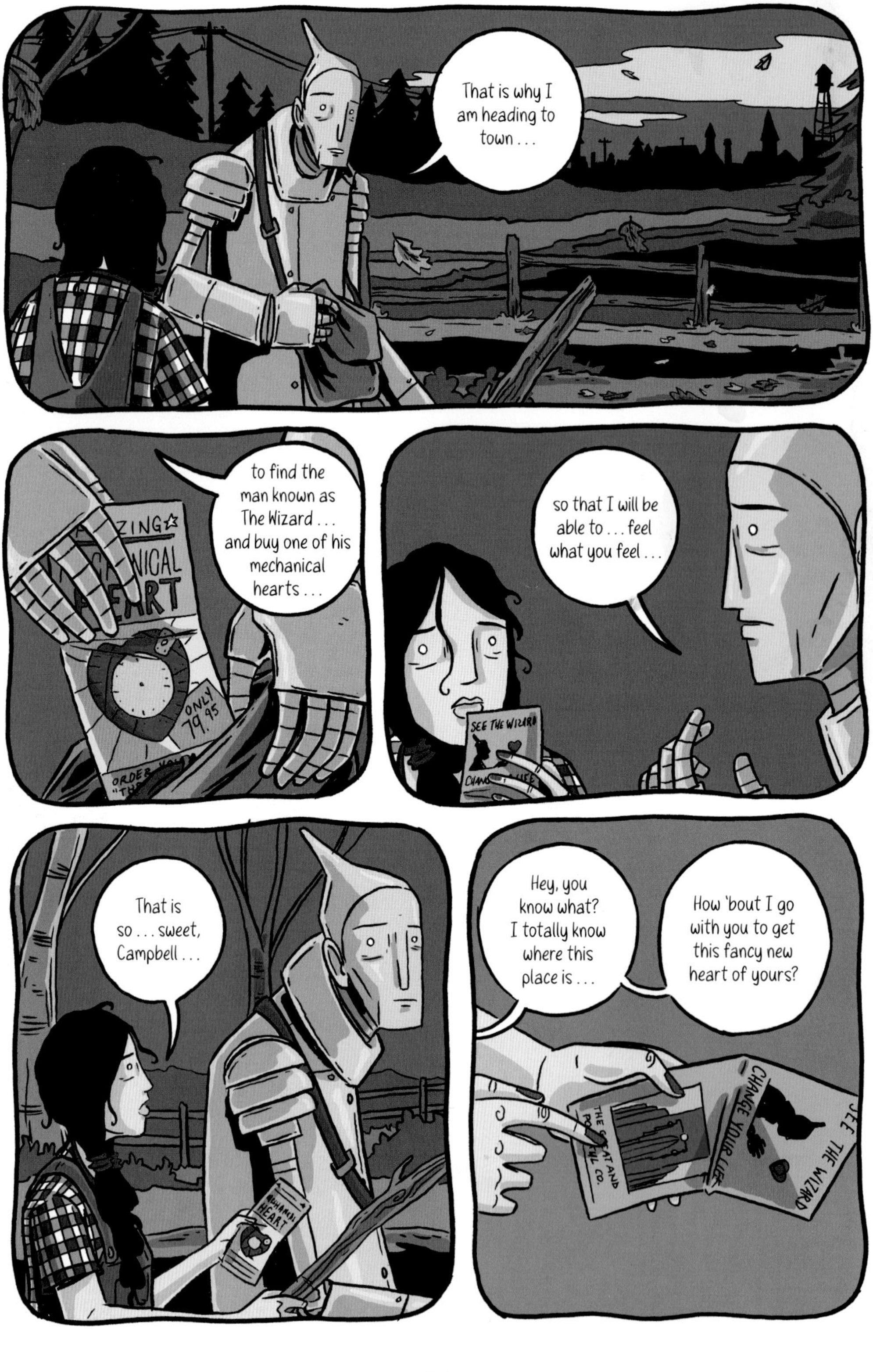
That is why I am heading to town . . .
to find the man known as The Wizard . . . and buy one of his mechanical hearts . . .
ONLY 79.95
so that I will be able to . . . feel what you feel . . .
SEE THE WIZARD
That is so . . . sweet, Campbell . . .
Hey, you know what? I totally know where this place is . . .
How 'bout I go with you to get this fancy new heart of yours?
CHANGE YOUR LIFE
SEE THE WIZARD

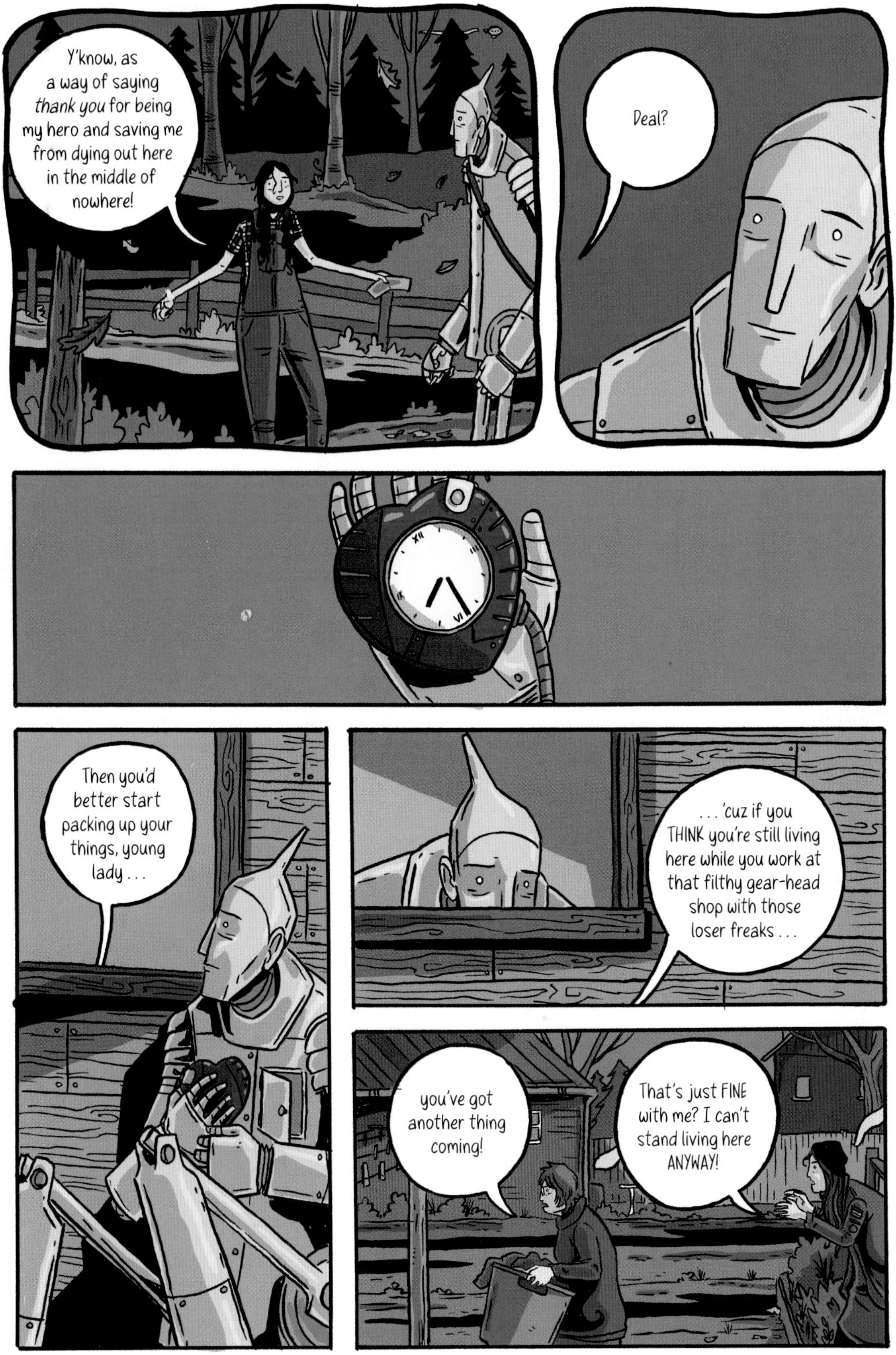
Y'know, as a way of saying *thank you* for being my hero and saving me from dying out here in the middle of nowhere!
Deal?
Then you'd better start packing up your things, young lady . . .
. . . 'cuz if you THINK you're still living here while you work at that filthy gear-head shop with those loser freaks . . .
you've got another thing coming!
That's just FINE with me? I can't stand living here ANYWAY!

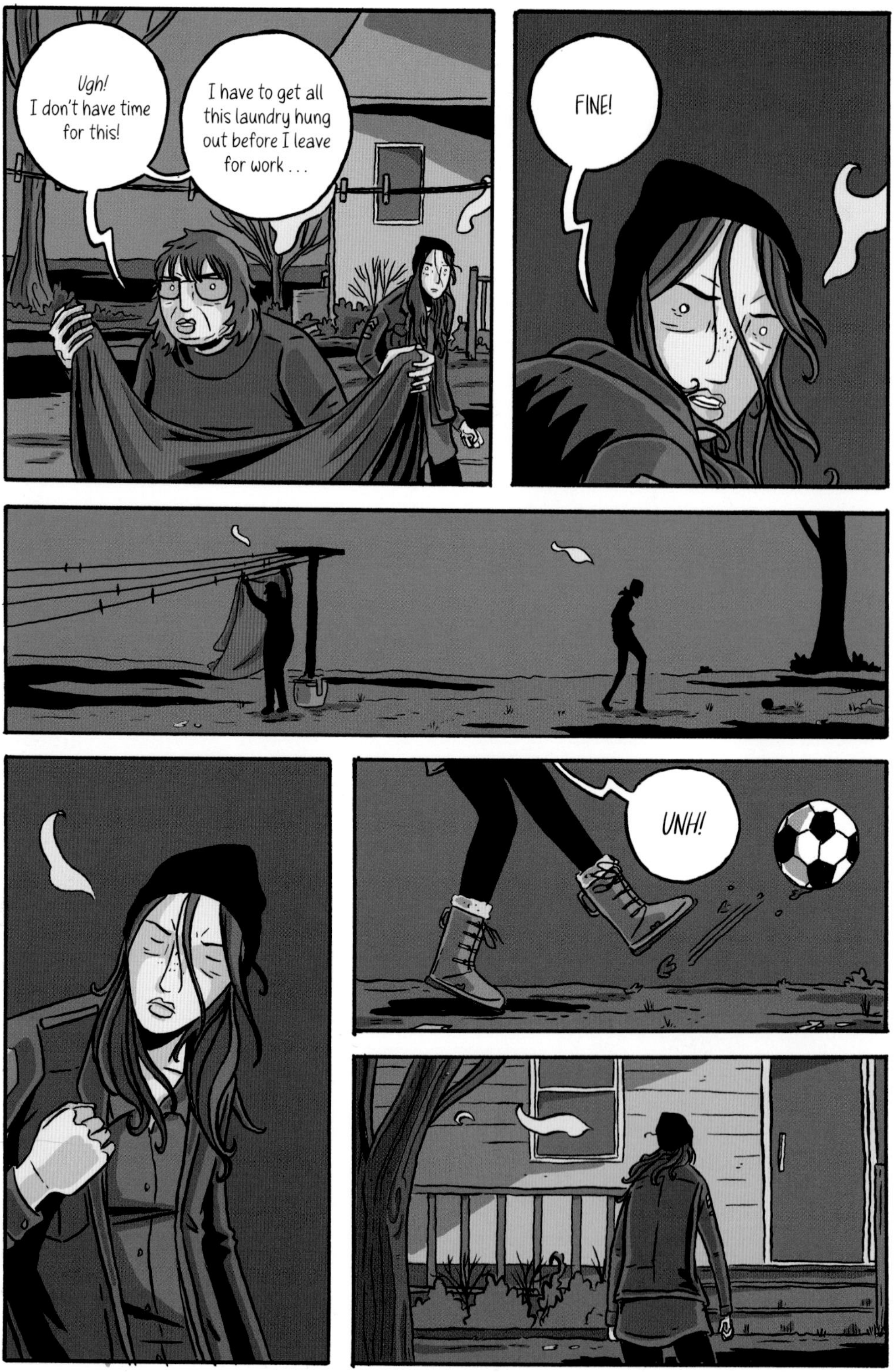
Ugh! I don't have time for this!
I have to get all this laundry hung out before I leave for work . . .
FINE!
UNH!

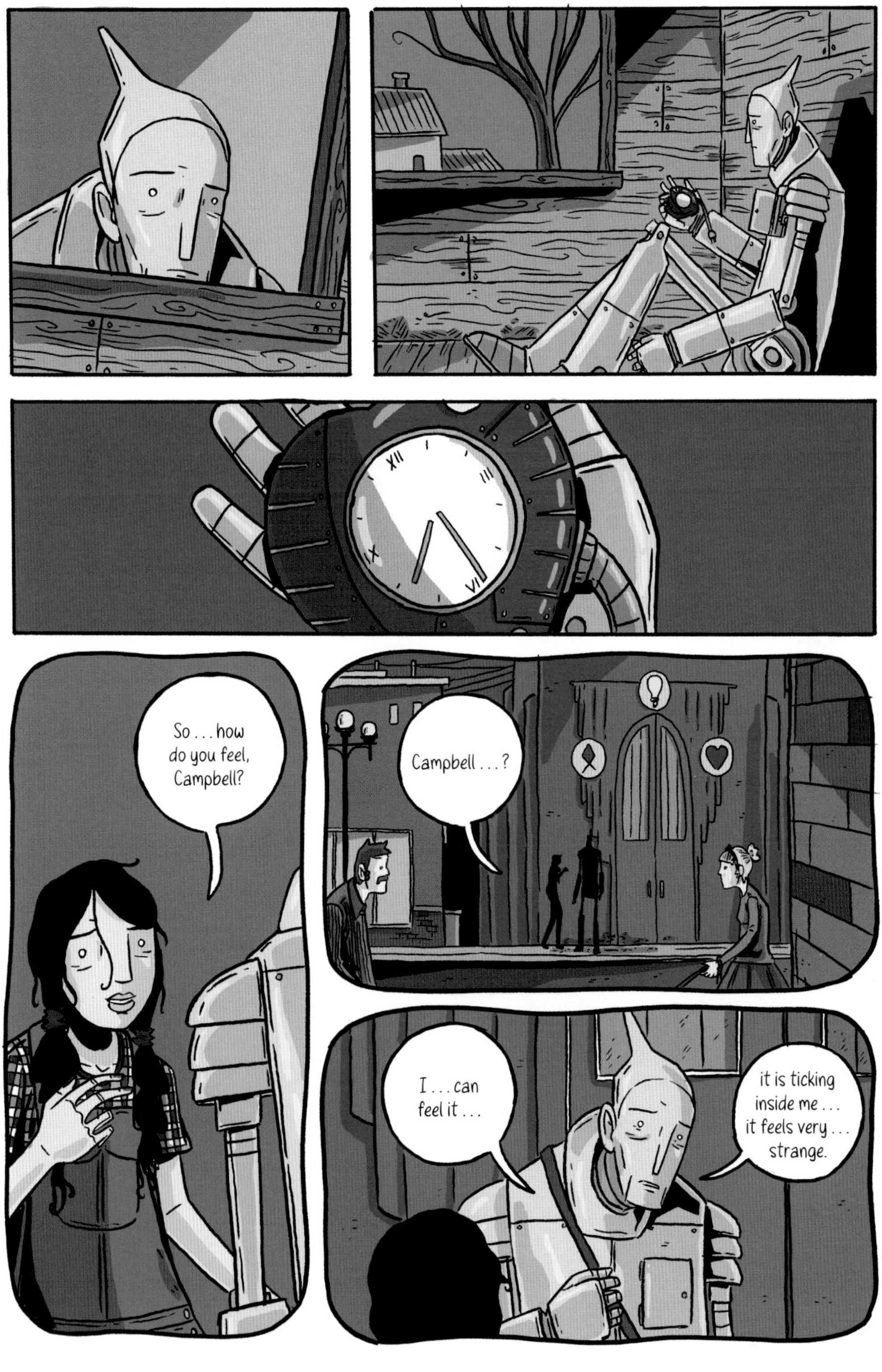
XII
I
III
VI
IX
So . . . how do you feel, Campbell?
Campbell . . . ?
I . . . can feel it . . .
it is ticking inside me . . . it feels very . . . strange.

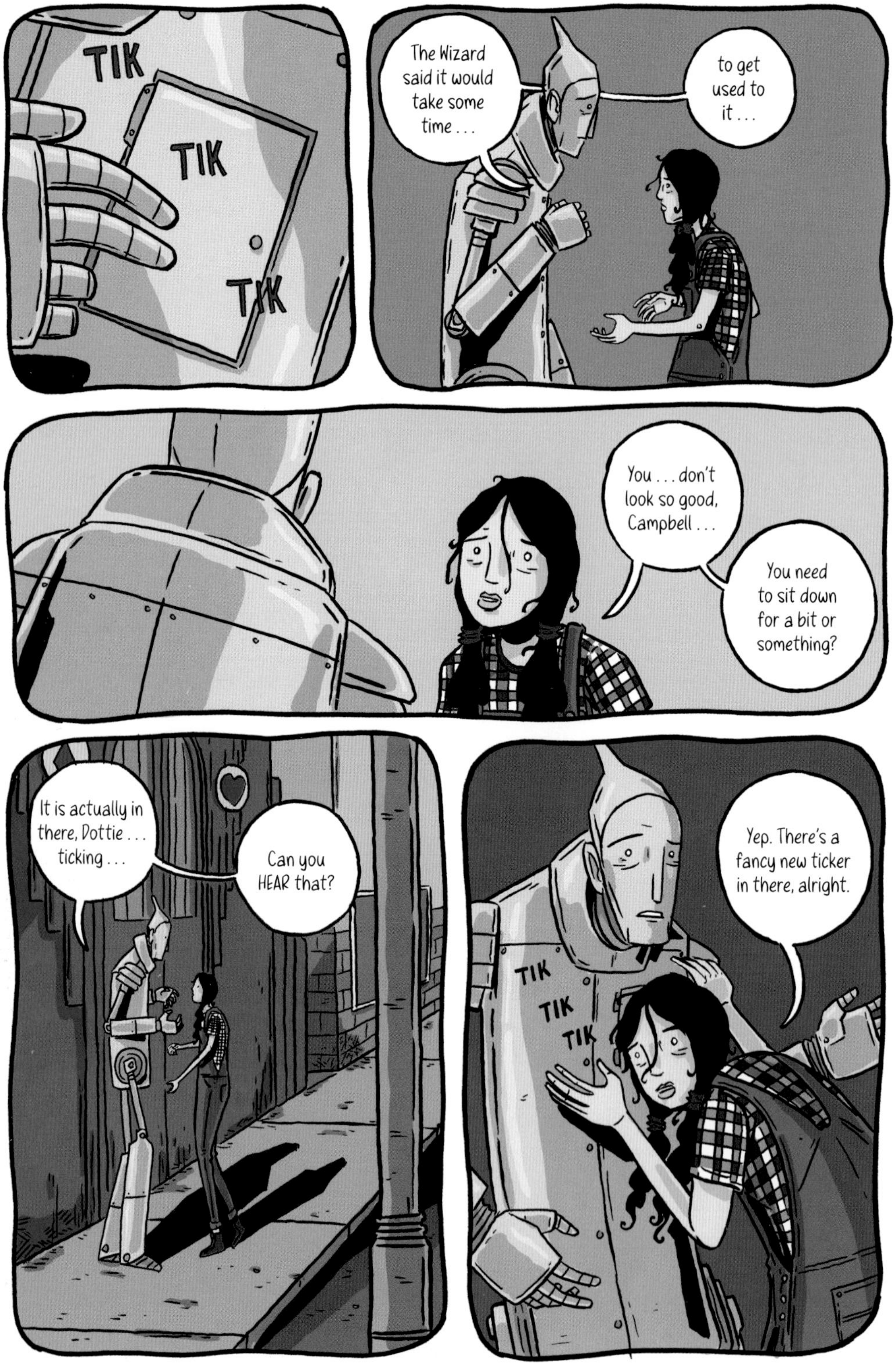
TIK
TIK
TIK
The Wizard said it would take some time . . .
to get used to it . . .
You . . . don't look so good, Campbell . . .
You need to sit down for a bit or something?
It is actually in there, Dottie . . . ticking . . .
Can you HEAR that?
TIK
TIK
TIK
Yep. There's a fancy new ticker in there, alright.

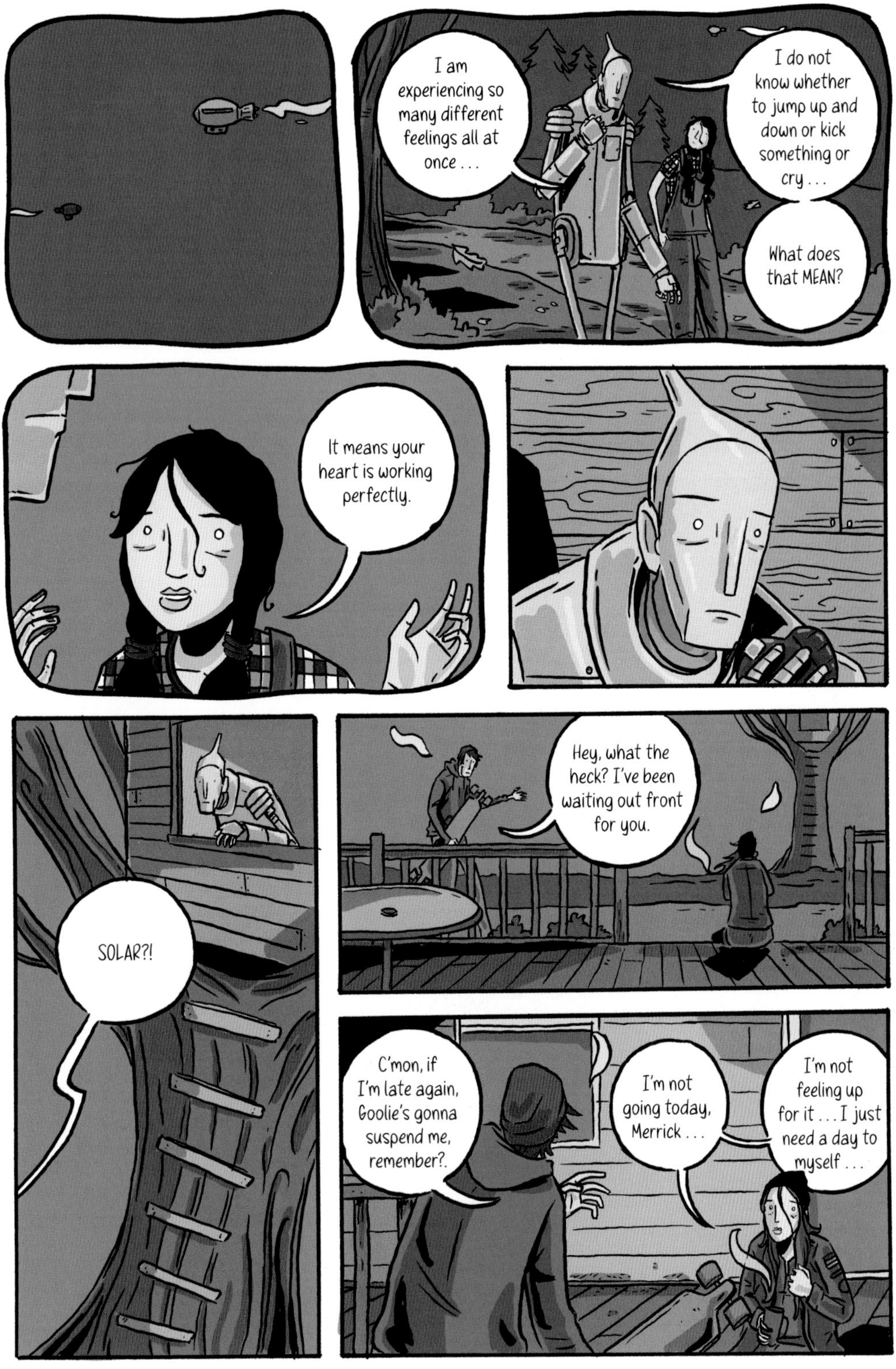
I am experiencing so many different feelings all at once . . .
I do not know whether to jump up and down or kick something or cry . . .
What does that MEAN?
It means your heart is working perfectly.
SOLAR?!
Hey, what the heck? I've been waiting out front for you.
C'mon, if I'm late again, Goolie's gonna suspend me, remember?.
I'm not going today, Merrick . . .
I'm not feeling up for it . . . I just need a day to myself . . .

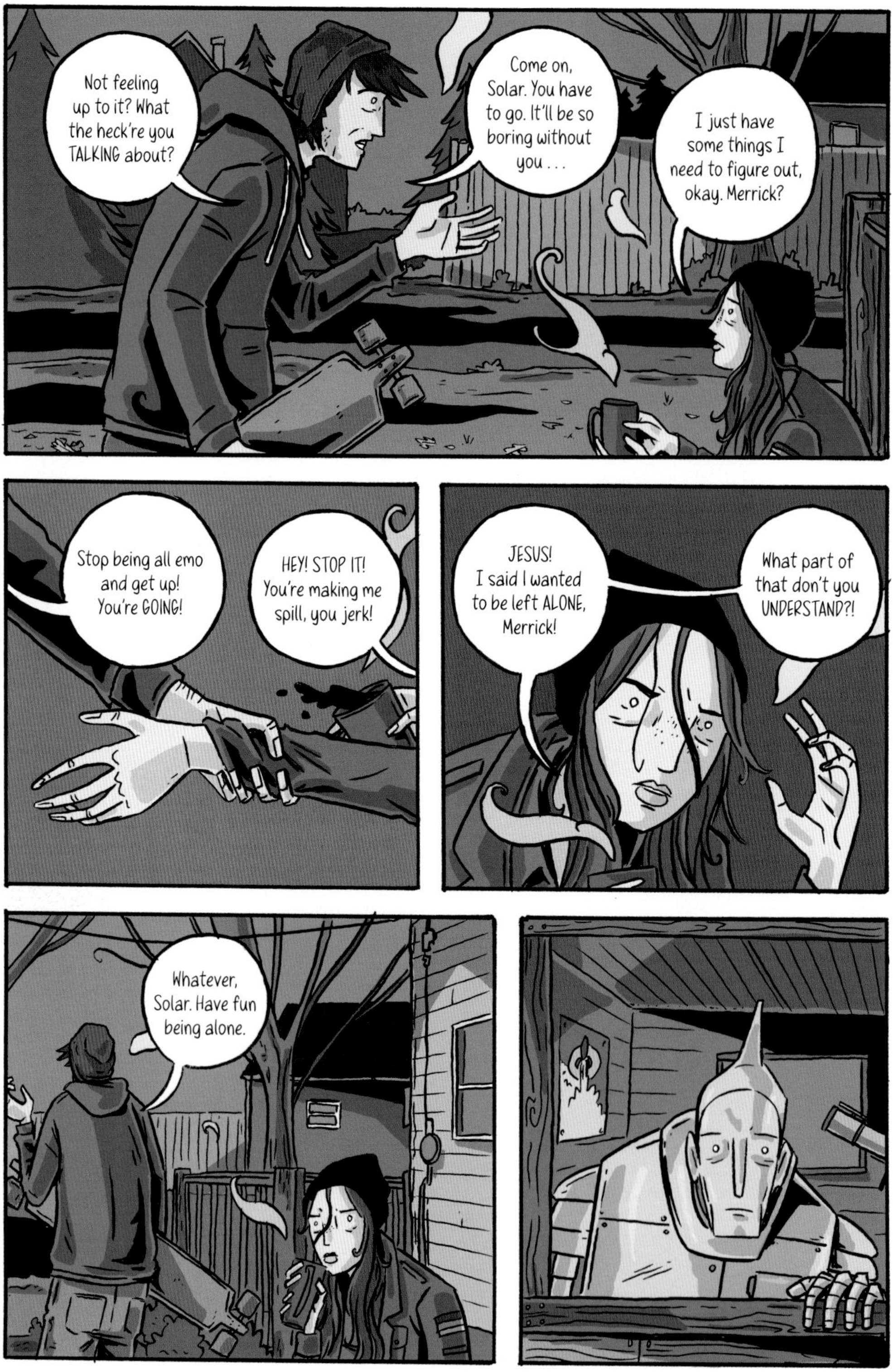
Not feeling up to it? What the heck're you TALKING about?
Come on, Solar. You have to go. It'll be so boring without you . . .
I just have some things I need to figure out, okay, Merrick?
Stop being all emo and get up! You're GOING!
HEY! STOP IT! You're making me spill, you jerk!
JESUS! I said I wanted to be left ALONE, Merrick!
What part of that don't you UNDERSTAND?!
Whatever, Solar. Have fun being alone.

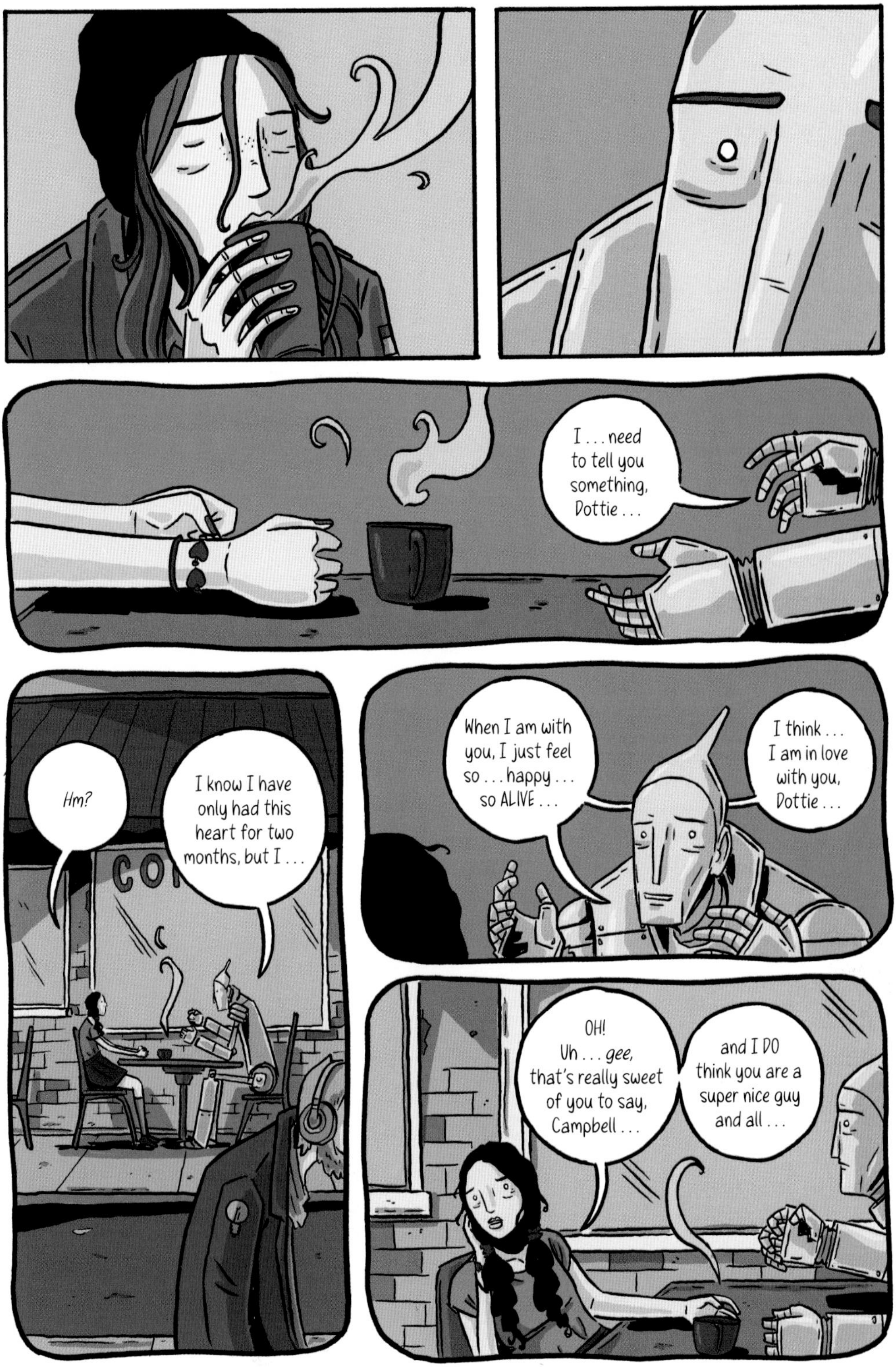
I . . . need to tell you something, Dottie . . .
Hm?
I know I have only had this heart for two months, but I . . .
When I am with you, I just feel so . . . happy . . . so ALIVE . . .
I think . . . I am in love with you, Dottie . . .
OH! Uh . . . *gee*, that's really sweet of you to say, Campbell . . .
and I DO think you are a super nice guy and all . . .

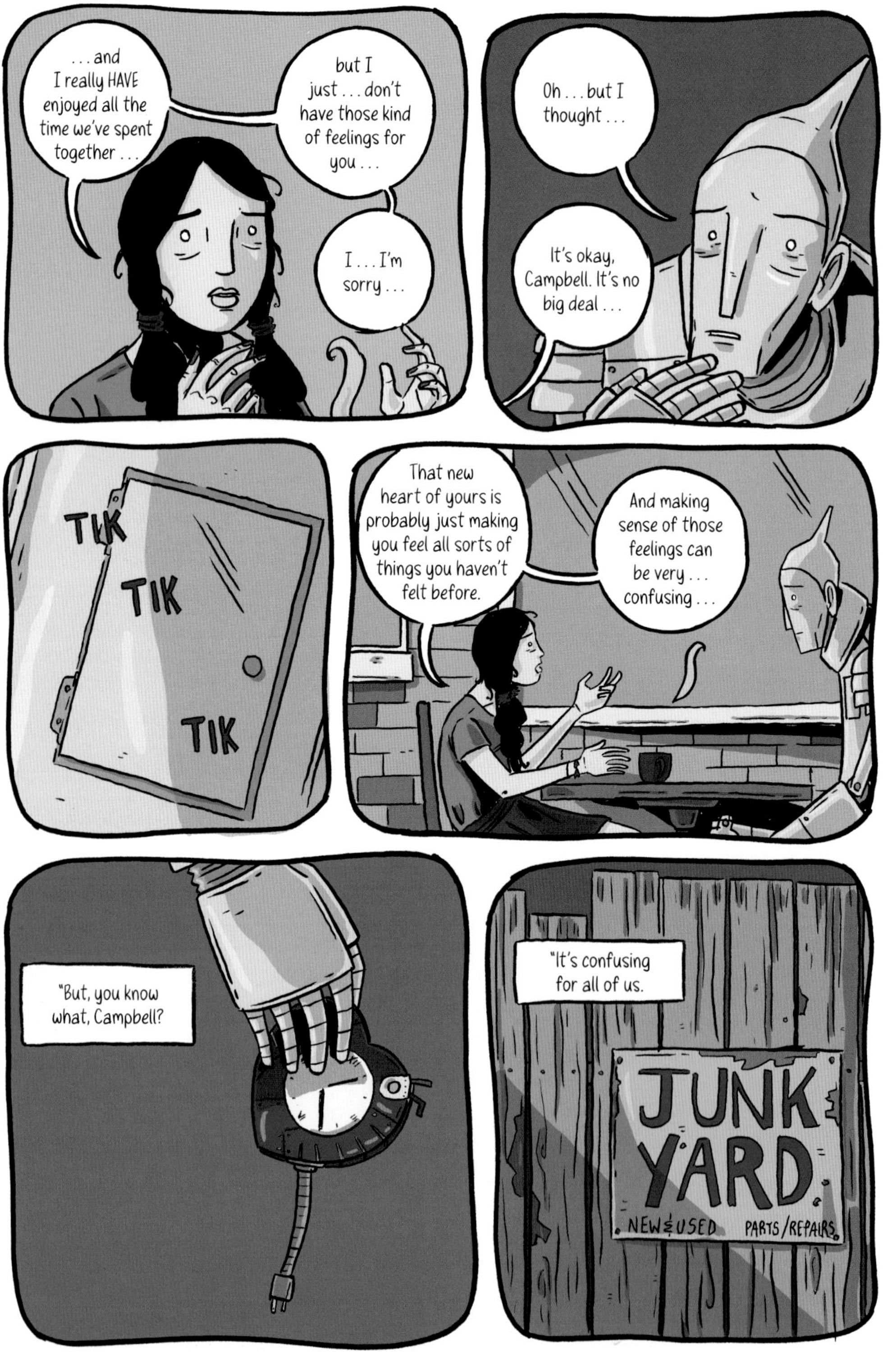
. . . and I really HAVE enjoyed all the time we've spent together . . .
but I just . . . don't have those kind of feelings for you . . .
I . . . I'm sorry . . .
Oh . . . but I thought . . .
It's okay, Campbell. It's no big deal . . .
TIK
TIK
TIK
That new heart of yours is probably just making you feel all sorts of things you haven't felt before.
And making sense of those feelings can be very . . . confusing . . .
"But, you know what, Campbell?
"It's confusing for all of us.
JUNK YARD
NEW & USED PARTS/REPAIRS

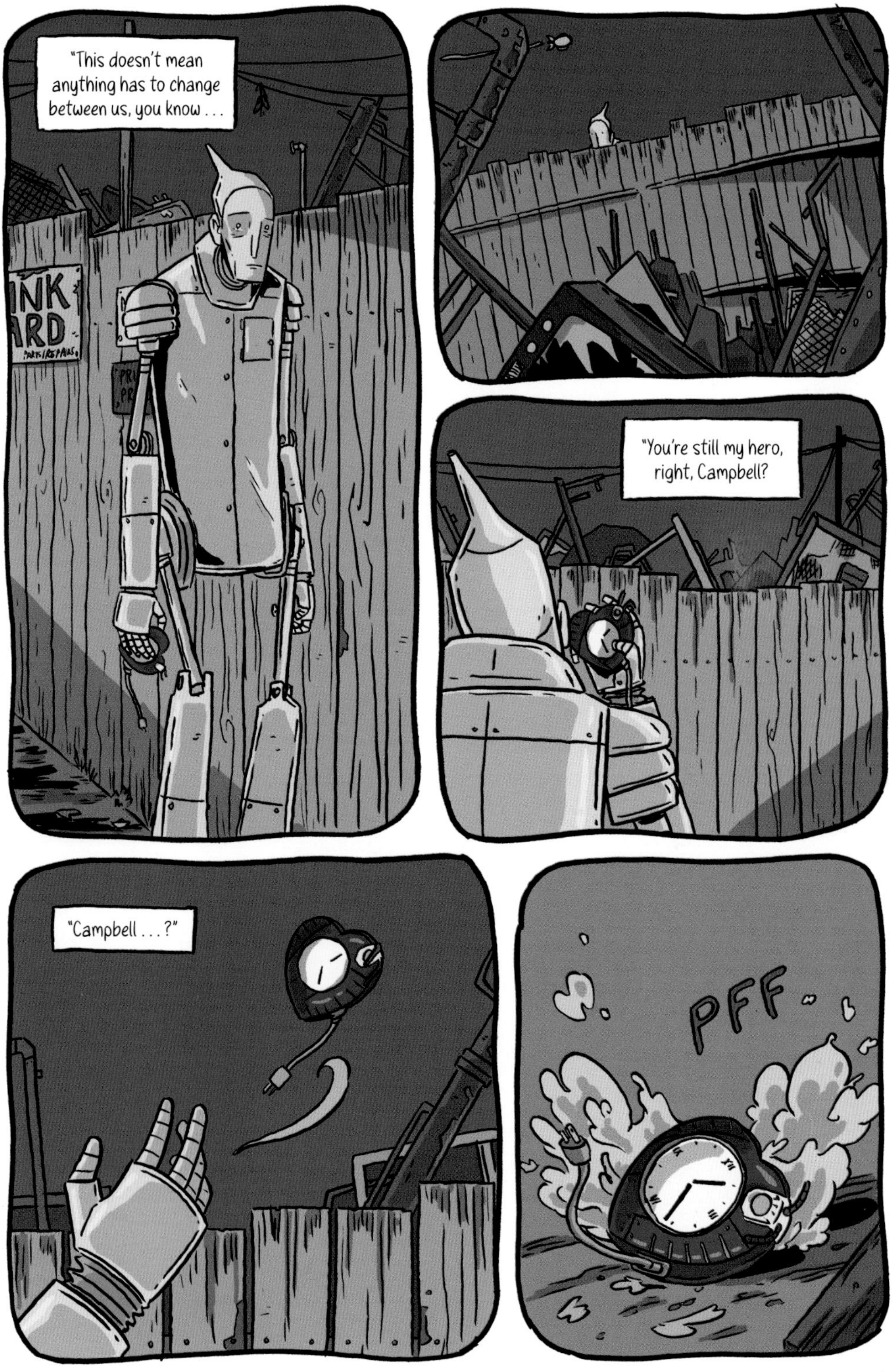
"This doesn't mean anything has to change between us, you know . . .
"You're still my hero, right, Campbell?
"Campbell . . . ?"
PFF

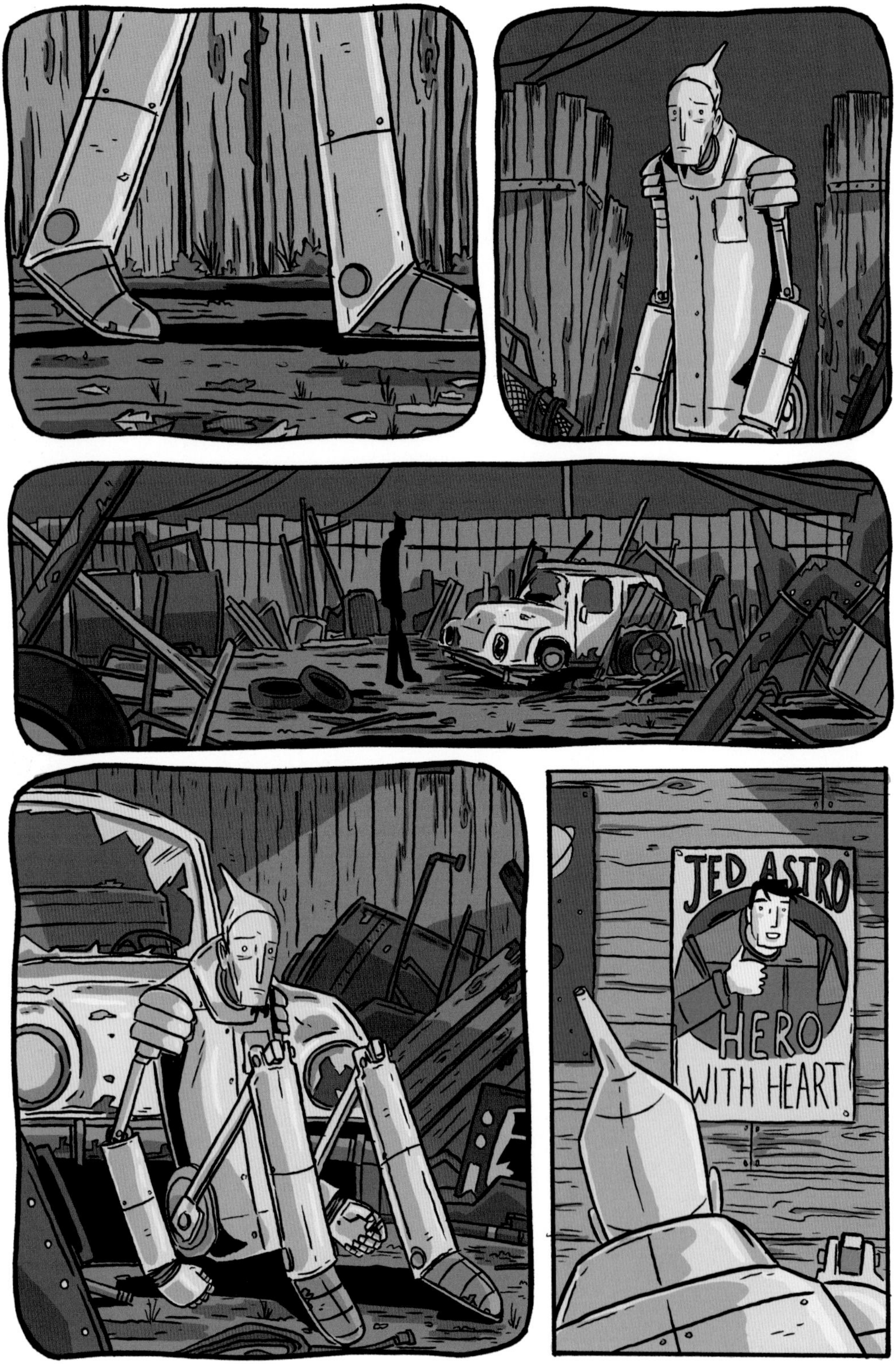
JED ASTRO
HERO
WITH HEART

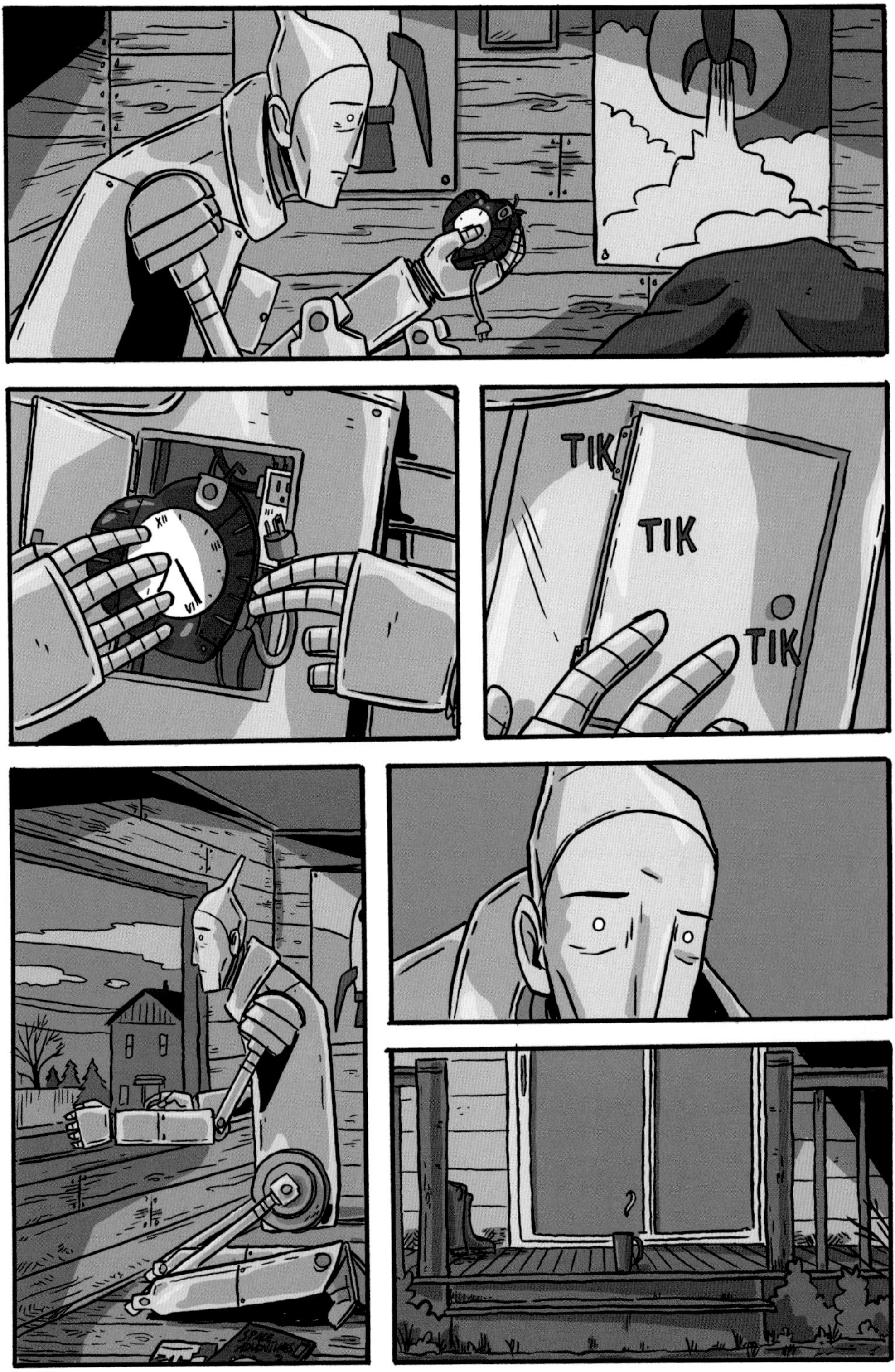
TIK
TIK
TIK
SPACE ADVENTURES

CHAPTER 8: Buried Treasure

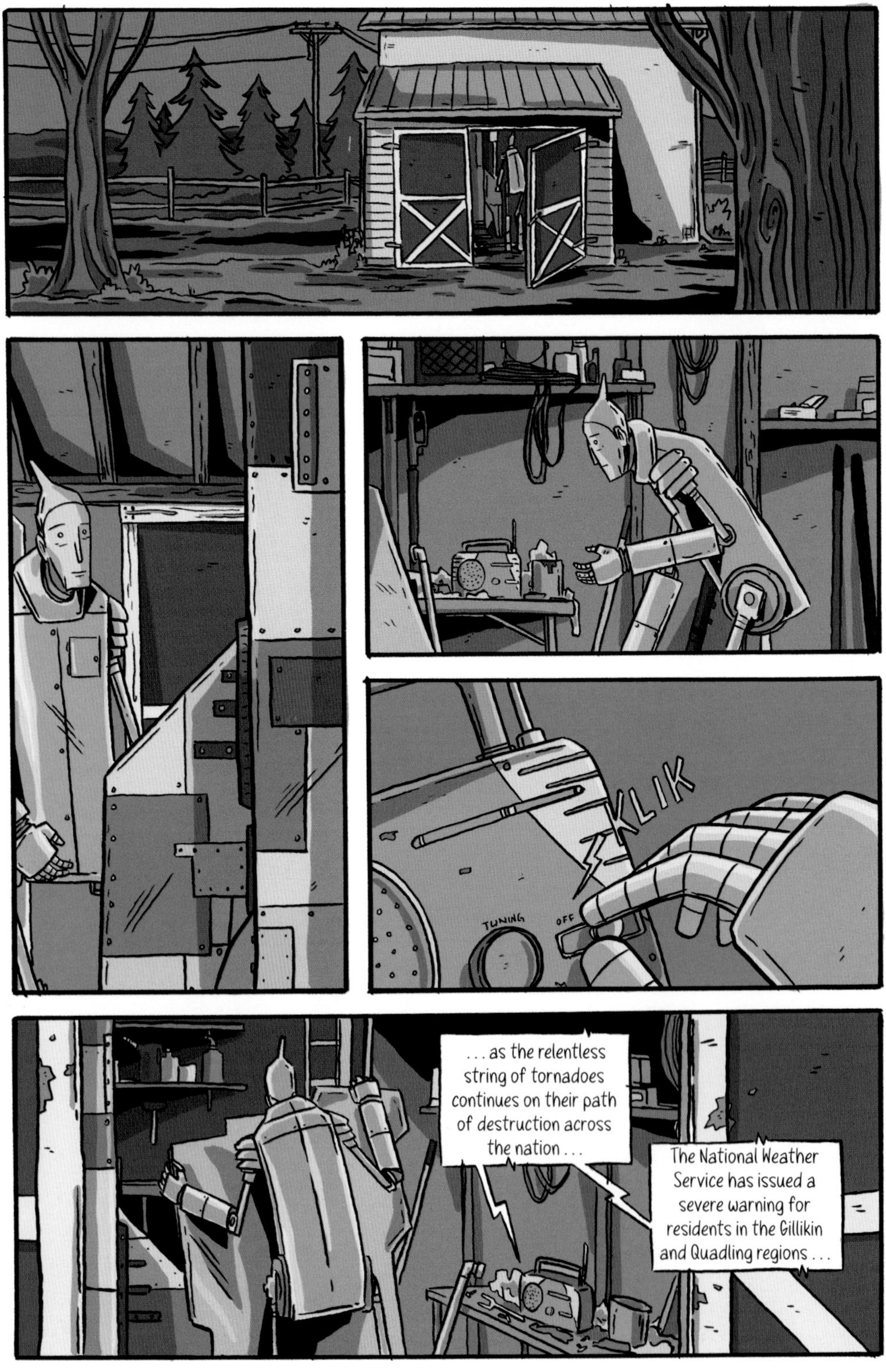
KLIK
TUNING
OFF
. . . as the relentless string of tornadoes continues on their path of destruction across the nation . . .
The National Weather Service has issued a severe warning for residents in the Gillikin and Quadling regions . . .

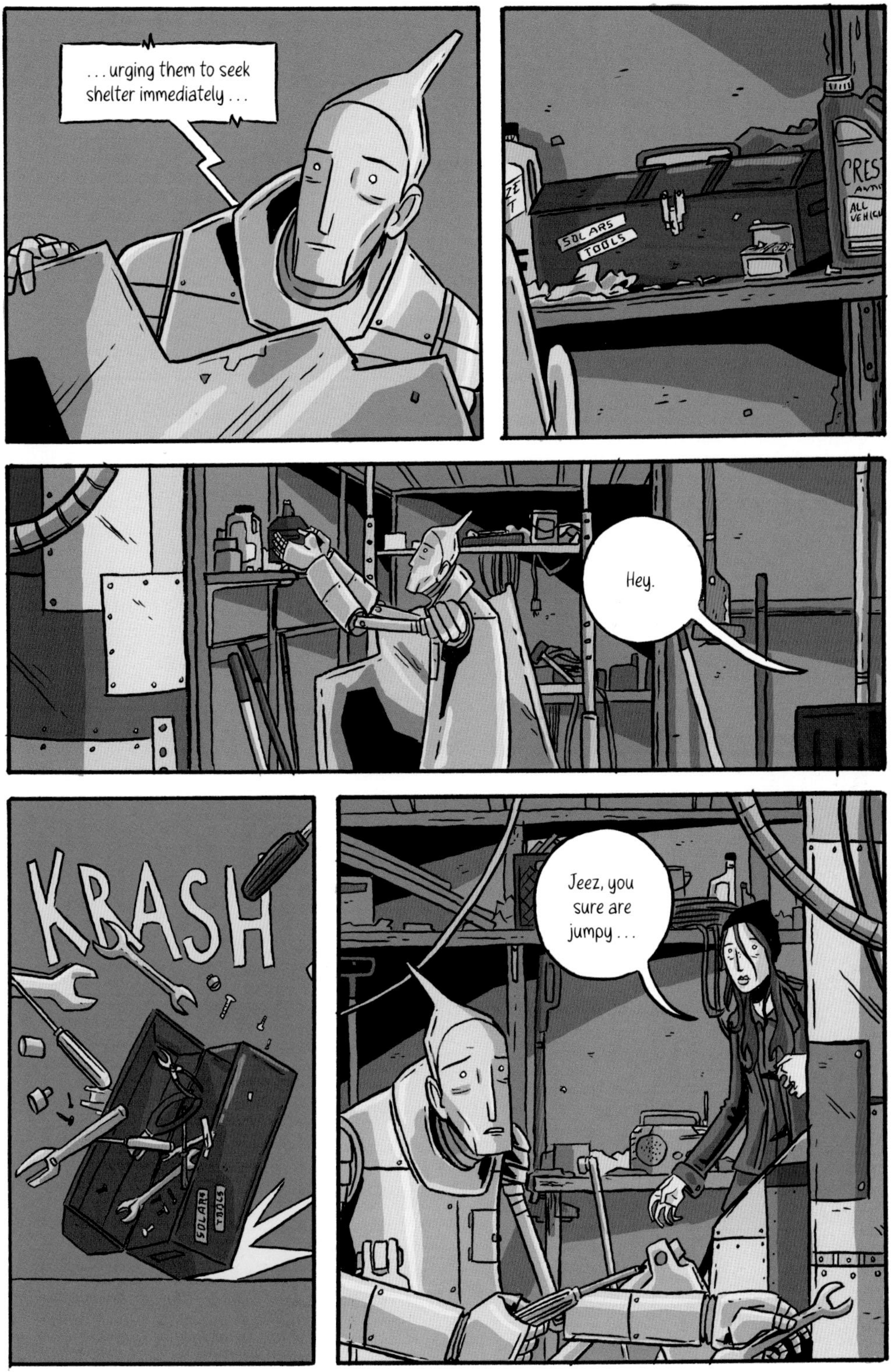

... urging them to seek shelter immediately ...
CREST
ALL VEHICLES
SOLARS TOOLS
Hey.
KRASH
SOLARS TOOLS
Jeez, you sure are jumpy ...

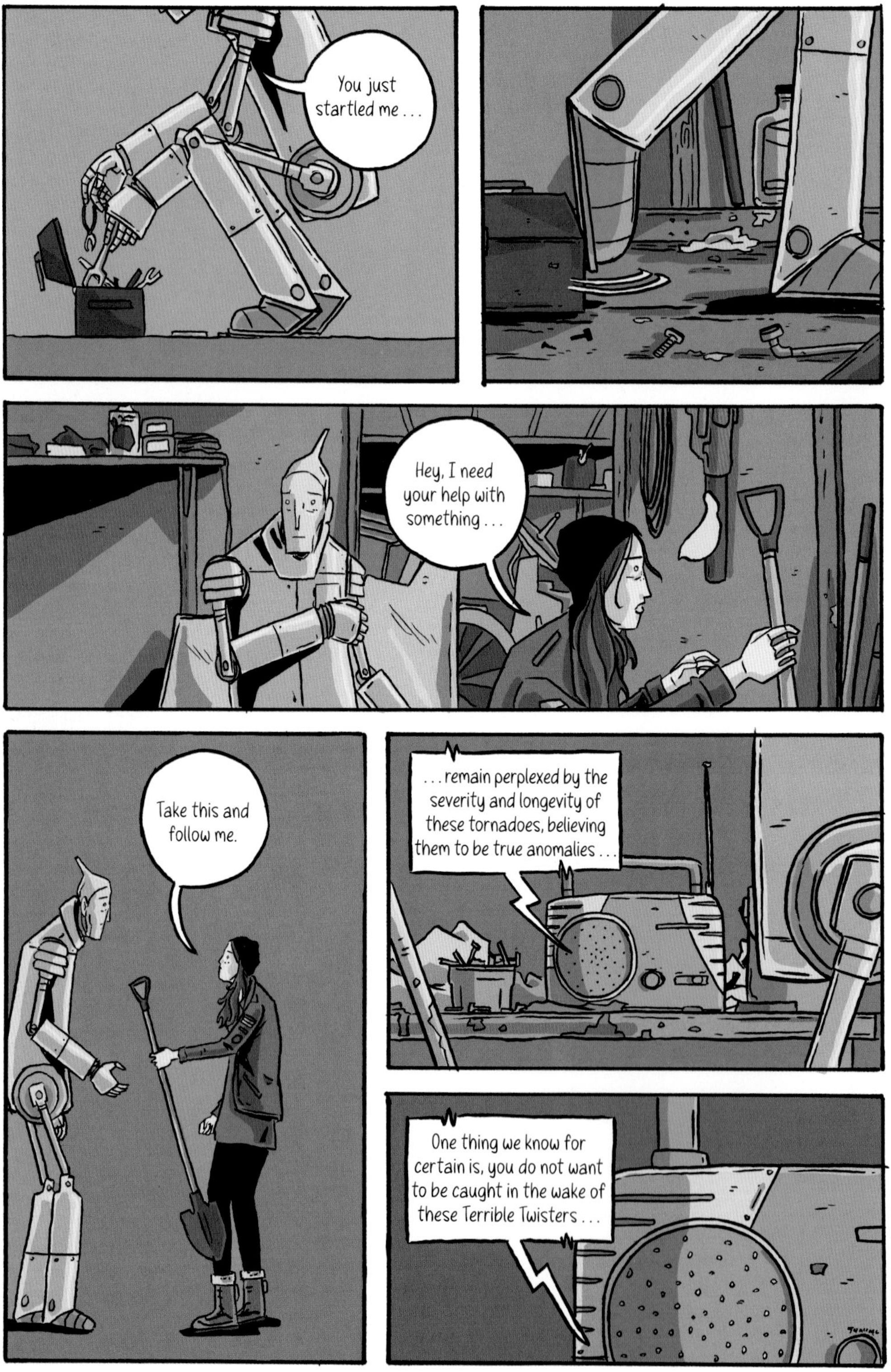
You just startled me . . .
Hey, I need your help with something . . .
Take this and follow me.
. . . remain perplexed by the severity and longevity of these tornadoes, believing them to be true anomalies . . .
One thing we know for certain is, you do not want to be caught in the wake of these Terrible Twisters . . .

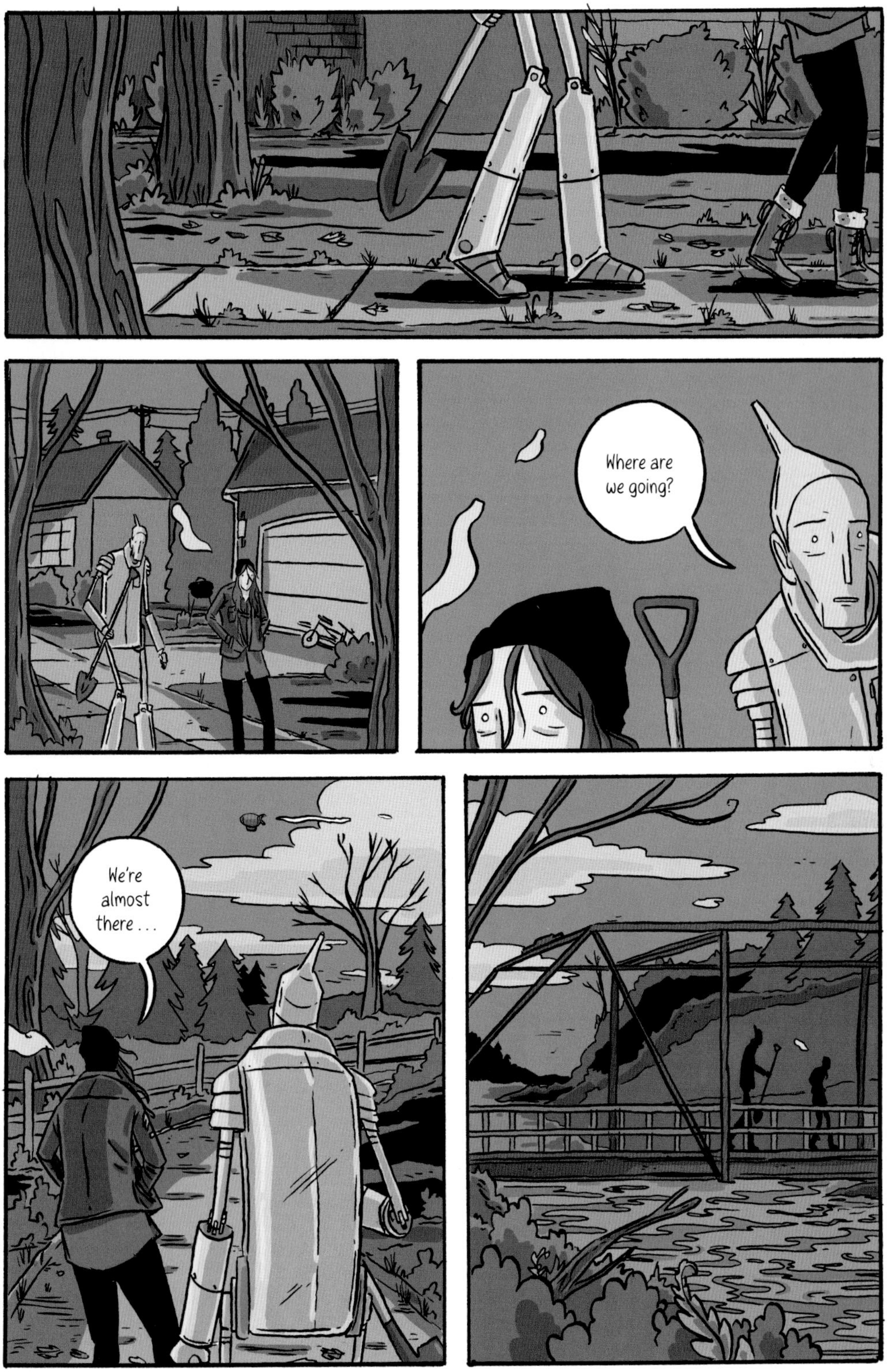
Where are we going?
We're almost there . . .

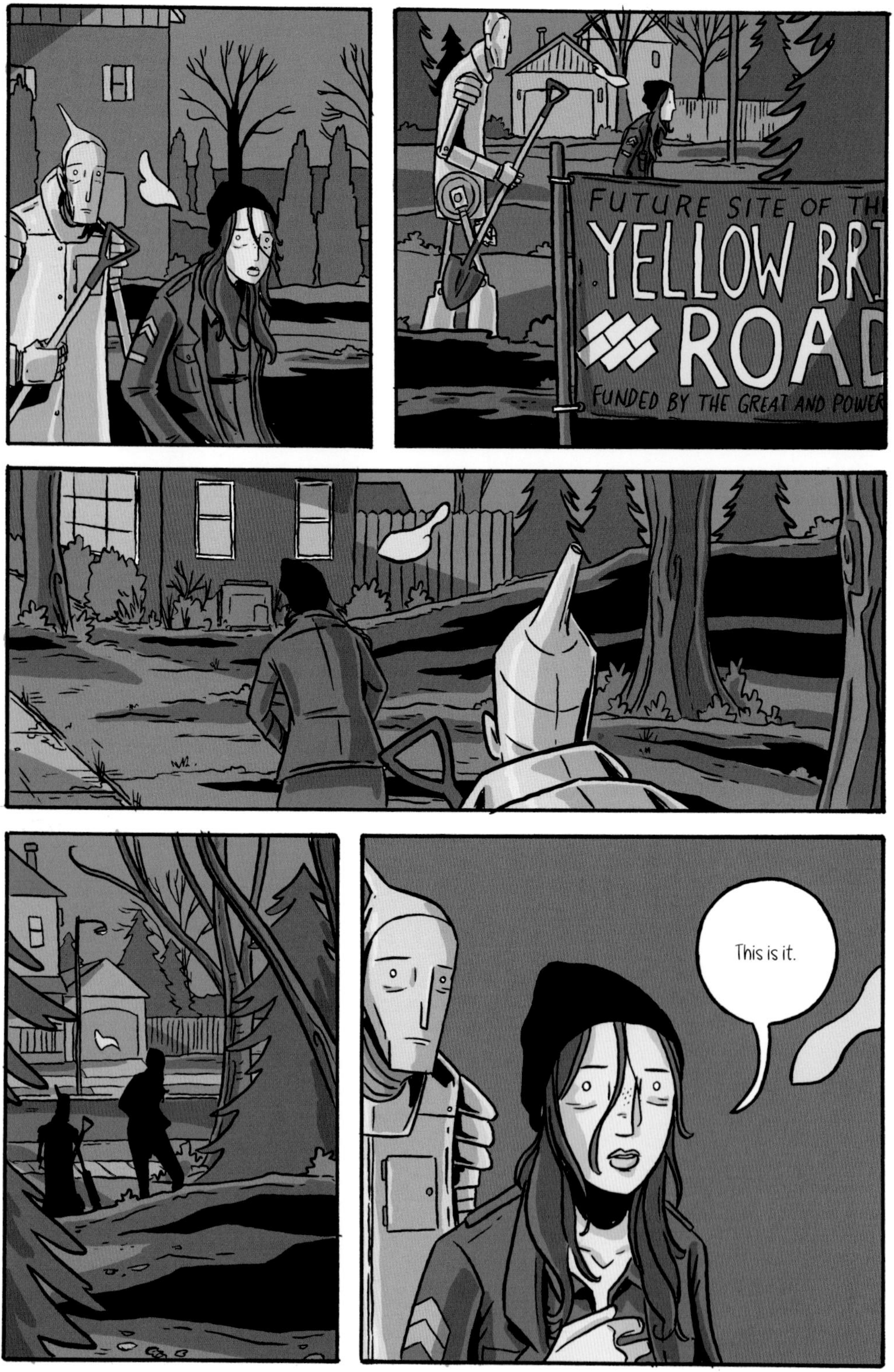
FUTURE SITE OF TH
YELLOW BRI
ROAD
FUNDED BY THE GREAT AND POWER
This is it.

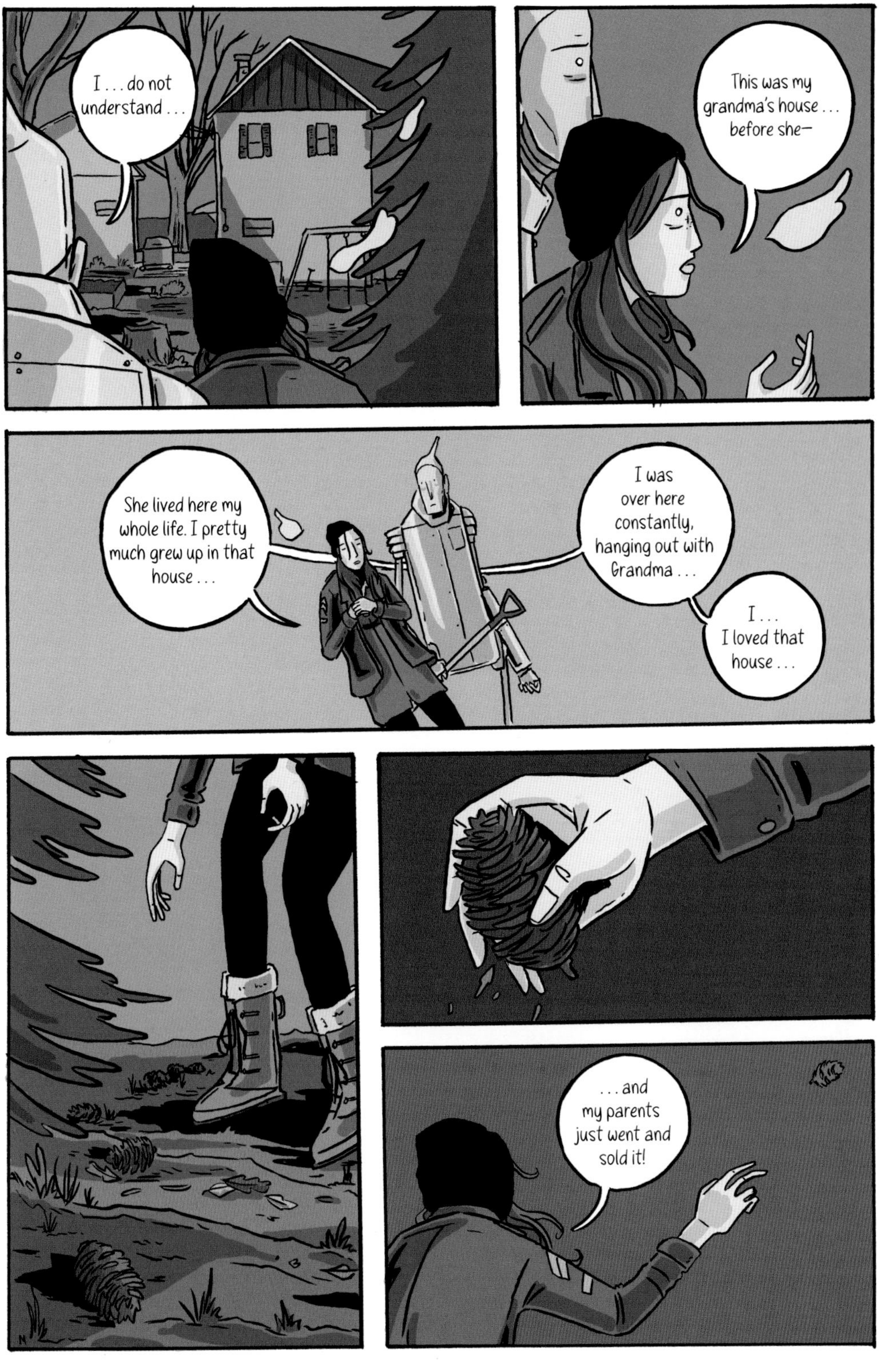

I . . . do not understand . . .
This was my grandma's house . . . before she—
She lived here my whole life. I pretty much grew up in that house . . .
I was over here constantly, hanging out with Grandma . . .
I . . . I loved that house . . .
. . . and my parents just went and sold it!

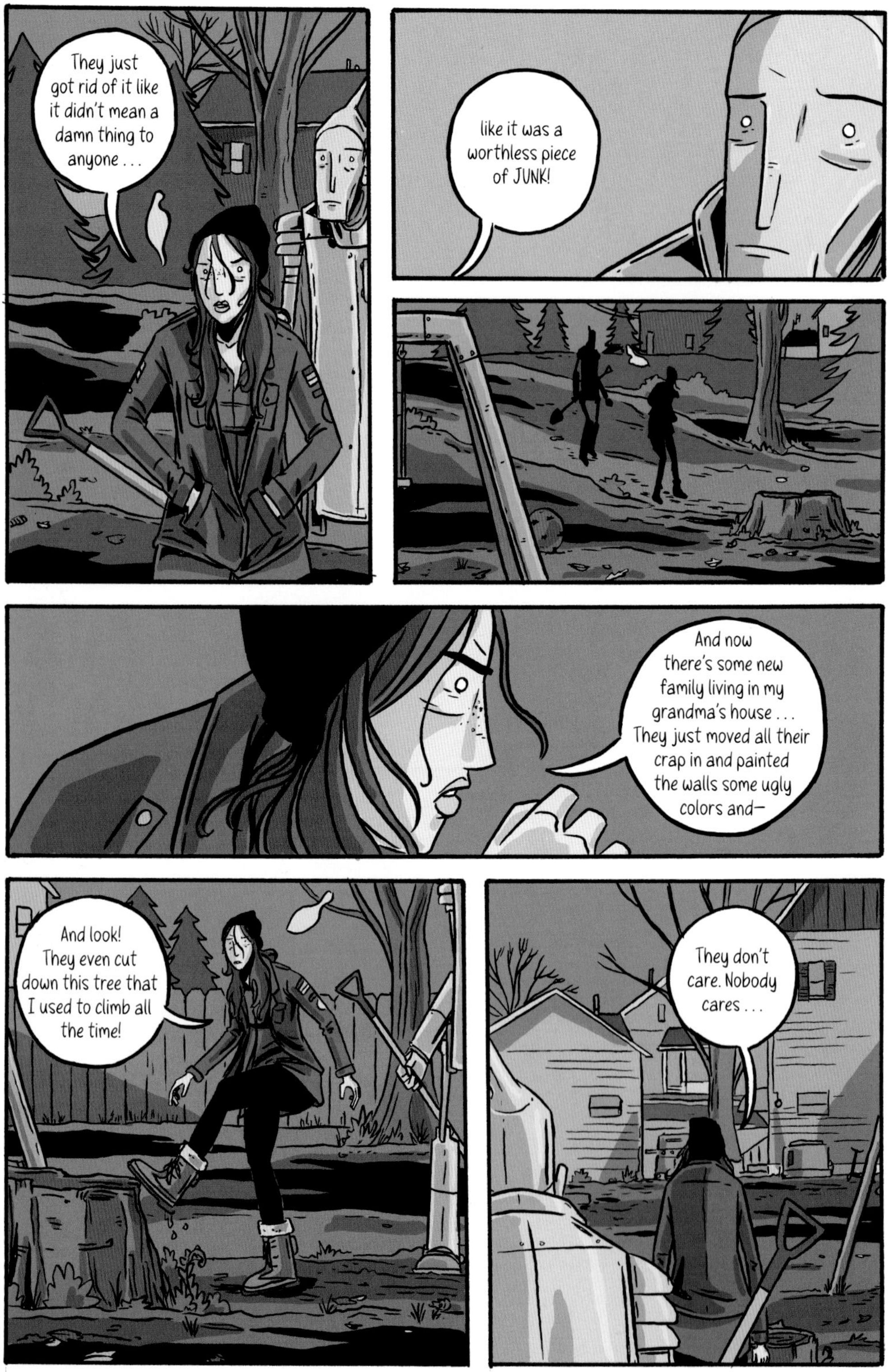
They just got rid of it like it didn't mean a damn thing to anyone . . .
like it was a worthless piece of JUNK!
And now there's some new family living in my grandma's house . . . They just moved all their crap in and painted the walls some ugly colors and—
And look! They even cut down this tree that I used to climb all the time!
They don't care. Nobody cares . . .

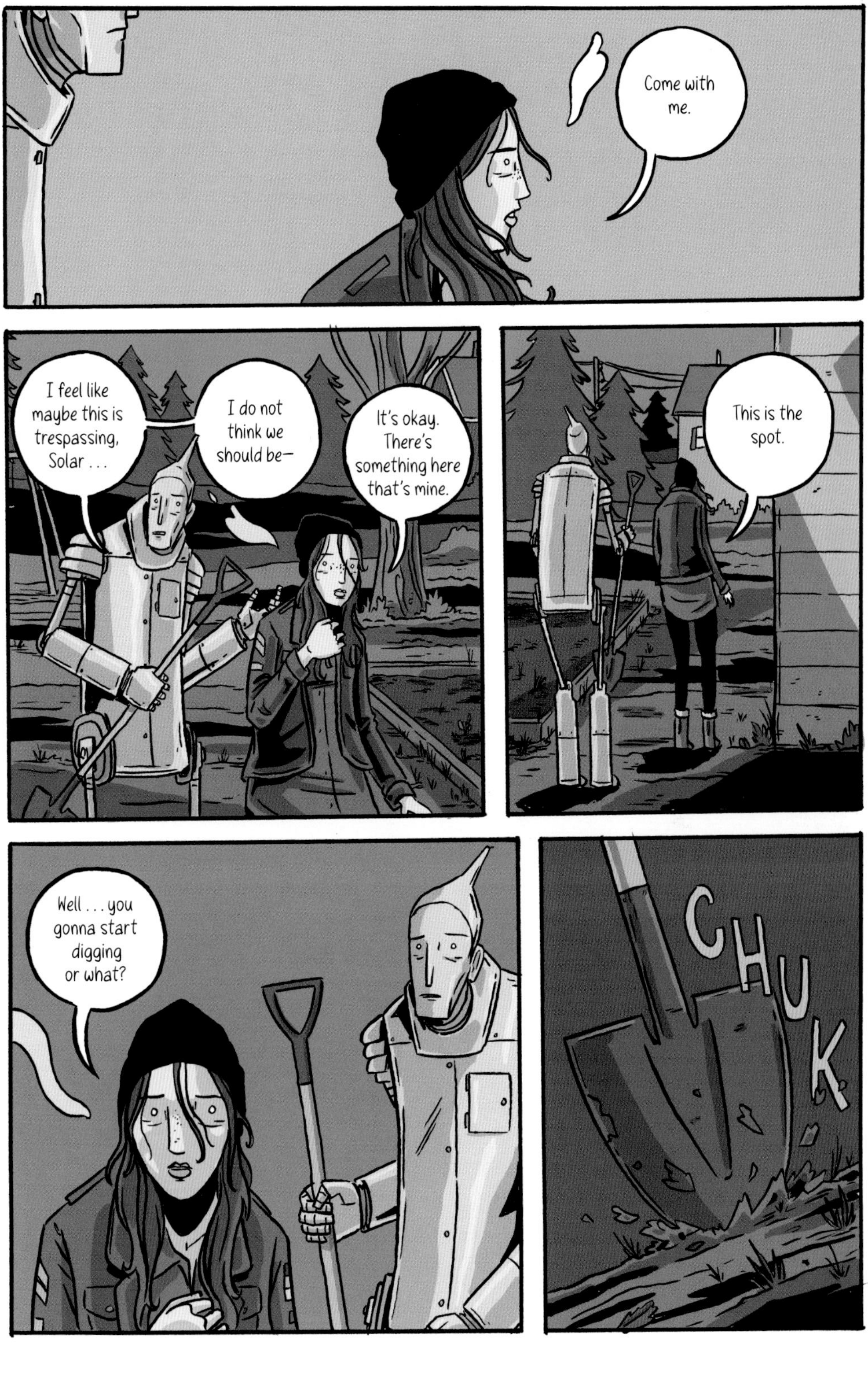
Come with me.
I feel like maybe this is trespassing, Solar . . .
I do not think we should be—
It's okay. There's something here that's mine.
This is the spot.
Well . . . you gonna start digging or what?
CHUK

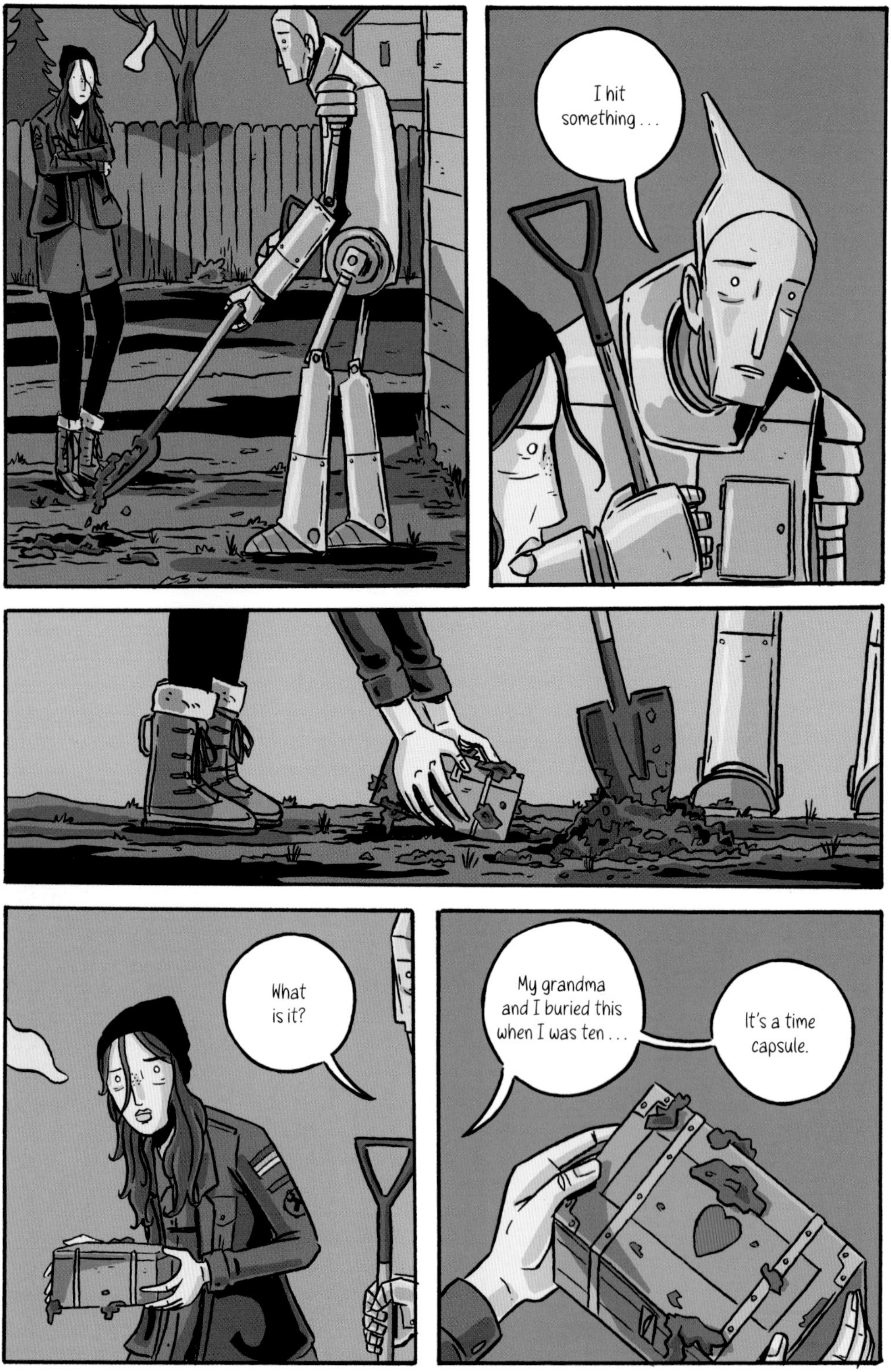
I hit something . . .
What is it?
My grandma and I buried this when I was ten . . .
It's a time capsule.

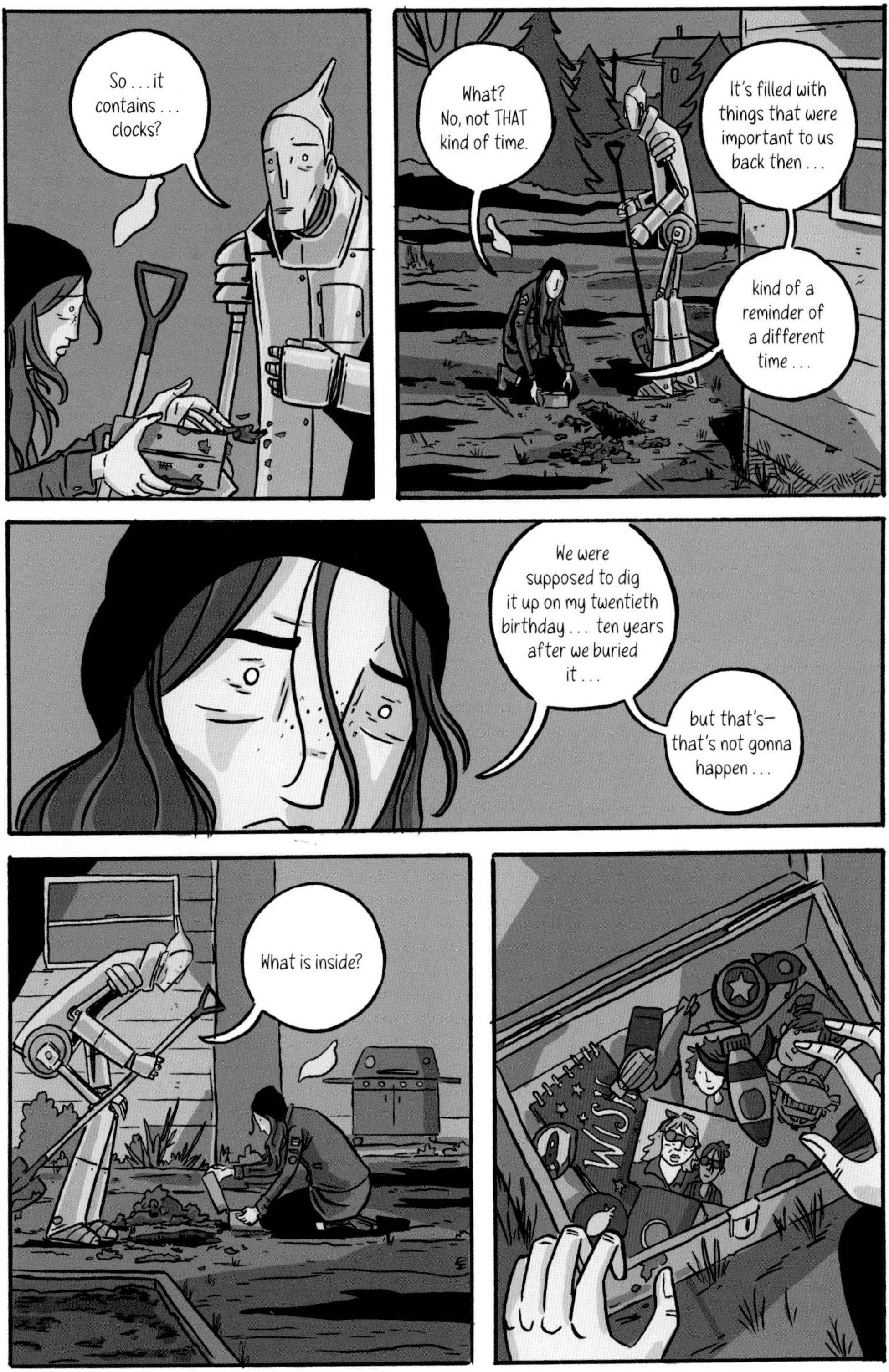
So . . . it contains . . . clocks?
What? No, not THAT kind of time.
It's filled with things that were important to us back then . . .
kind of a reminder of a different time . . .
We were supposed to dig it up on my twentieth birthday . . . ten years after we buried it . . .
but that's— that's not gonna happen . . .
What is inside?
WISH

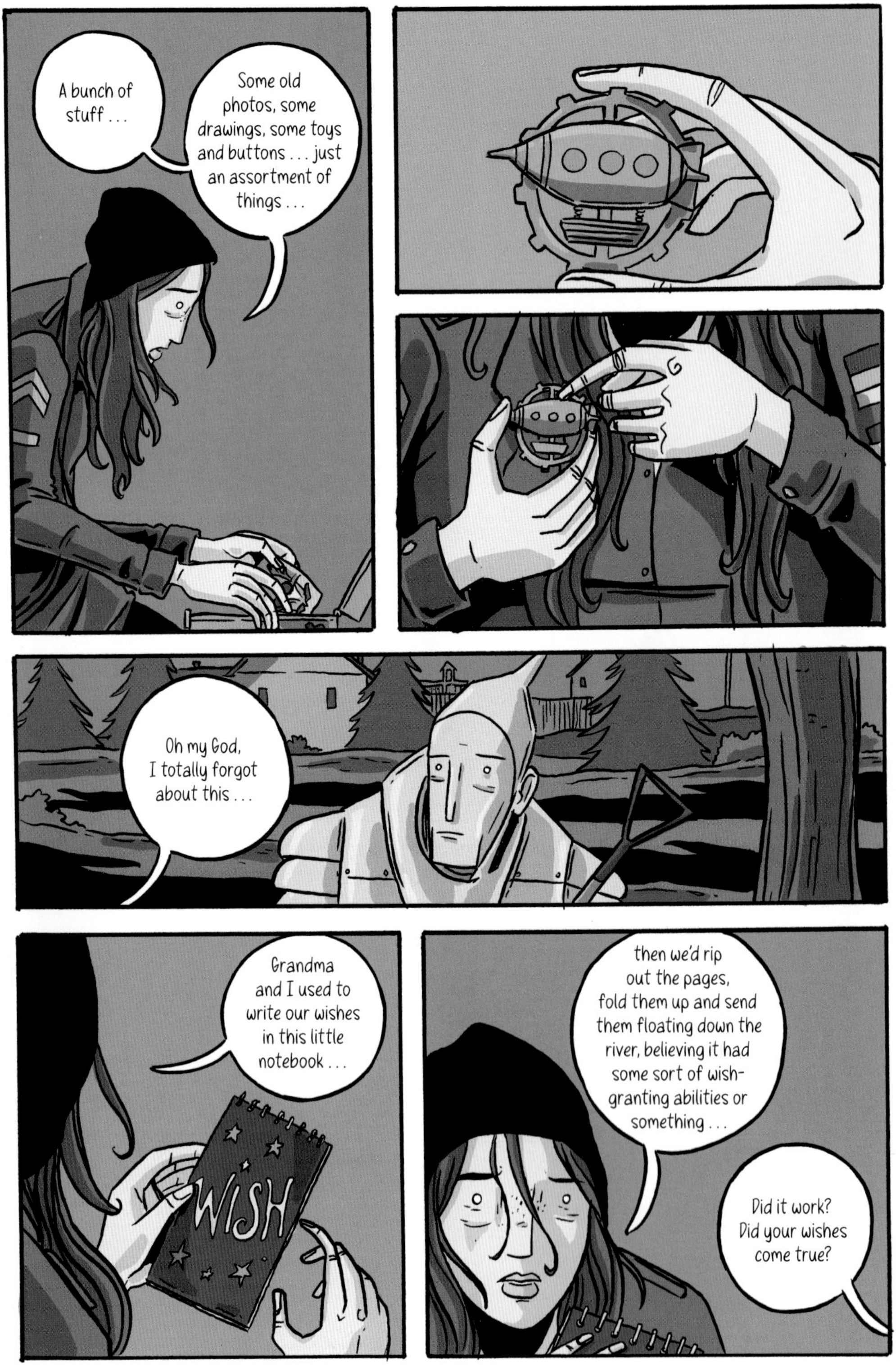
A bunch of stuff . . .
Some old photos, some drawings, some toys and buttons . . . just an assortment of things . . .
Oh my God, I totally forgot about this . . .
Grandma and I used to write our wishes in this little notebook . . .
WISH
then we'd rip out the pages, fold them up and send them floating down the river, believing it had some sort of wish-granting abilities or something . . .
Did it work? Did your wishes come true?

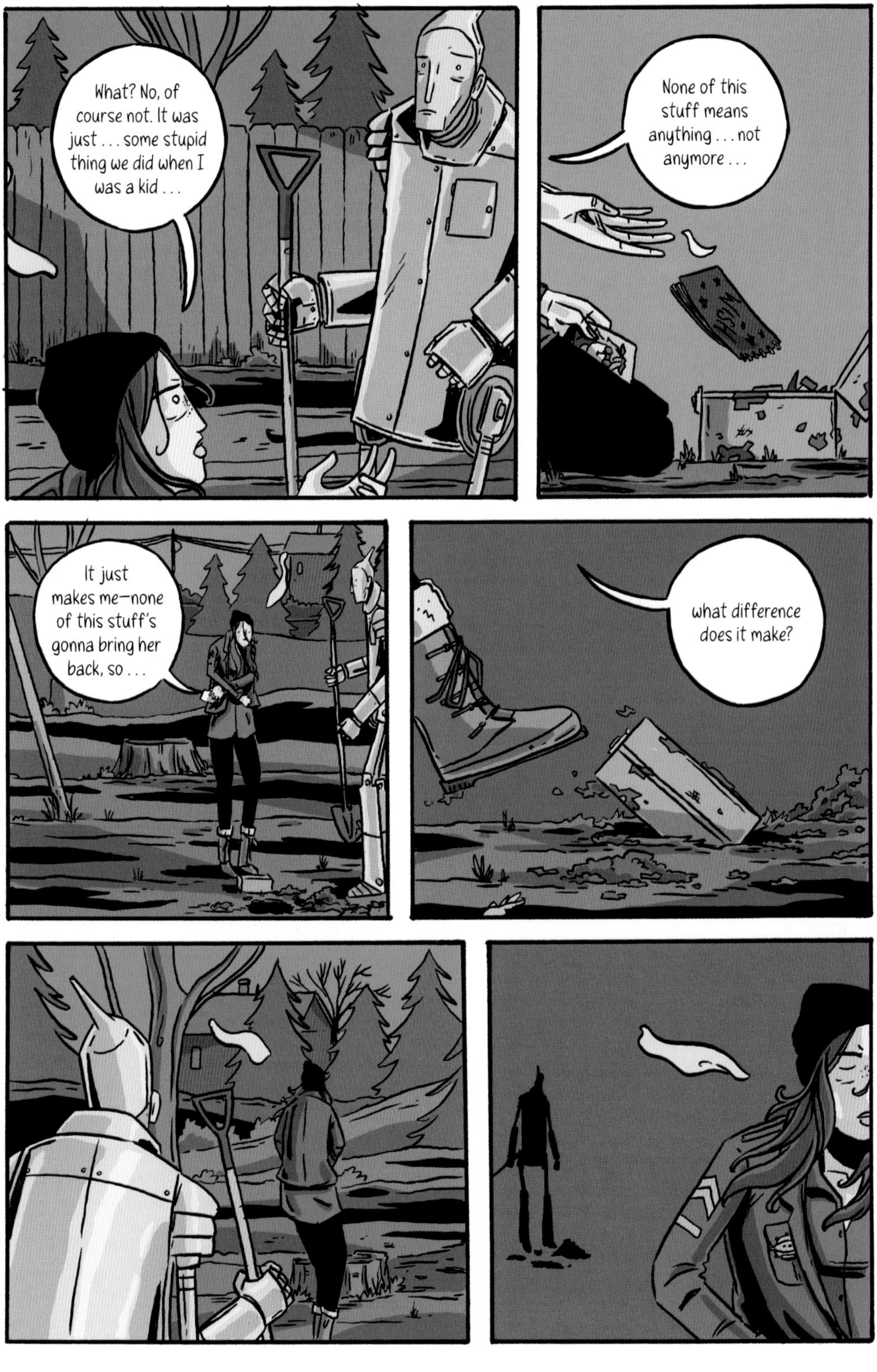
What? No, of course not. It was just . . . some stupid thing we did when I was a kid . . .
None of this stuff means anything . . . not anymore . . .
It just makes me—none of this stuff's gonna bring her back, so . . .
what difference does it make?

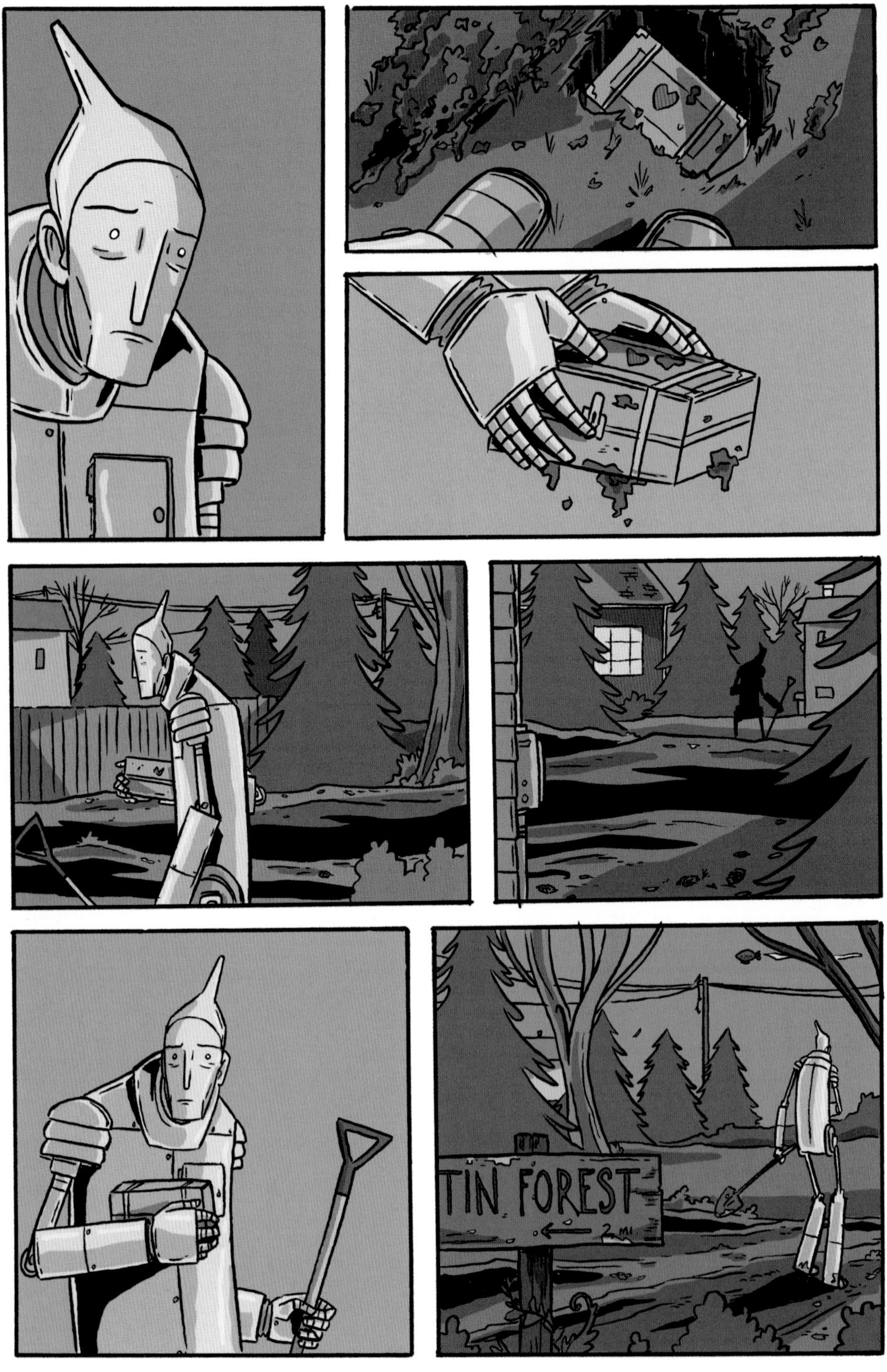
TIN FOREST
2 MI

CHAPTER 9: B.O.S.F.

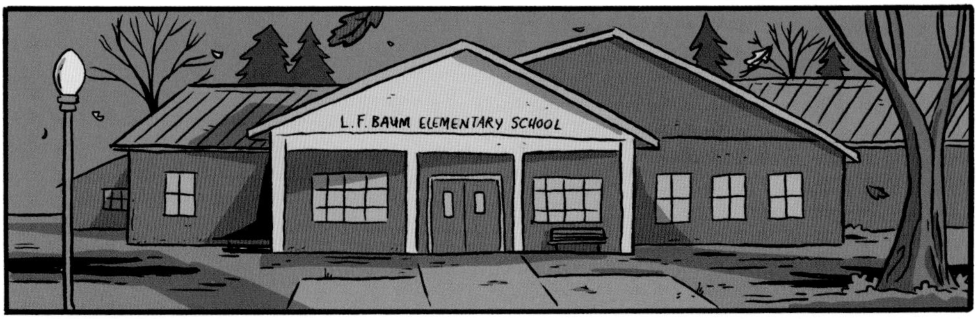
L. F. BAUM ELEMENTARY SCHOOL

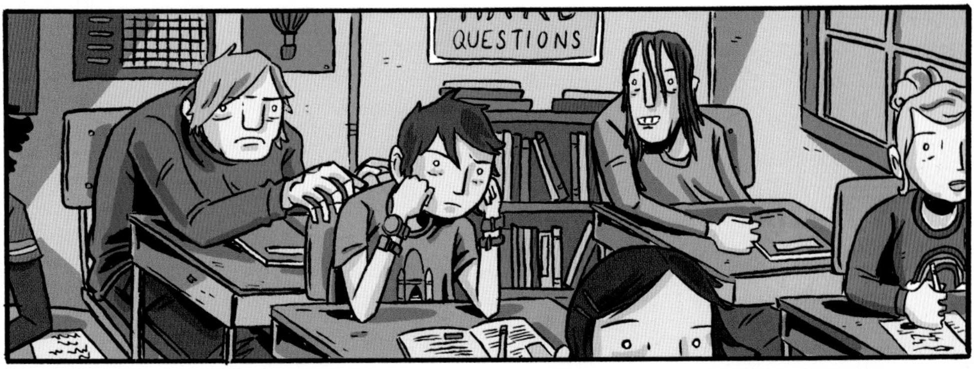
QUESTIONS

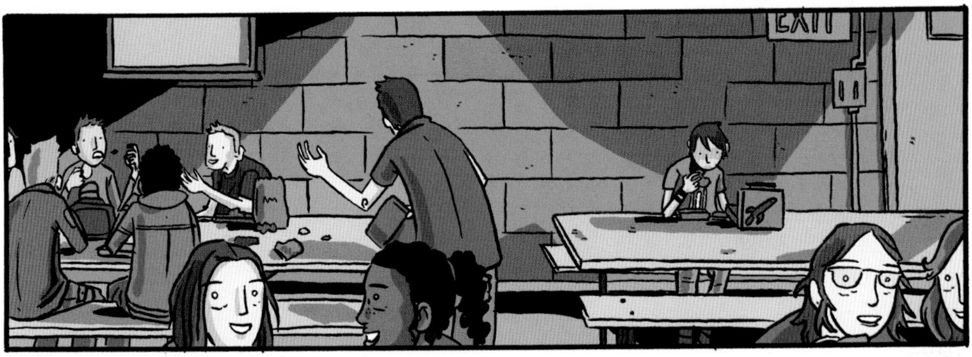
EXIT

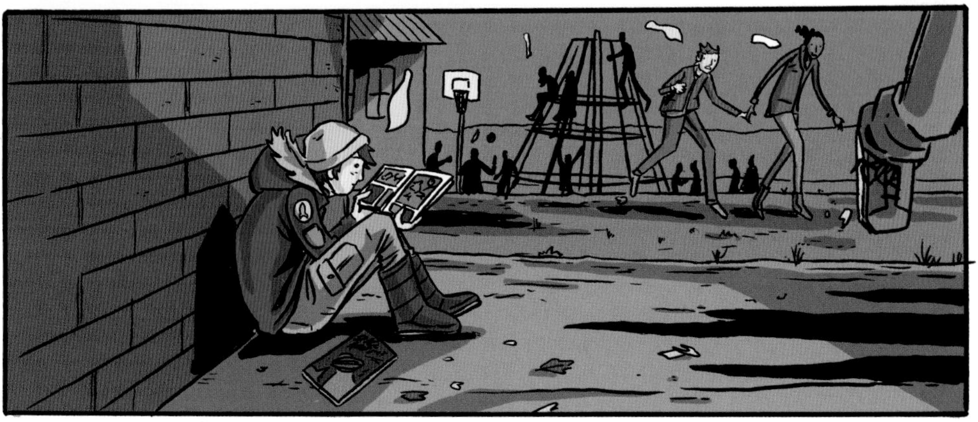

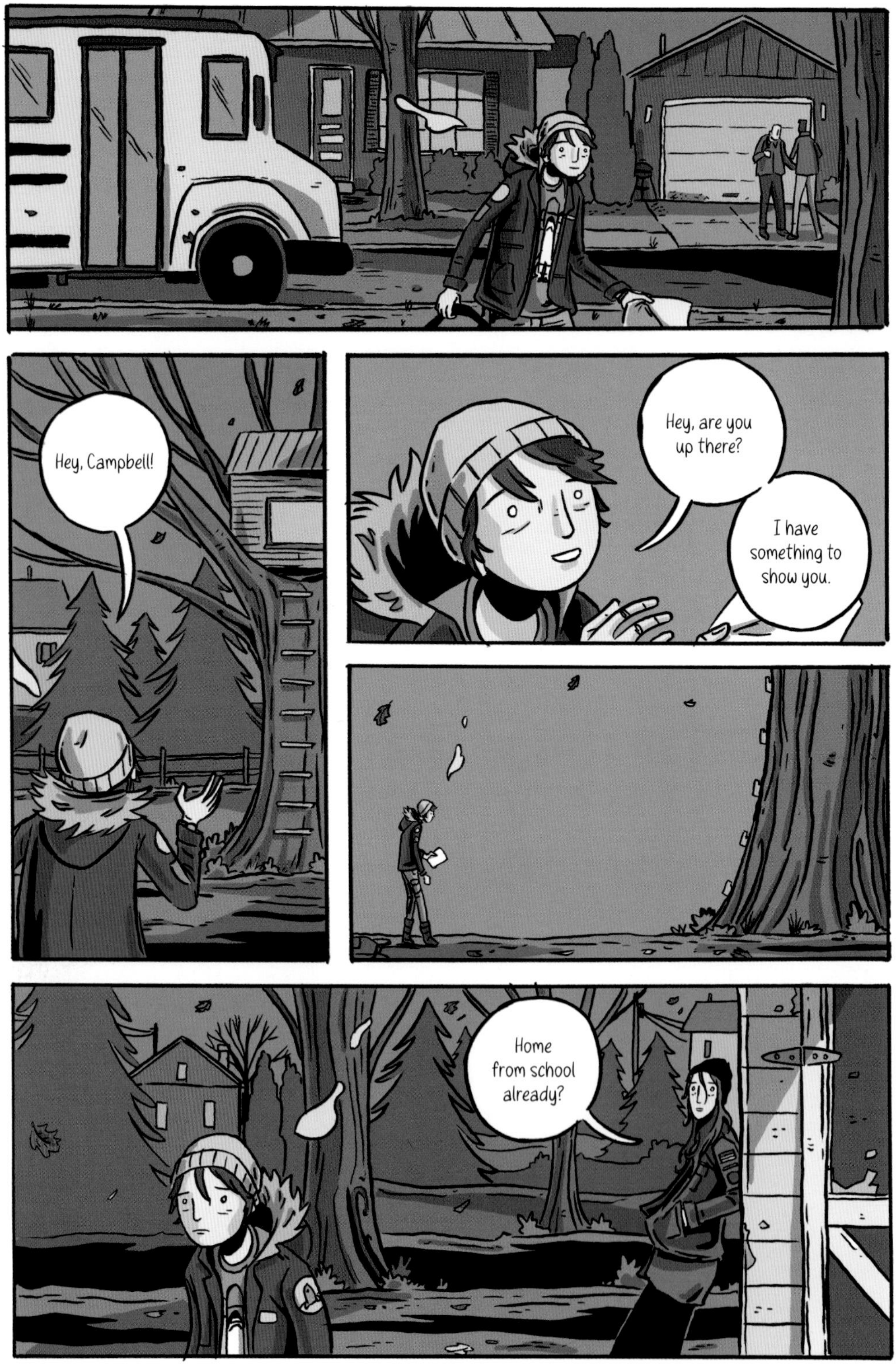
Hey, Campbell!
Hey, are you up there?
I have something to show you.
Home from school already?

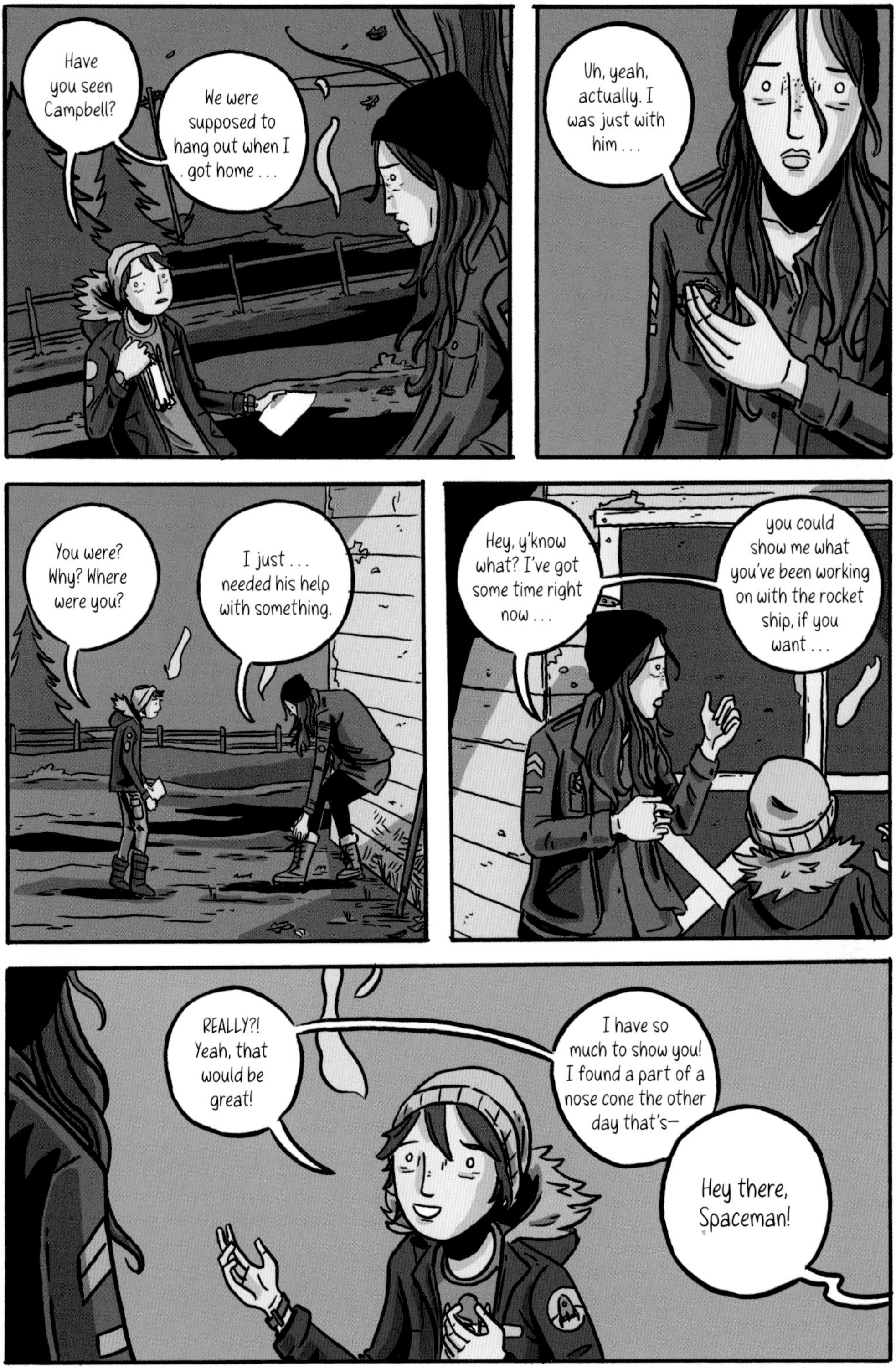
Have you seen Campbell?
We were supposed to hang out when I got home . . .
Uh, yeah, actually. I was just with him . . .
You were? Why? Where were you?
I just . . . needed his help with something.
Hey, y'know what? I've got some time right now . . .
you could show me what you've been working on with the rocket ship, if you want . . .
REALLY?! Yeah, that would be great!
I have so much to show you! I found a part of a nose cone the other day that's—
Hey there, Spaceman!

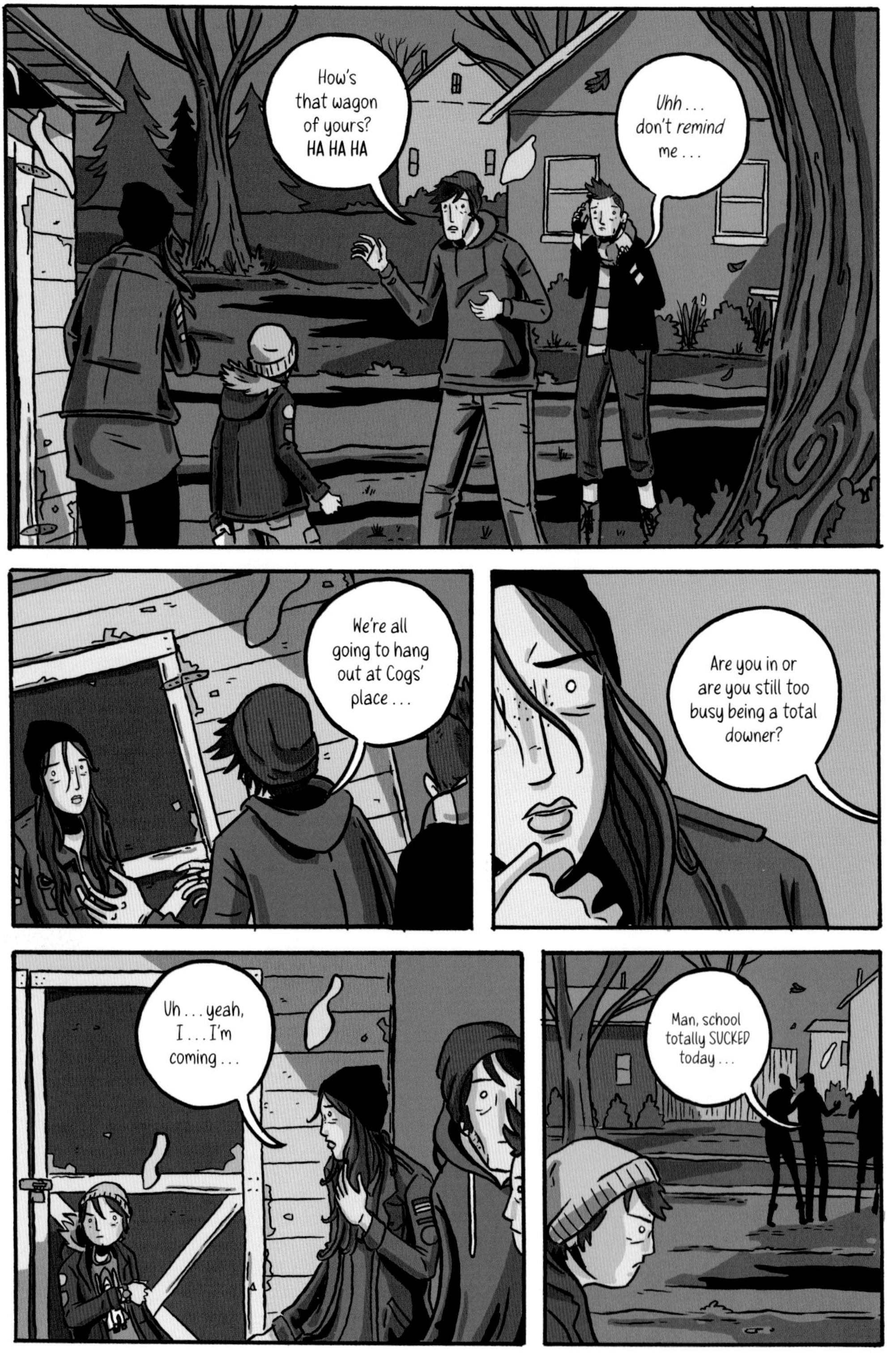
How's that wagon of yours? HA HA HA
Uhh . . . don't remind me . . .
We're all going to hang out at Cogs' place . . .
Are you in or are you still too busy being a total downer?
Uh . . . yeah, I . . . I'm coming . . .
Man, school totally SUCKED today . . .

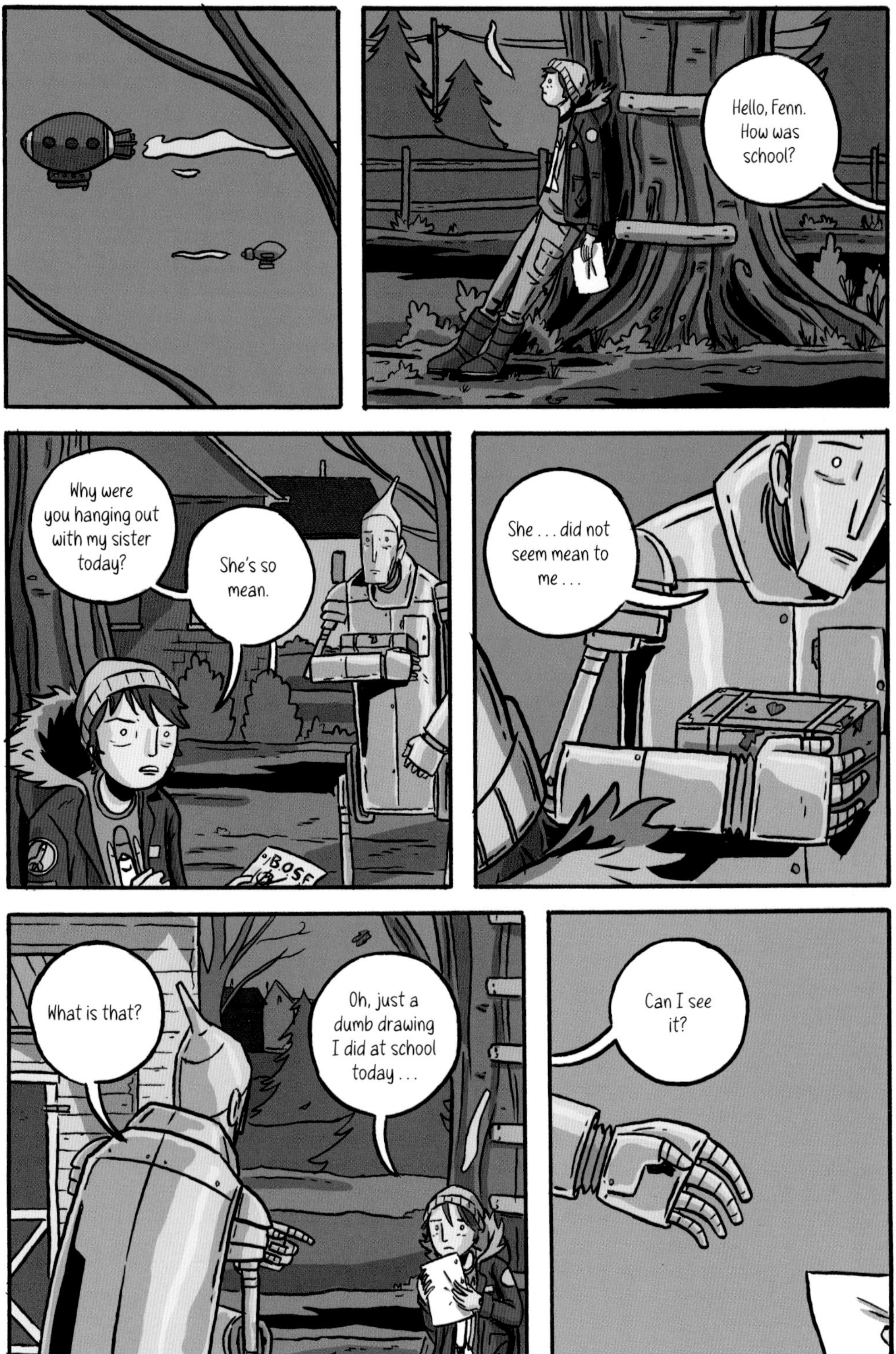
Hello, Fenn.
How was
school?
Why were
you hanging out
with my sister
today?
She's so
mean.
She . . . did not
seem mean to
me . . .
What is that?
Oh, just a
dumb drawing
I did at school
today . . .
Can I see
it?

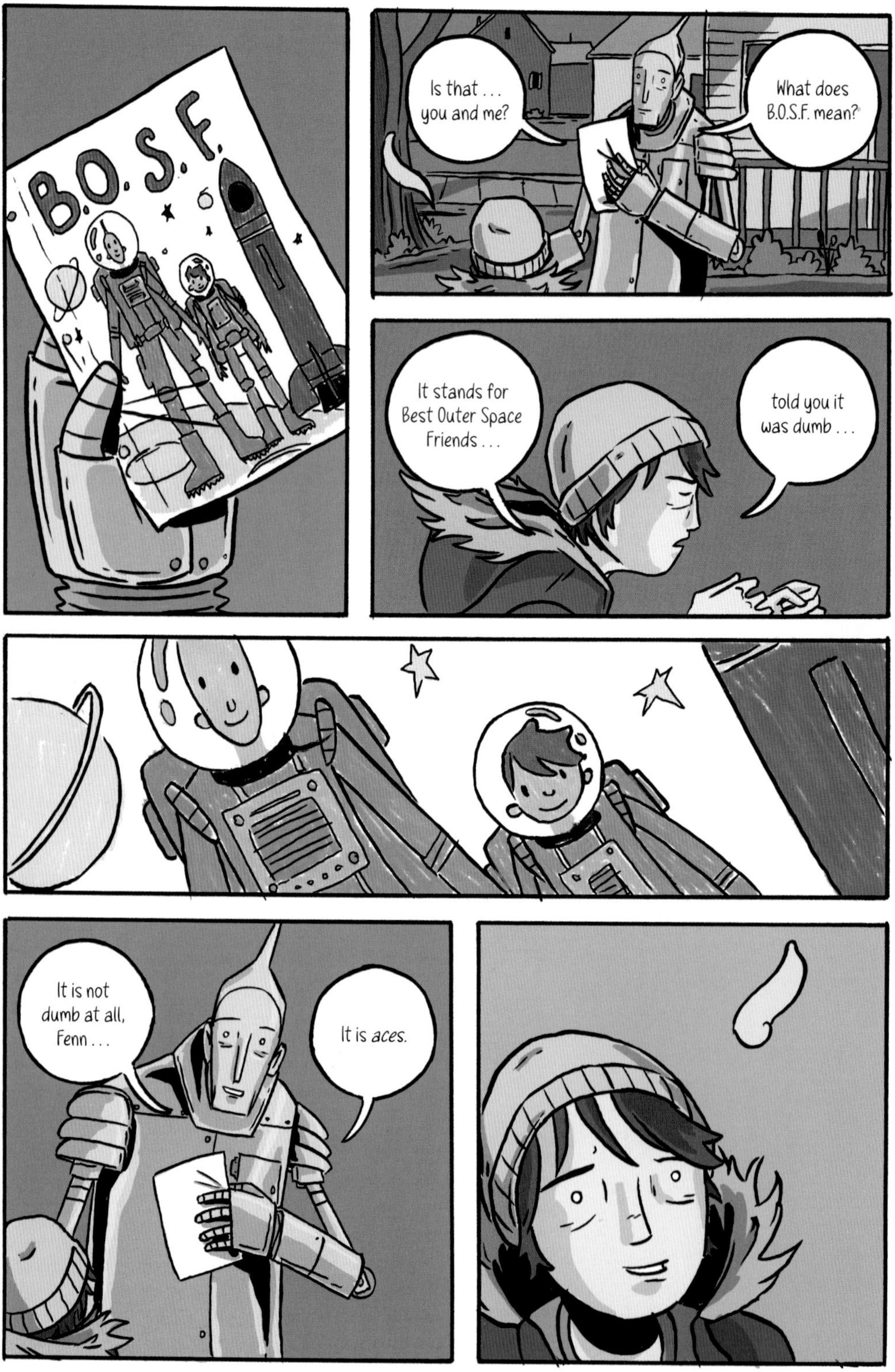
B.O.S.F.
Is that . . . you and me?
What does B.O.S.F. mean?
It stands for Best Outer Space Friends . . .
told you it was dumb . . .
It is not dumb at all, Fenn . . .
It is *aces*.

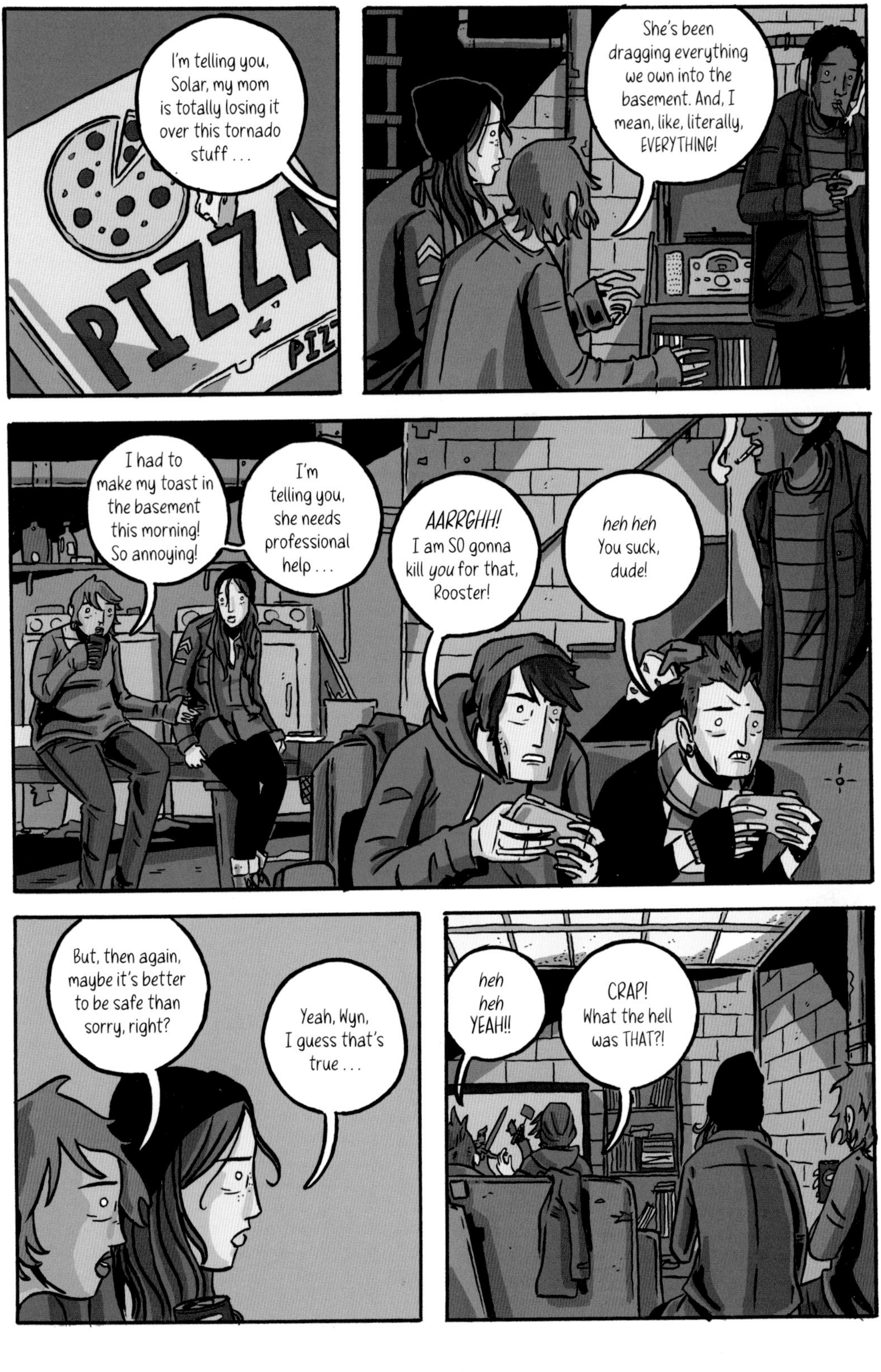
I'm telling you, Solar, my mom is totally losing it over this tornado stuff . . .
PIZZA
She's been dragging everything we own into the basement. And, I mean, like, literally, EVERYTHING!
I had to make my toast in the basement this morning! So annoying!
I'm telling you, she needs professional help . . .
AARRGHH! I am SO gonna kill *you* for that, Rooster!
heh heh You suck, dude!
But, then again, maybe it's better to be safe than sorry, right?
Yeah, Wyn, I guess that's true . . .
heh heh YEAH!!
CRAP! What the hell was THAT?!

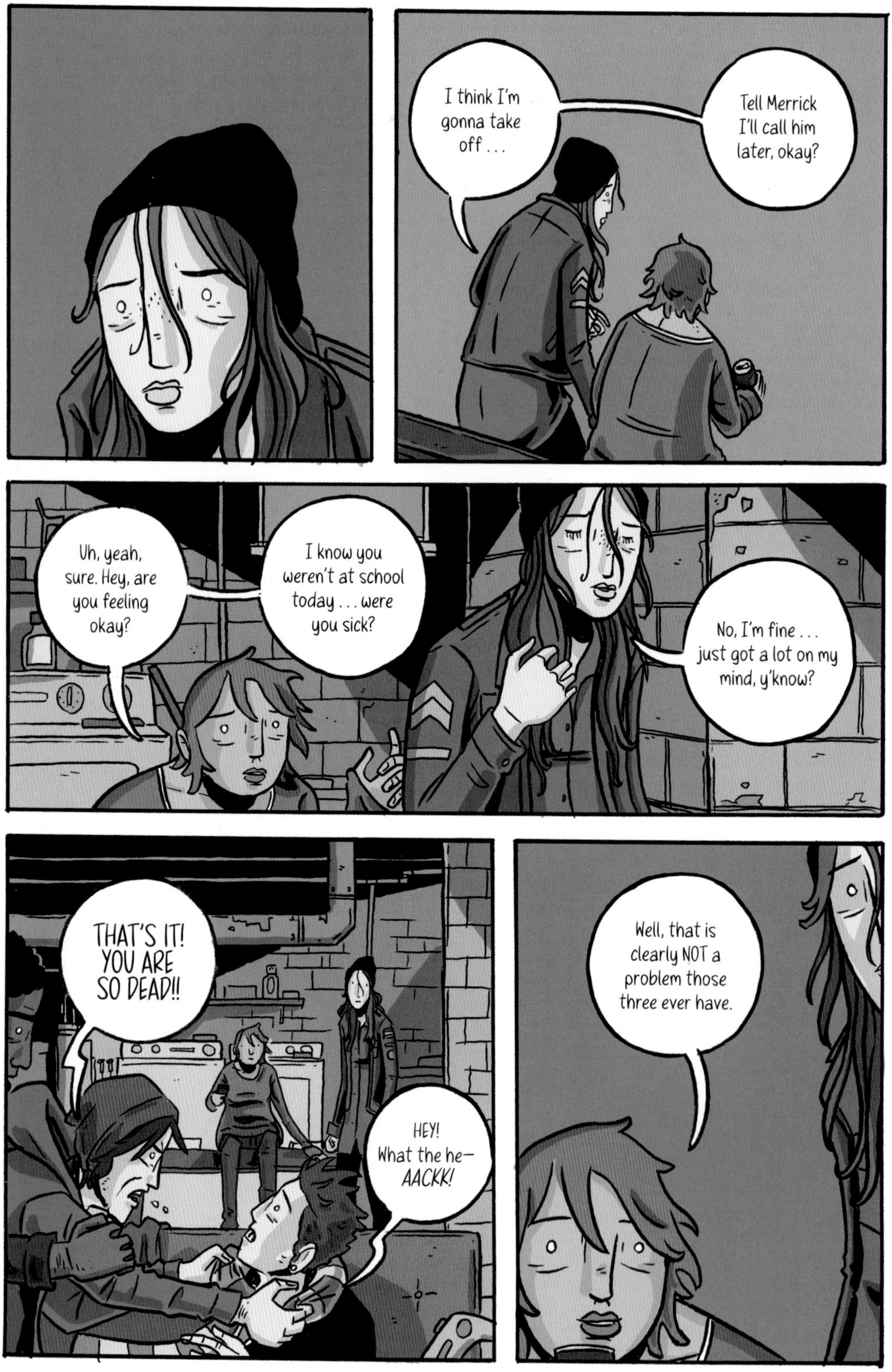
I think I'm gonna take off . . .
Tell Merrick I'll call him later, okay?
Uh, yeah, sure. Hey, are you feeling okay?
I know you weren't at school today . . . were you sick?
No, I'm fine . . . just got a lot on my mind, y'know?
THAT'S IT! YOU ARE SO DEAD!!
HEY! What the he— AACKK!
Well, that is clearly NOT a problem those three ever have.

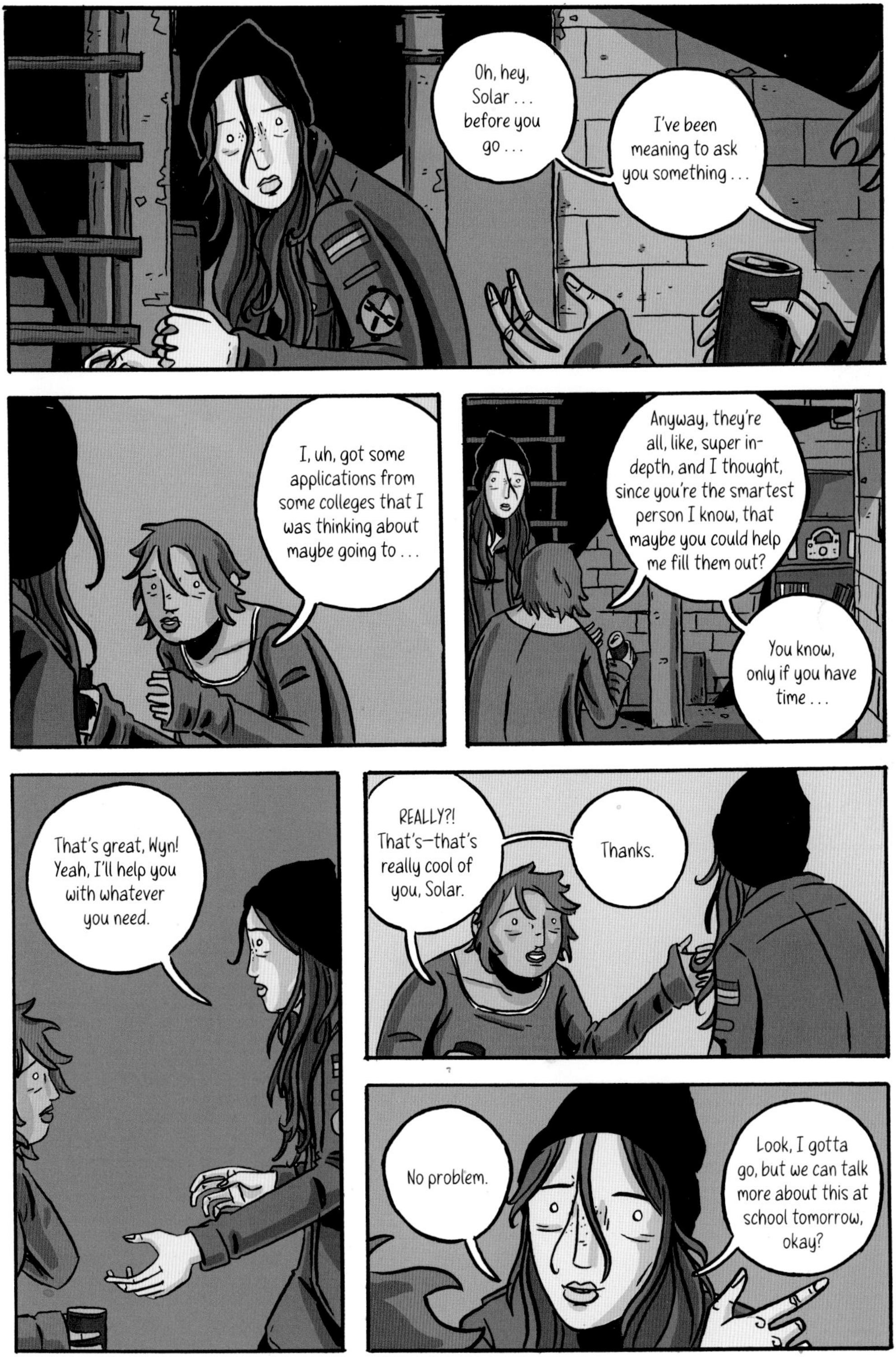
Oh, hey, Solar . . . before you go . . .
I've been meaning to ask you something . . .
I, uh, got some applications from some colleges that I was thinking about maybe going to . . .
Anyway, they're all, like, super in-depth, and I thought, since you're the smartest person I know, that maybe you could help me fill them out?
You know, only if you have time . . .
That's great, Wyn! Yeah, I'll help you with whatever you need.
REALLY?! That's—that's really cool of you, Solar.
Thanks.
No problem.
Look, I gotta go, but we can talk more about this at school tomorrow, okay?

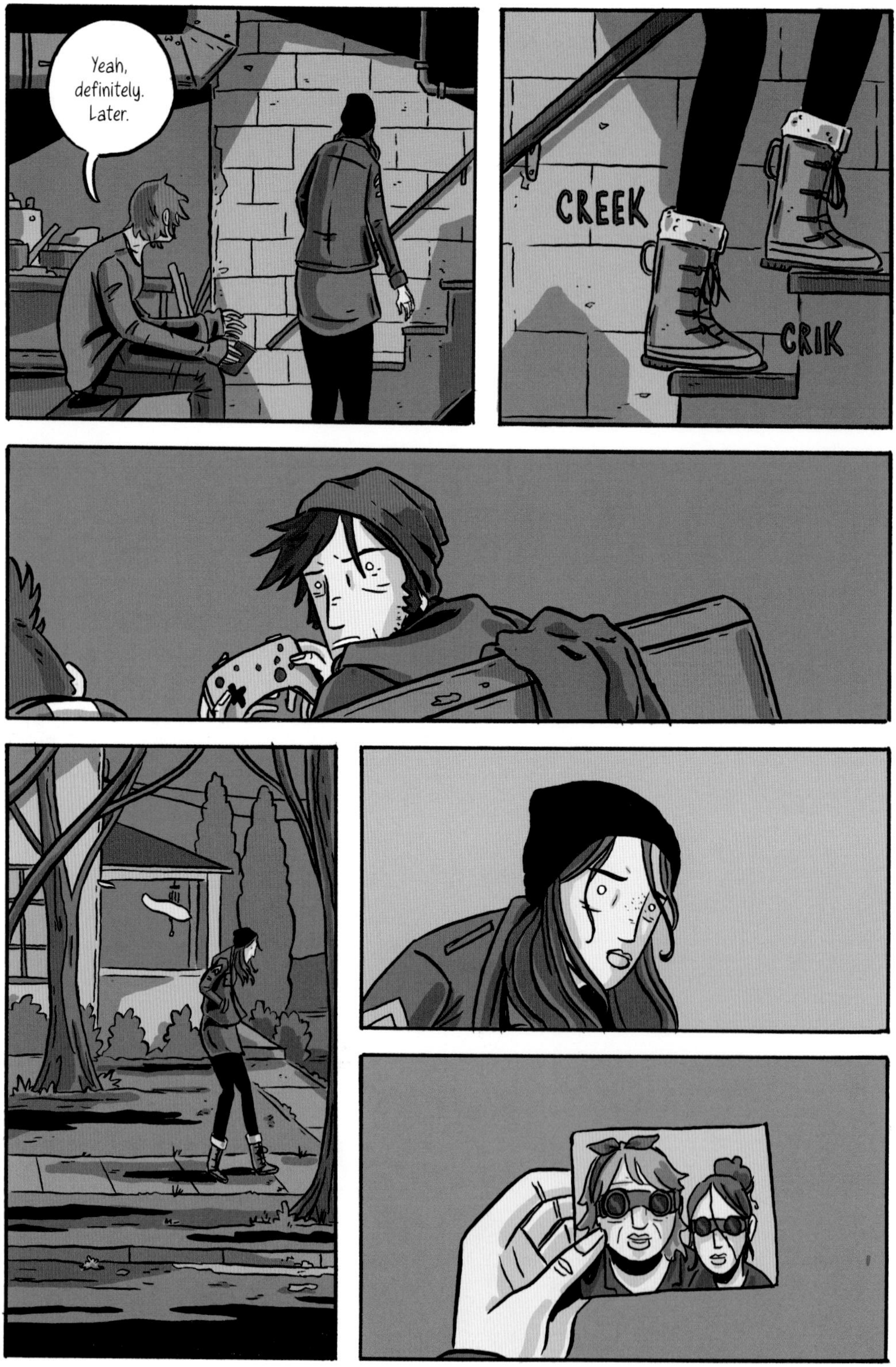
Yeah, definitely. Later.
CREEK
CRIK

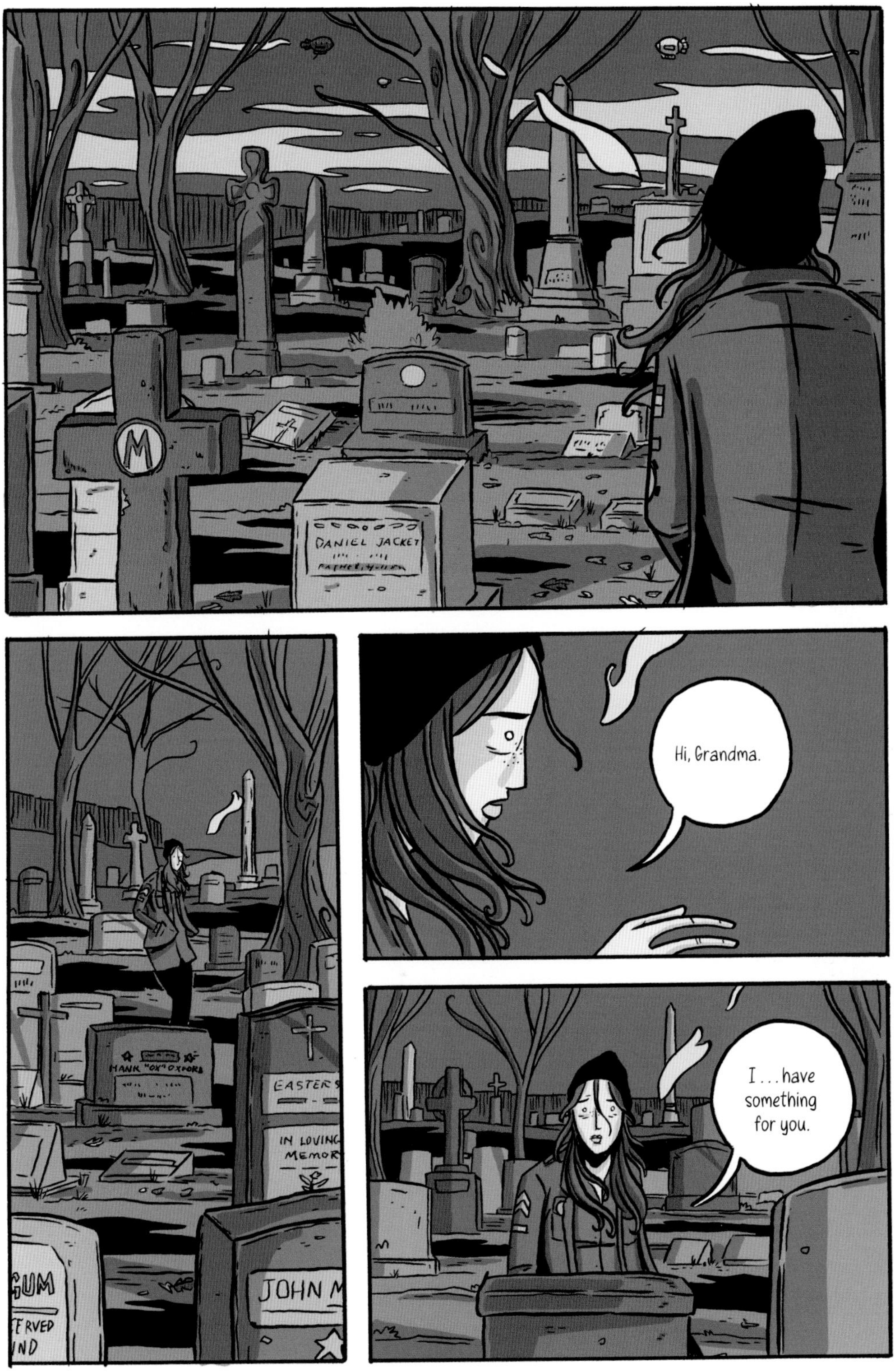
DANIEL JACKET
HANK "OX" OXFORD
Hi, Grandma.
I . . . have something for you.

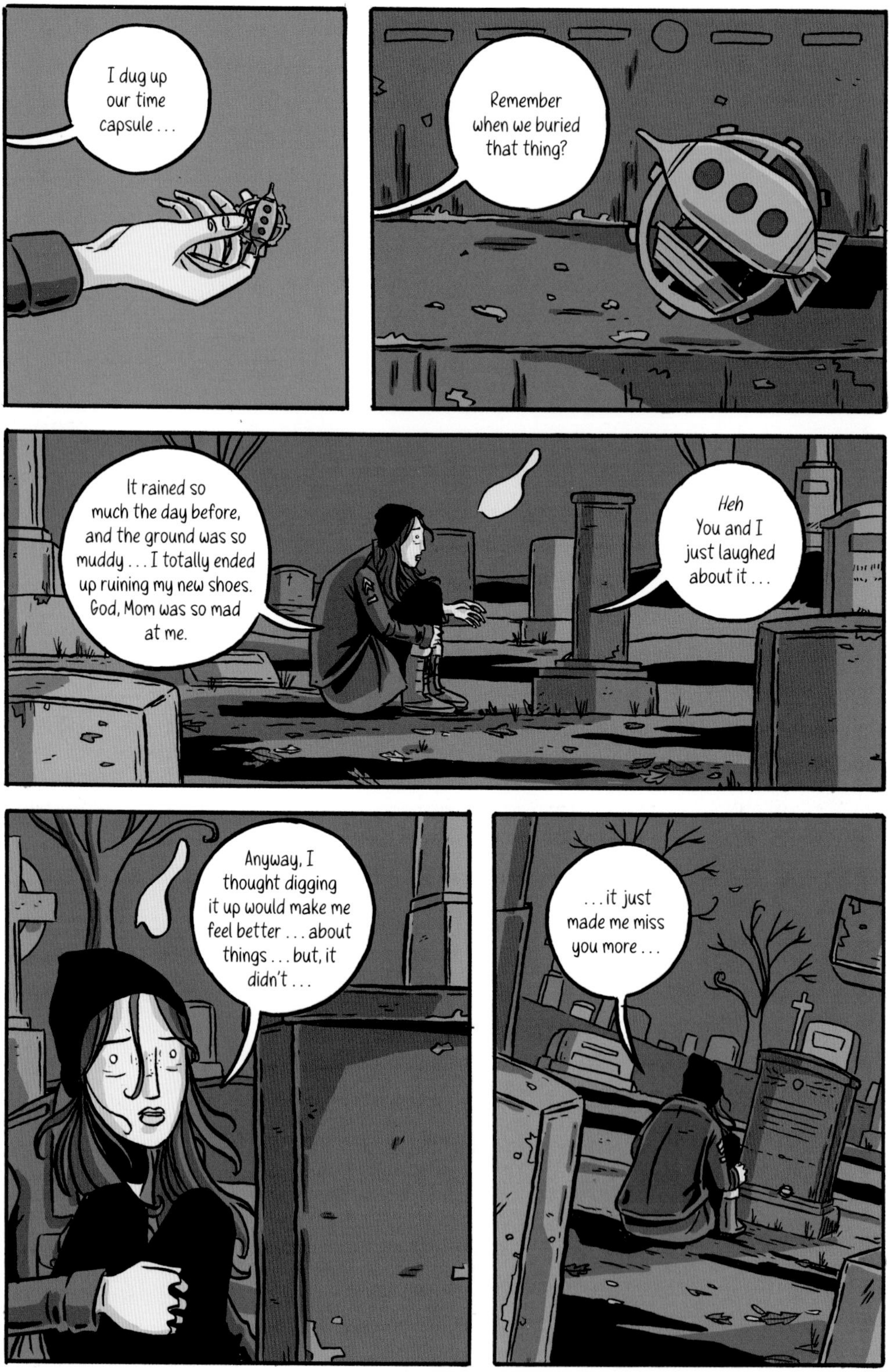
I dug up our time capsule . . .
Remember when we buried that thing?
It rained so much the day before, and the ground was so muddy . . . I totally ended up ruining my new shoes. God, Mom was so mad at me.
Heh You and I just laughed about it . . .
Anyway, I thought digging it up would make me feel better . . . about things . . . but, it didn't . . .
. . . it just made me miss you more . . .

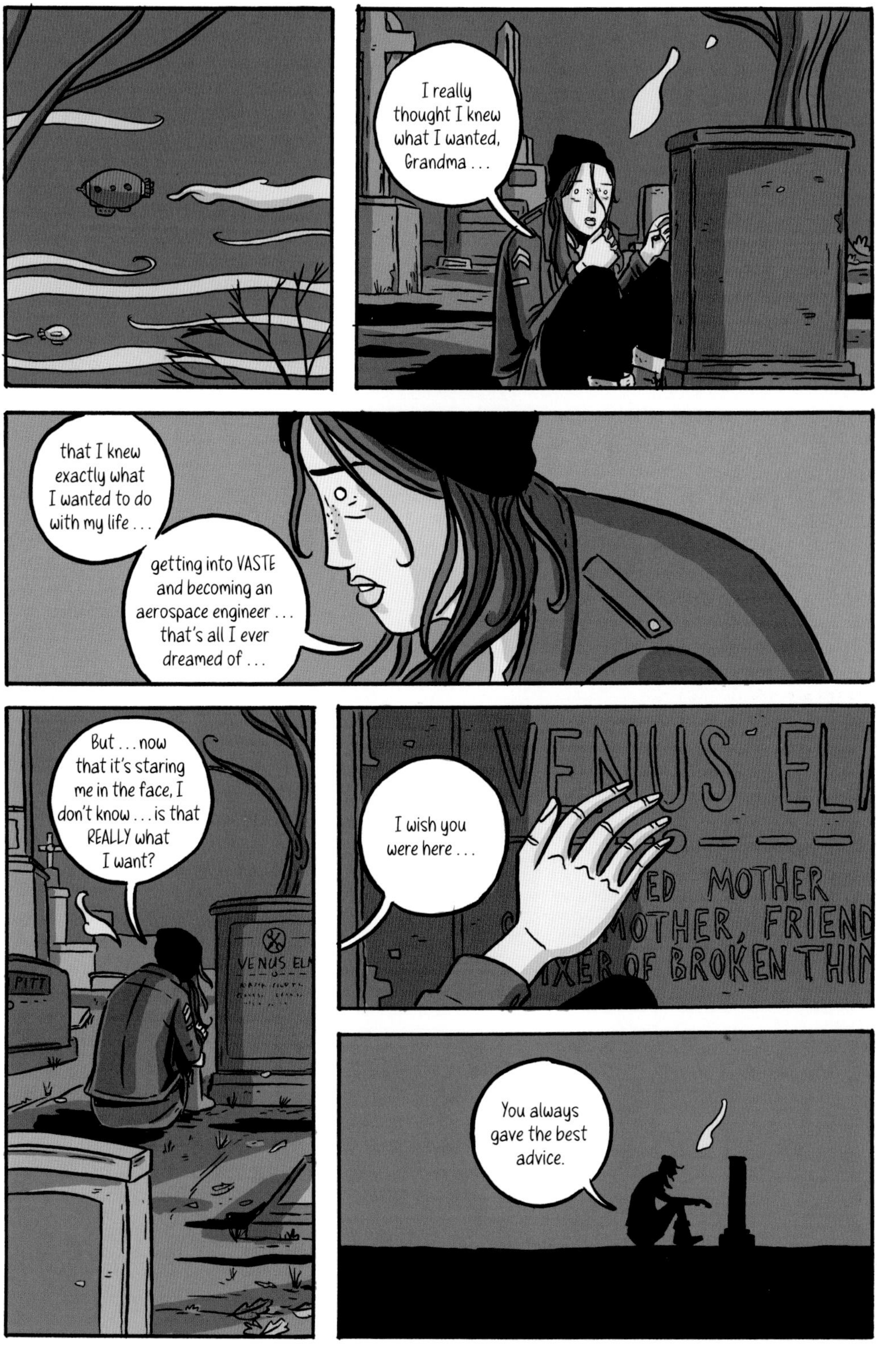
I really thought I knew what I wanted, Grandma . . .
that I knew exactly what I wanted to do with my life . . .
getting into VASTE and becoming an aerospace engineer . . . that's all I ever dreamed of . . .
But . . . now that it's staring me in the face, I don't know . . . is that REALLY what I want?
I wish you were here . . .
You always gave the best advice.

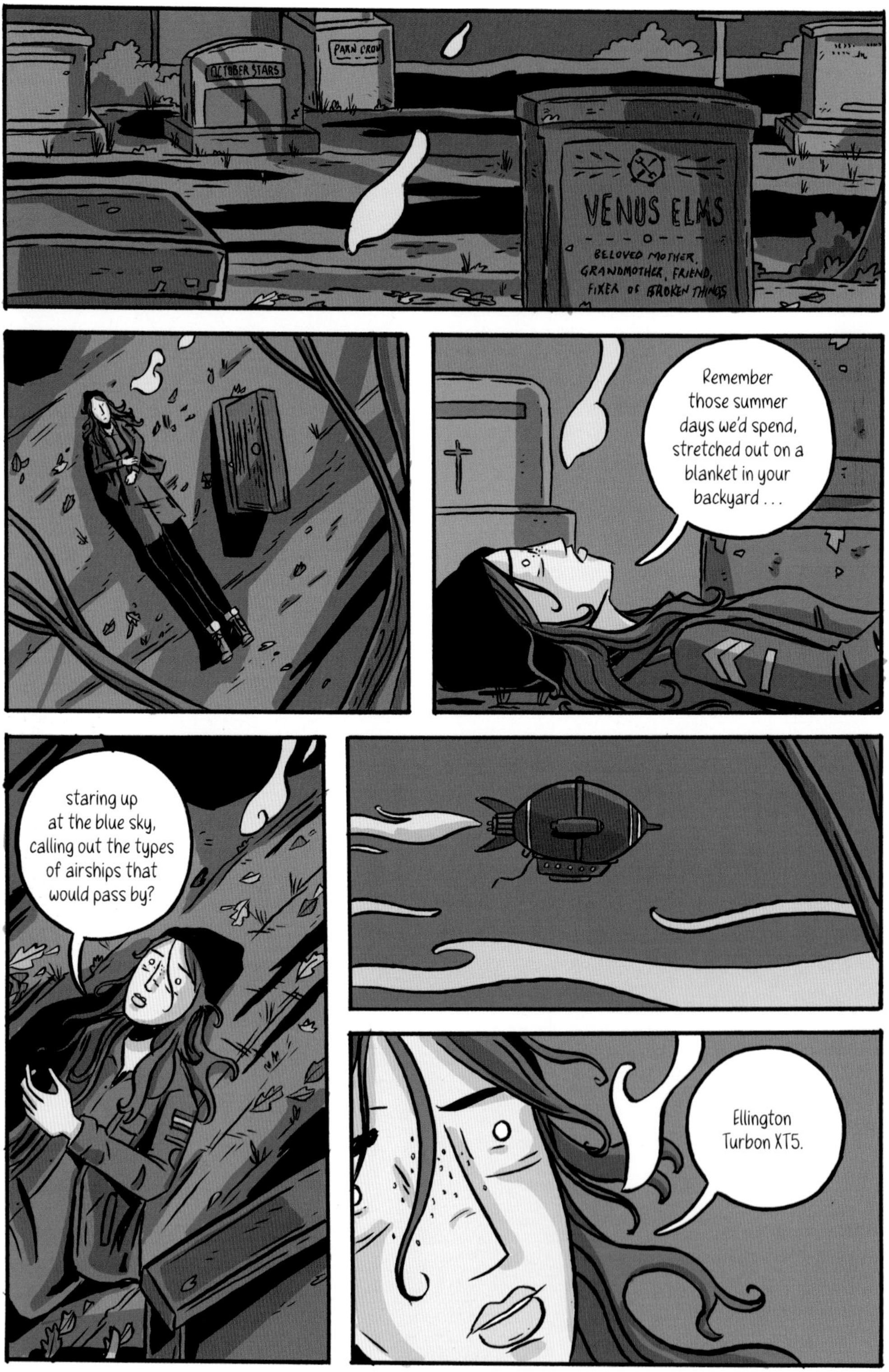
OCTOBER STARS
VENUS ELMS
BELOVED MOTHER, GRANDMOTHER, FRIEND, FIXER OF BROKEN THINGS
Remember those summer days we'd spend, stretched out on a blanket in your backyard . . .
staring up at the blue sky, calling out the types of airships that would pass by?
Ellington Turbon XT5.

CHAPTER 10: Heartache

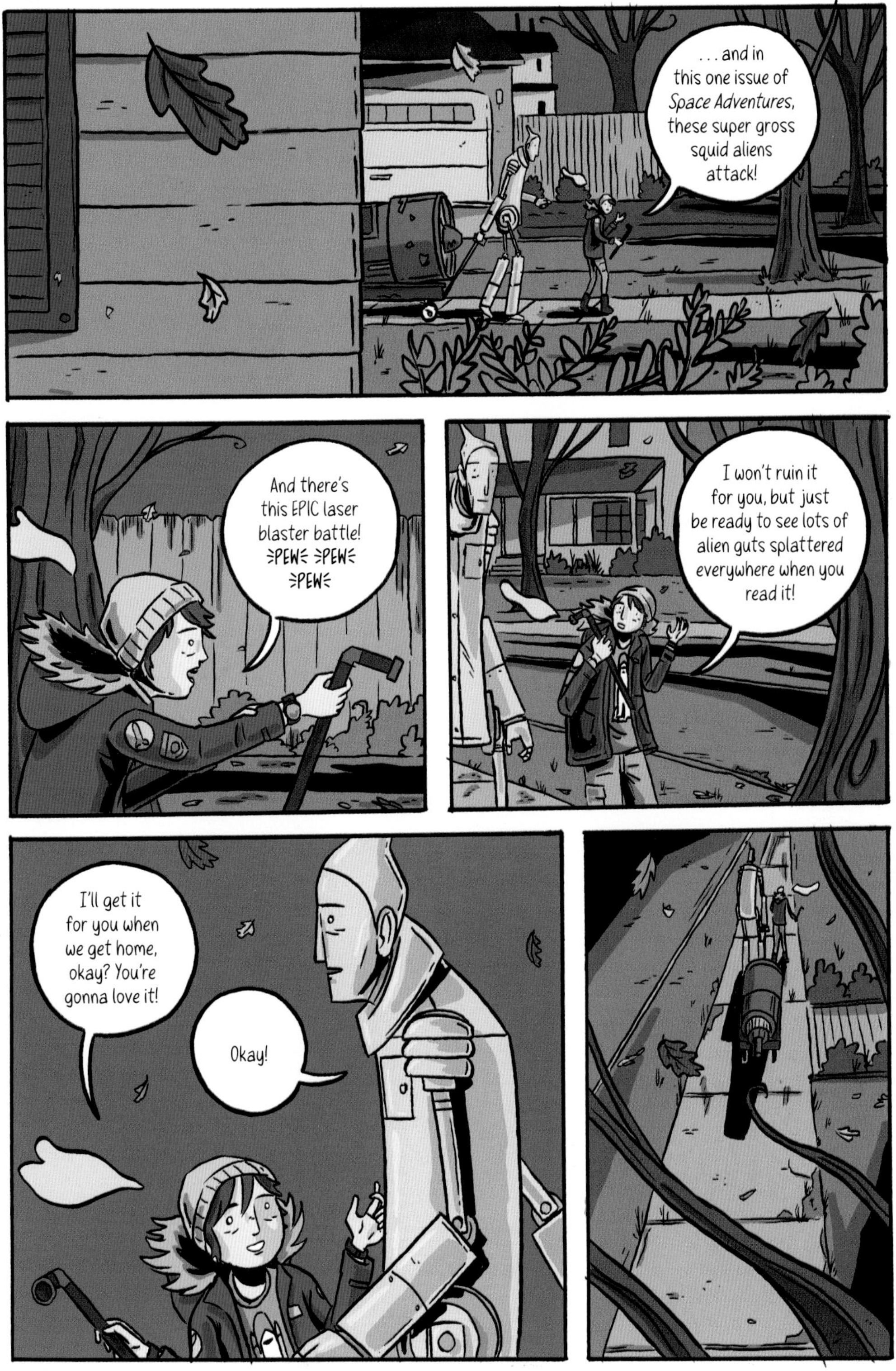

. . . and in this one issue of *Space Adventures*, these super gross squid aliens attack!
And there's this EPIC laser blaster battle! PEW PEW PEW
I won't ruin it for you, but just be ready to see lots of alien guts splattered everywhere when you read it!
I'll get it for you when we get home, okay? You're gonna love it!
Okay!

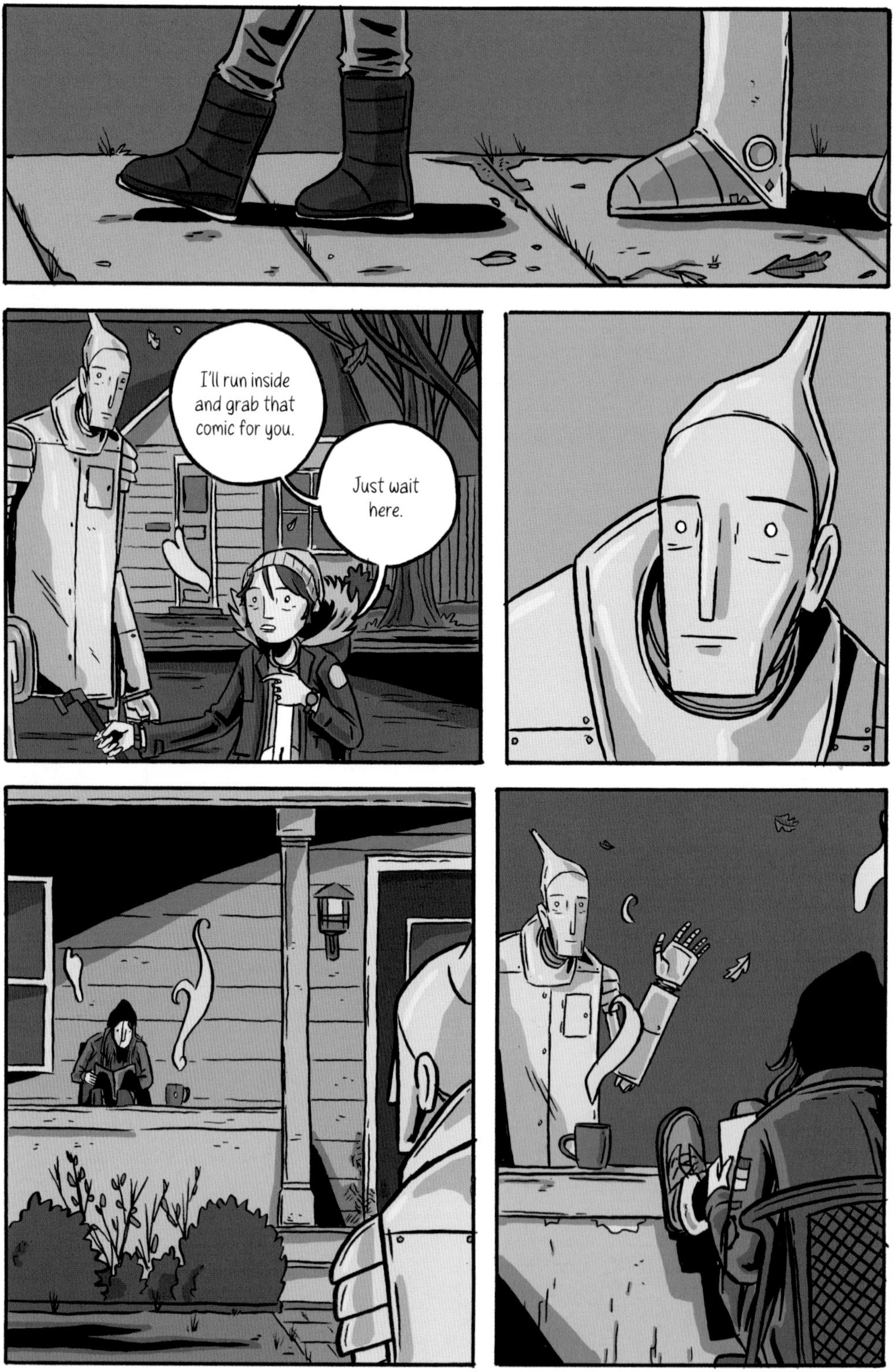
I'll run inside and grab that comic for you.
Just wait here.

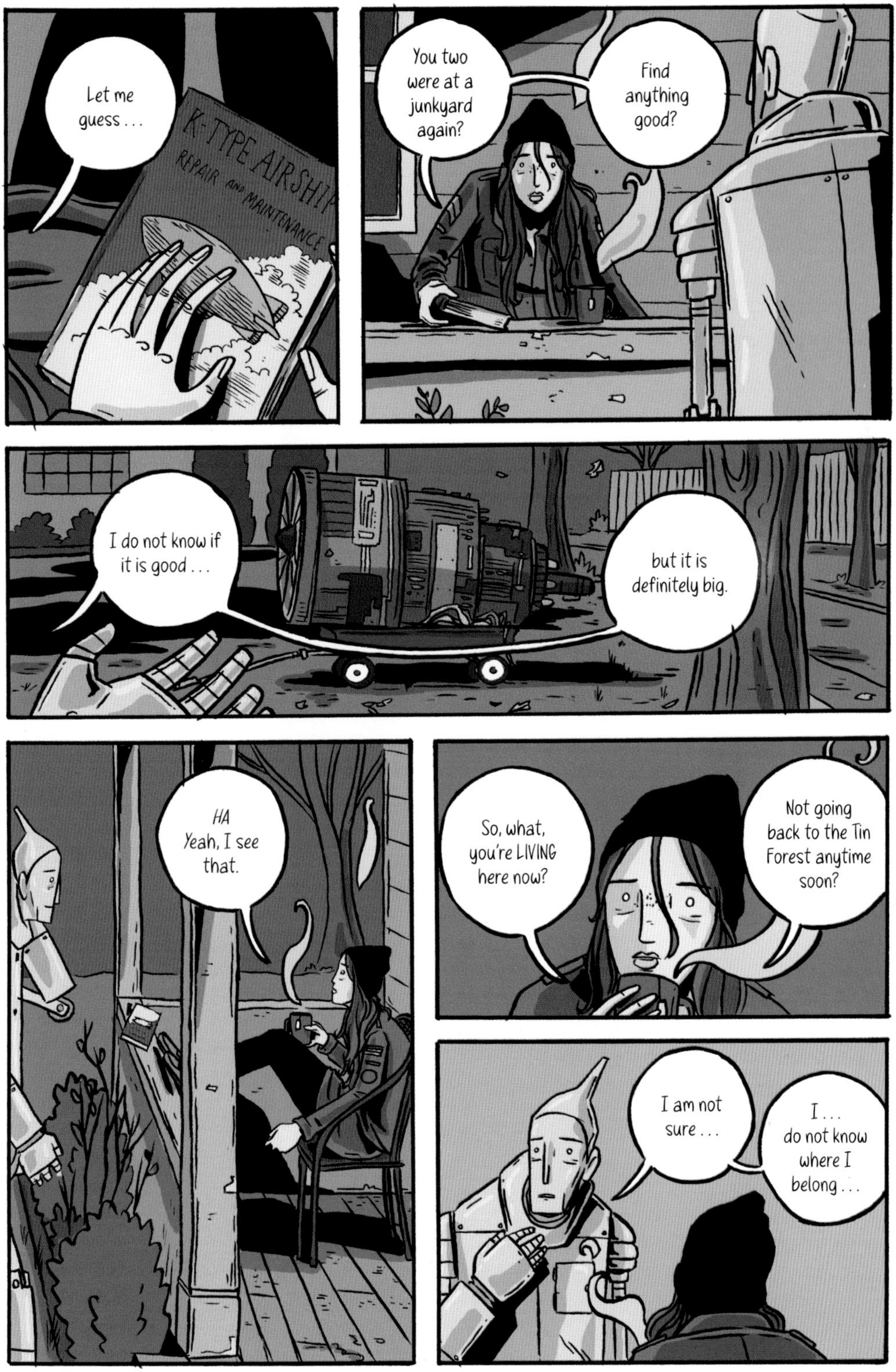
Let me guess . . .
K-TYPE AIRSHIP
REPAIR AND MAINTENANCE
You two were at a junkyard again?
Find anything good?
I do not know if it is good . . .
but it is definitely big.
HA
Yeah, I see that.
So, what, you're LIVING here now?
Not going back to the Tin Forest anytime soon?
I am not sure . . .
I . . . do not know where I belong . . .

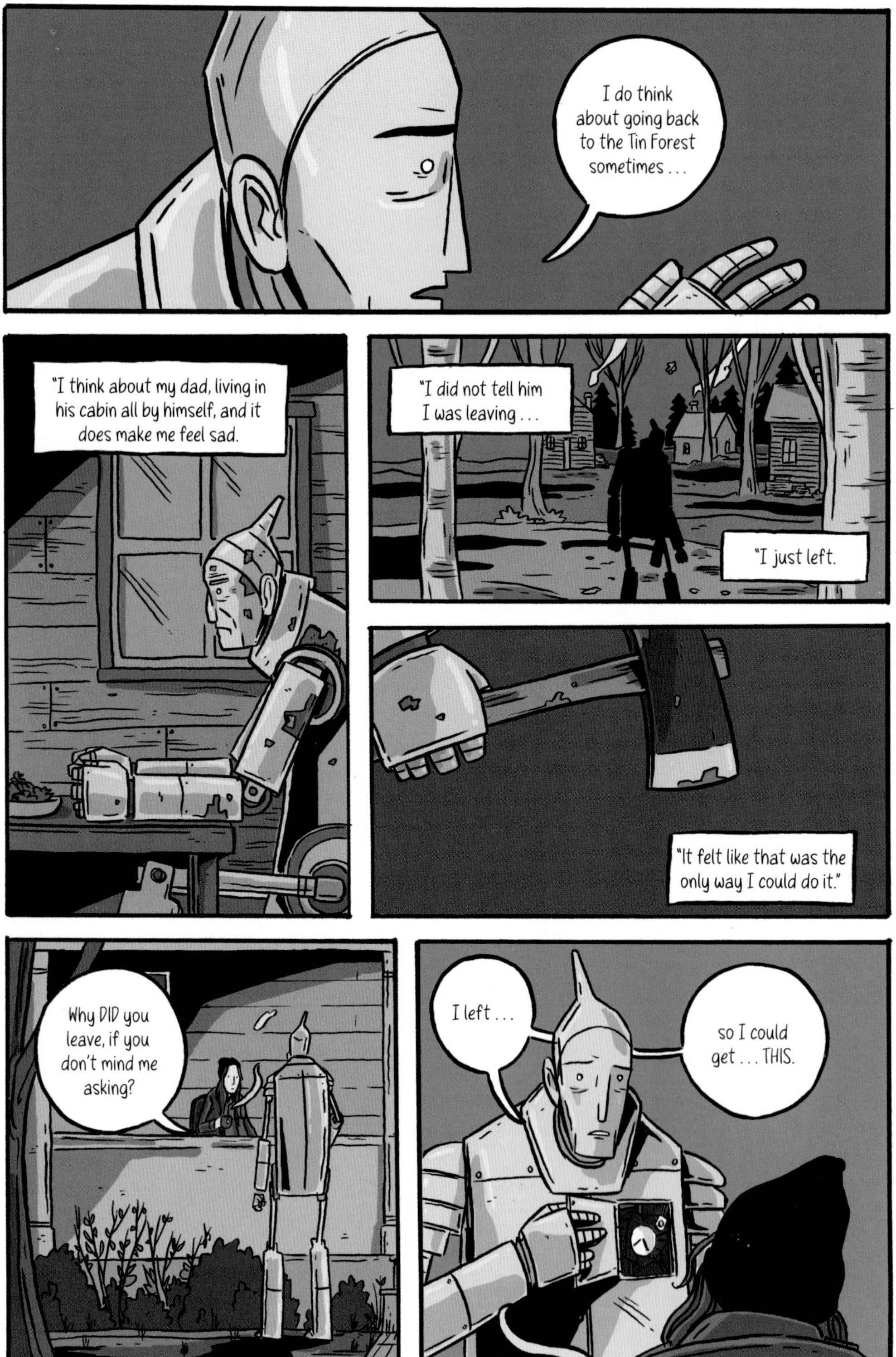
I do think about going back to the Tin Forest sometimes . . .
"I think about my dad, living in his cabin all by himself, and it does make me feel sad.
"I did not tell him I was leaving . . .
"I just left.
"It felt like that was the only way I could do it."
Why DID you leave, if you don't mind me asking?
I left . . .
so I could get . . . THIS.

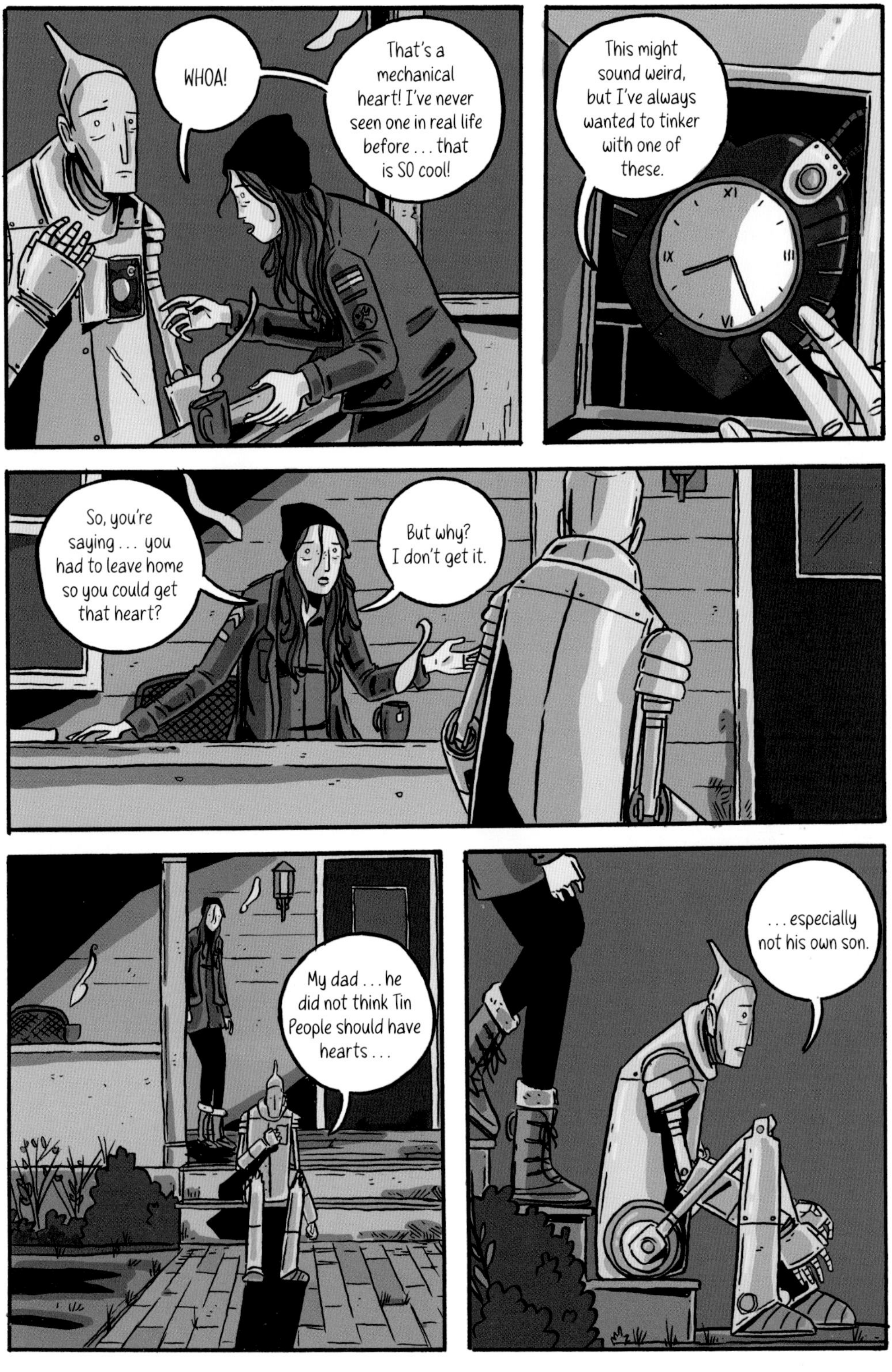
WHOA!
That's a mechanical heart! I've never seen one in real life before . . . that is SO cool!
This might sound weird, but I've always wanted to tinker with one of these.
So, you're saying . . . you had to leave home so you could get that heart?
But why? I don't get it.
My dad . . . he did not think Tin People should have hearts . . .
. . . especially not his own son.

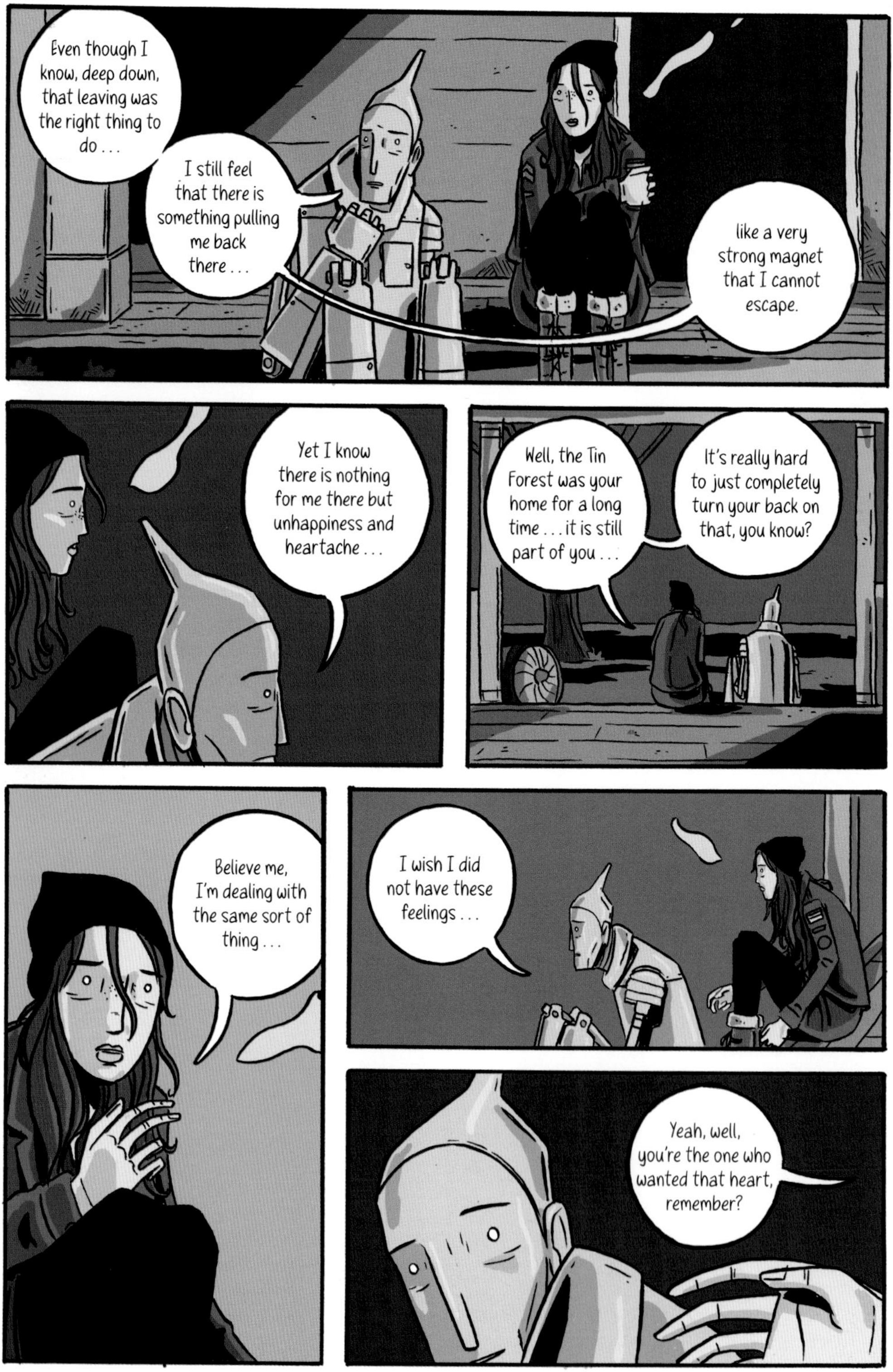
Even though I know, deep down, that leaving was the right thing to do . . .
I still feel that there is something pulling me back there . . .
like a very strong magnet that I cannot escape.
Yet I know there is nothing for me there but unhappiness and heartache . . .
Well, the Tin Forest was your home for a long time . . . it is still part of you . . .
It's really hard to just completely turn your back on that, you know?
Believe me, I'm dealing with the same sort of thing . . .
I wish I did not have these feelings . . .
Yeah, well, you're the one who wanted that heart, remember?

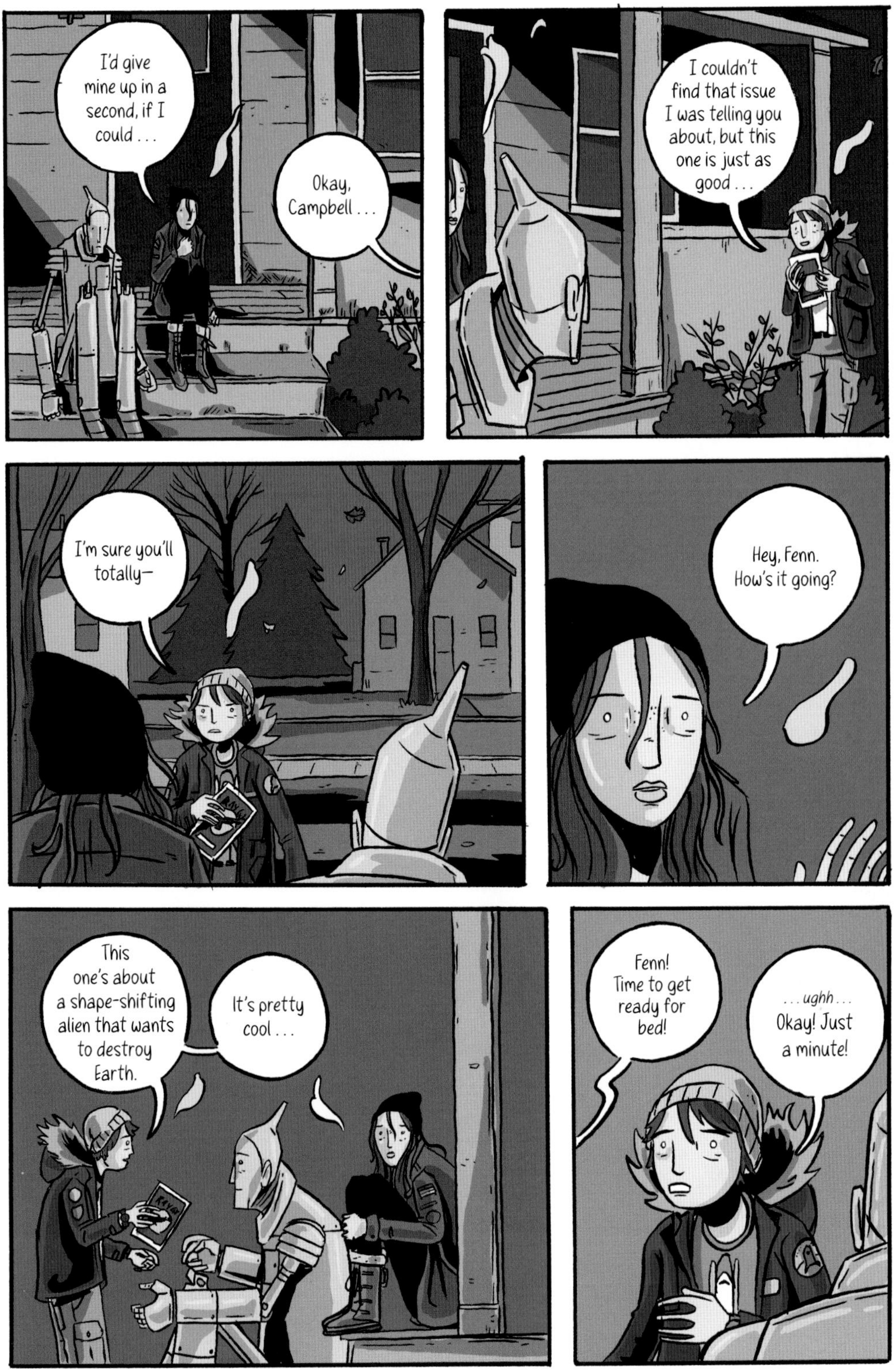

I'd give mine up in a second, if I could . . .
Okay, Campbell . . .
I couldn't find that issue I was telling you about, but this one is just as good . . .
I'm sure you'll totally—
Hey, Fenn. How's it going?
This one's about a shape-shifting alien that wants to destroy Earth.
It's pretty cool . . .
Fenn! Time to get ready for bed!
. . . ughh . . . Okay! Just a minute!

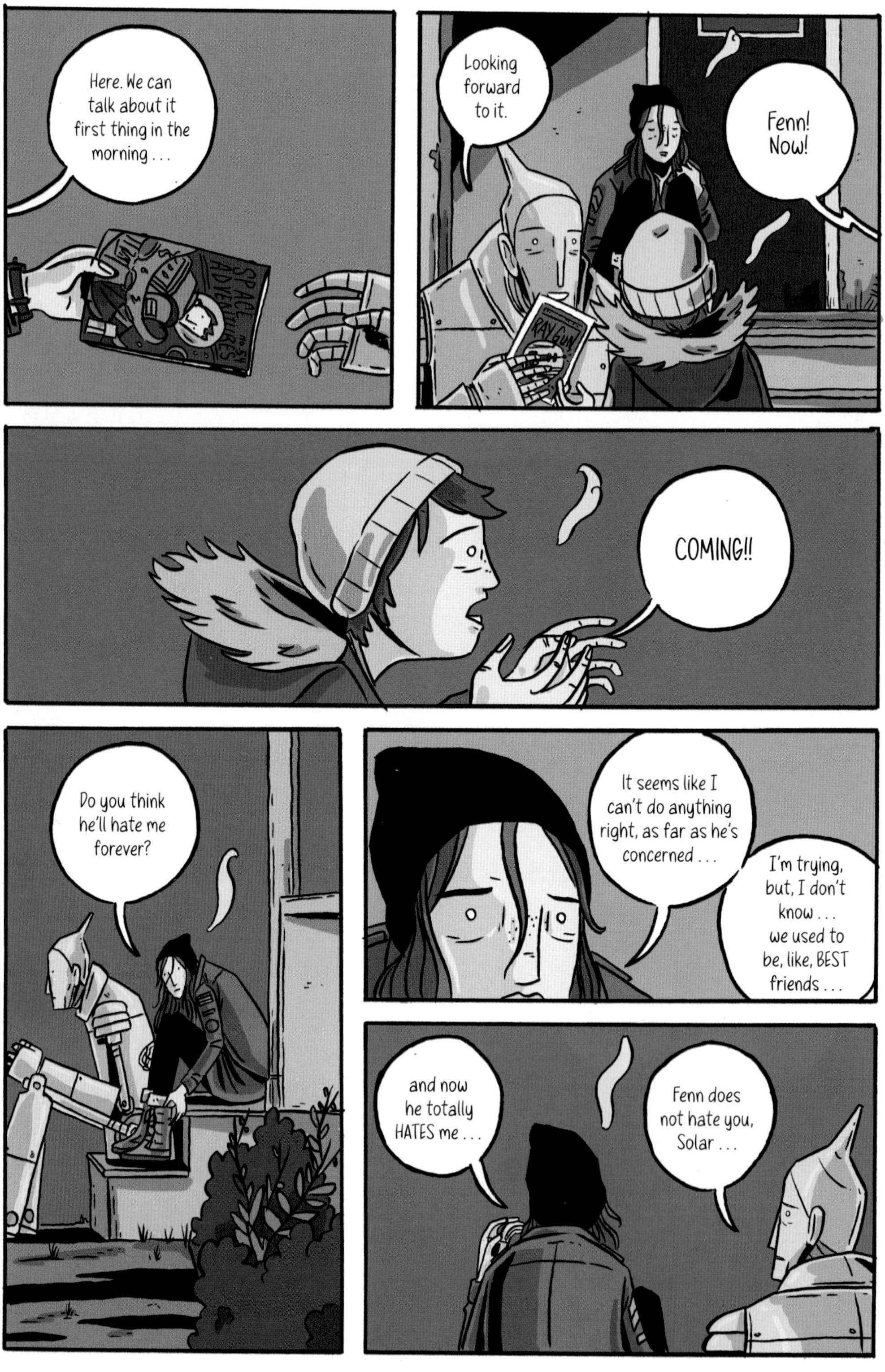
Here. We can talk about it first thing in the morning . . .
SPACE ADVENTURES
Looking forward to it.
RAY GUN
Fenn! Now!
COMING!!
Do you think he'll hate me forever?
It seems like I can't do anything right, as far as he's concerned . . .
I'm trying, but, I don't know . . . we used to be, like, BEST friends . . .
and now he totally HATES me . . .
Fenn does not hate you, Solar . . .

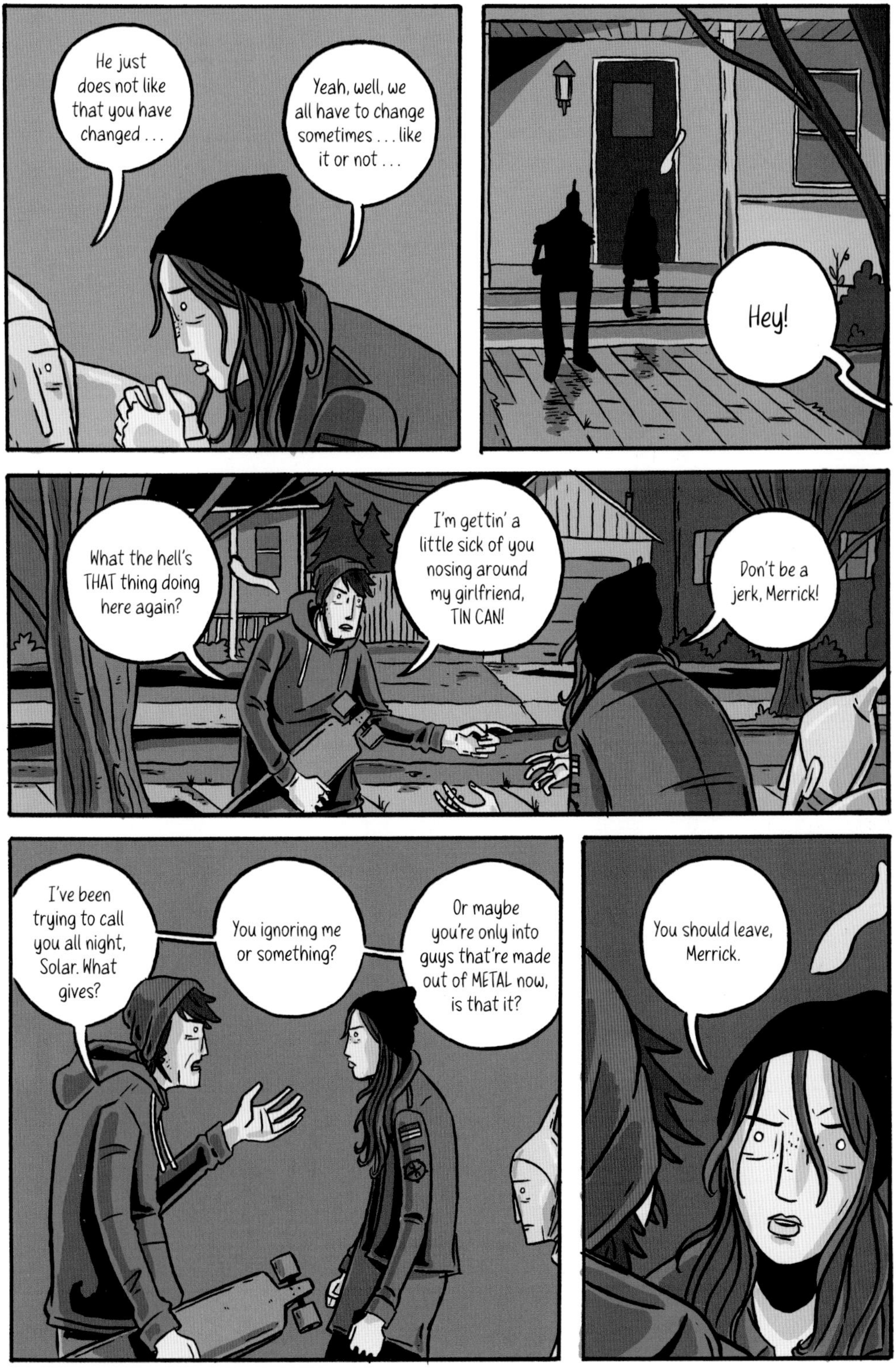
He just does not like that you have changed . . .
Yeah, well, we all have to change sometimes . . . like it or not . . .
Hey!
What the hell's THAT thing doing here again?
I'm gettin' a little sick of you nosing around my girlfriend, TIN CAN!
Don't be a jerk, Merrick!
I've been trying to call you all night, Solar. What gives?
You ignoring me or something?
Or maybe you're only into guys that're made out of METAL now, is that it?
You should leave, Merrick.

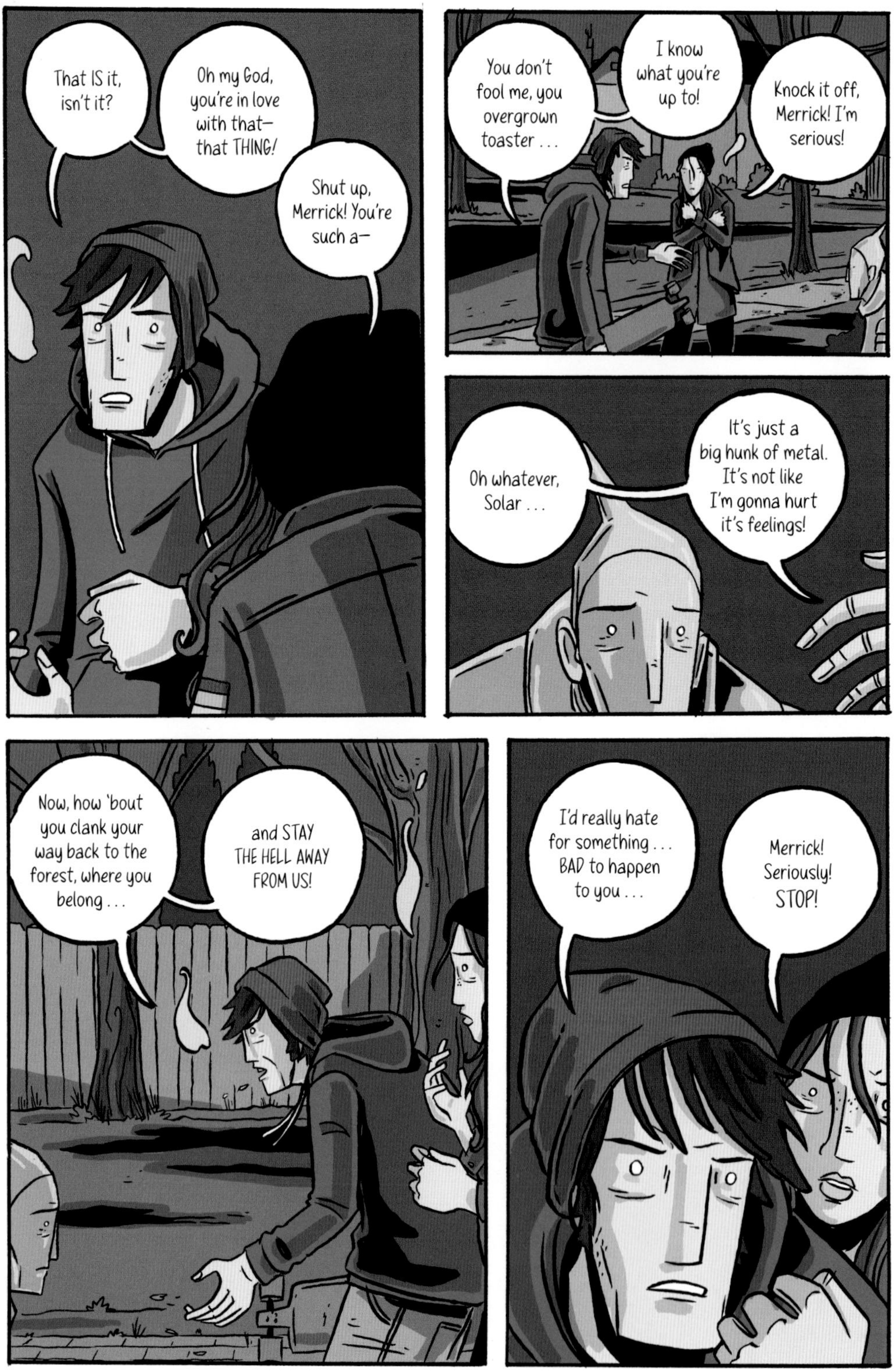
That IS it, isn't it?
Oh my God, you're in love with that— that THING!
Shut up, Merrick! You're such a—
You don't fool me, you overgrown toaster . . .
I know what you're up to!
Knock it off, Merrick! I'm serious!
Oh whatever, Solar . . .
It's just a big hunk of metal. It's not like I'm gonna hurt it's feelings!
Now, how 'bout you clank your way back to the forest, where you belong . . .
and STAY THE HELL AWAY FROM US!
I'd really hate for something . . . BAD to happen to you . . .
Merrick! Seriously! STOP!

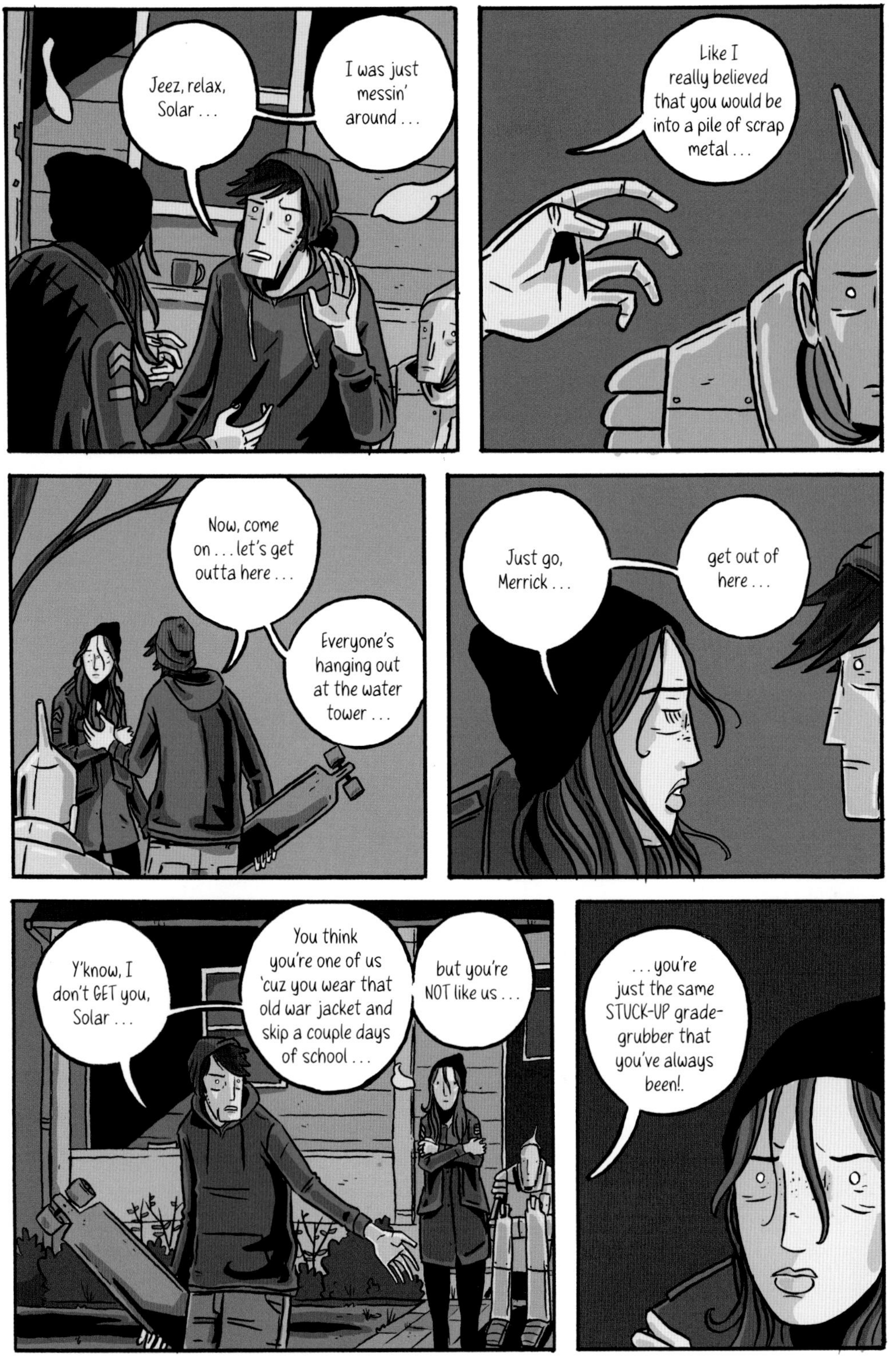
Jeez, relax, Solar . . .
I was just messin' around . . .
Like I really believed that you would be into a pile of scrap metal . . .
Now, come on . . . let's get outta here . . .
Everyone's hanging out at the water tower . . .
Just go, Merrick . . .
get out of here . . .
Y'know, I don't GET you, Solar . . .
You think you're one of us 'cuz you wear that old war jacket and skip a couple days of school . . .
but you're NOT like us . . .
. . . you're just the same STUCK-UP grade-grubber that you've always been!.

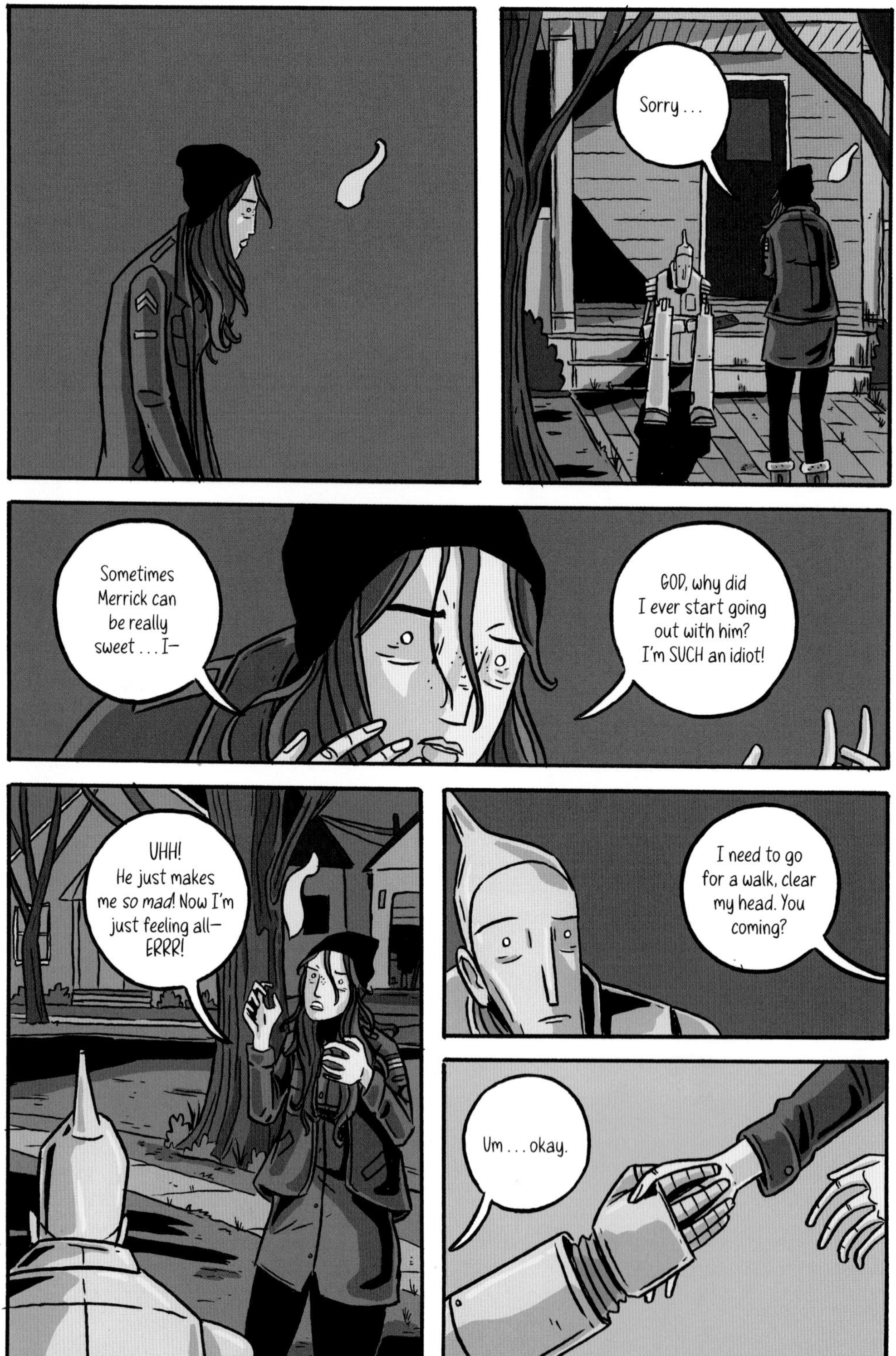
Sorry . . .
Sometimes Merrick can be really sweet . . . I—
GOD, why did I ever start going out with him? I'm SUCH an idiot!
UHH! He just makes me so mad! Now I'm just feeling all— ERRR!
I need to go for a walk, clear my head. You coming?
Um . . . okay.

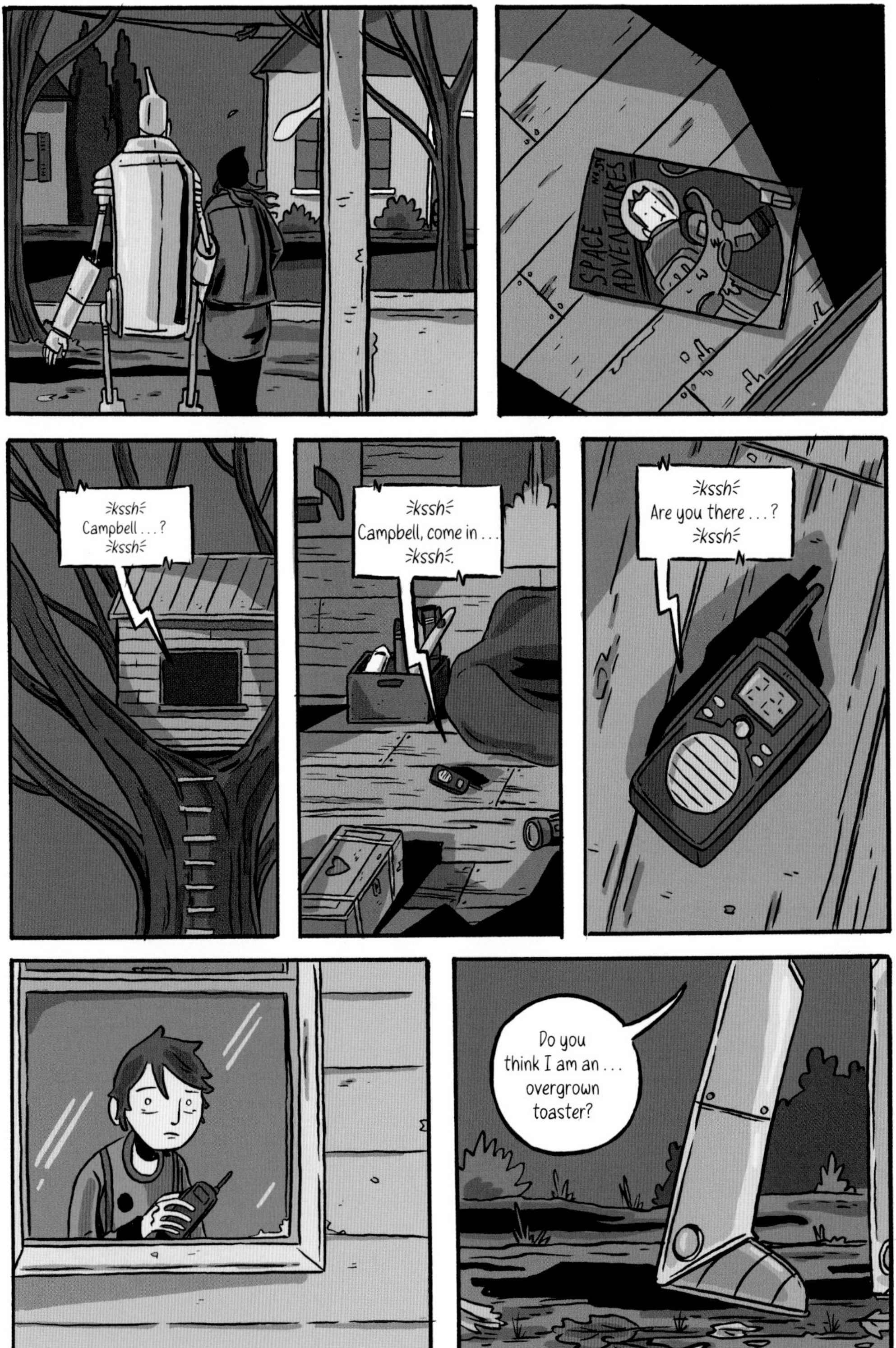
SPACE ADVENTURES
≷kssh≶ Campbell . . . ? ≷kssh≶
≷kssh≶ Campbell, come in . . . ≷kssh≶.
≷kssh≶ Are you there . . . ? ≷kssh≶
Do you think I am an . . . overgrown toaster?

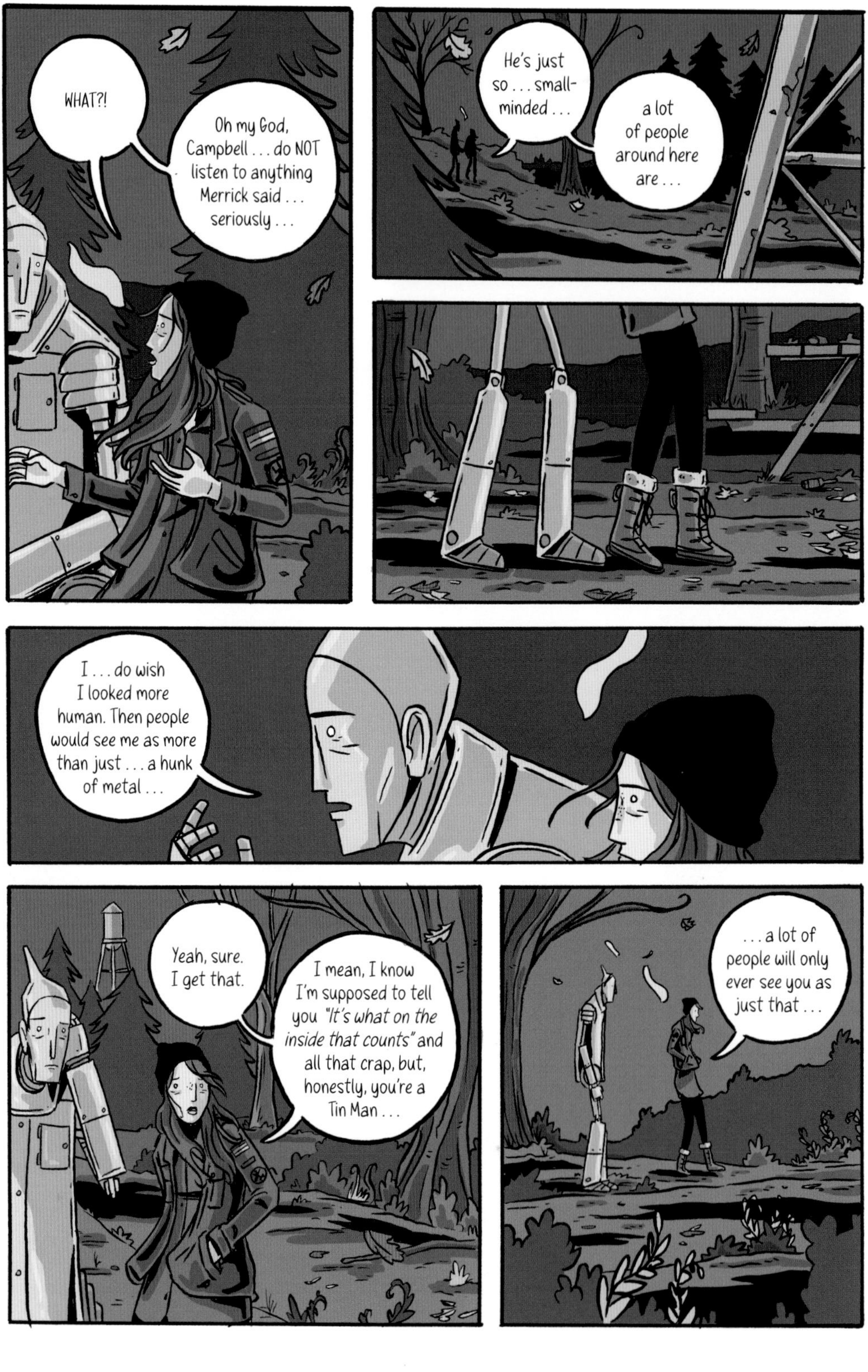
WHAT?!
Oh my God, Campbell . . . do NOT listen to anything Merrick said . . . seriously . . .
He's just so . . . small-minded . . .
a lot of people around here are . . .
I . . . do wish I looked more human. Then people would see me as more than just . . . a hunk of metal . . .
Yeah, sure. I get that.
I mean, I know I'm supposed to tell you *"It's what on the inside that counts"* and all that crap, but, honestly, you're a Tin Man . . .
. . . a lot of people will only ever see you as just that . . .

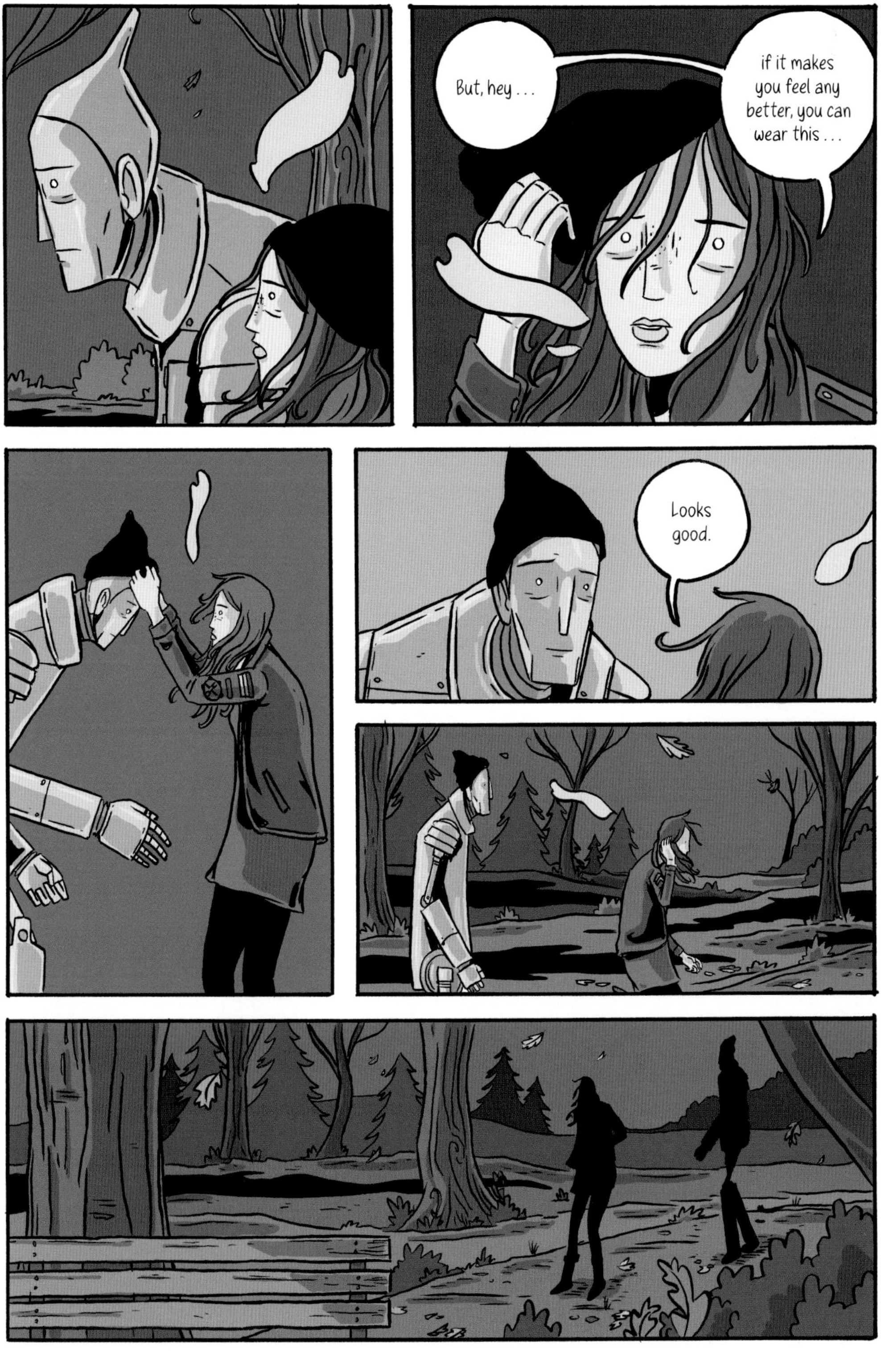
But, hey . . .
if it makes you feel any better, you can wear this . . .
Looks good.

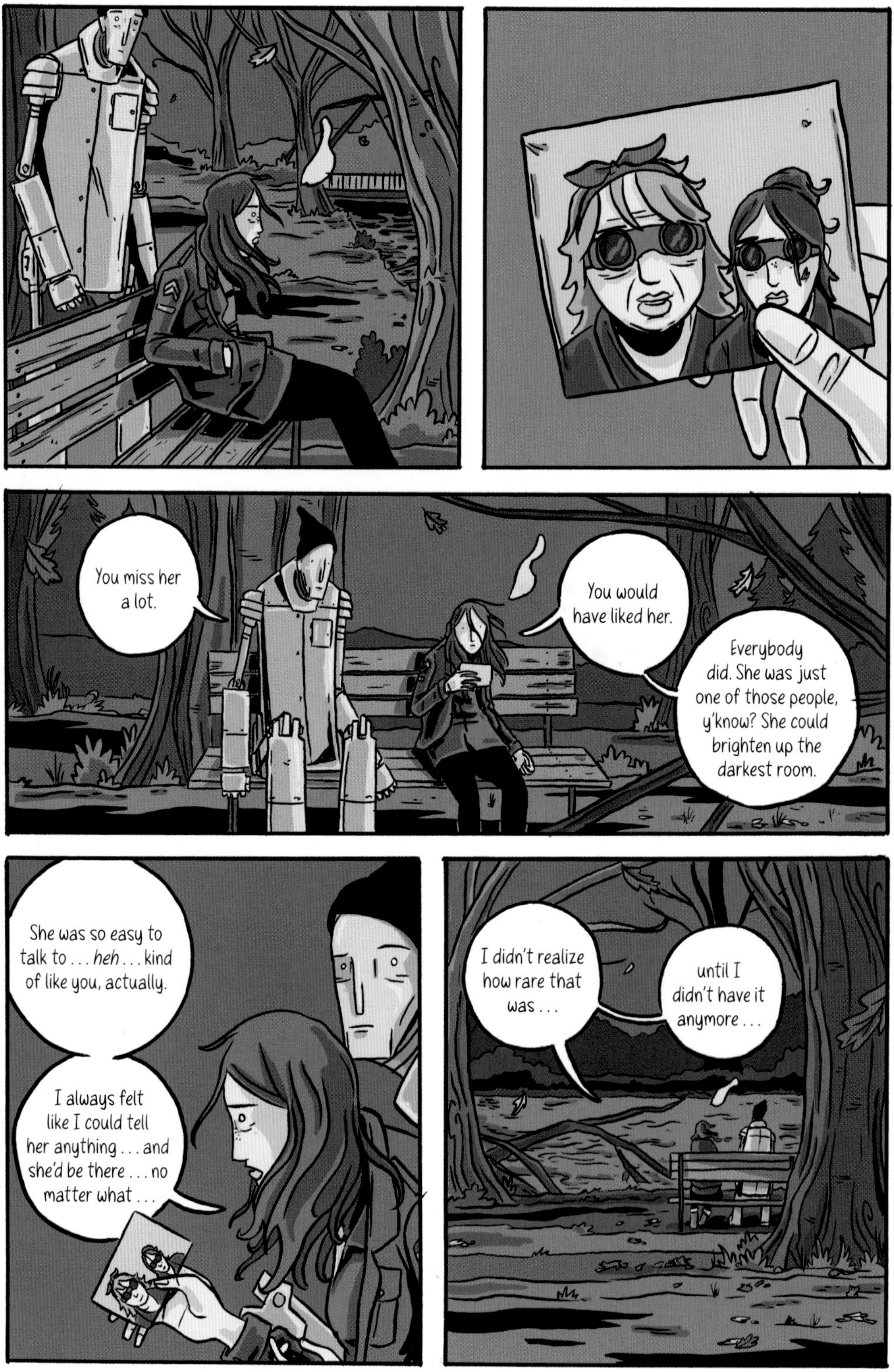
You miss her a lot.
You would have liked her.
Everybody did. She was just one of those people, y'know? She could brighten up the darkest room.
She was so easy to talk to . . . *heh* . . . kind of like you, actually.
I always felt like I could tell her anything . . . and she'd be there . . . no matter what . . .
I didn't realize how rare that was . . .
until I didn't have it anymore . . .

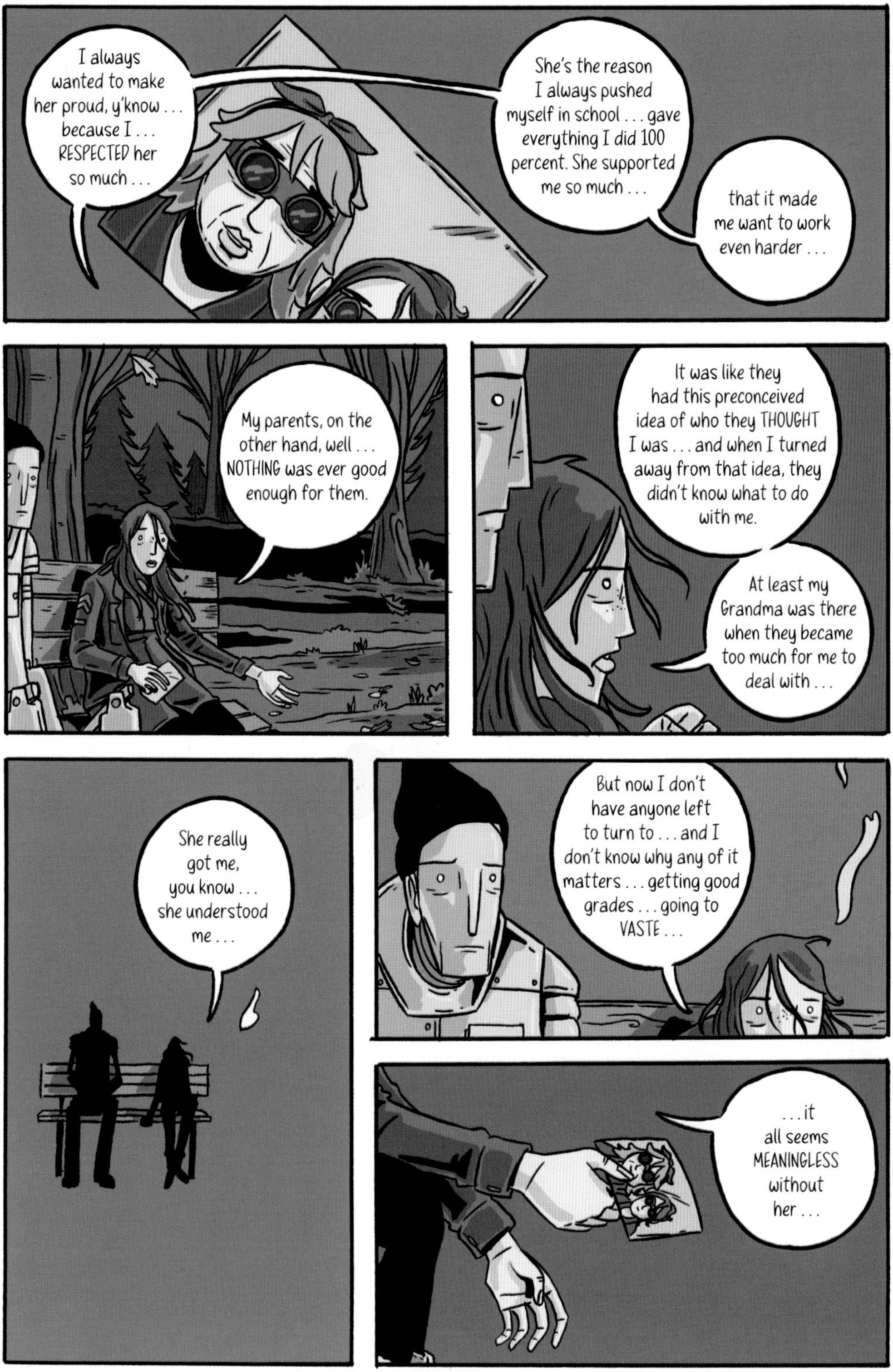
I always wanted to make her proud, y'know . . . because I . . . RESPECTED her so much . . .
She's the reason I always pushed myself in school . . . gave everything I did 100 percent. She supported me so much . . .
that it made me want to work even harder . . .
My parents, on the other hand, well . . . NOTHING was ever good enough for them.
It was like they had this preconceived idea of who they THOUGHT I was . . . and when I turned away from that idea, they didn't know what to do with me.
At least my Grandma was there when they became too much for me to deal with . . .
She really got me, you know . . . she understood me . . .
But now I don't have anyone left to turn to . . . and I don't know why any of it matters . . . getting good grades . . . going to VASTE . . .
. . . it all seems MEANINGLESS without her . . .

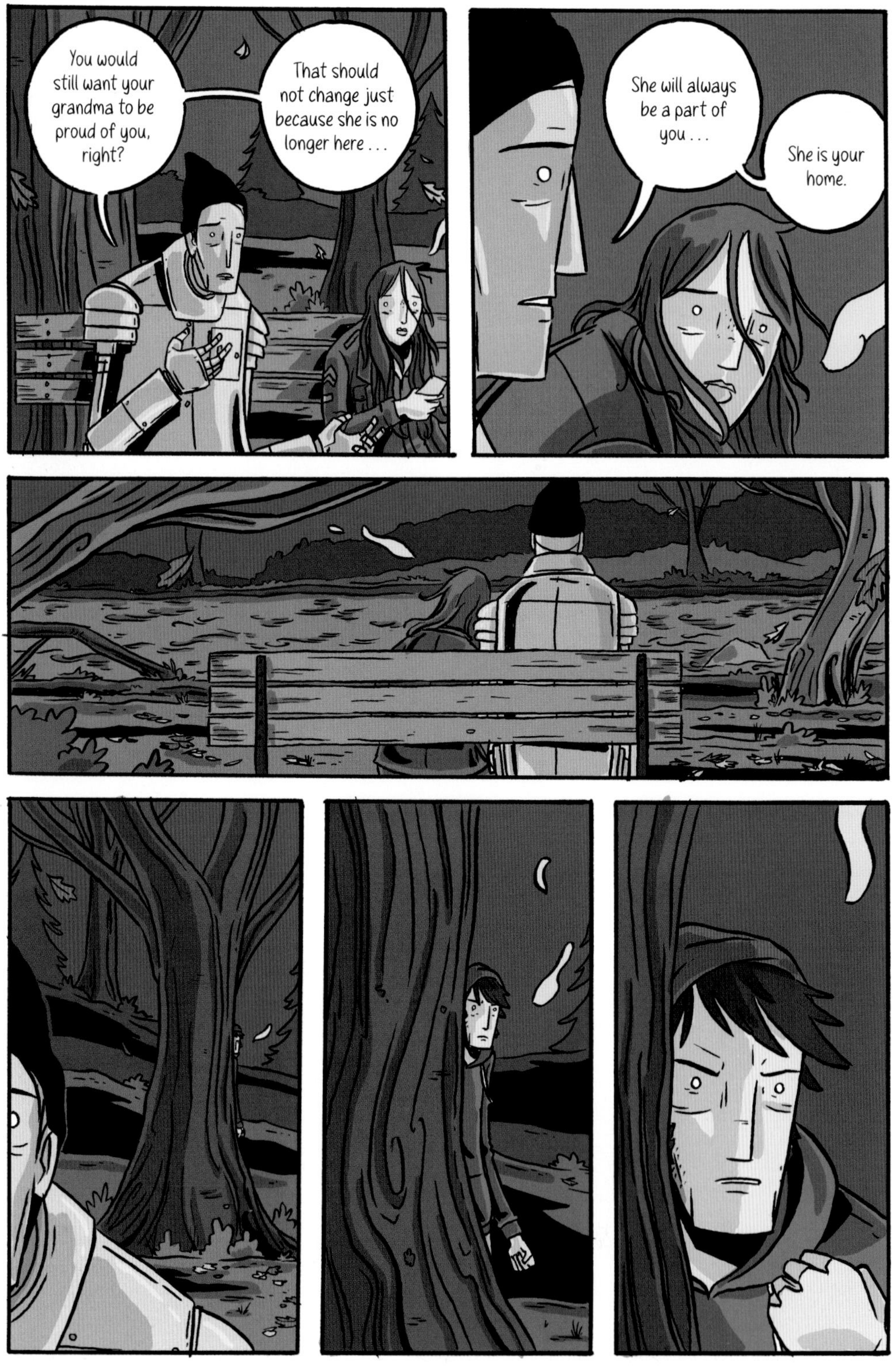

You would still want your grandma to be proud of you, right?
That should not change just because she is no longer here . . .
She will always be a part of you . . .
She is your home.

CHAPTER 11: A Ton of Bricks

...standing just outside Wamego, where a series of tornadoes has just swept through the town...

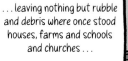

...leaving nothing but rubble and debris where once stood houses, farms and schools and churches...

...residents of this once-peaceful town are now left to pick up the pieces after this devastating ordeal...

≥YAWN≤

Morning, Mom.
Morning, Dad.

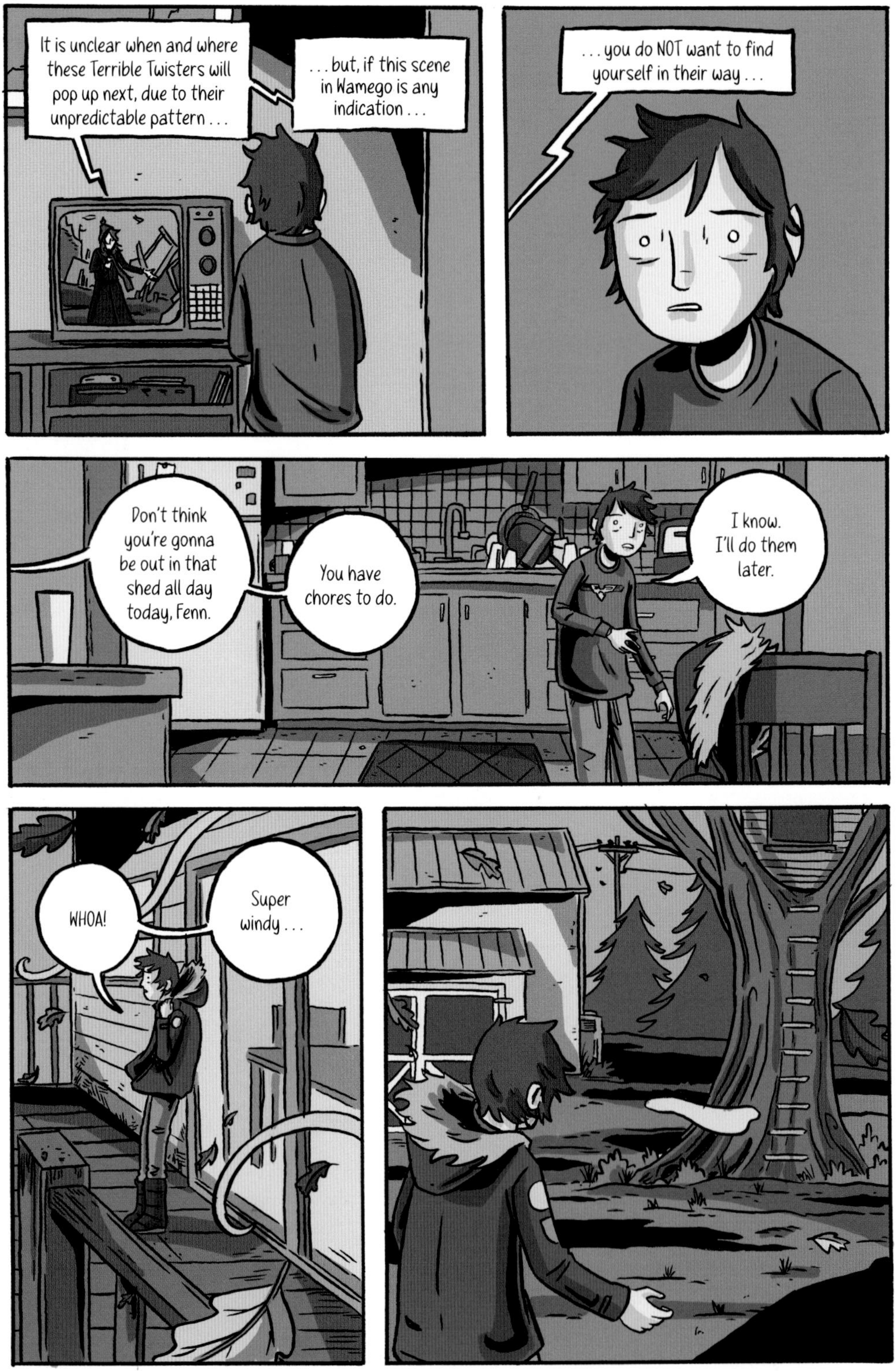
It is unclear when and where these Terrible Twisters will pop up next, due to their unpredictable pattern . . .
. . . but, if this scene in Wamego is any indication . . .
. . . you do NOT want to find yourself in their way . . .
Don't think you're gonna be out in that shed all day today, Fenn.
You have chores to do.
I know. I'll do them later.
WHOA!
Super windy . . .

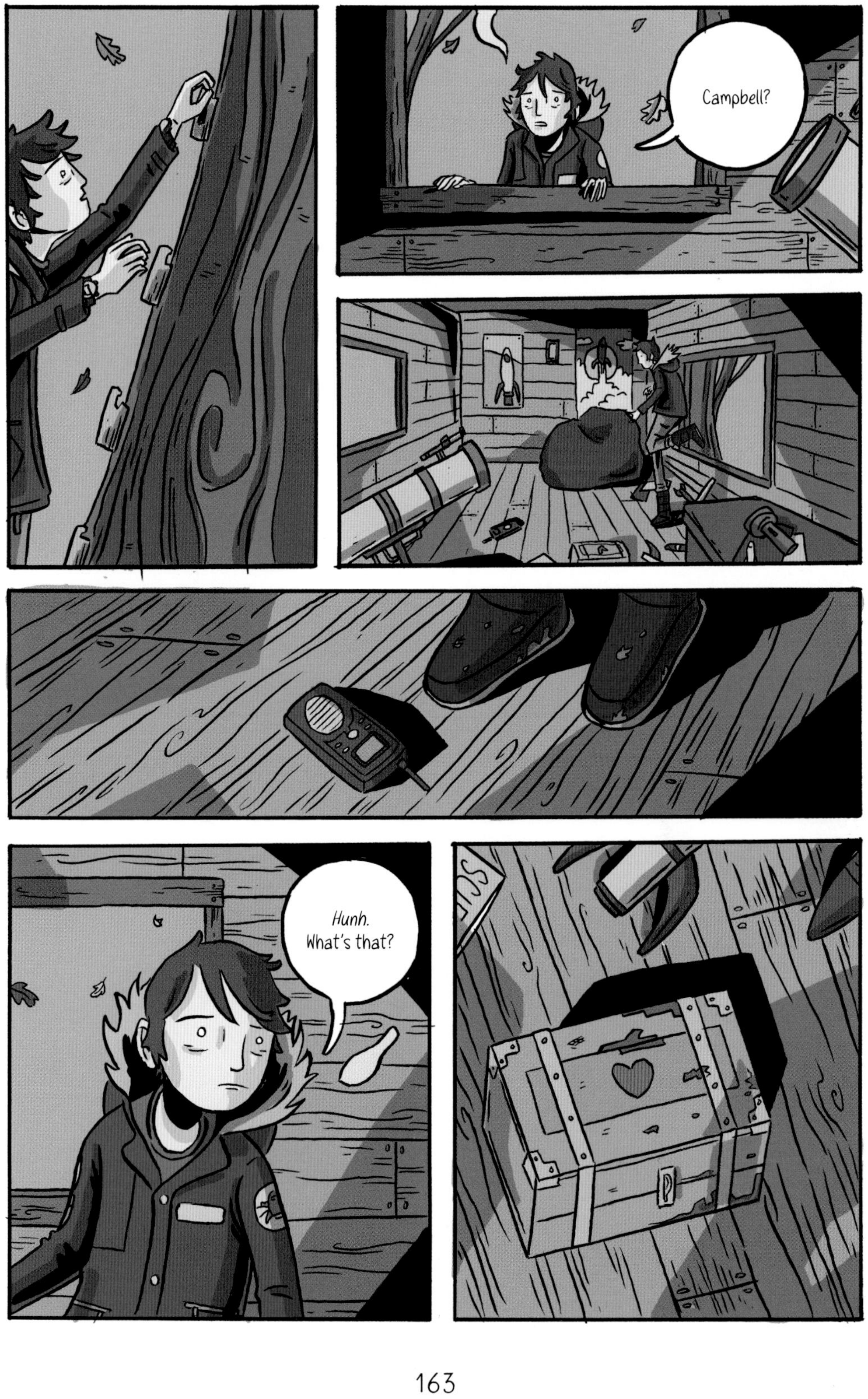
Campbell?
Hunh. What's that?

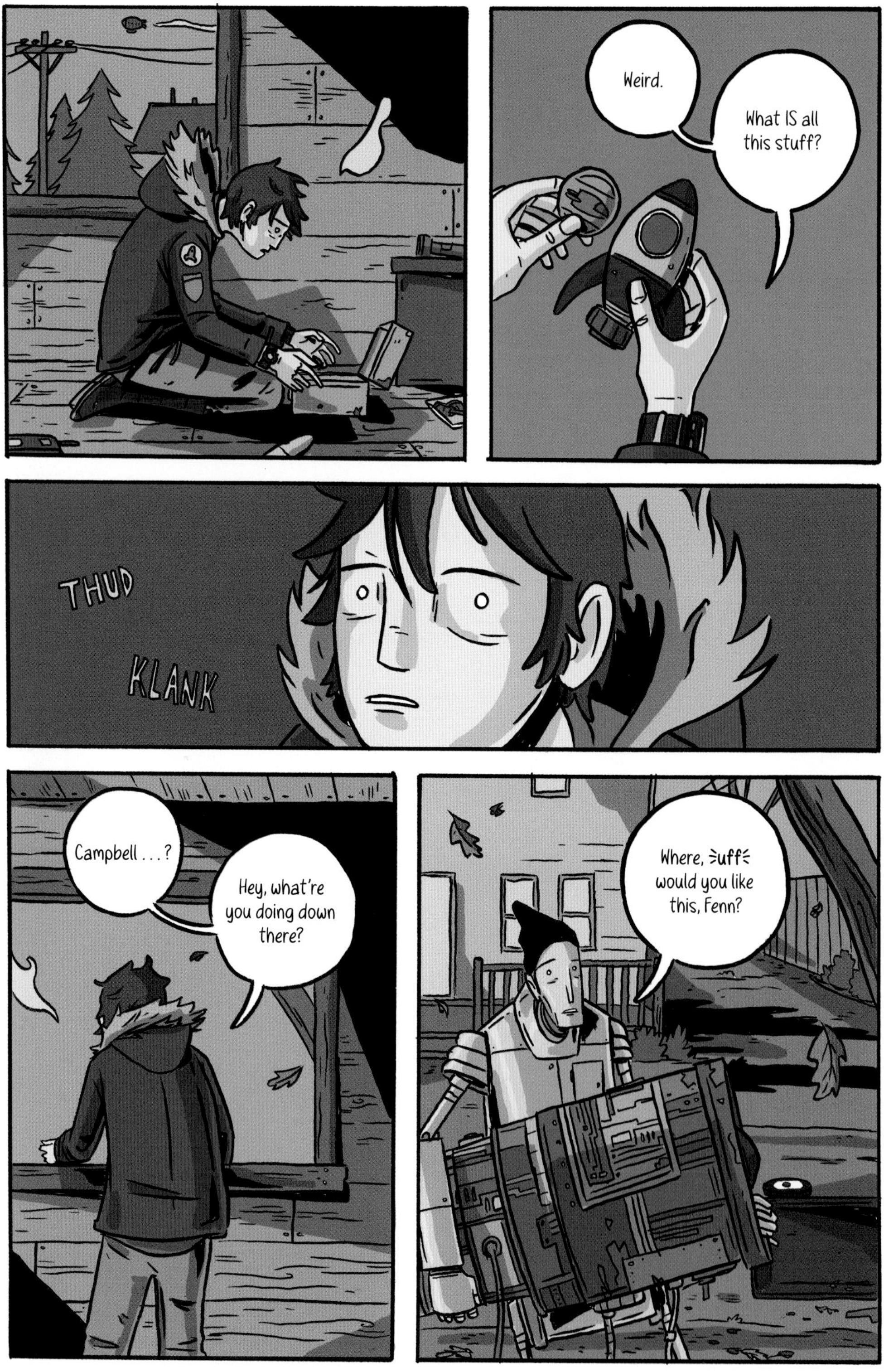
Weird.
What IS all this stuff?
THUD
KLANK
Campbell . . . ?
Hey, what're you doing down there?
Where, ≥uff≤ would you like this, Fenn?

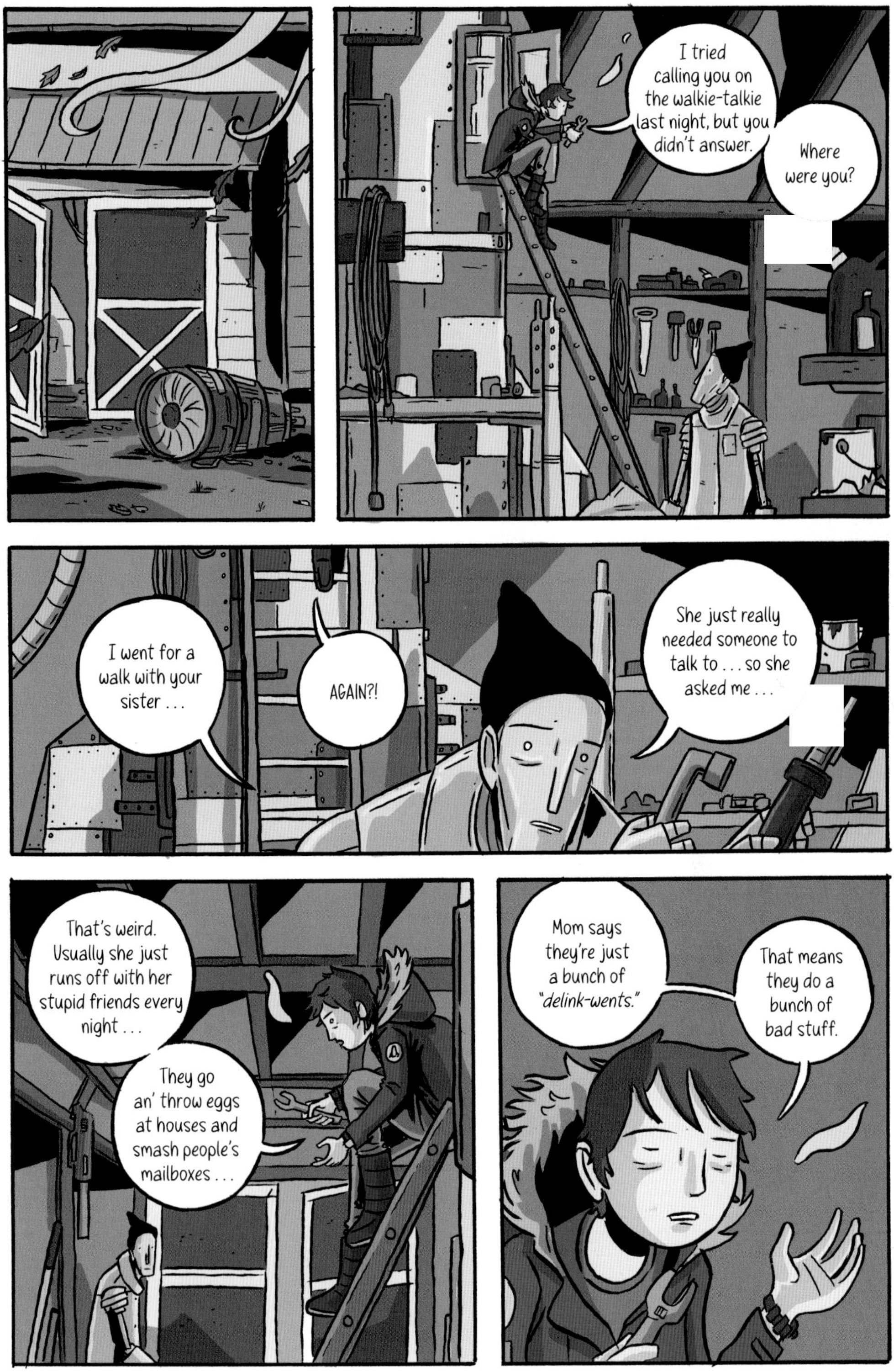
I tried calling you on the walkie-talkie last night, but you didn't answer.
Where were you?
I went for a walk with your sister . . .
AGAIN?!
She just really needed someone to talk to . . . so she asked me . . .
That's weird. Usually she just runs off with her stupid friends every night . . .
They go an' throw eggs at houses and smash people's mailboxes . . .
Mom says they're just a bunch of *"delink-wents."*
That means they do a bunch of bad stuff.

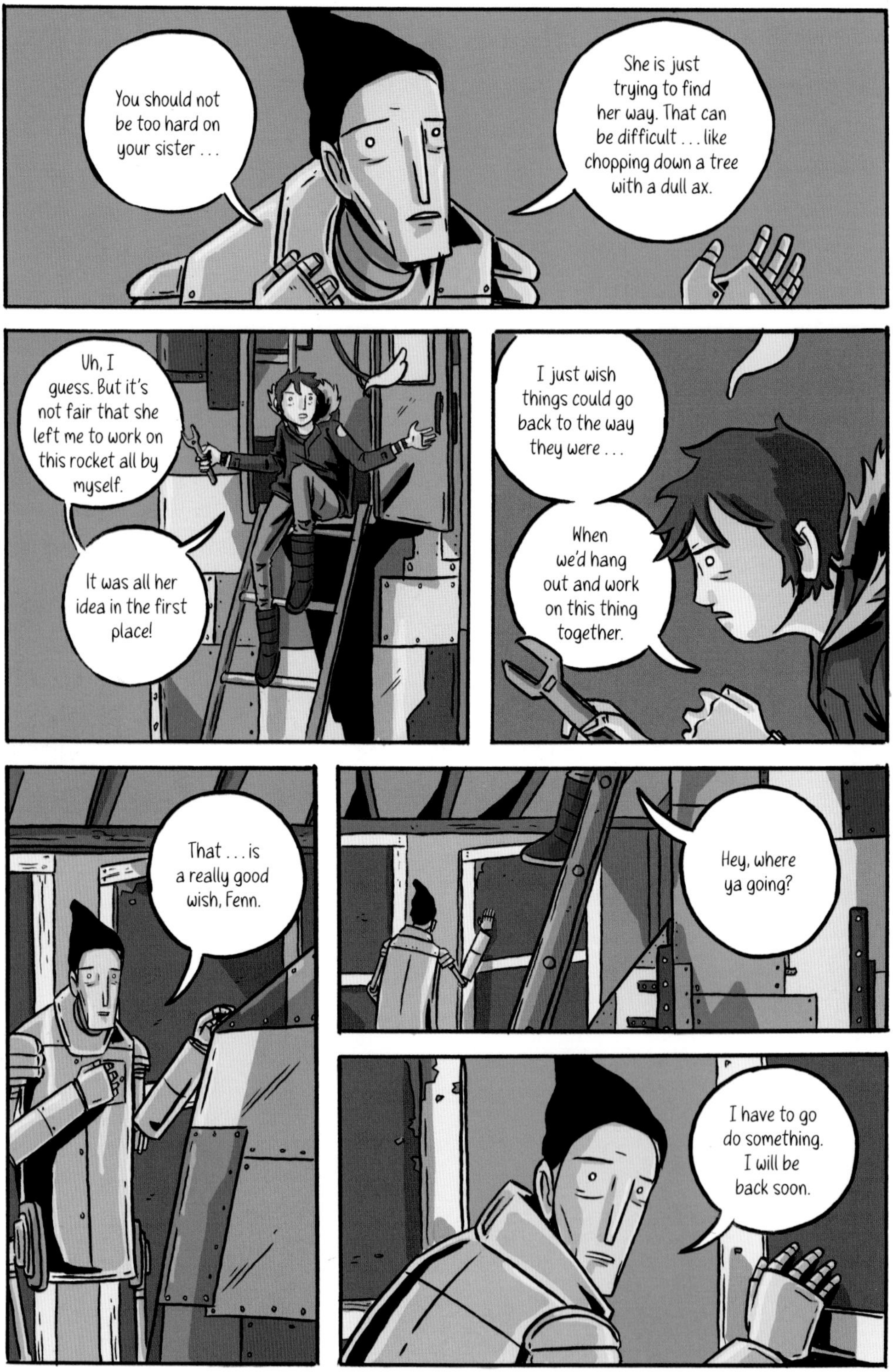
You should not be too hard on your sister . . .
She is just trying to find her way. That can be difficult . . . like chopping down a tree with a dull ax.
Uh, I guess. But it's not fair that she left me to work on this rocket all by myself.
It was all her idea in the first place!
I just wish things could go back to the way they were . . .
When we'd hang out and work on this thing together.
That . . . is a really good wish, Fenn.
Hey, where ya going?
I have to go do something. I will be back soon.

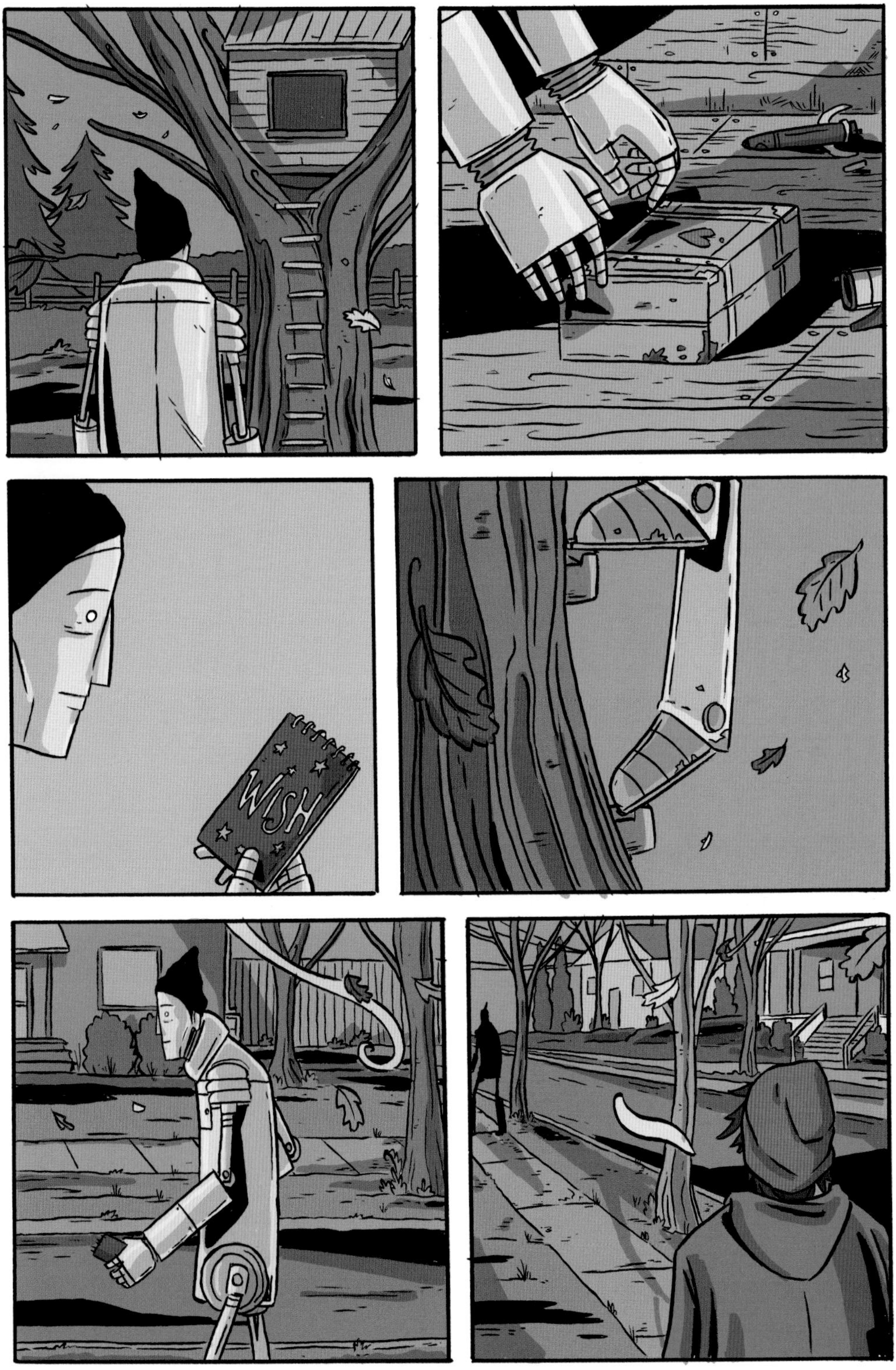
WISH

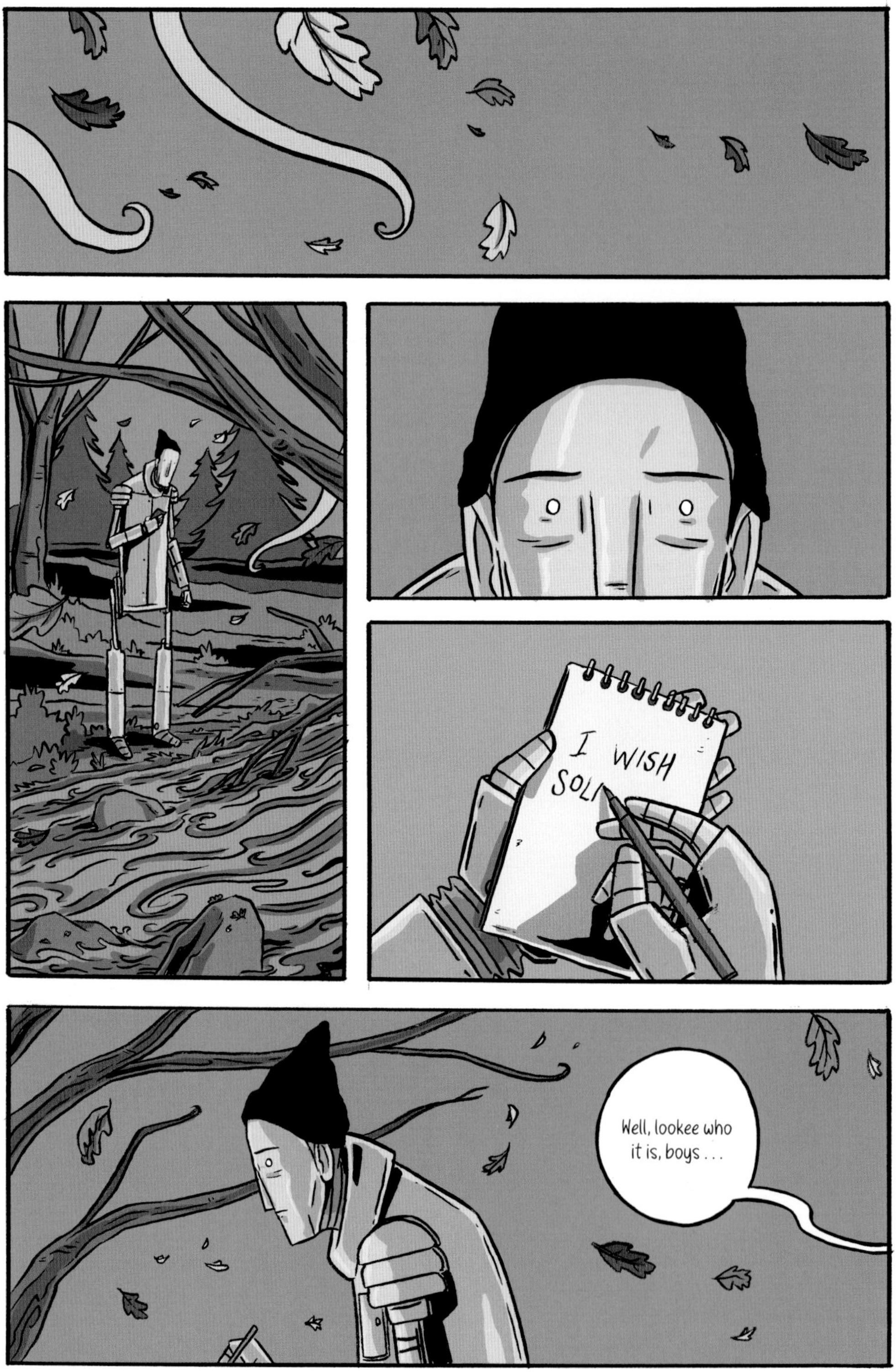
I WISH
SOL
Well, lookee who it is, boys . . .

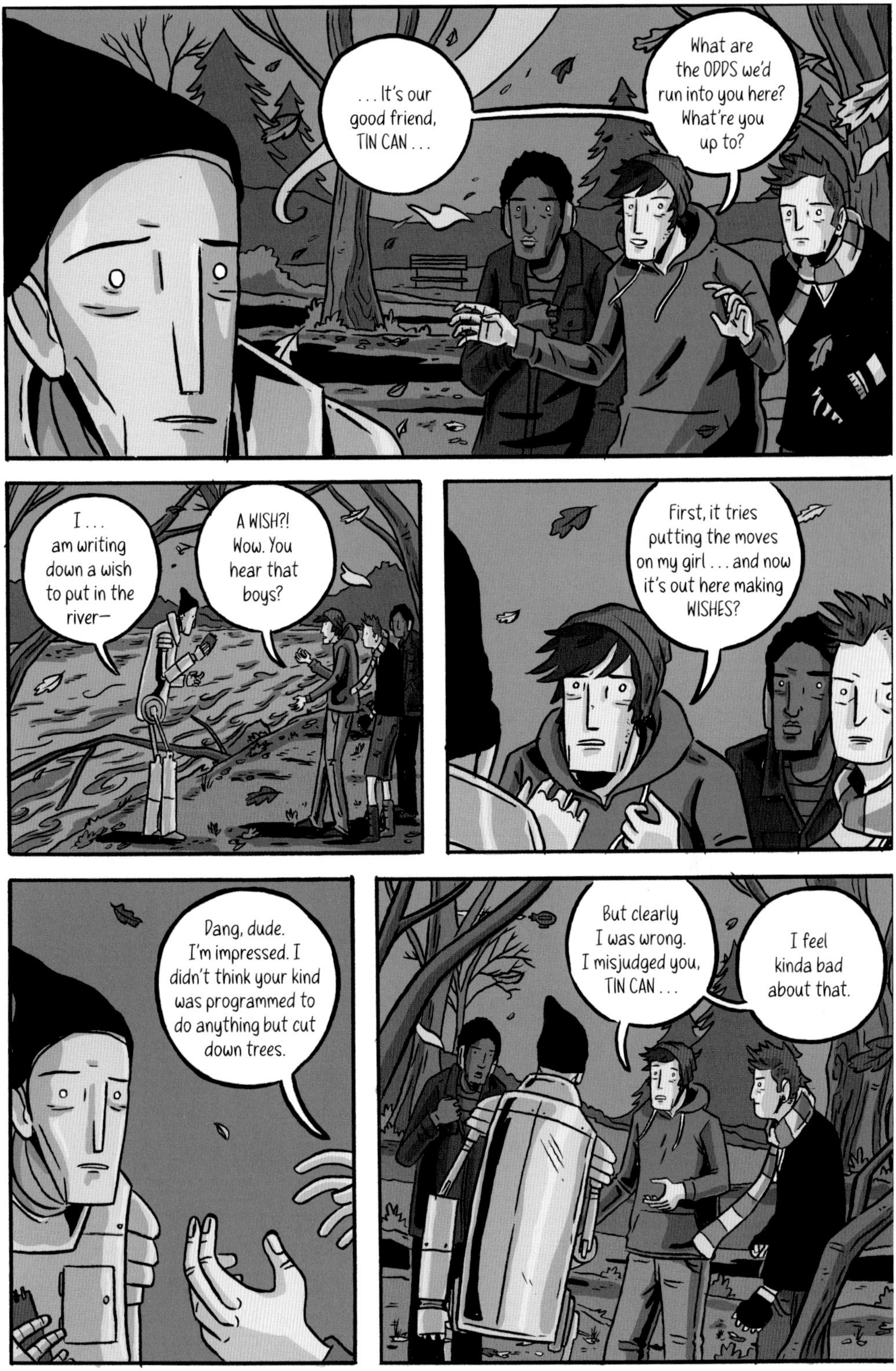
. . . It's our good friend, TIN CAN . . .
What are the ODDS we'd run into you here? What're you up to?
I . . . am writing down a wish to put in the river—
A WISH?! Wow. You hear that boys?
First, it tries putting the moves on my girl . . . and now it's out here making WISHES?
Dang, dude. I'm impressed. I didn't think your kind was programmed to do anything but cut down trees.
But clearly I was wrong. I misjudged you, TIN CAN . . .
I feel kinda bad about that.

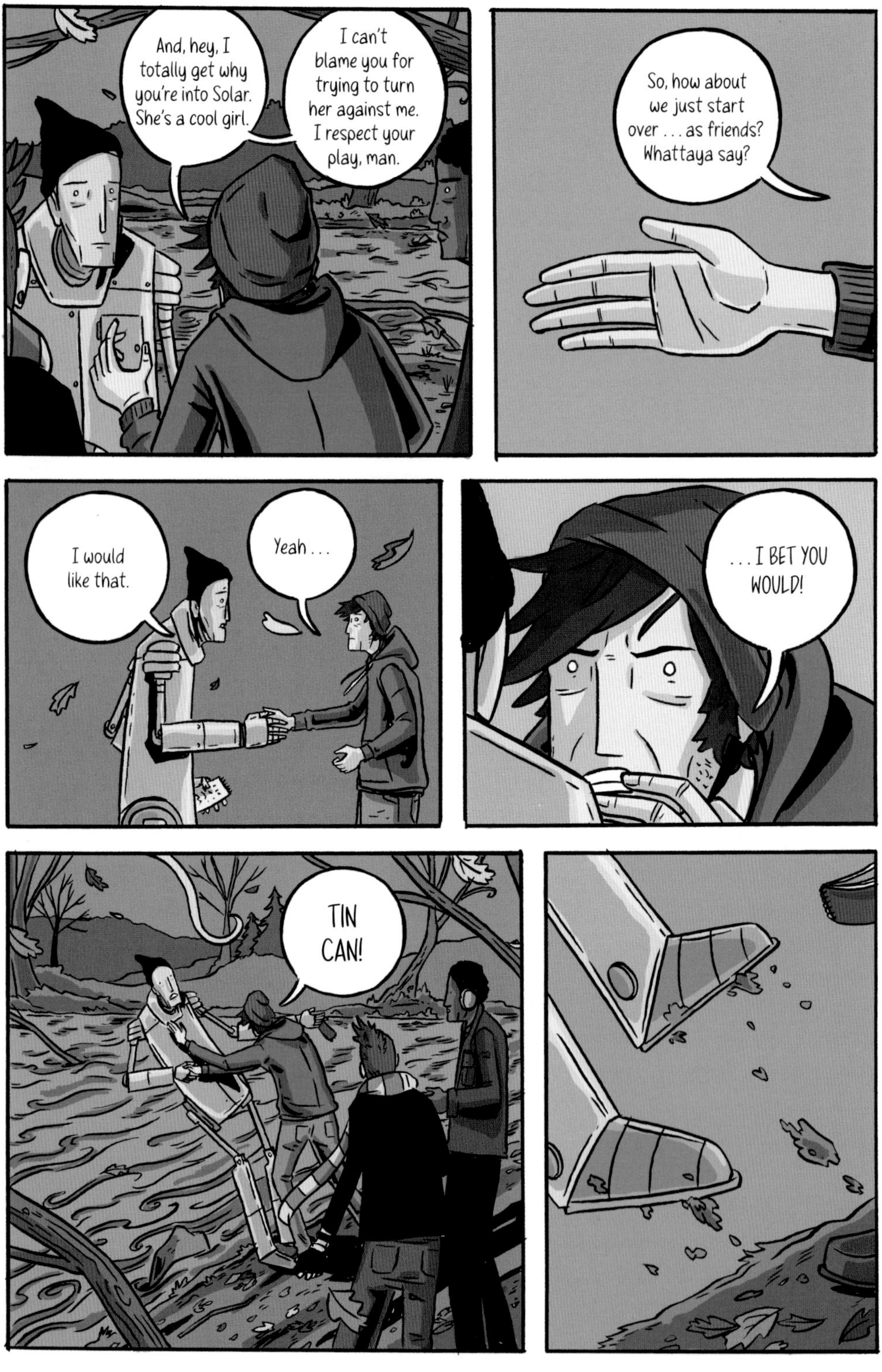
And, hey, I totally get why you're into Solar. She's a cool girl.
I can't blame you for trying to turn her against me. I respect your play, man.
So, how about we just start over . . . as friends? Whattaya say?
I would like that.
Yeah . . .
. . . I BET YOU WOULD!
TIN CAN!

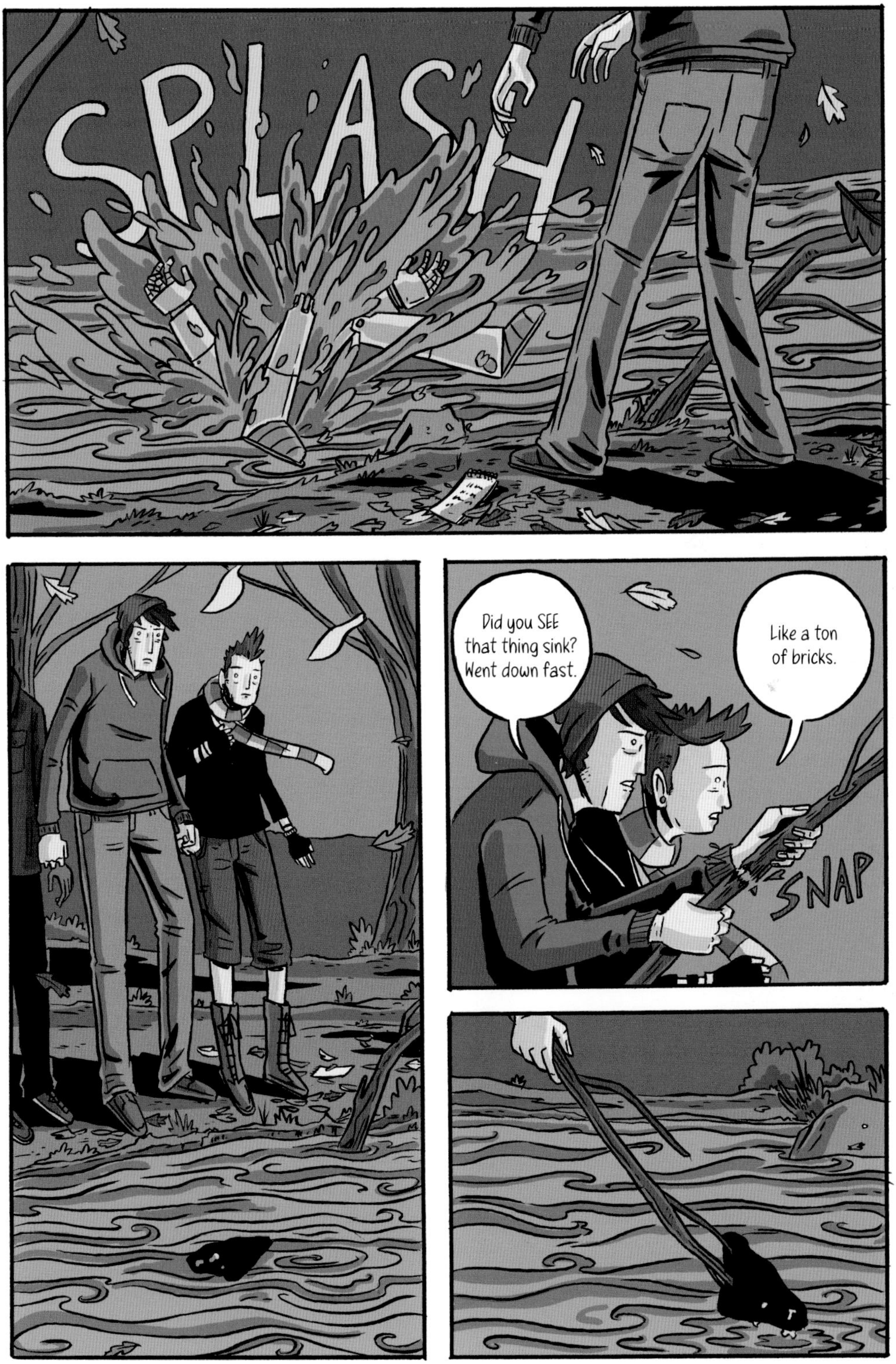
SPLASH
Did you SEE that thing sink? Went down fast.
Like a ton of bricks.
SNAP

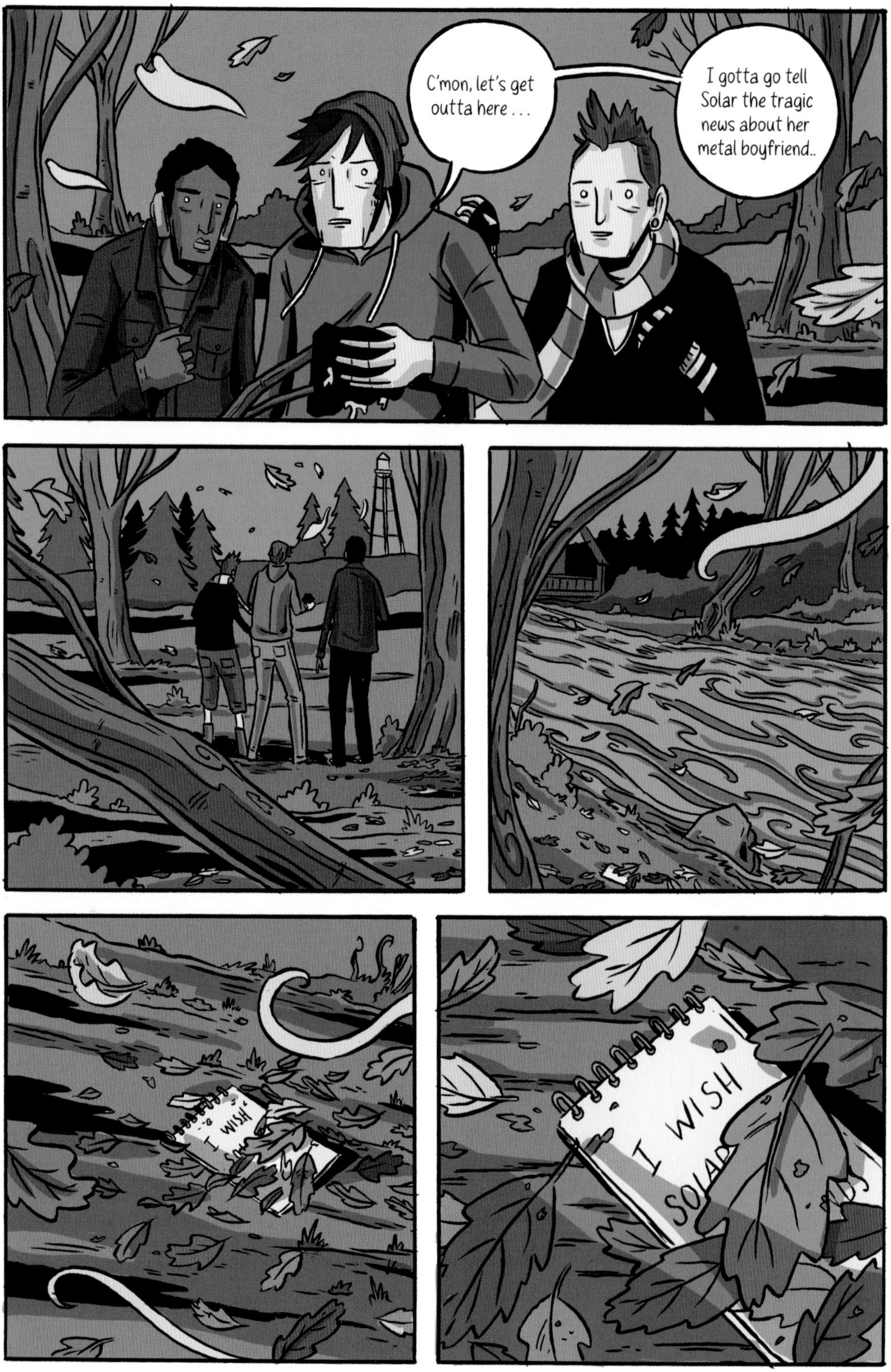
C'mon, let's get outta here . . .
I gotta go tell Solar the tragic news about her metal boyfriend..
I WISH
I WISH

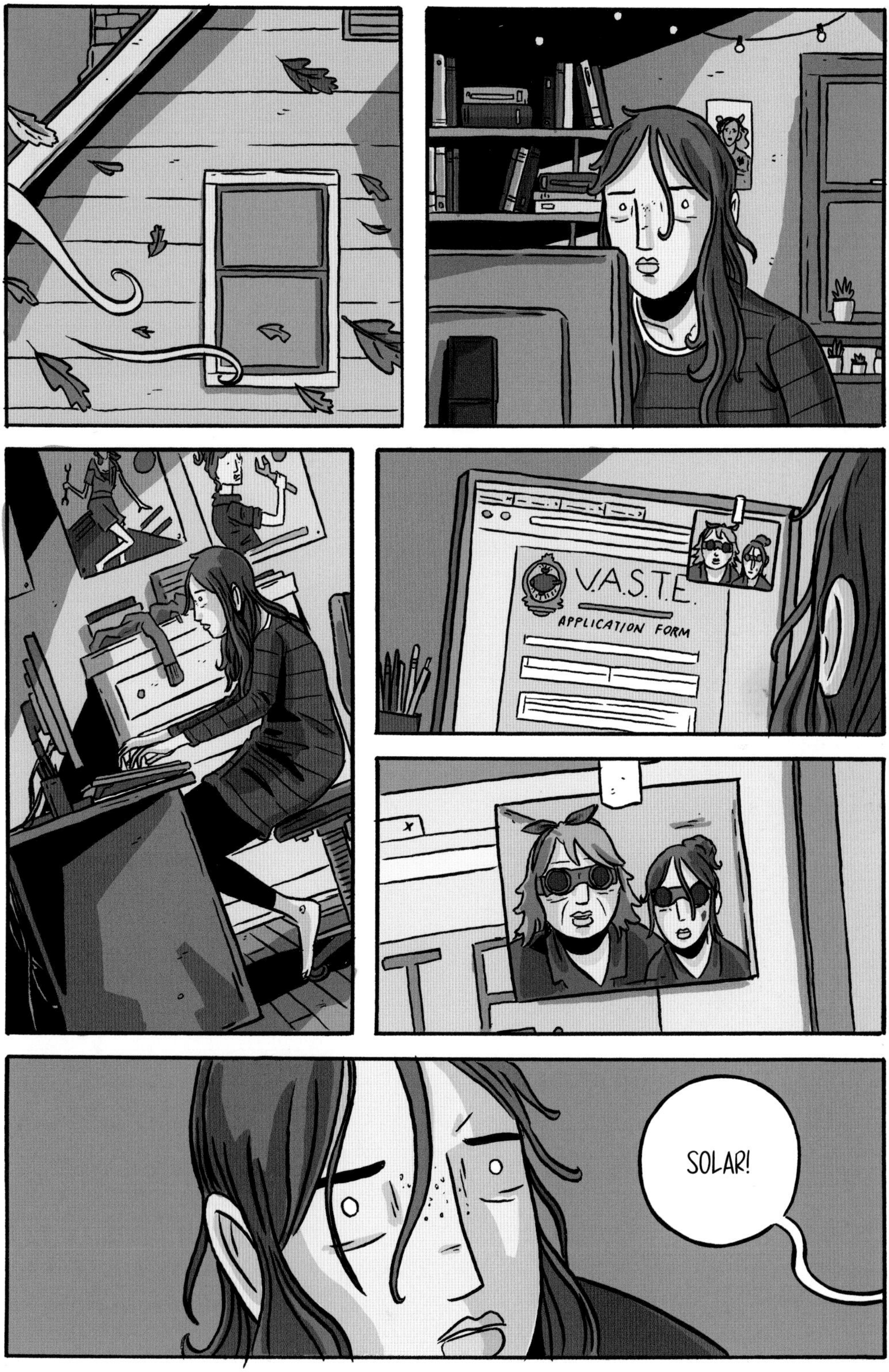
V.A.S.T.E.
APPLICATION FORM
SOLAR!

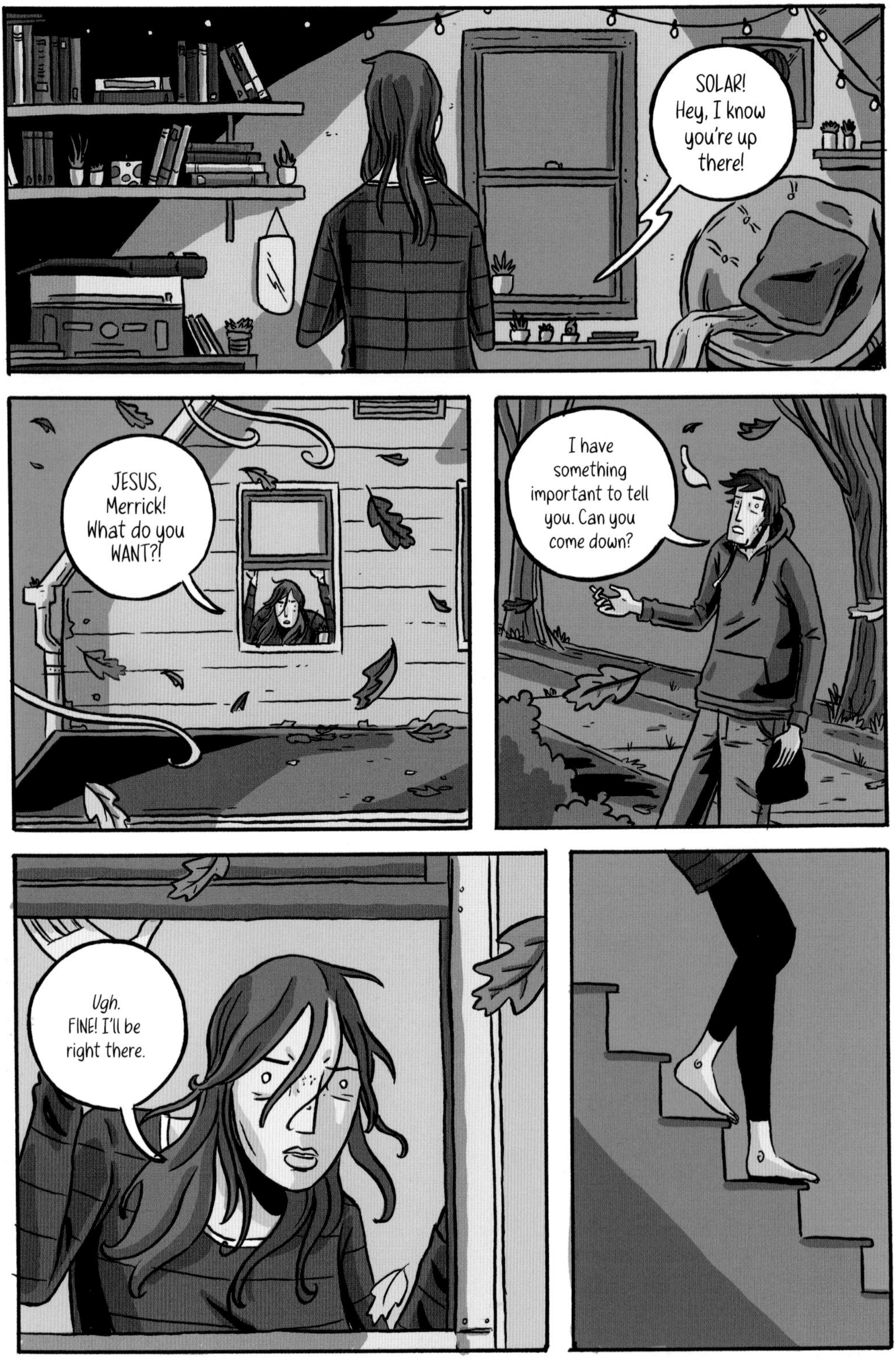
SOLAR! Hey, I know you're up there!
JESUS, Merrick! What do you WANT?!
I have something important to tell you. Can you come down?
Ugh. FINE! I'll be right there.

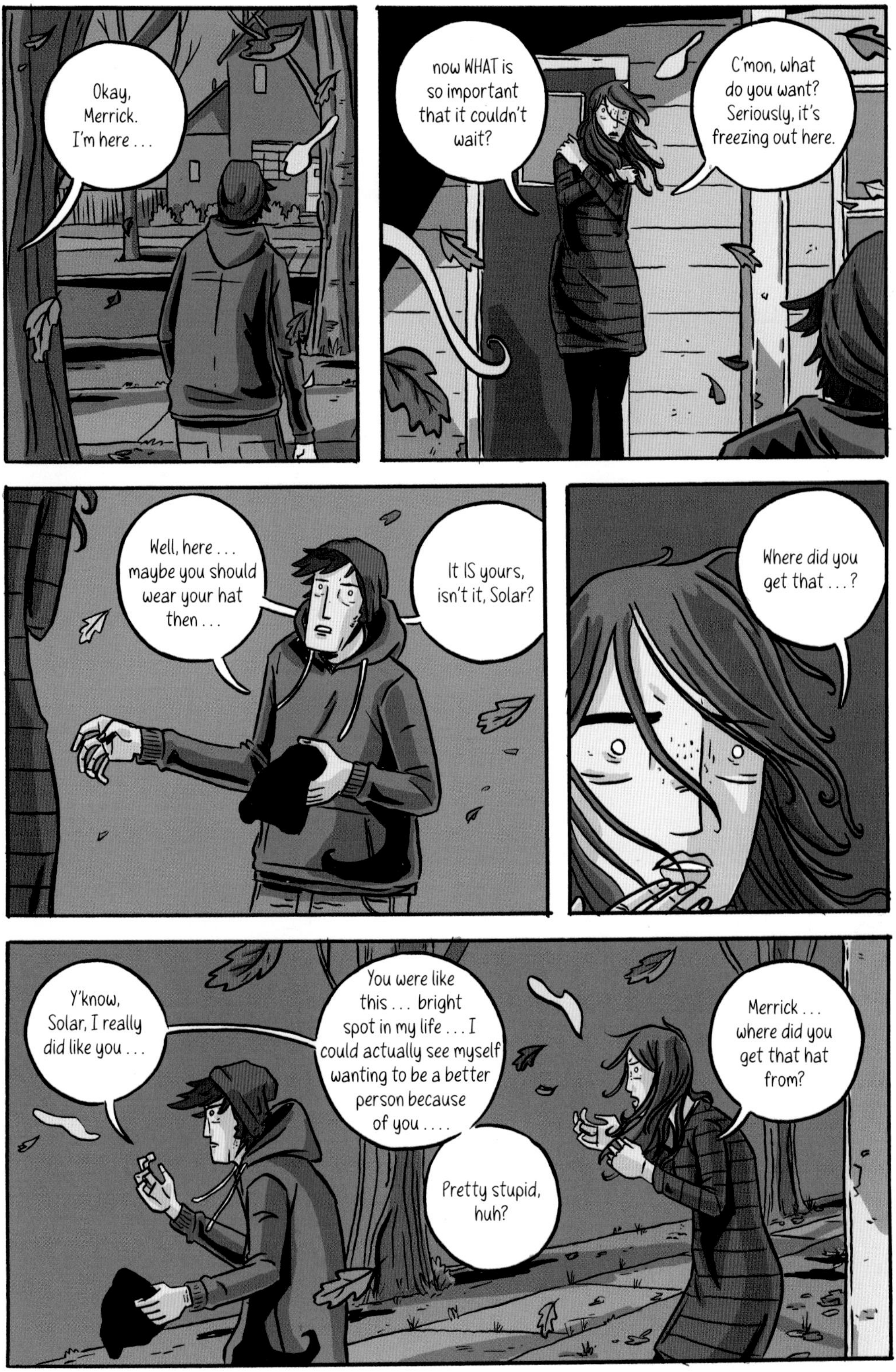

Okay, Merrick. I'm here . . .
now WHAT is so important that it couldn't wait?
C'mon, what do you want? Seriously, it's freezing out here.
Well, here . . . maybe you should wear your hat then . . .
It IS yours, isn't it, Solar?
Where did you get that . . . ?
Y'know, Solar, I really did like you . . .
You were like this . . . bright spot in my life . . . I could actually see myself wanting to be a better person because of you . . . .
Pretty stupid, huh?
Merrick . . . where did you get that hat from?

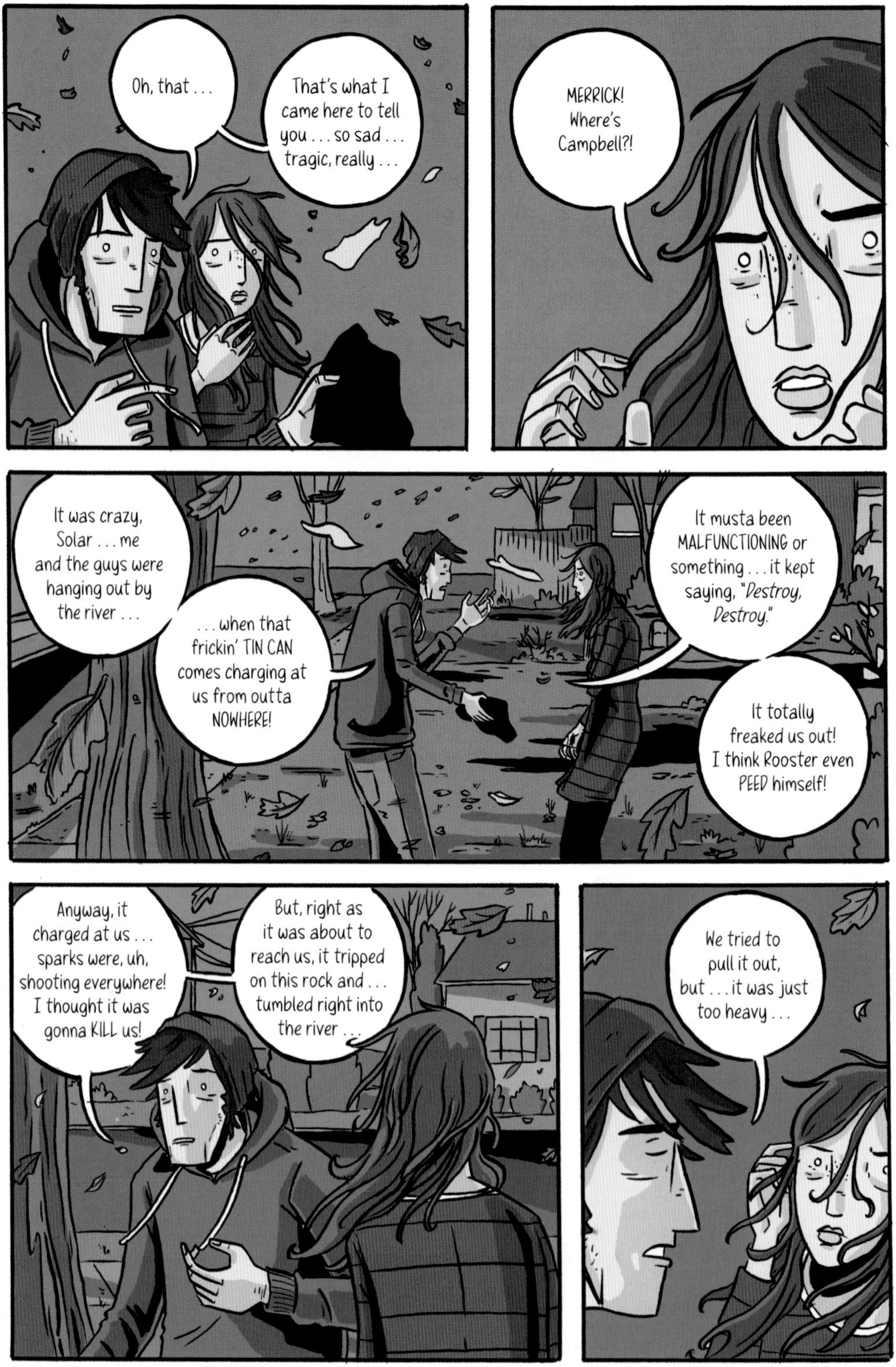
Oh, that . . .
That's what I came here to tell you . . . so sad . . . tragic, really . . .
MERRICK! Where's Campbell?!
It was crazy, Solar . . . me and the guys were hanging out by the river . . .
. . . when that frickin' TIN CAN comes charging at us from outta NOWHERE!
It musta been MALFUNCTIONING or something . . . it kept saying, "Destroy, Destroy."
It totally freaked us out! I think Rooster even PEED himself!
Anyway, it charged at us . . . sparks were, uh, shooting everywhere! I thought it was gonna KILL us!
But, right as it was about to reach us, it tripped on this rock and . . . tumbled right into the river . . .
We tried to pull it out, but . . . it was just too heavy . . .

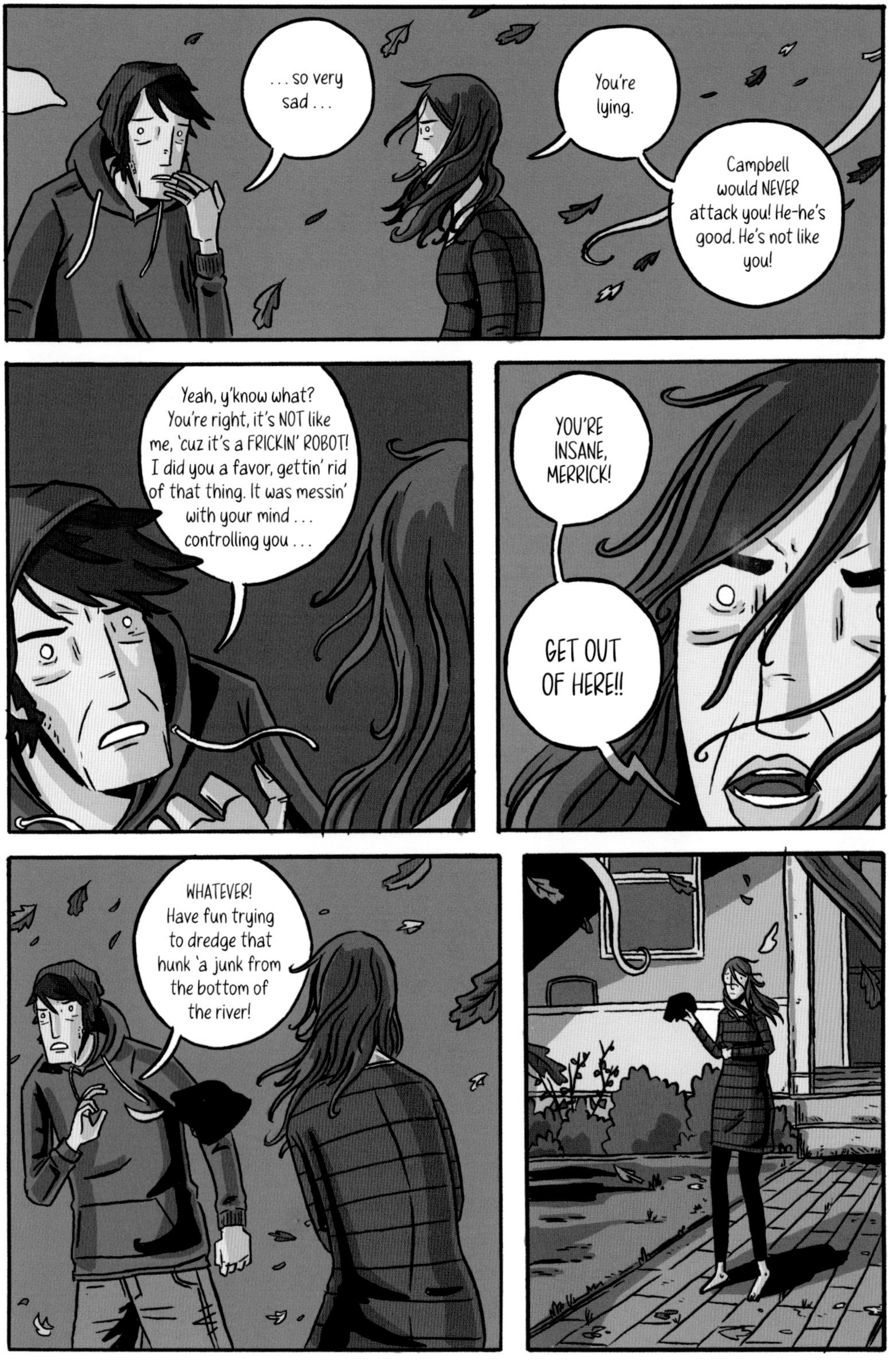

. . . so very sad . . .
You're lying.
Campbell would NEVER attack you! He-he's good. He's not like you!
Yeah, y'know what? You're right, it's NOT like me, 'cuz it's a FRICKIN' ROBOT! I did you a favor, gettin' rid of that thing. It was messin' with your mind . . . controlling you . . .
YOU'RE INSANE, MERRICK!
GET OUT OF HERE!!
WHATEVER! Have fun trying to dredge that hunk 'a junk from the bottom of the river!

CHAPTER 12: Blastoff

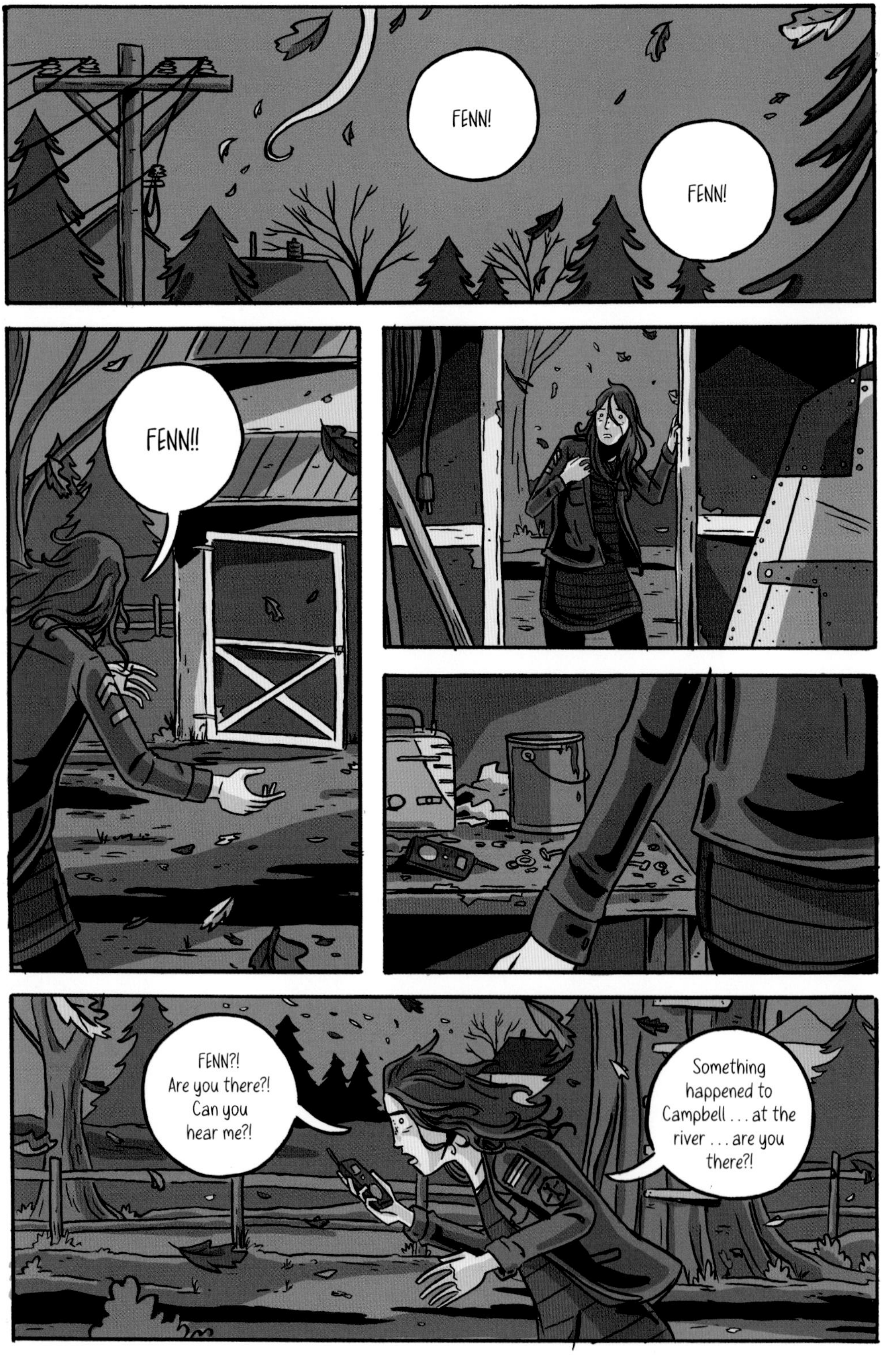
FENN!
FENN!
FENN!!
FENN?! Are you there?! Can you hear me?!
Something happened to Campbell . . . at the river . . . are you there?!

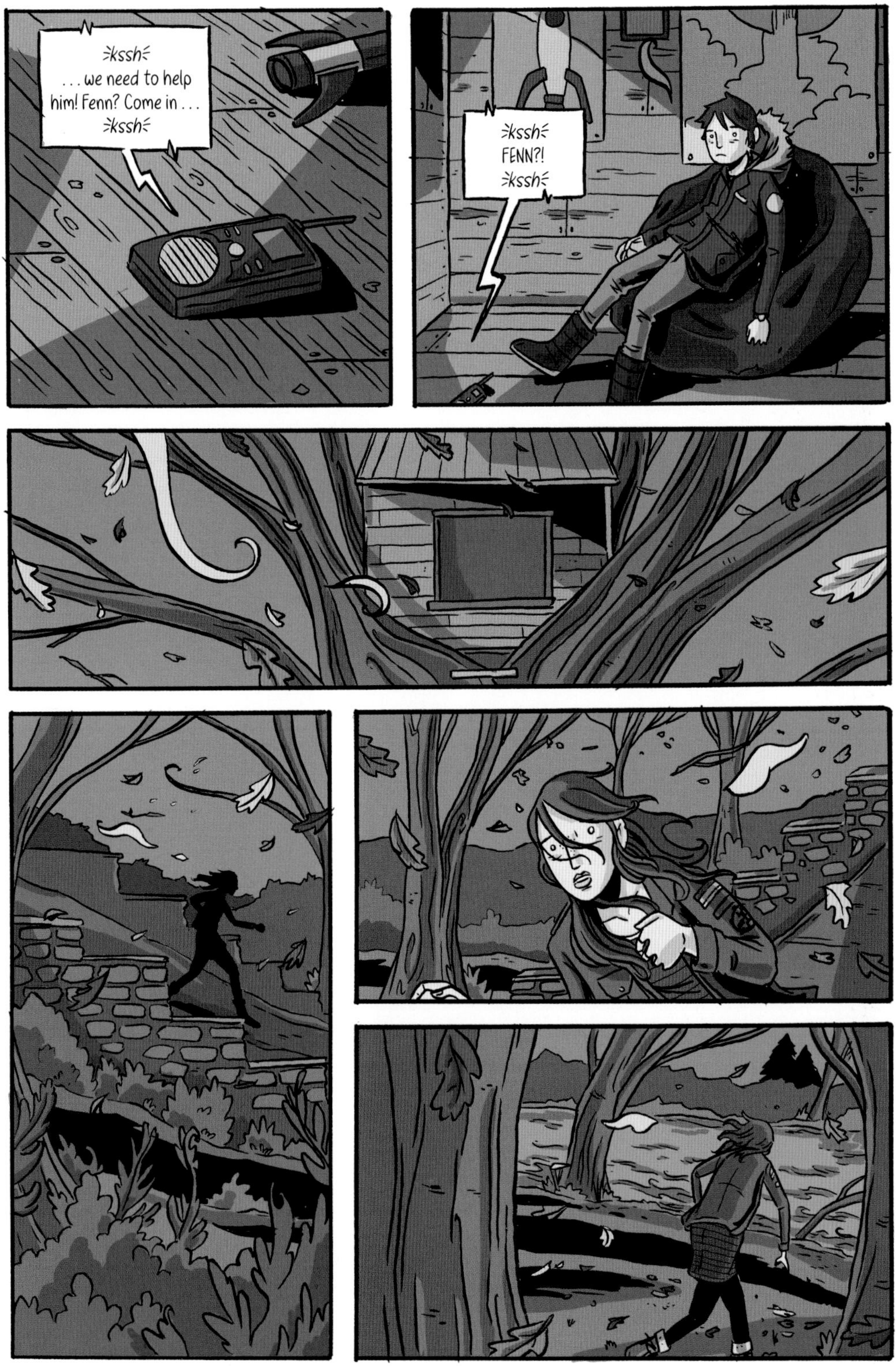
kssh
. . . we need to help him! Fenn? Come in . . .
kssh
kssh
FENN?!
kssh

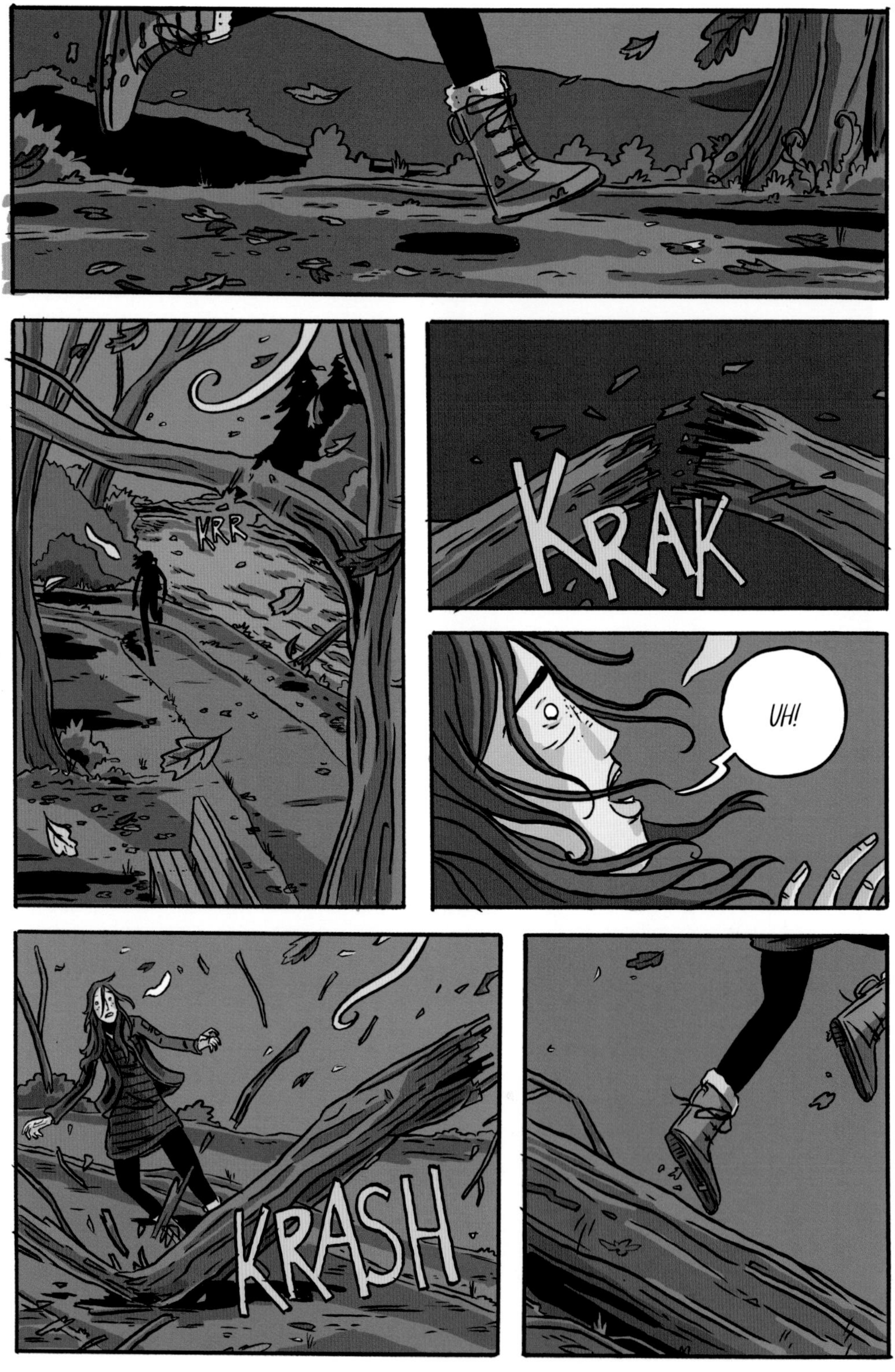
KRR
KRAK
UH!
KRASH

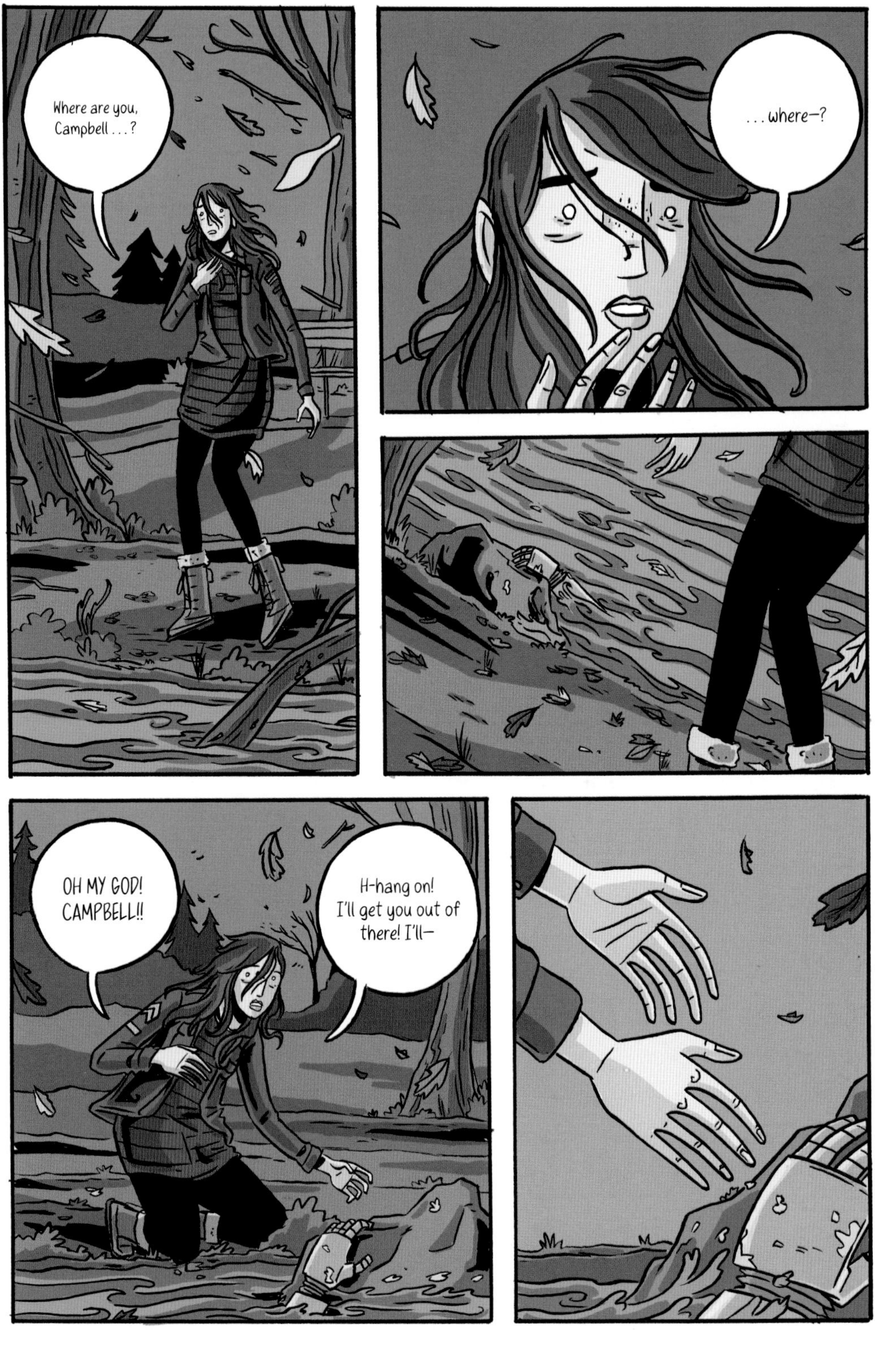
Where are you, Campbell . . . ?
. . . where—?
OH MY GOD! CAMPBELL!!
H-hang on! I'll get you out of there! I'll—

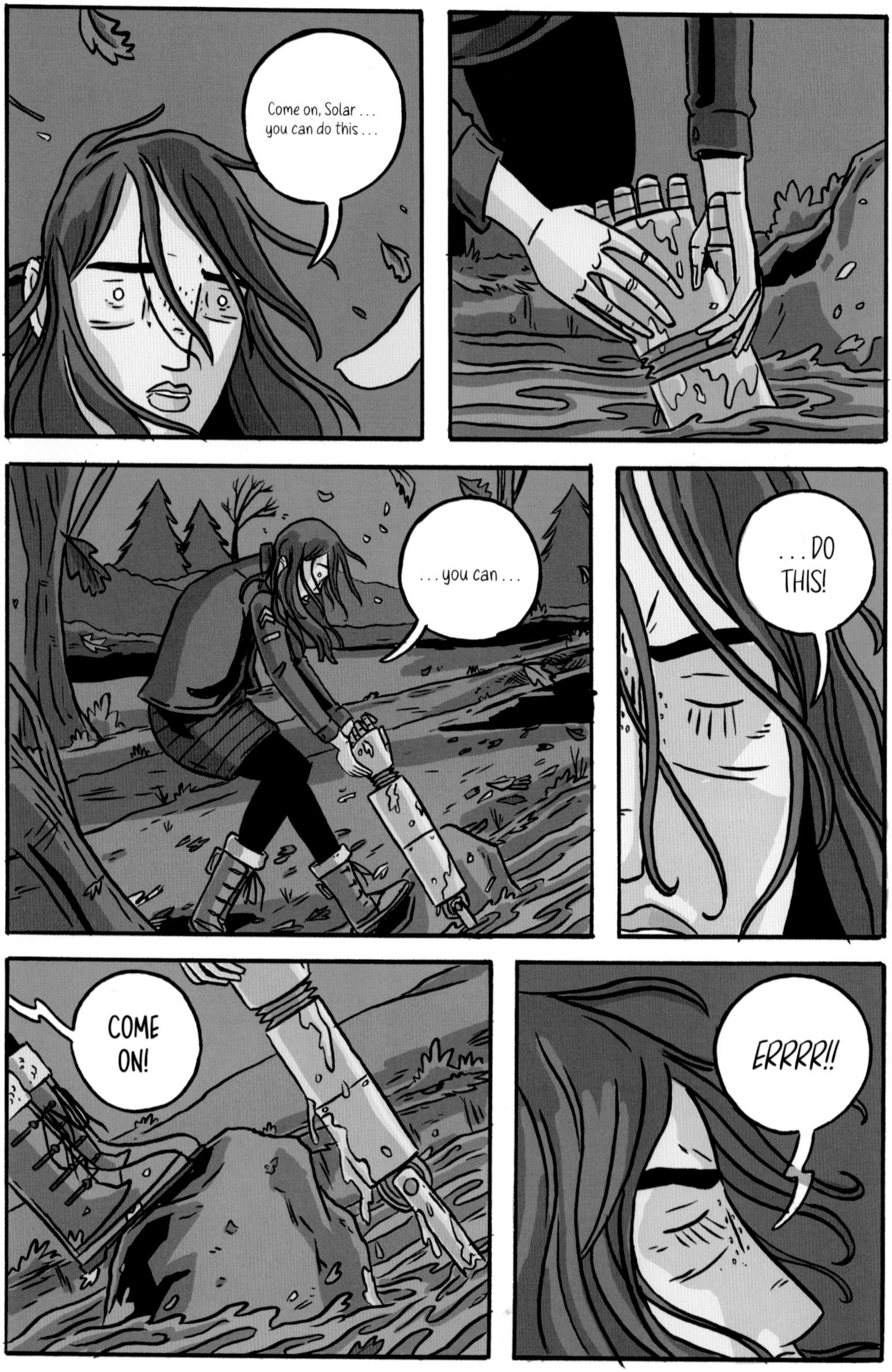
Come on, Solar . . . you can do this . . .
. . . you can . . .
. . . DO THIS!
COME ON!
ERRRR!!

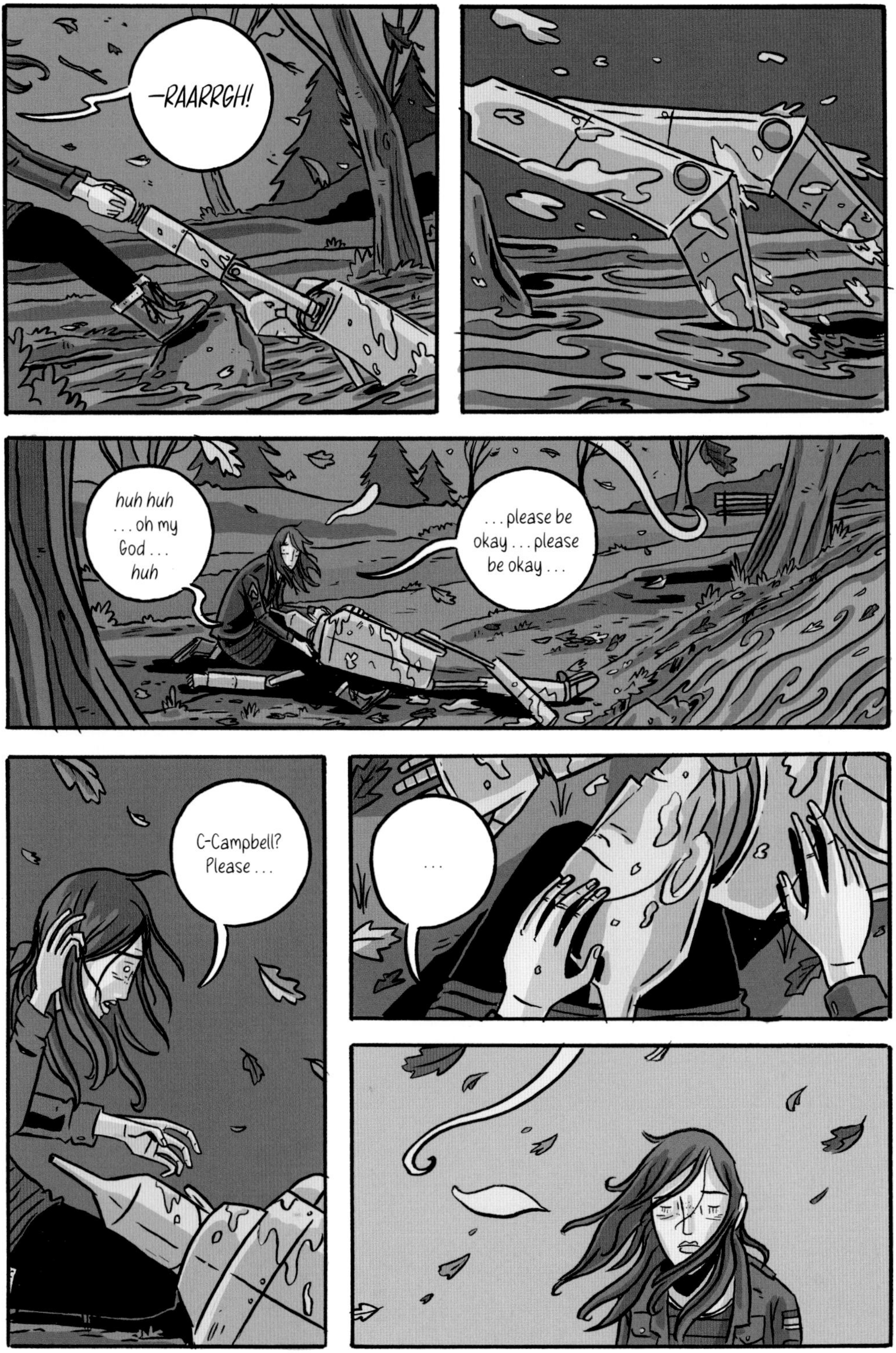
—RAARRGH!
huh huh
...oh my
God...
huh
...please be
okay...please
be okay...
C-Campbell?
Please...
...

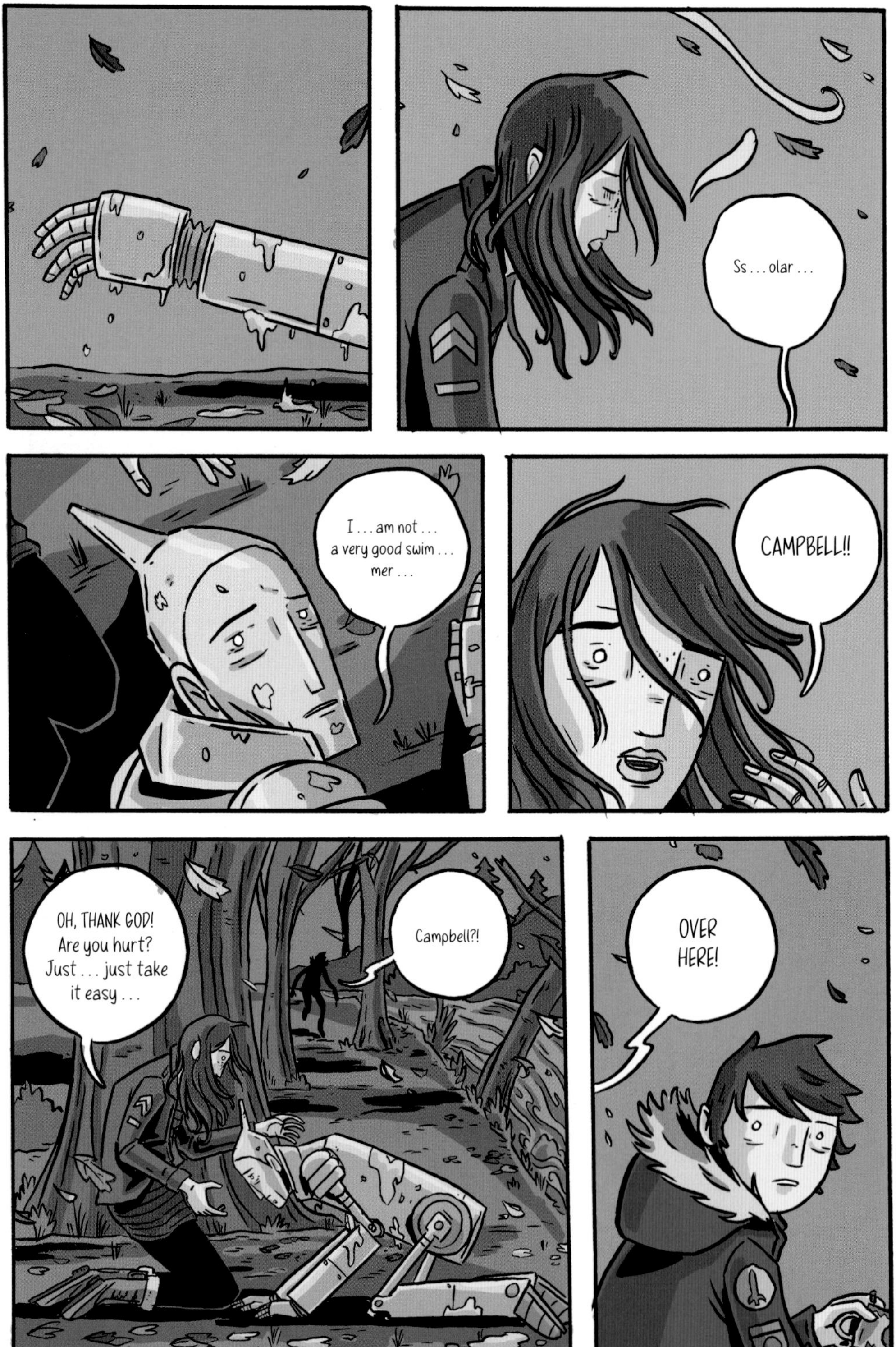
Ss . . . olar . . .
I . . . am not . . . a very good swim . . . mer . . .
CAMPBELL!!
OH, THANK GOD! Are you hurt? Just . . . just take it easy . . .
Campbell?!
OVER HERE!

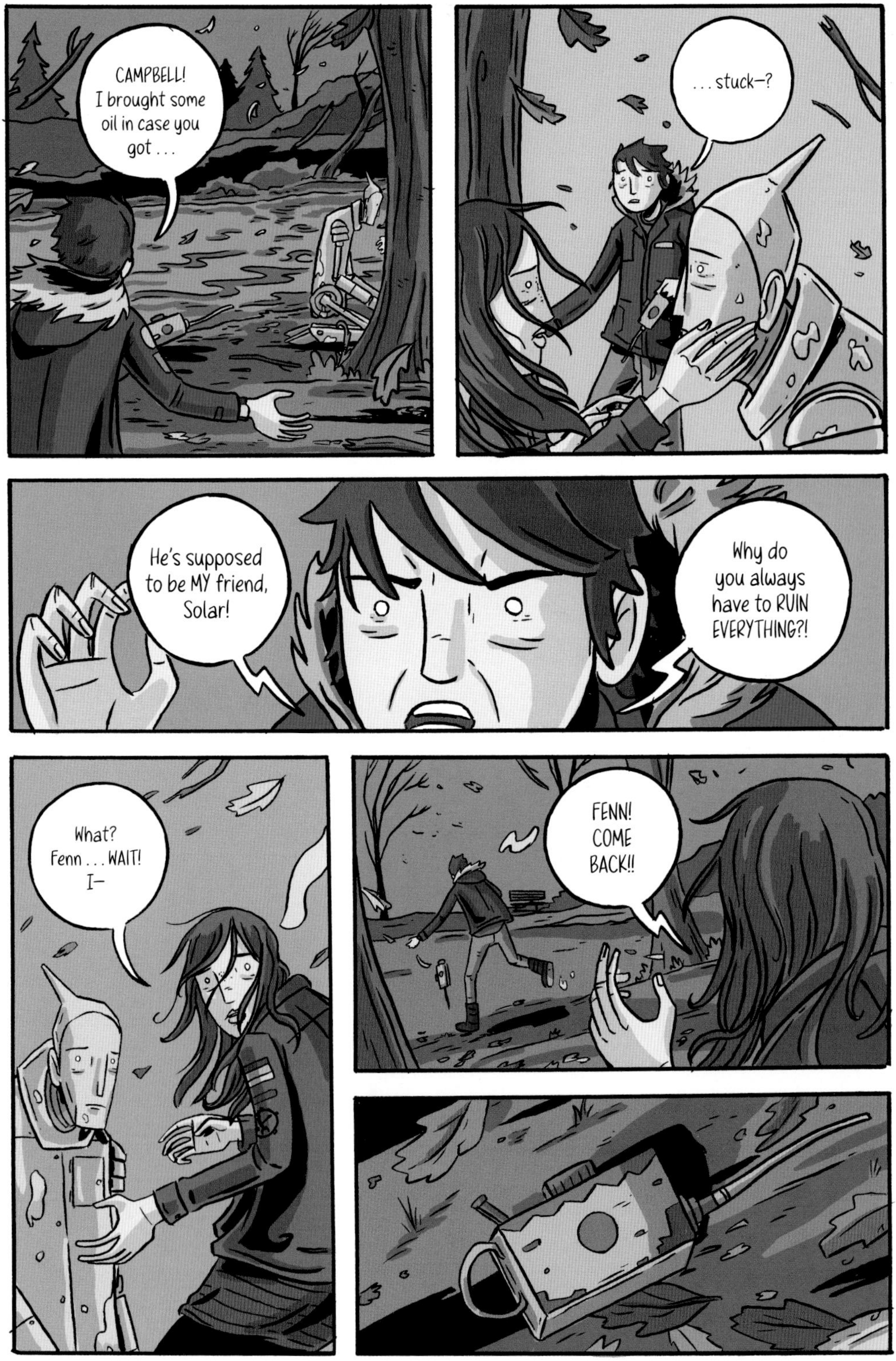
CAMPBELL! I brought some oil in case you got . . .
. . . stuck—?
He's supposed to be MY friend, Solar!
Why do you always have to RUIN EVERYTHING?!
What? Fenn . . . WAIT! I—
FENN! COME BACK!!

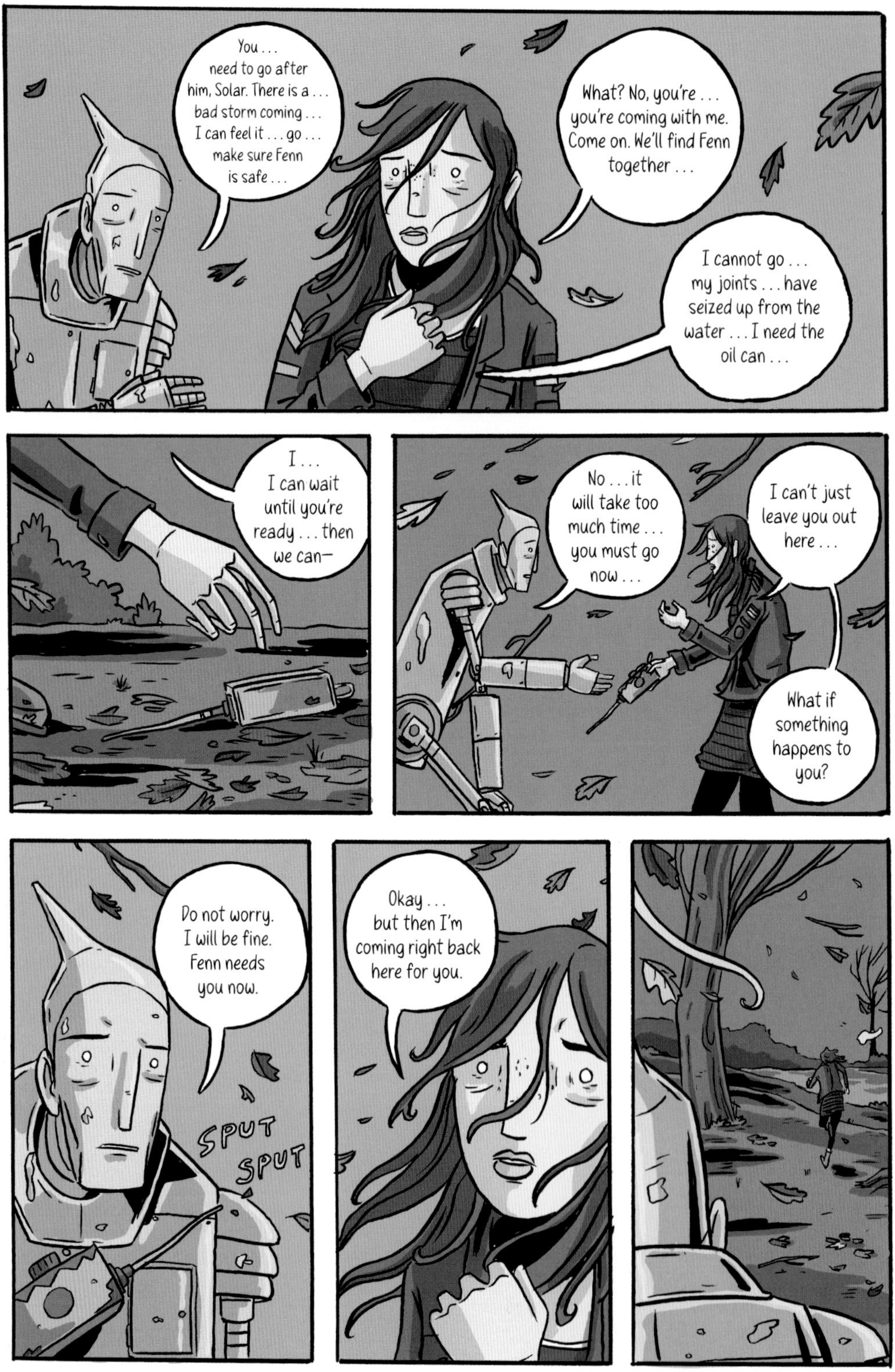
You . . . need to go after him, Solar. There is a . . . bad storm coming . . . I can feel it . . . go . . . make sure Fenn is safe . . .
What? No, you're . . . you're coming with me. Come on. We'll find Fenn together . . .
I cannot go . . . my joints . . . have seized up from the water . . . I need the oil can . . .
I . . . I can wait until you're ready . . . then we can—
No . . . it will take too much time . . . you must go now . . .
I can't just leave you out here . . .
What if something happens to you?
Do not worry. I will be fine. Fenn needs you now.
SPUT SPUT
Okay . . . but then I'm coming right back here for you.

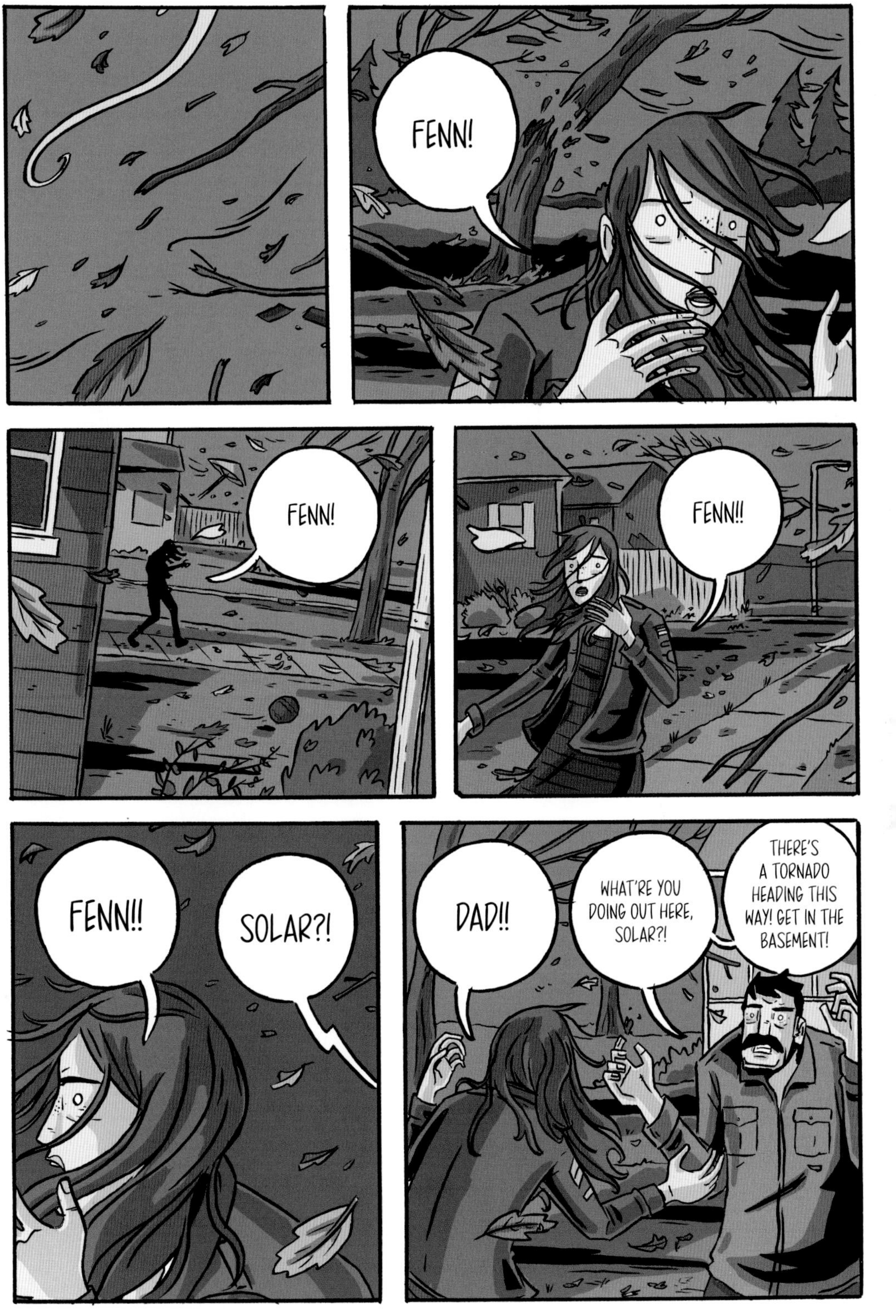
FENN!
FENN!
FENN!!
FENN!!
SOLAR?!
DAD!!
WHAT'RE YOU DOING OUT HERE, SOLAR?!
THERE'S A TORNADO HEADING THIS WAY! GET IN THE BASEMENT!

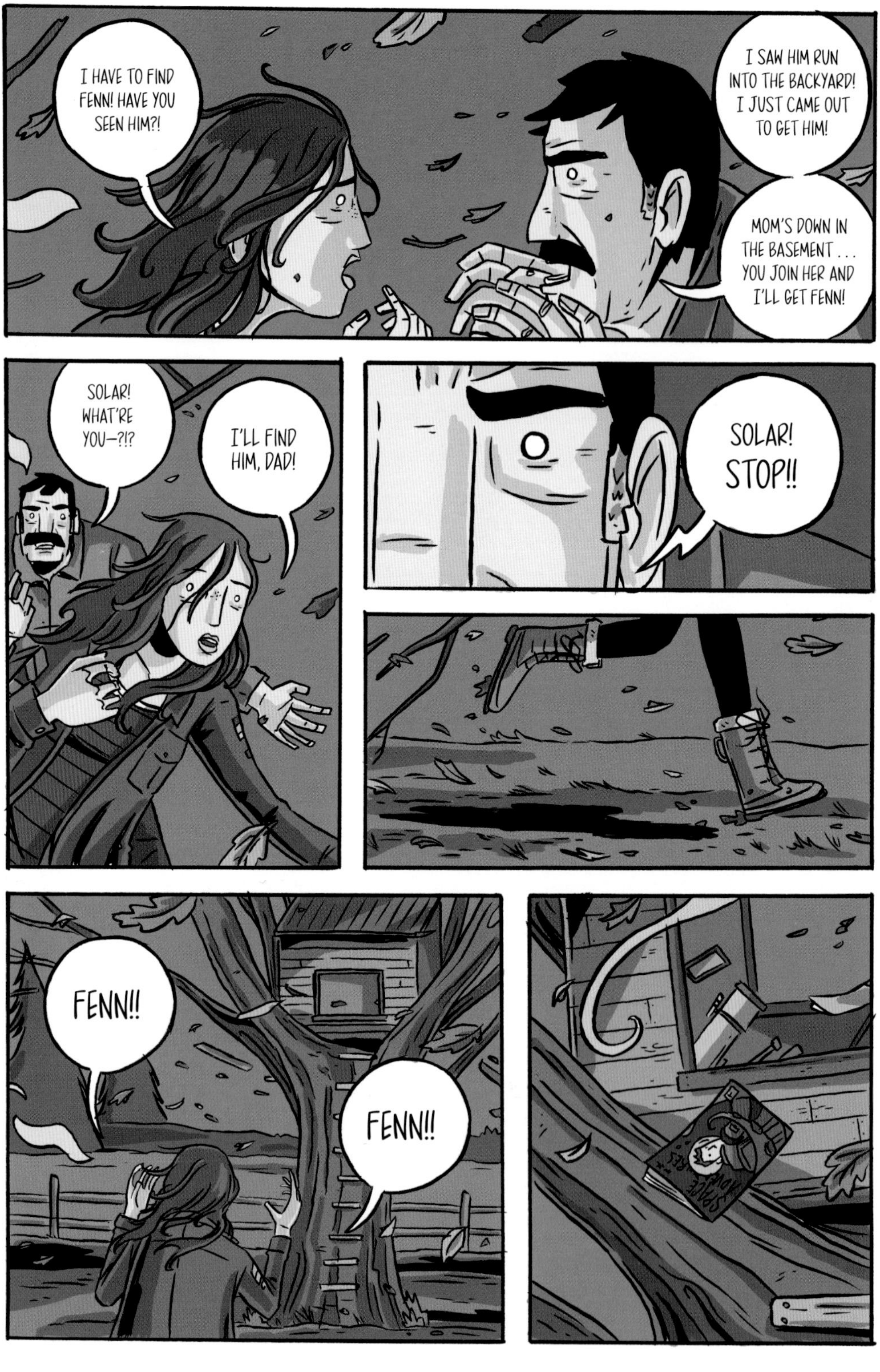
I HAVE TO FIND FENN! HAVE YOU SEEN HIM?!
I SAW HIM RUN INTO THE BACKYARD! I JUST CAME OUT TO GET HIM!
MOM'S DOWN IN THE BASEMENT . . . YOU JOIN HER AND I'LL GET FENN!
SOLAR! WHAT'RE YOU—?!?
I'LL FIND HIM, DAD!
SOLAR! STOP!!
FENN!!
FENN!!

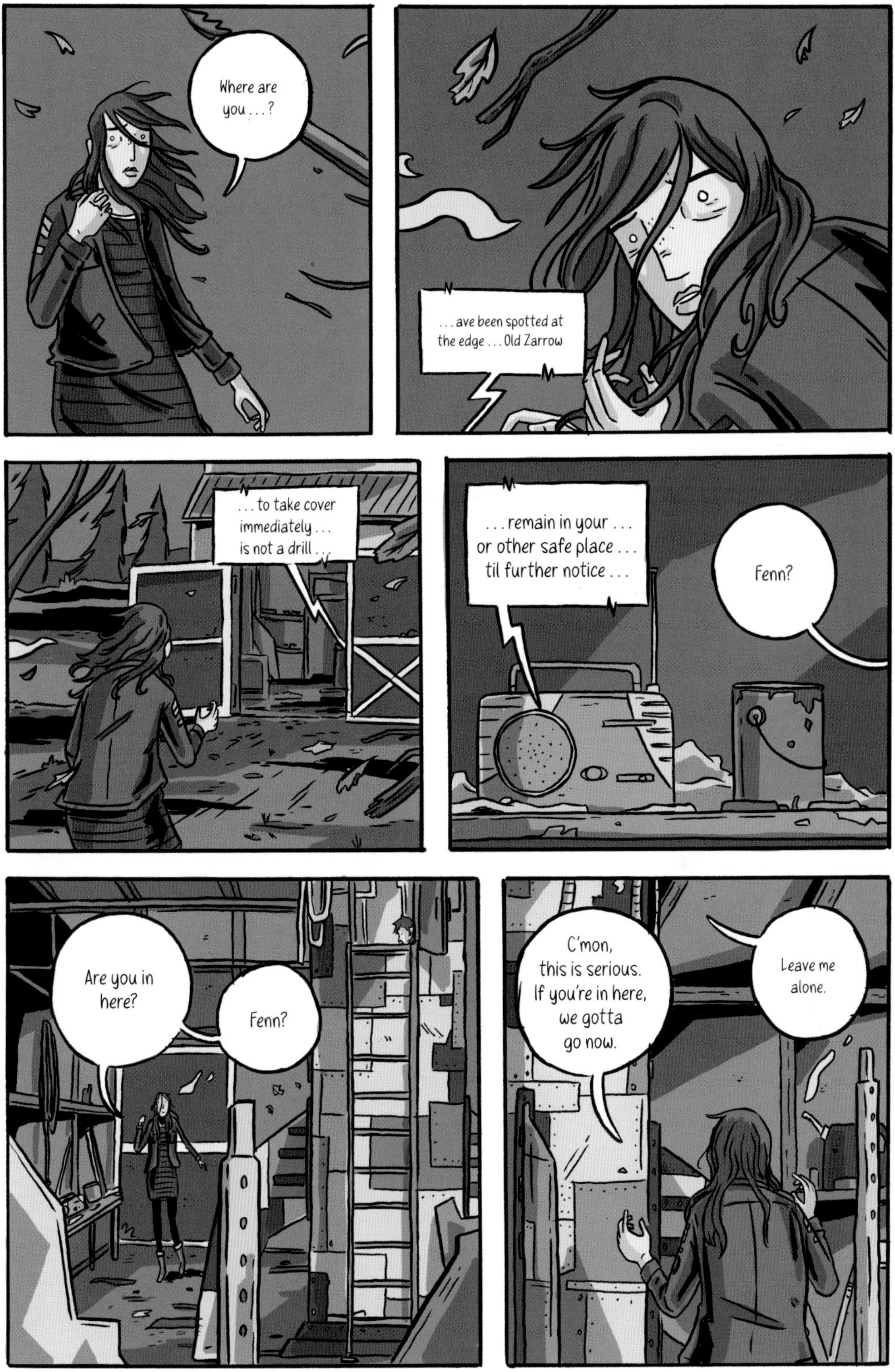
Where are you . . . ?
. . . ave been spotted at the edge . . . Old Zarrow
. . . to take cover immediately . . . is not a drill . . .
. . . remain in your . . . or other safe place . . . til further notice . . .
Fenn?
Are you in here?
Fenn?
C'mon, this is serious. If you're in here, we gotta go now.
Leave me alone.

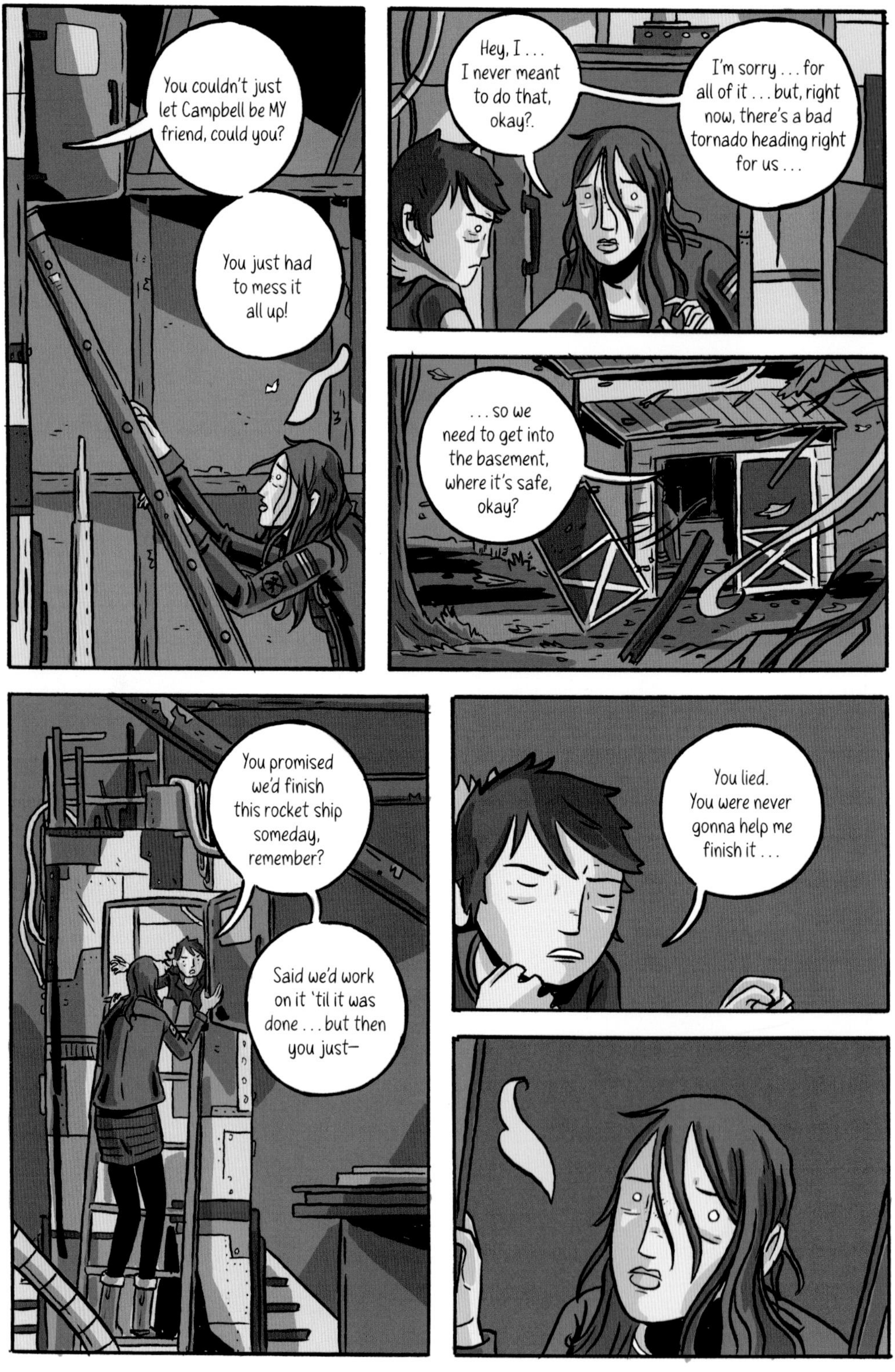
You couldn't just let Campbell be MY friend, could you?
You just had to mess it all up!
Hey, I . . . I never meant to do that, okay?.
I'm sorry . . . for all of it . . . but, right now, there's a bad tornado heading right for us . . .
. . . so we need to get into the basement, where it's safe, okay?
You promised we'd finish this rocket ship someday, remember?
Said we'd work on it 'til it was done . . . but then you just—
You lied. You were never gonna help me finish it . . .

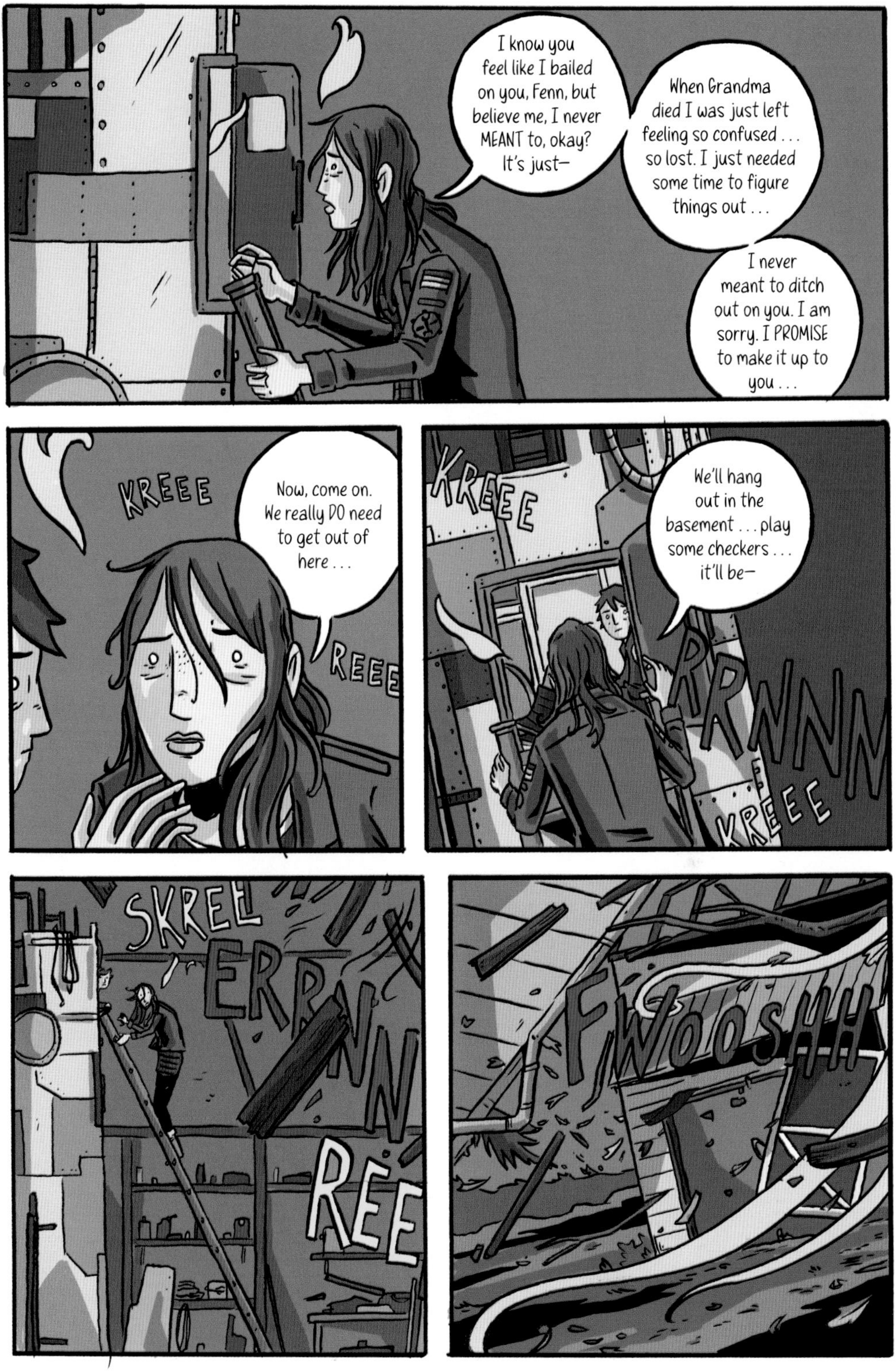
I know you feel like I bailed on you, Fenn, but believe me, I never MEANT to, okay? It's just—
When Grandma died I was just left feeling so confused . . . so lost. I just needed some time to figure things out . . .
I never meant to ditch out on you. I am sorry. I PROMISE to make it up to you . . .
KREEE
Now, come on. We really DO need to get out of here . . .
REEE
KREEE
We'll hang out in the basement . . . play some checkers . . . it'll be—
RRNNM
KREEE
SKREE
ERRNN
REE
FWOOSHH

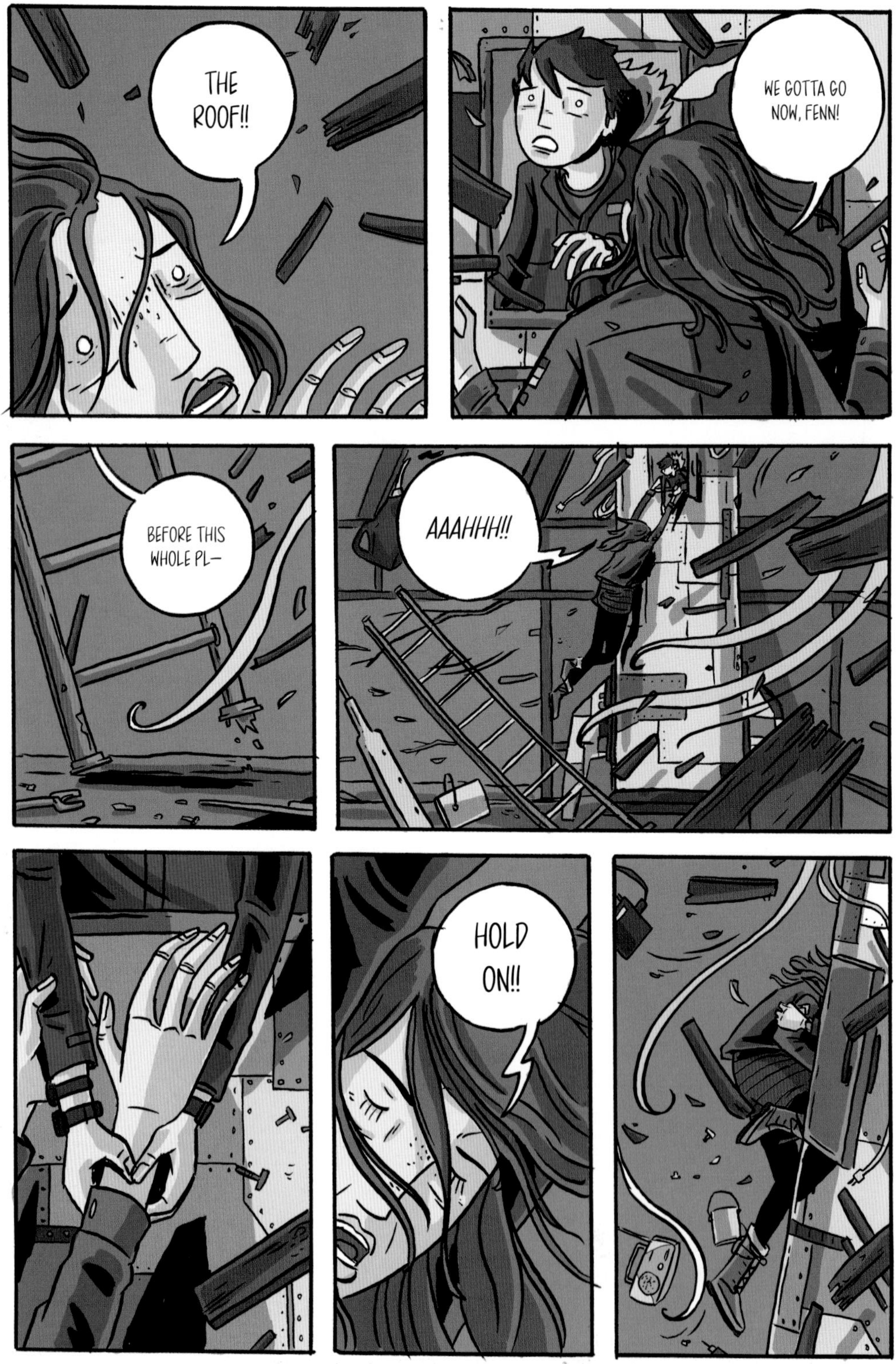
THE ROOF!!
WE GOTTA GO NOW, FENN!
BEFORE THIS WHOLE PL—
AAAHHH!!
HOLD ON!!

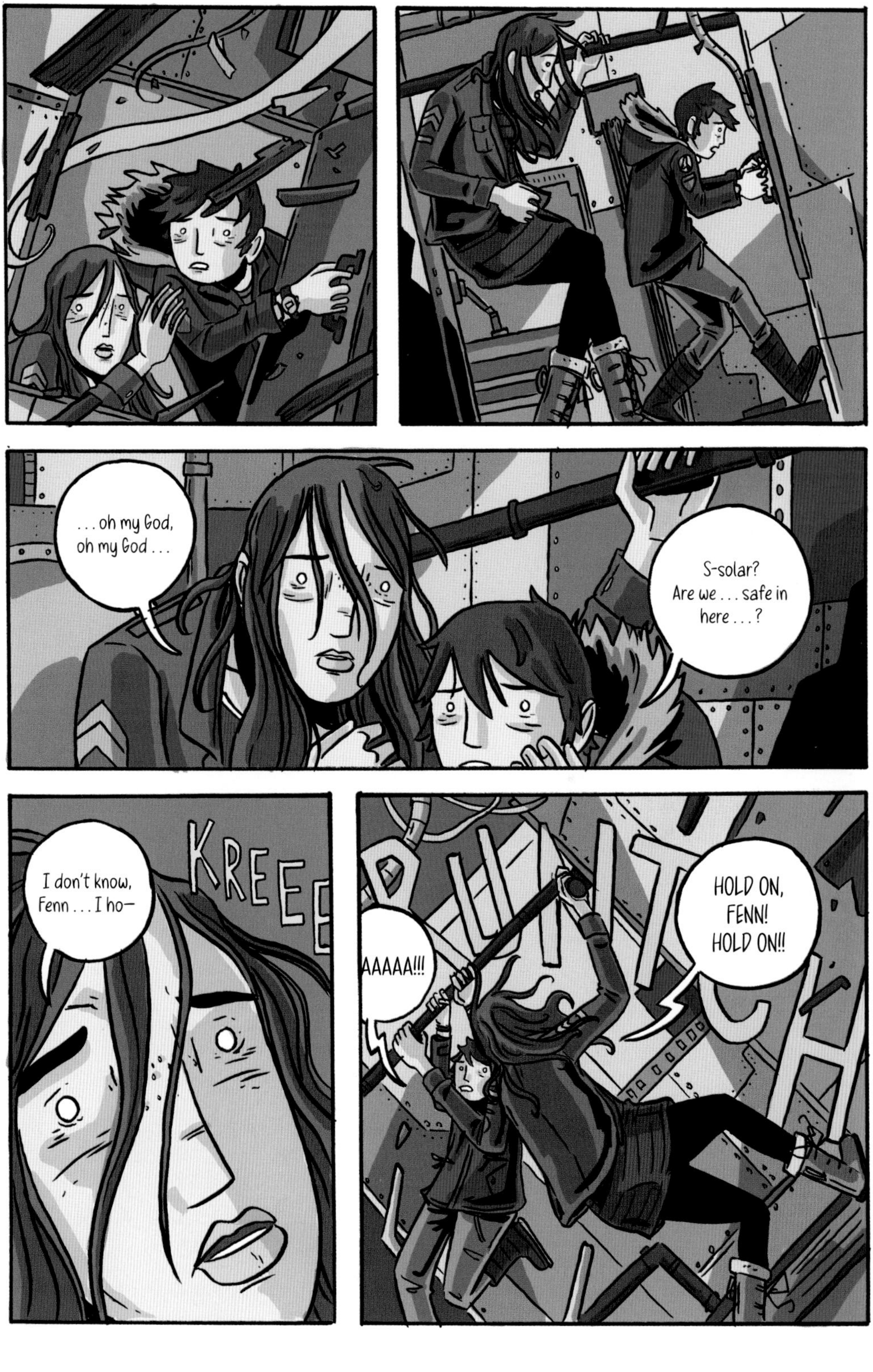
. . . oh my God,
oh my God . . .
S-solar?
Are we . . . safe in
here . . . ?
I don't know,
Fenn . . . I ho—
KREEE
AAAAA!!!
HOLD ON,
FENN!
HOLD ON!!

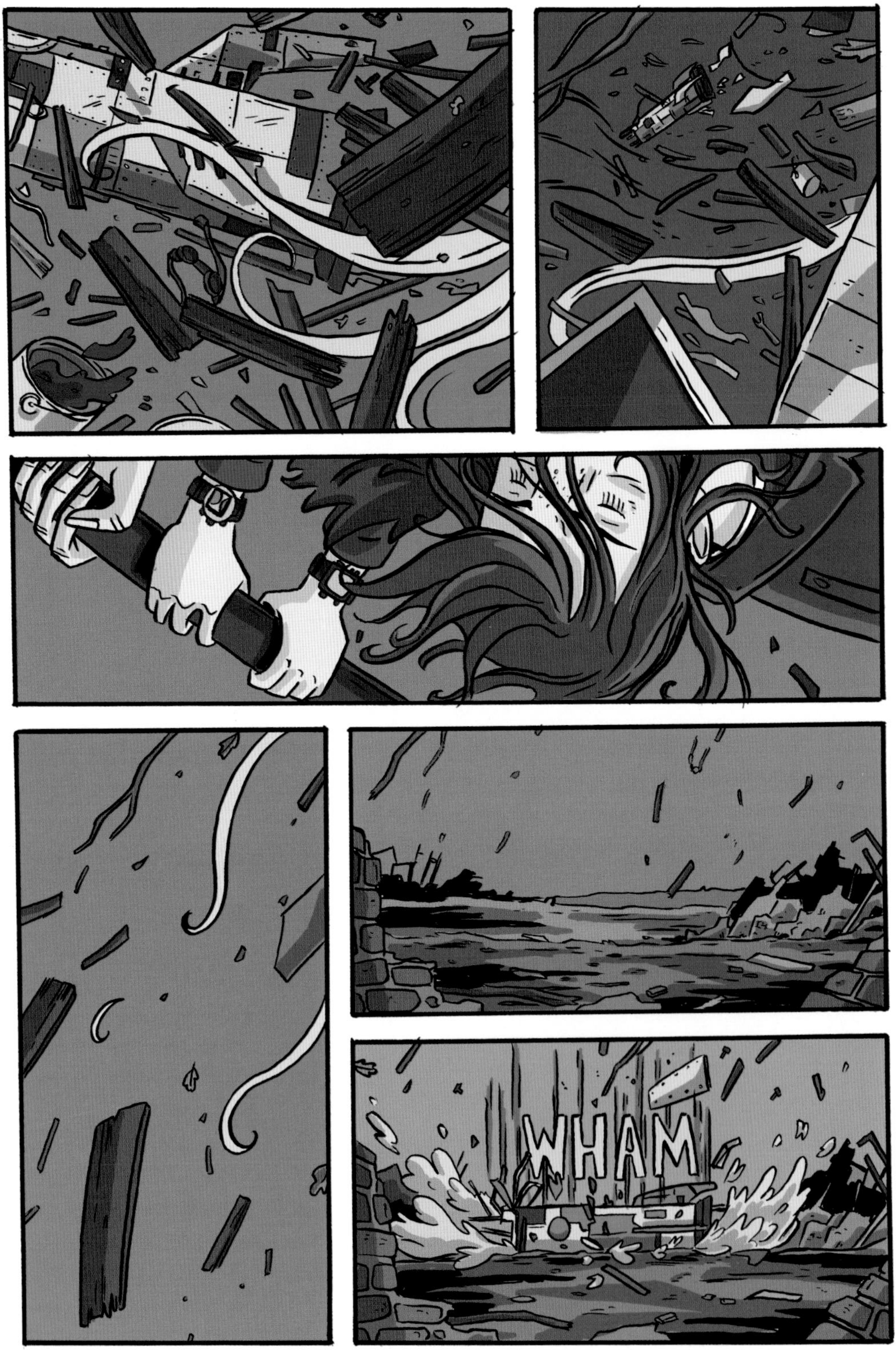
WHAM

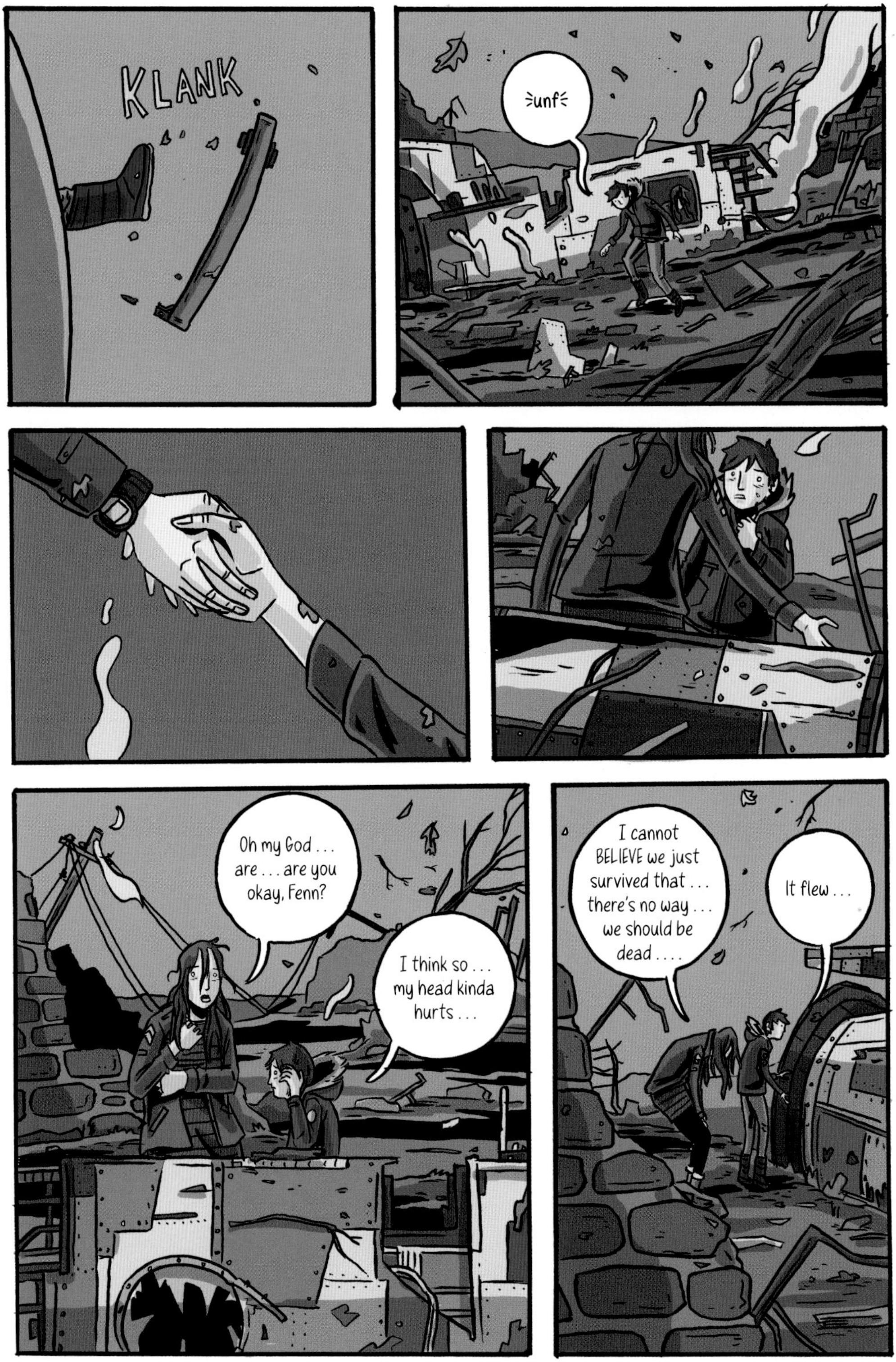
KLANK
unf
Oh my God . . . are . . . are you okay, Fenn?
I think so . . . my head kinda hurts . . .
I cannot BELIEVE we just survived that . . . there's no way . . . we should be dead . . . .
It flew . . .

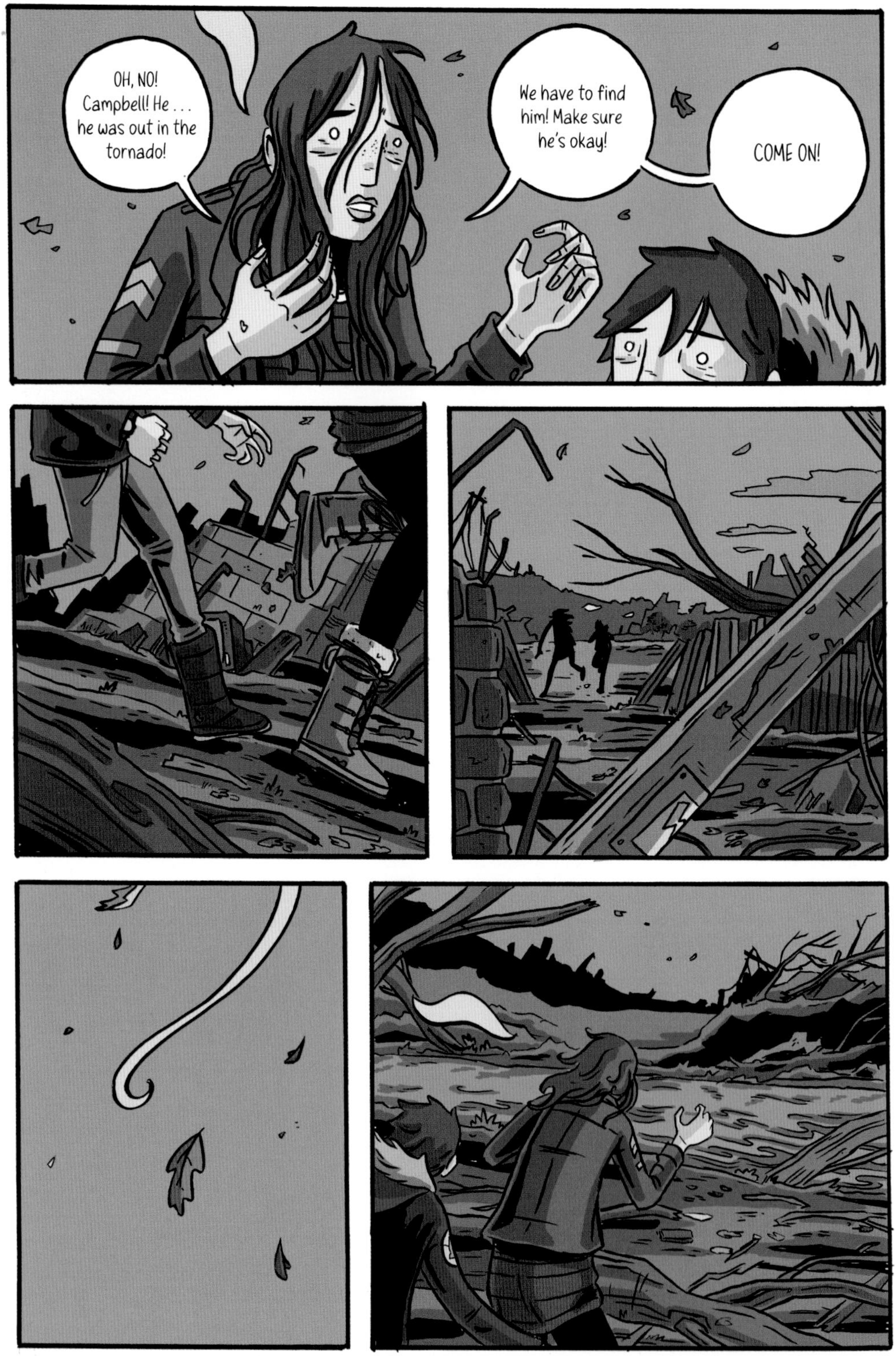

OH, NO! Campbell! He . . . he was out in the tornado!
We have to find him! Make sure he's okay!
COME ON!

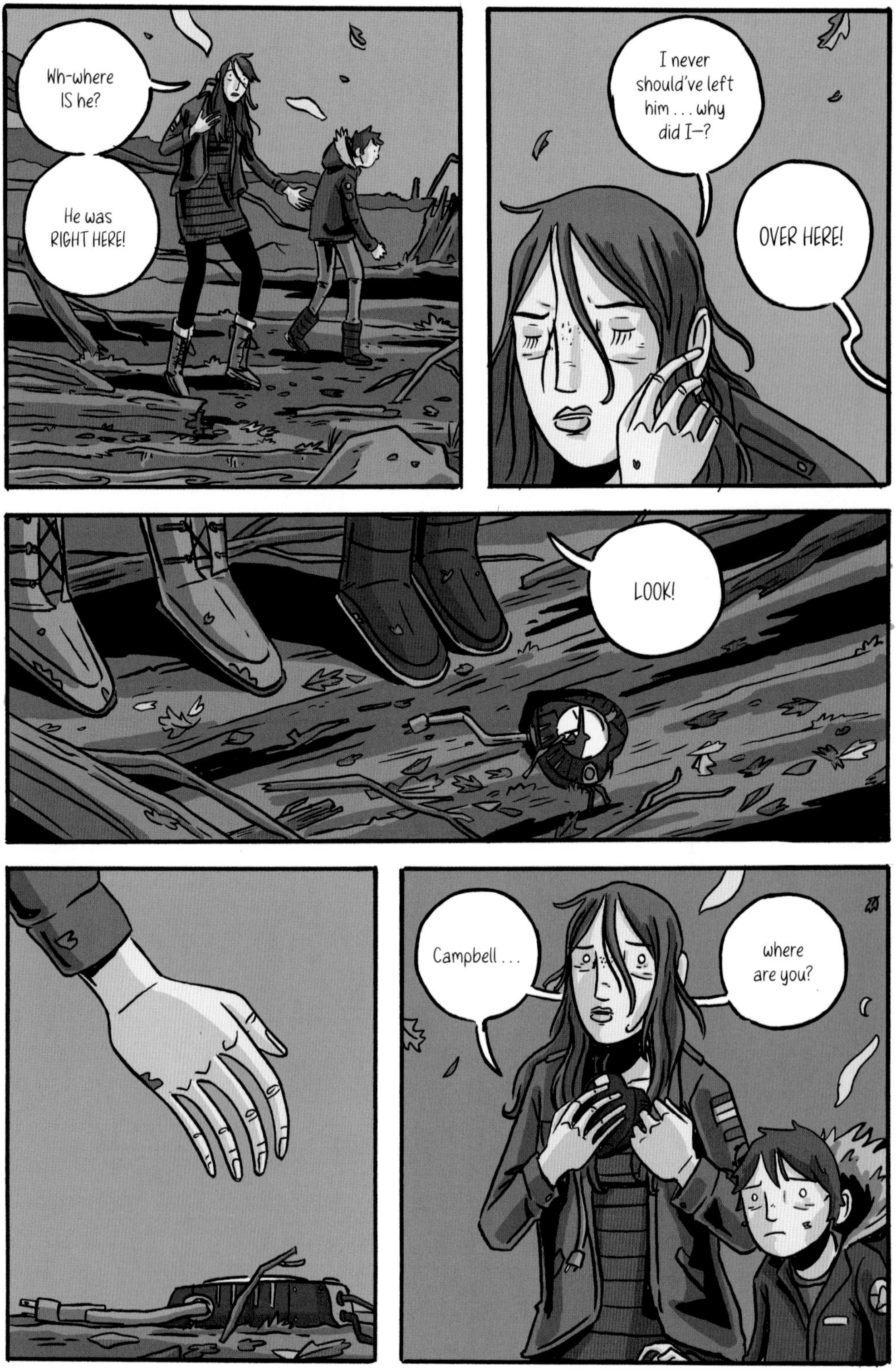
Wh-where IS he?
He was RIGHT HERE!
I never should've left him . . . why did I–?
OVER HERE!
LOOK!
Campbell . . .
where are you?

CHAPTER 13: New and Improved

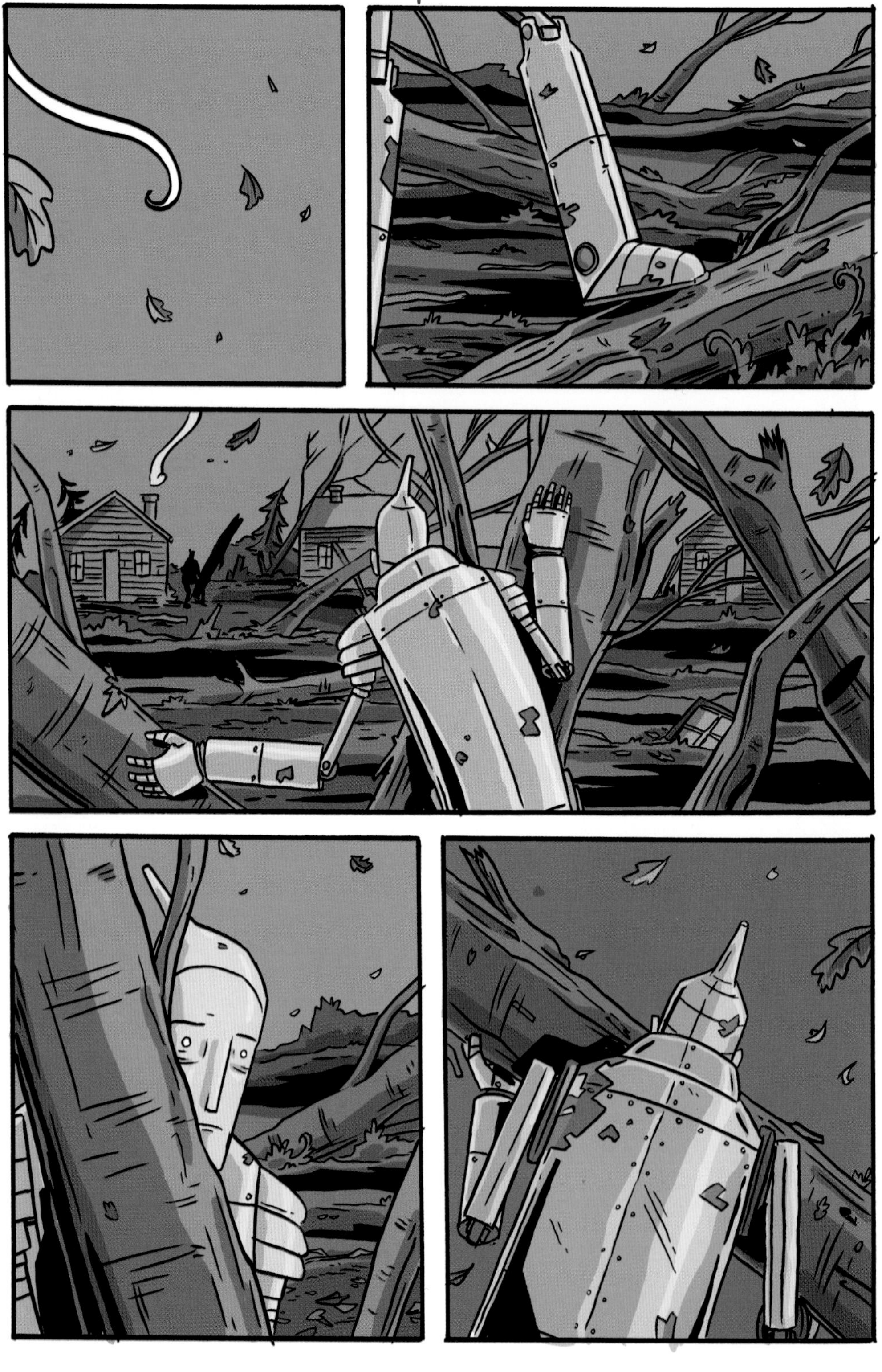

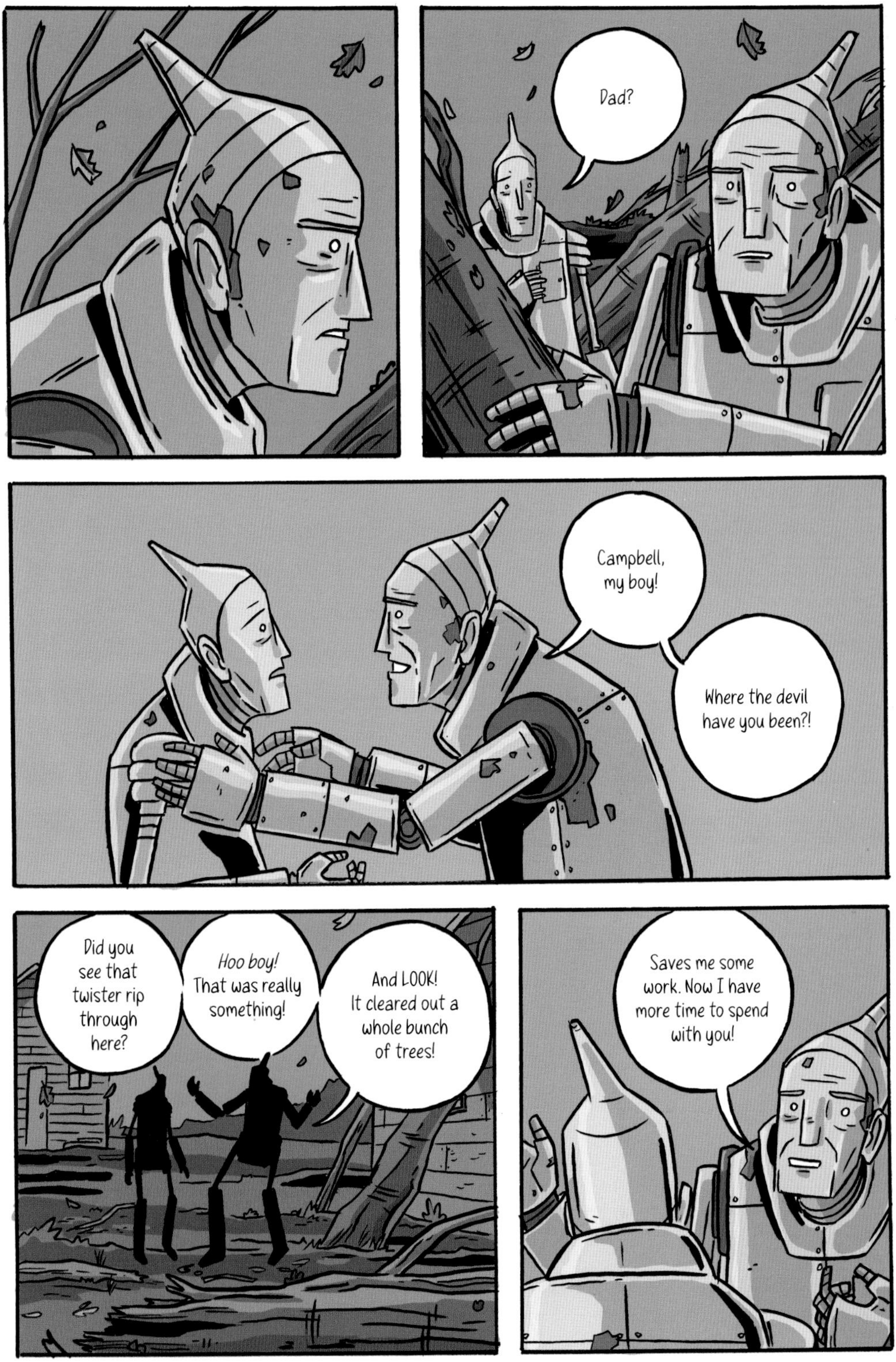
Dad?
Campbell, my boy!
Where the devil have you been?!
Did you see that twister rip through here?
Hoo boy! That was really something!
And LOOK! It cleared out a whole bunch of trees!
Saves me some work. Now I have more time to spend with you!

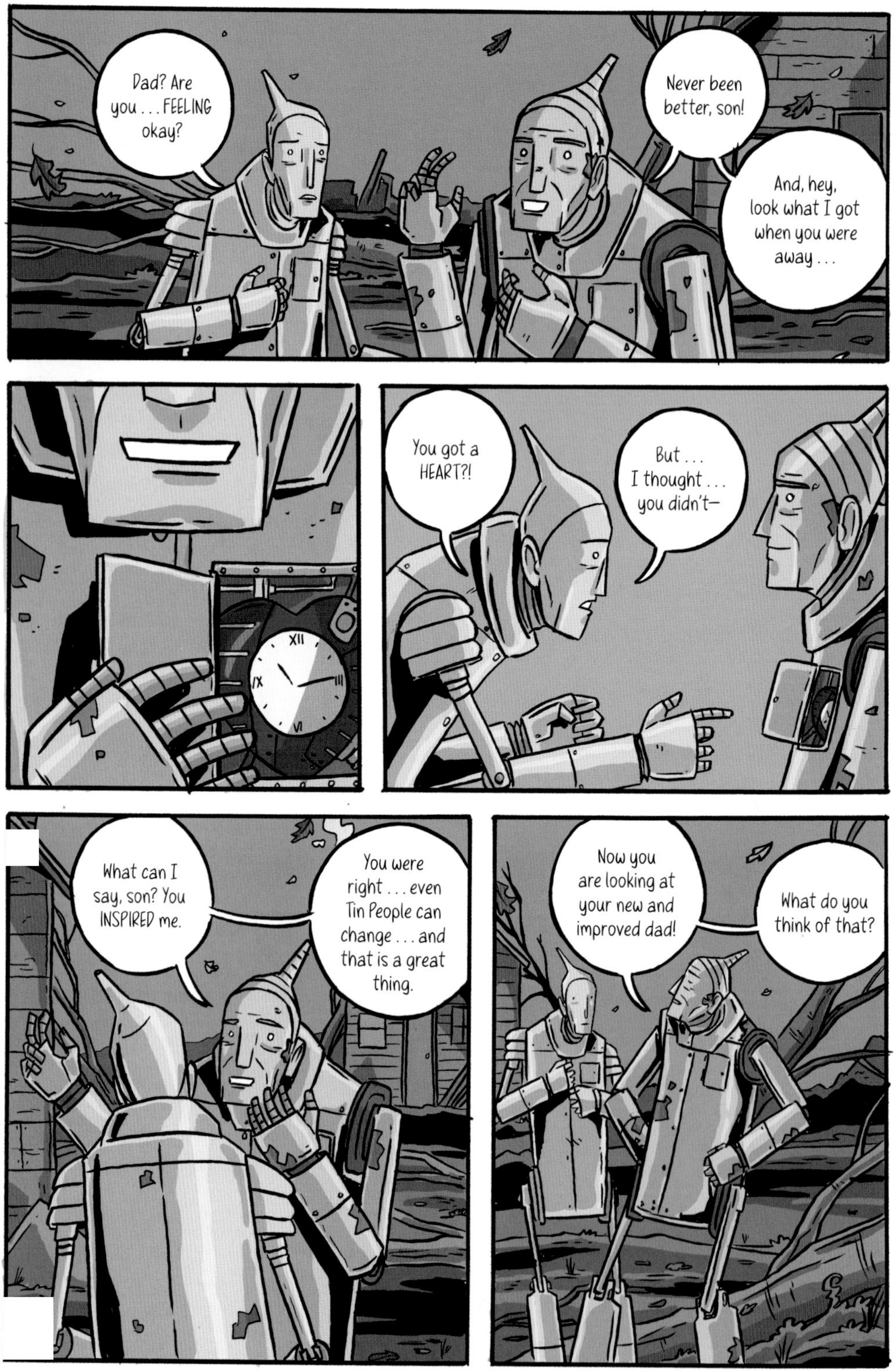
Dad? Are you . . . FEELING okay?
Never been better, son!
And, hey, look what I got when you were away . . .
You got a HEART?!
But . . . I thought . . . you didn't—
What can I say, son? You INSPIRED me.
You were right . . . even Tin People can change . . . and that is a great thing.
Now you are looking at your new and improved dad!
What do you think of that?

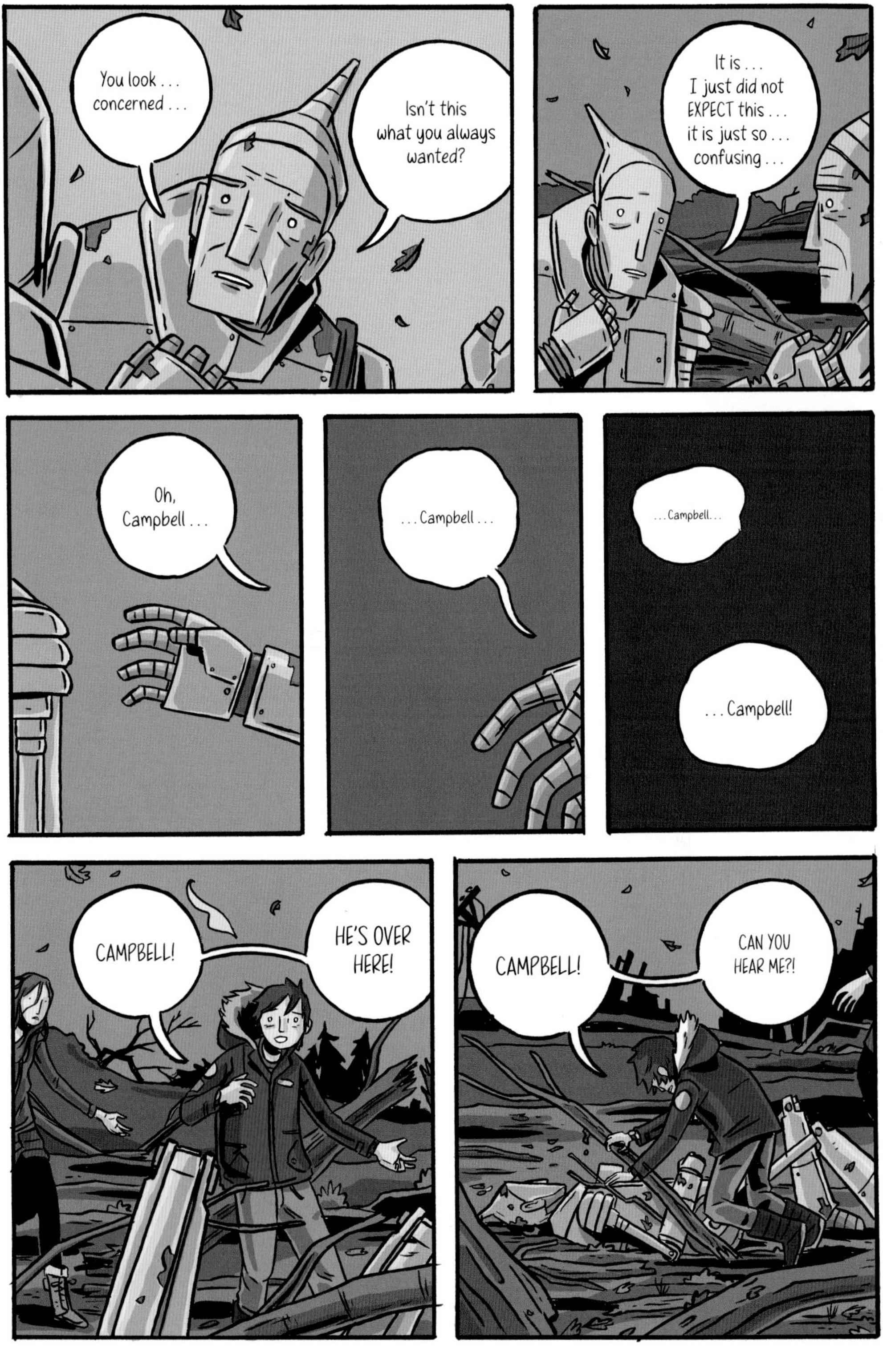

You look . . . concerned . . .
Isn't this what you always wanted?
It is . . . I just did not EXPECT this . . . it is just so . . . confusing . . .
Oh, Campbell . . .
. . . Campbell . . .
. . . Campbell . . .
. . . Campbell!
CAMPBELL!
HE'S OVER HERE!
CAMPBELL!
CAN YOU HEAR ME?!

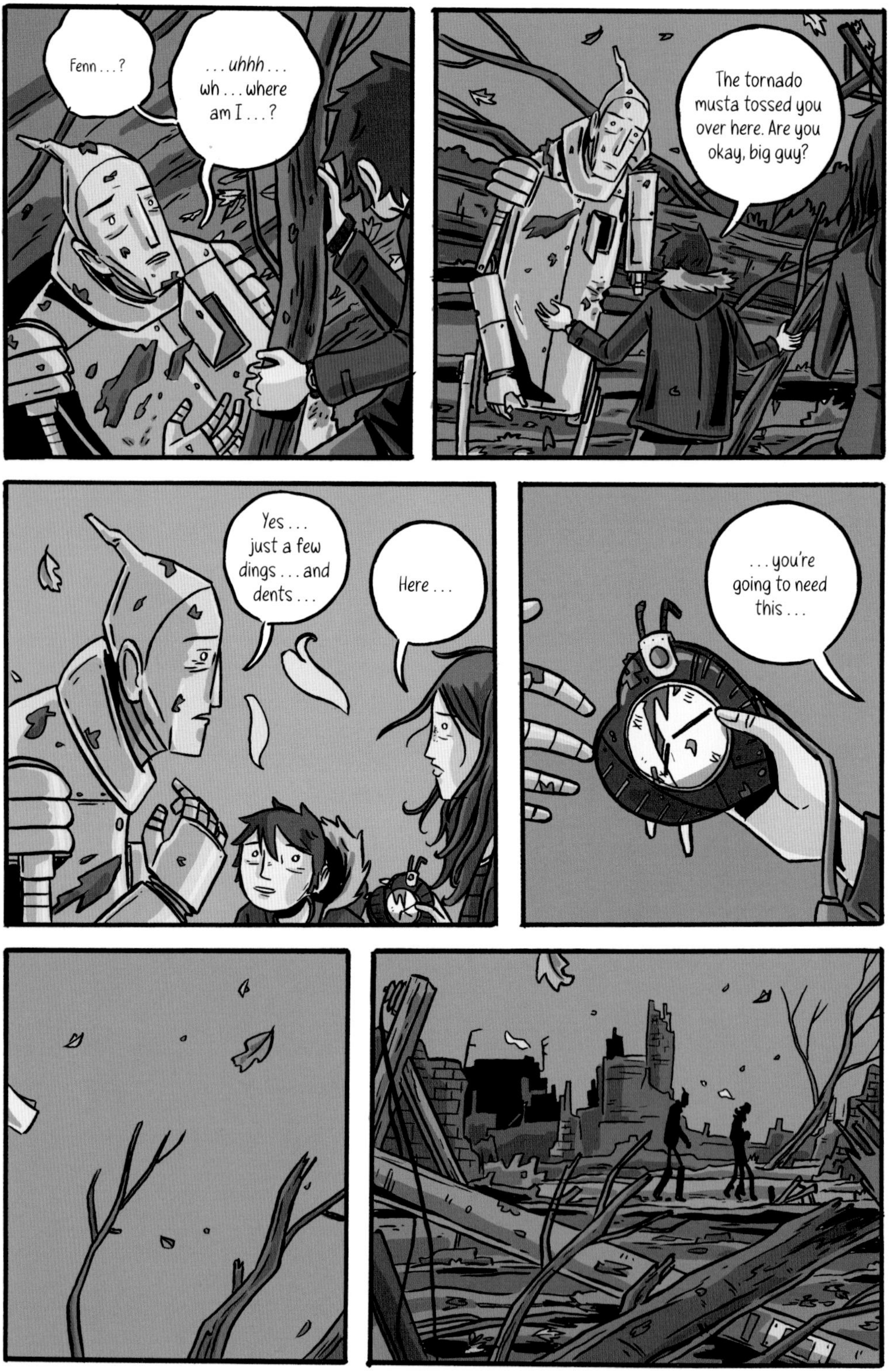
Fenn . . . ?
. . . uhhh . . . wh . . . where am I . . . ?
The tornado musta tossed you over here. Are you okay, big guy?
Yes . . . just a few dings . . . and dents . . .
Here . . .
. . . you're going to need this . . .

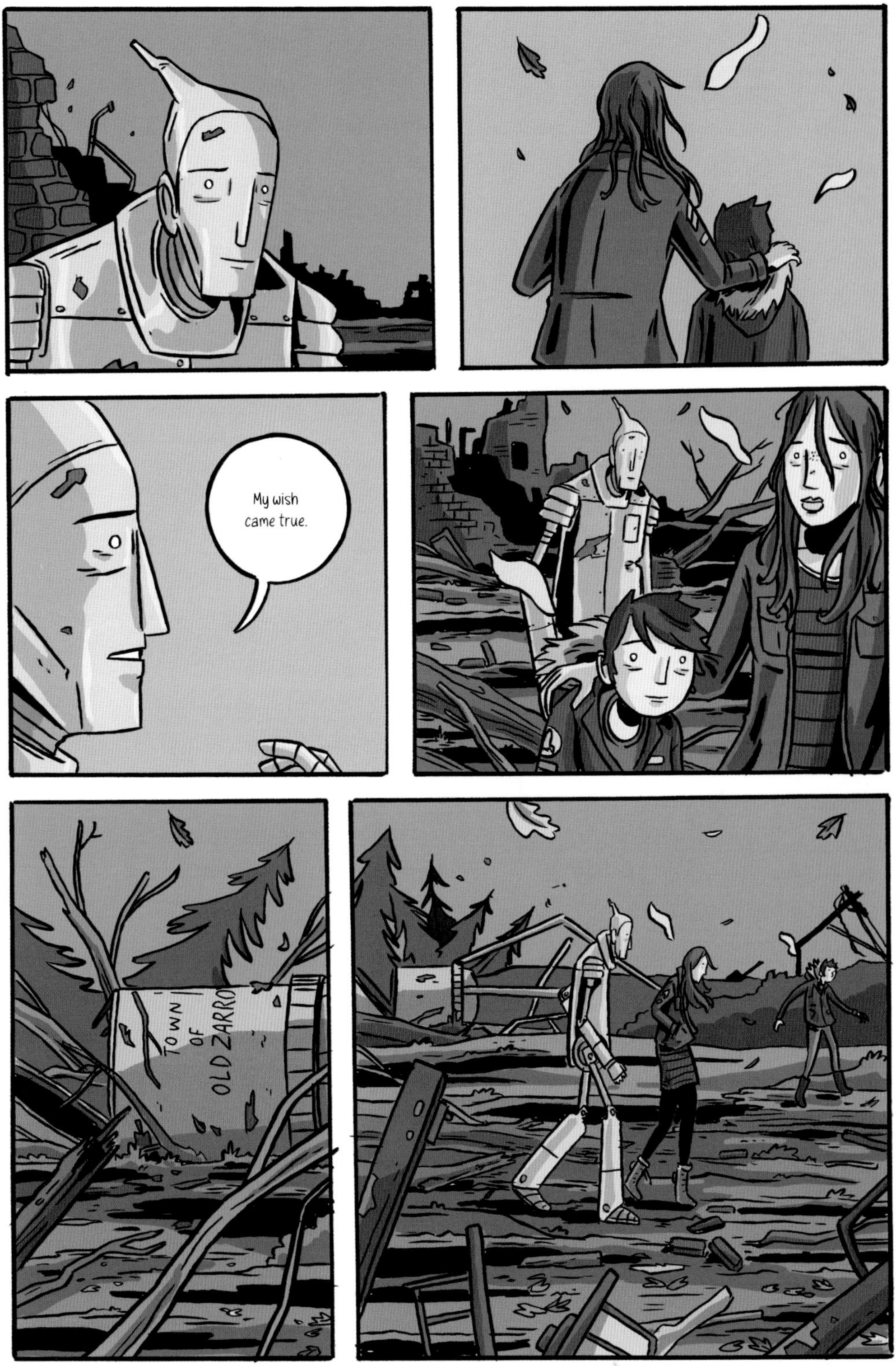
My wish came true.
TOWN OF OLD ZARRO

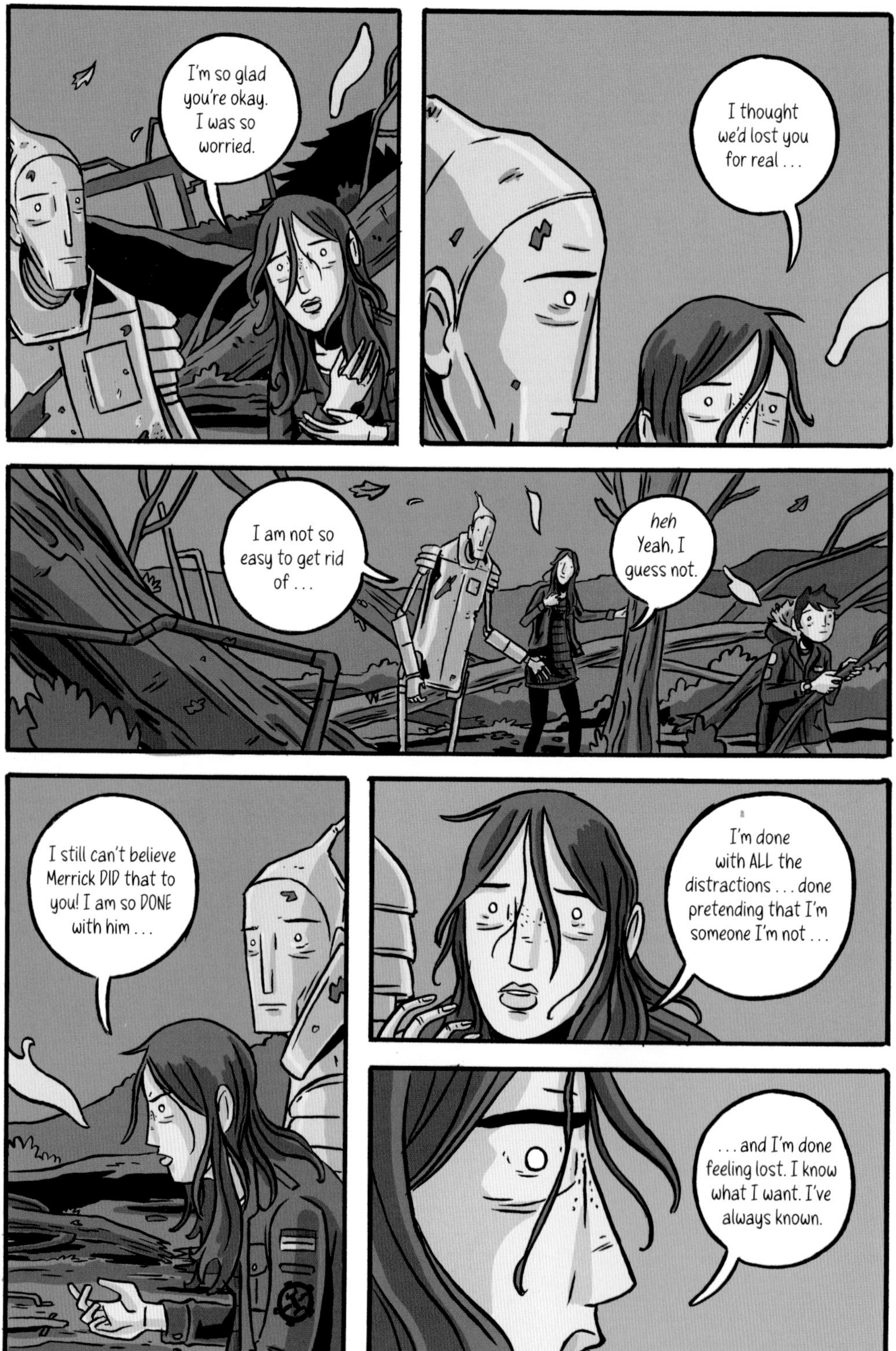
I'm so glad you're okay. I was so worried.
I thought we'd lost you for real . . .
I am not so easy to get rid of . . .
heh Yeah, I guess not.
I still can't believe Merrick DID that to you! I am so DONE with him . . .
I'm done with ALL the distractions . . . done pretending that I'm someone I'm not . . .
. . . and I'm done feeling lost. I know what I want. I've always known.

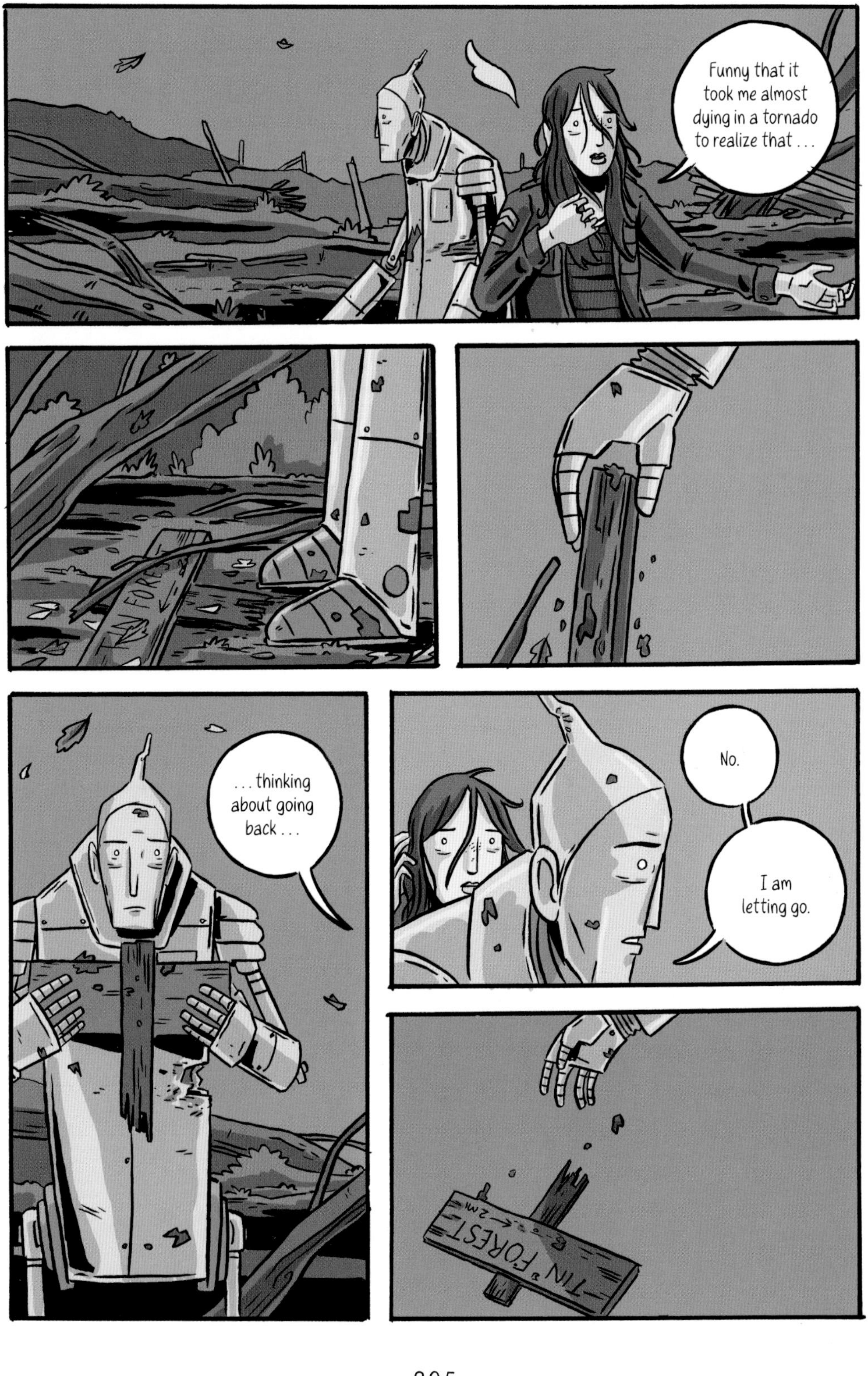
Funny that it took me almost dying in a tornado to realize that . . .
. . . thinking about going back . . .
No.
I am letting go.
TIN FOREST
2 MI →

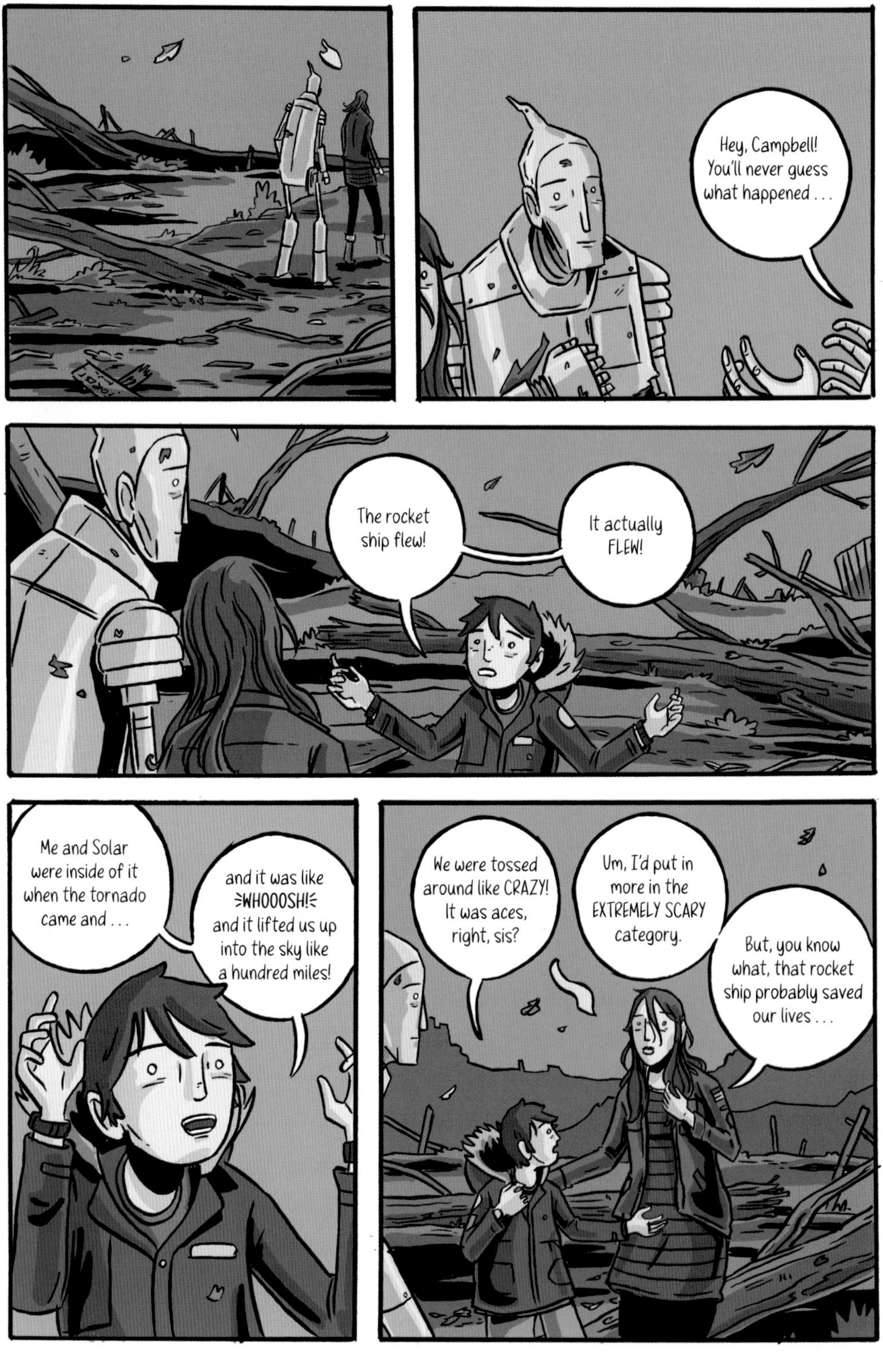
Hey, Campbell! You'll never guess what happened . . .
The rocket ship flew!
It actually FLEW!
Me and Solar were inside of it when the tornado came and . . .
and it was like ⋚WHOOOSH!⋚ and it lifted us up into the sky like a hundred miles!
We were tossed around like CRAZY! It was aces, right, sis?
Um, I'd put in more in the EXTREMELY SCARY category.
But, you know what, that rocket ship probably saved our lives . . .

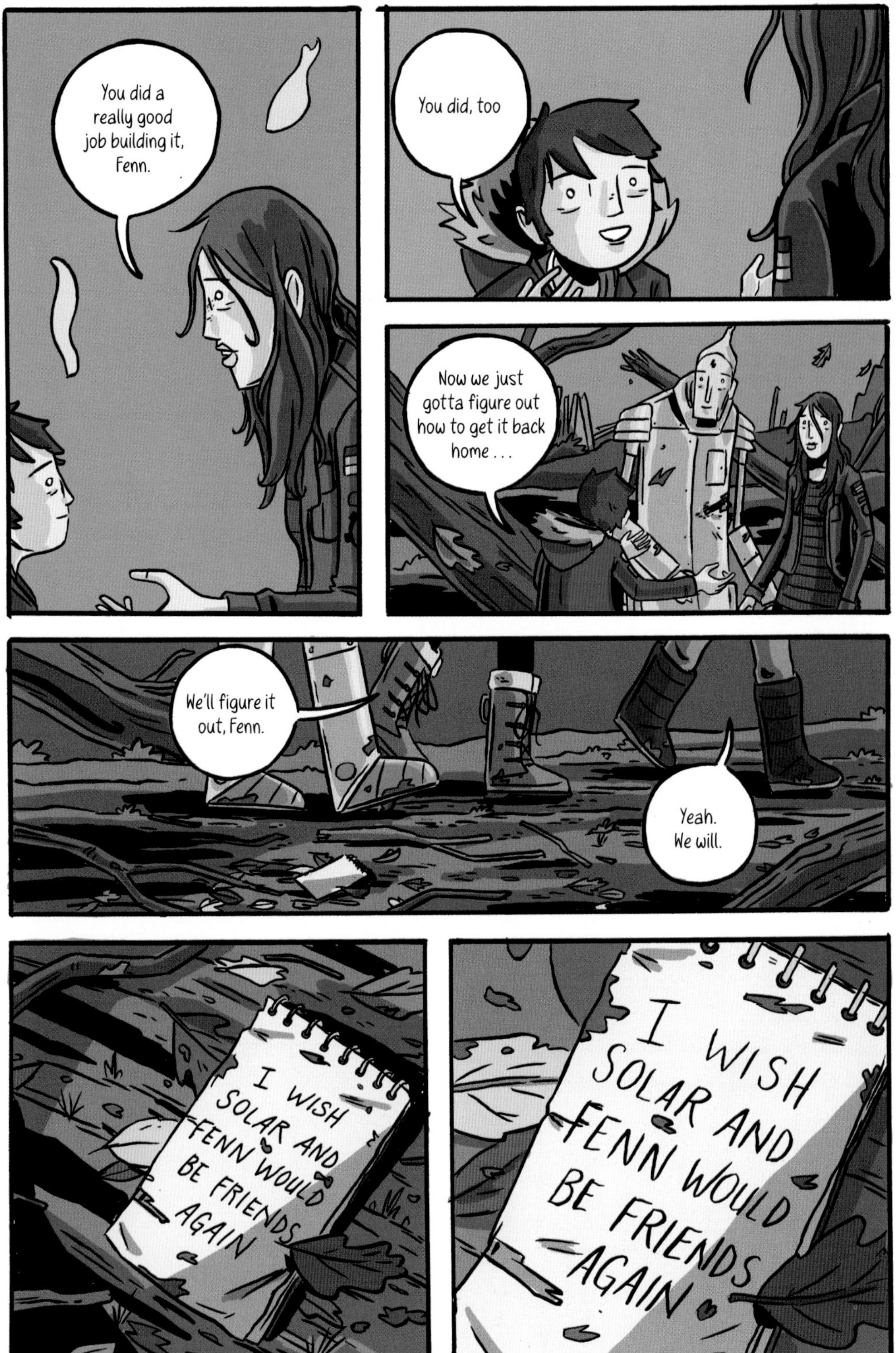
You did a really good job building it, Fenn.
You did, too
Now we just gotta figure out how to get it back home . . .
We'll figure it out, Fenn.
Yeah. We will.
I WISH SOLAR AND FENN WOULD BE FRIENDS AGAIN
I WISH SOLAR AND FENN WOULD BE FRIENDS AGAIN

CHAPTER 14: Home

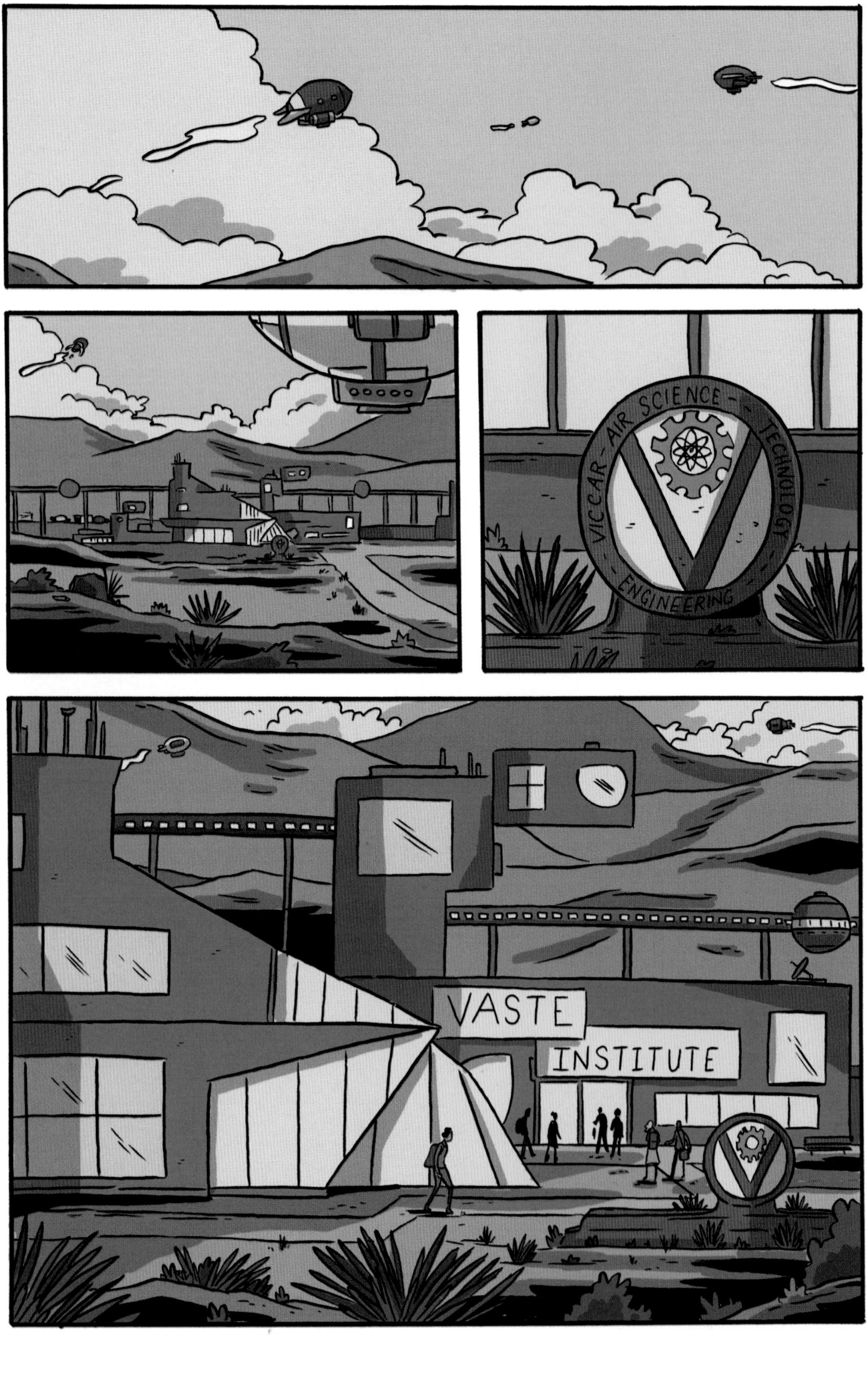
VICCAR - AIR SCIENCE - TECHNOLOGY - ENGINEERING
VASTE
INSTITUTE

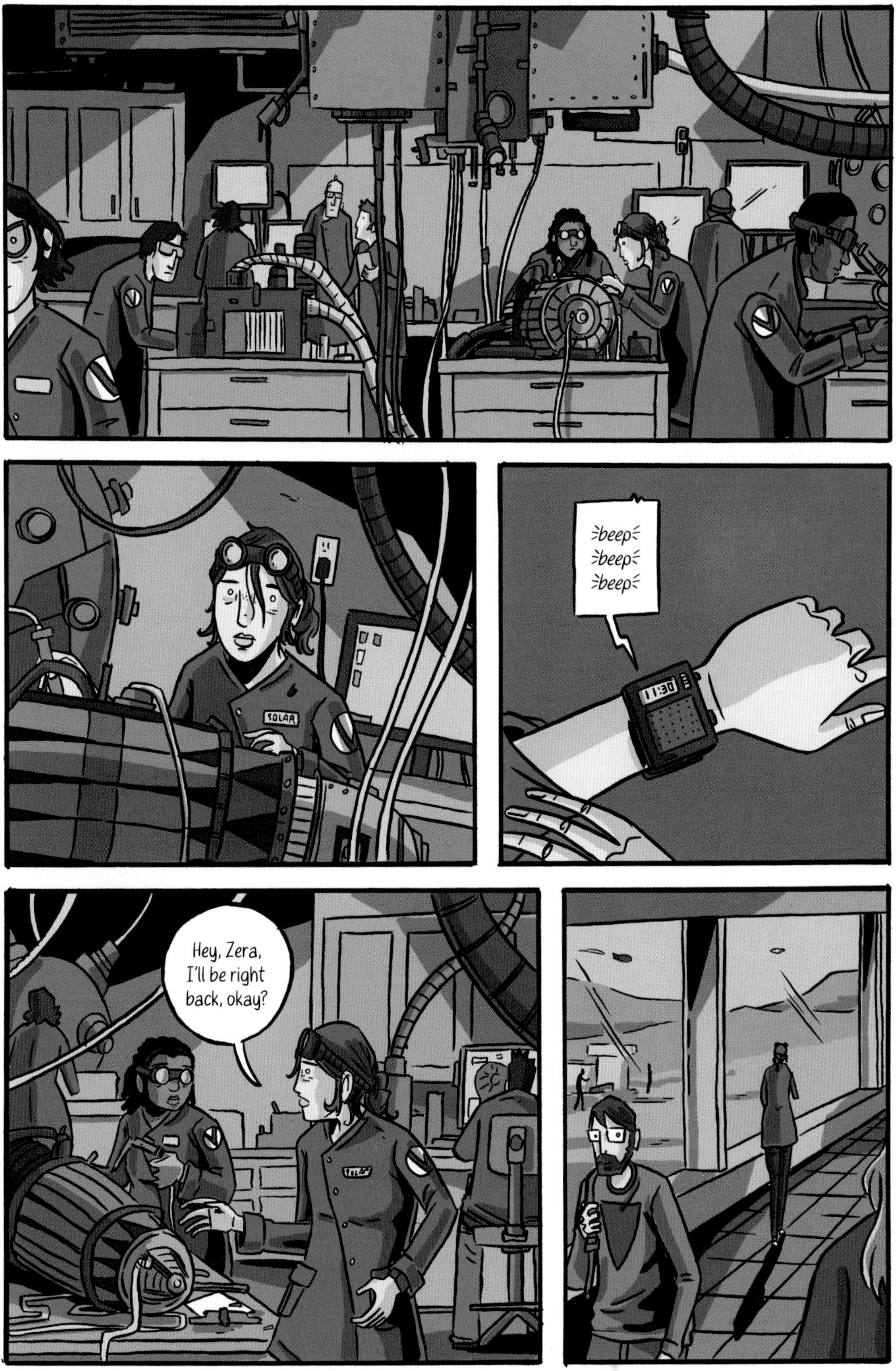
SOLAR
beep
beep
beep
11:30
Hey, Zera, I'll be right back, okay?
SOLAR

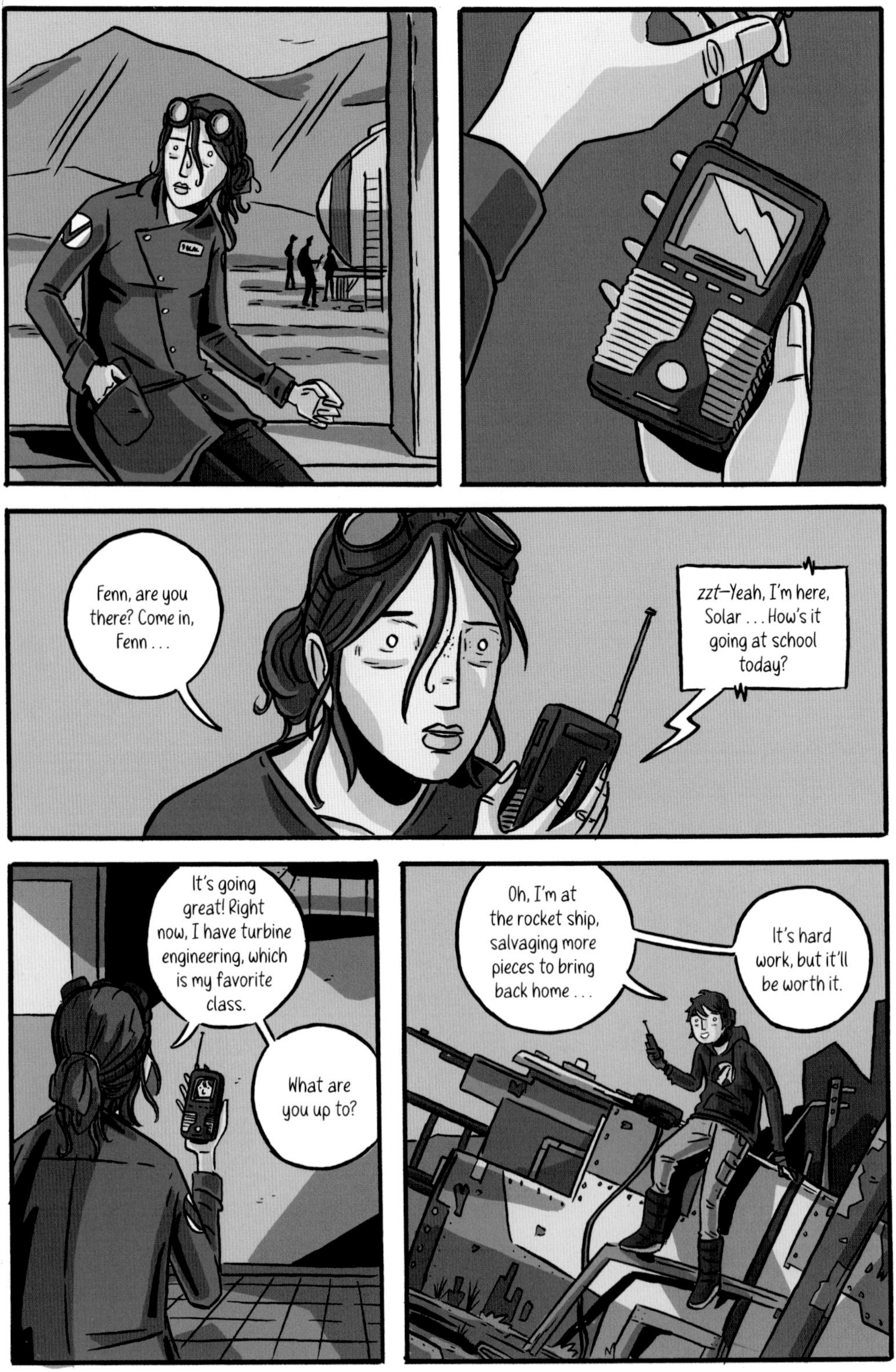

Fenn, are you there? Come in, Fenn . . .
zzt—Yeah, I'm here, Solar . . . How's it going at school today?
It's going great! Right now, I have turbine engineering, which is my favorite class.
What are you up to?
Oh, I'm at the rocket ship, salvaging more pieces to bring back home . . .
It's hard work, but it'll be worth it.

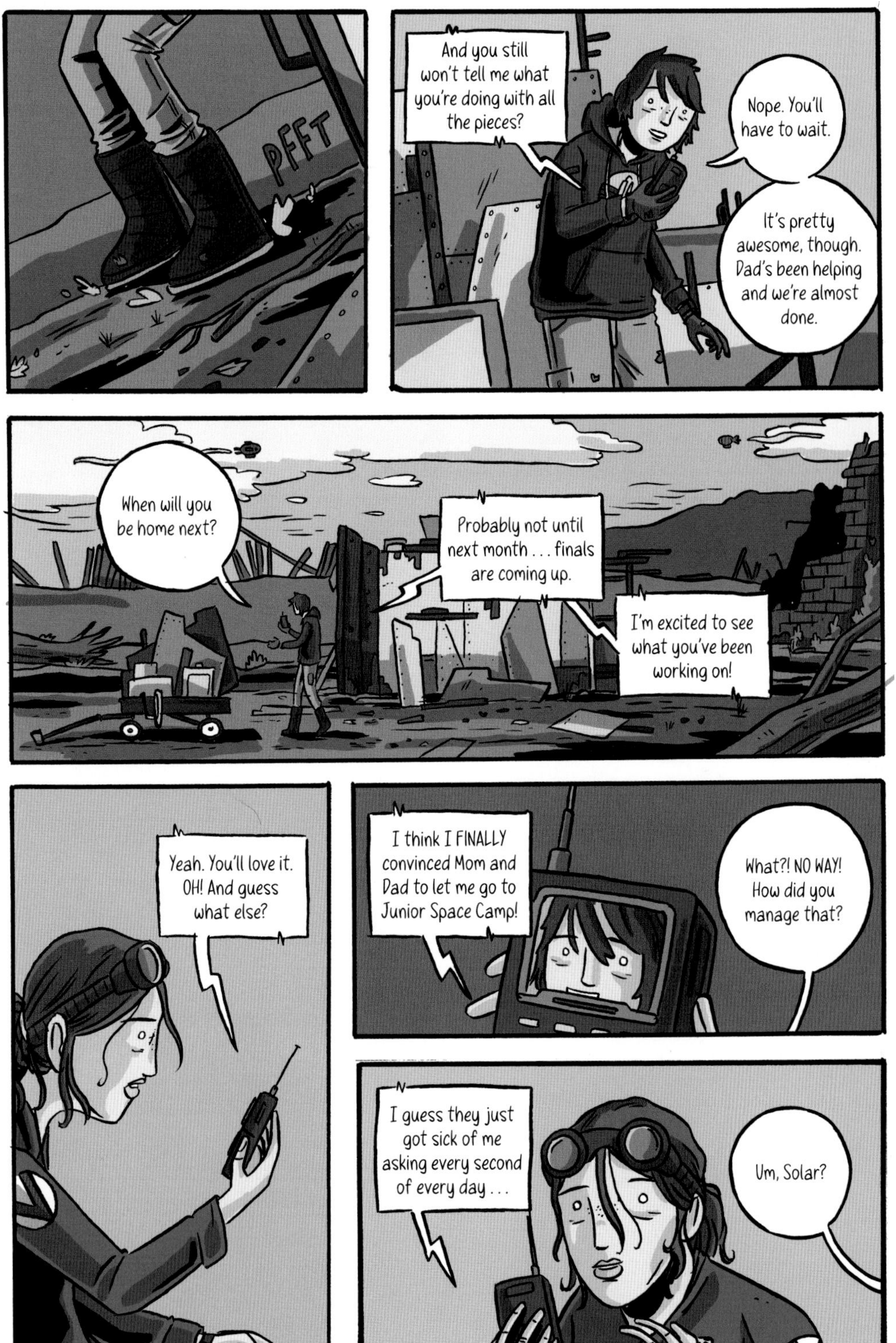
PFFT
And you still won't tell me what you're doing with all the pieces?
Nope. You'll have to wait.
It's pretty awesome, though. Dad's been helping and we're almost done.
When will you be home next?
Probably not until next month . . . finals are coming up.
I'm excited to see what you've been working on!
Yeah. You'll love it. OH! And guess what else?
I think I FINALLY convinced Mom and Dad to let me go to Junior Space Camp!
What?! NO WAY! How did you manage that?
I guess they just got sick of me asking every second of every day . . .
Um, Solar?

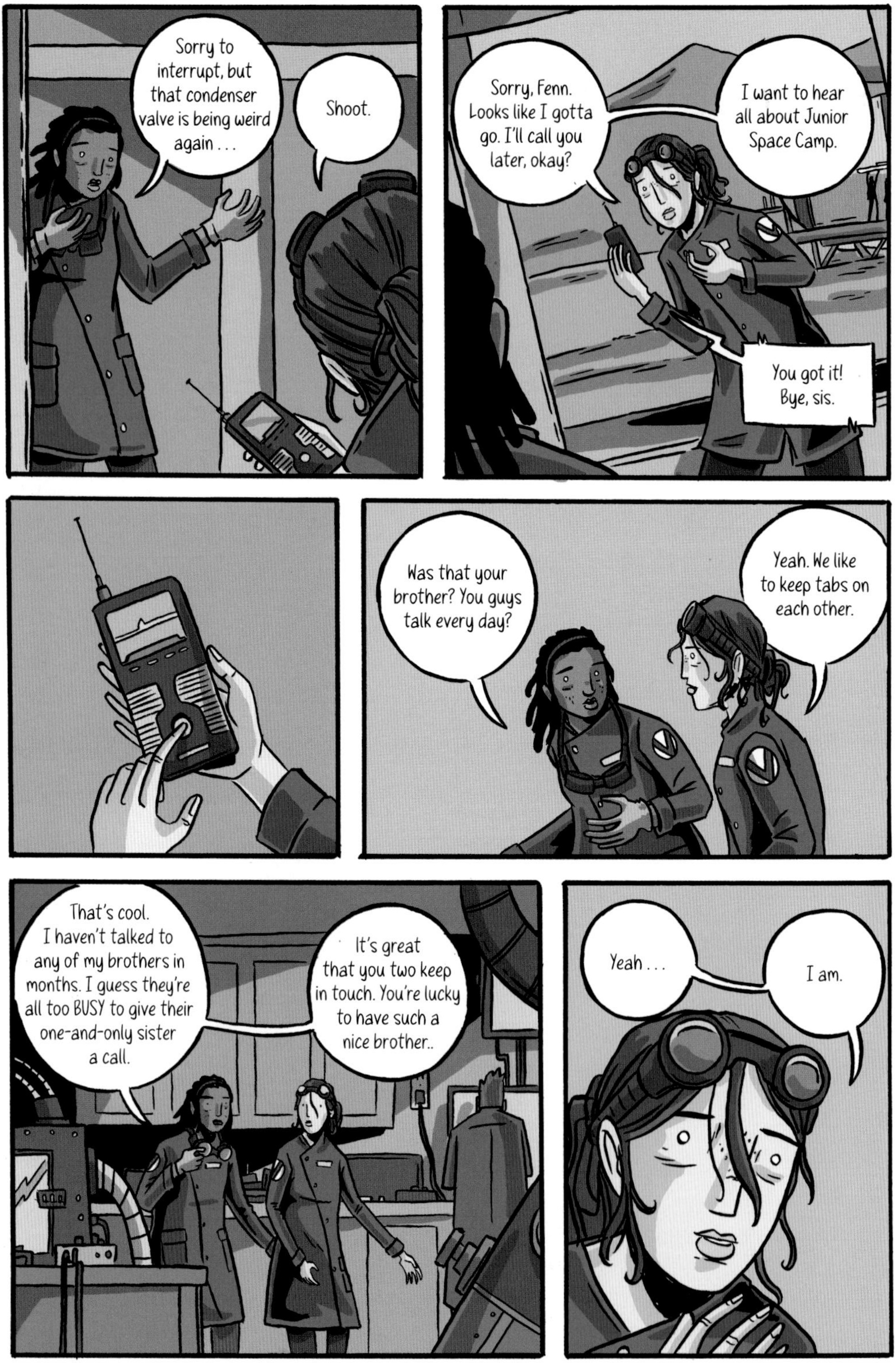
Sorry to interrupt, but that condenser valve is being weird again . . .
Shoot.
Sorry, Fenn. Looks like I gotta go. I'll call you later, okay?
I want to hear all about Junior Space Camp.
You got it! Bye, sis.
Was that your brother? You guys talk every day?
Yeah. We like to keep tabs on each other.
That's cool. I haven't talked to any of my brothers in months. I guess they're all too BUSY to give their one-and-only sister a call.
It's great that you two keep in touch. You're lucky to have such a nice brother..
Yeah . . .
I am.

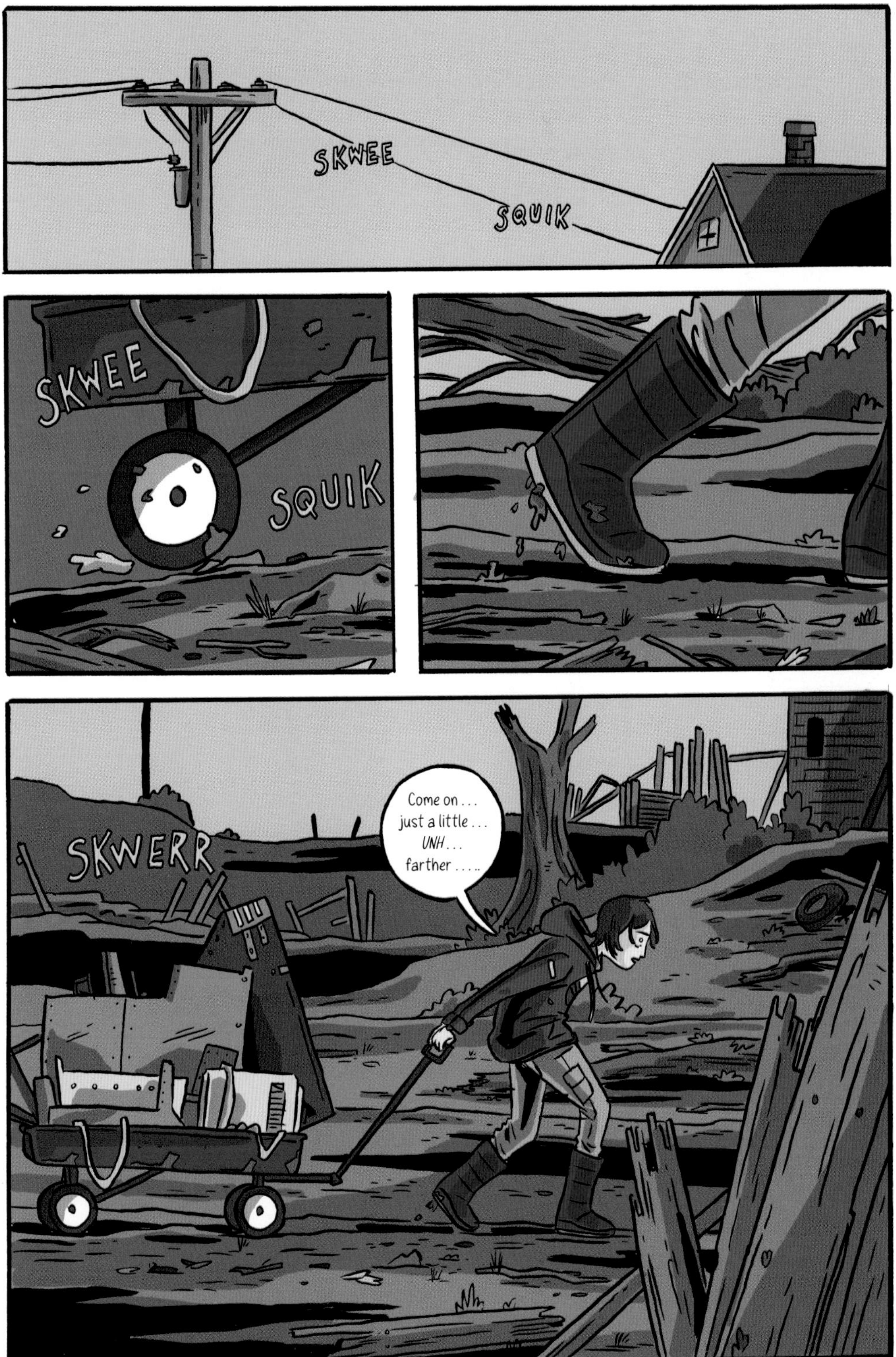
SKWEE
SQUIK
SKWEE
SQUIK
SKWERR
Come on . . . just a little . . . *UNH* . . . farther . . . . .

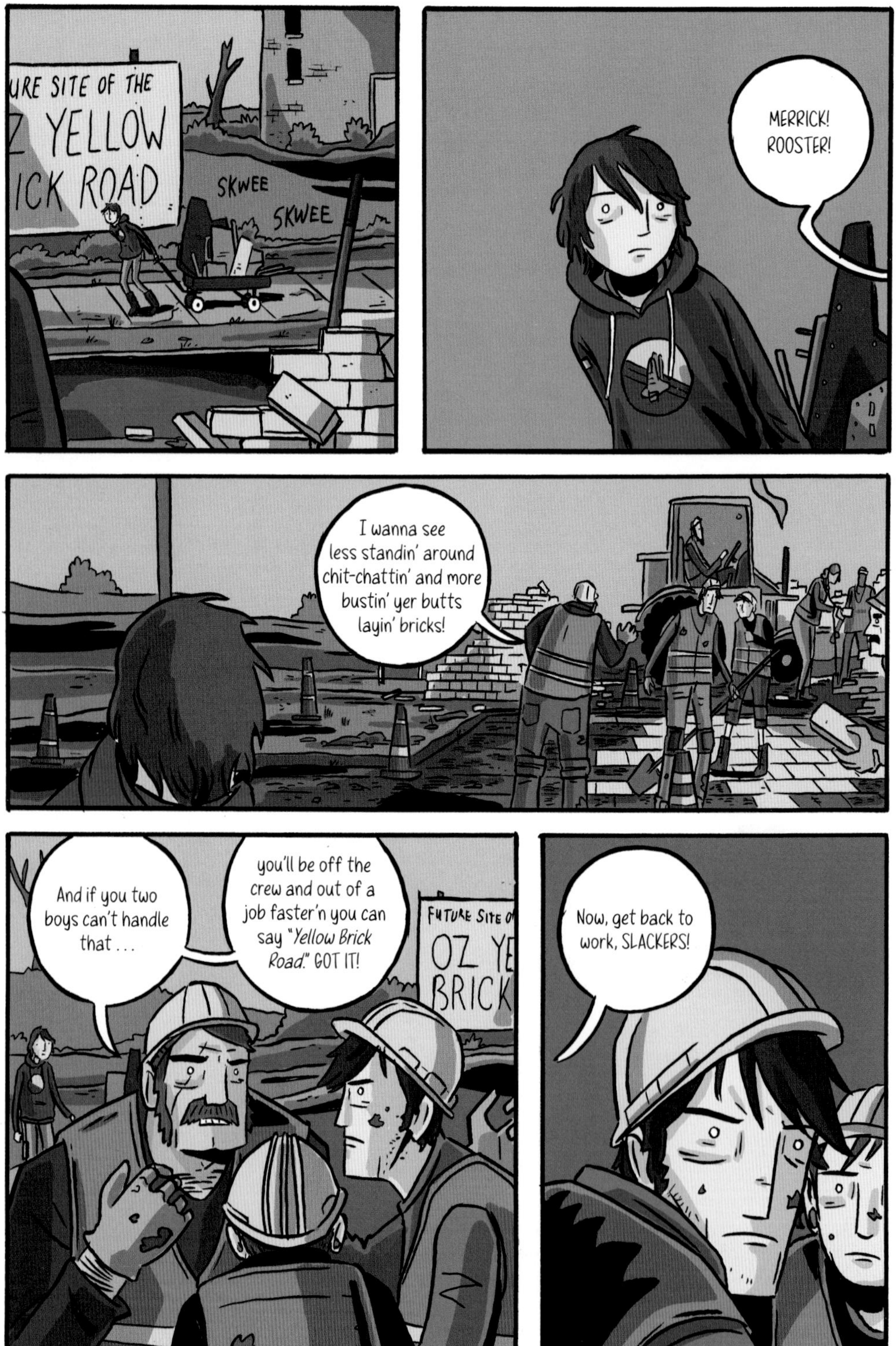
URE SITE OF THE
Z YELLOW
ICK ROAD
SKWEE
SKWEE
MERRICK! ROOSTER!
I wanna see less standin' around chit-chattin' and more bustin' yer butts layin' bricks!
And if you two boys can't handle that . . .
you'll be off the crew and out of a job faster'n you can say "*Yellow Brick Road*." GOT IT!
FUTURE SITE OF
OZ YE
BRICK
Now, get back to work, SLACKERS!

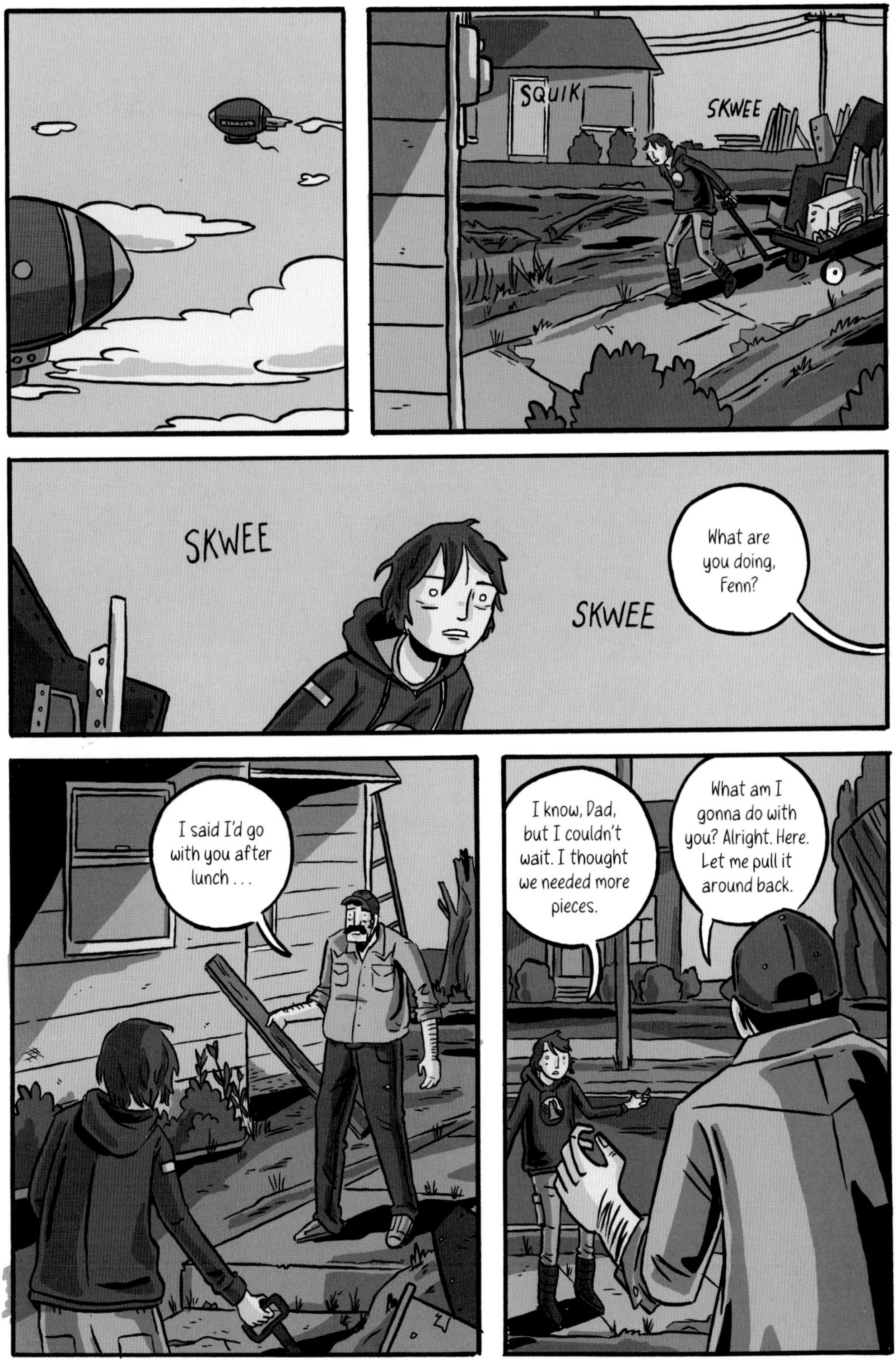
SQUIK
SKWEE
SKWEE
SKWEE
What are you doing, Fenn?
I said I'd go with you after lunch . . .
I know, Dad, but I couldn't wait. I thought we needed more pieces.
What am I gonna do with you? Alright. Here. Let me pull it around back.

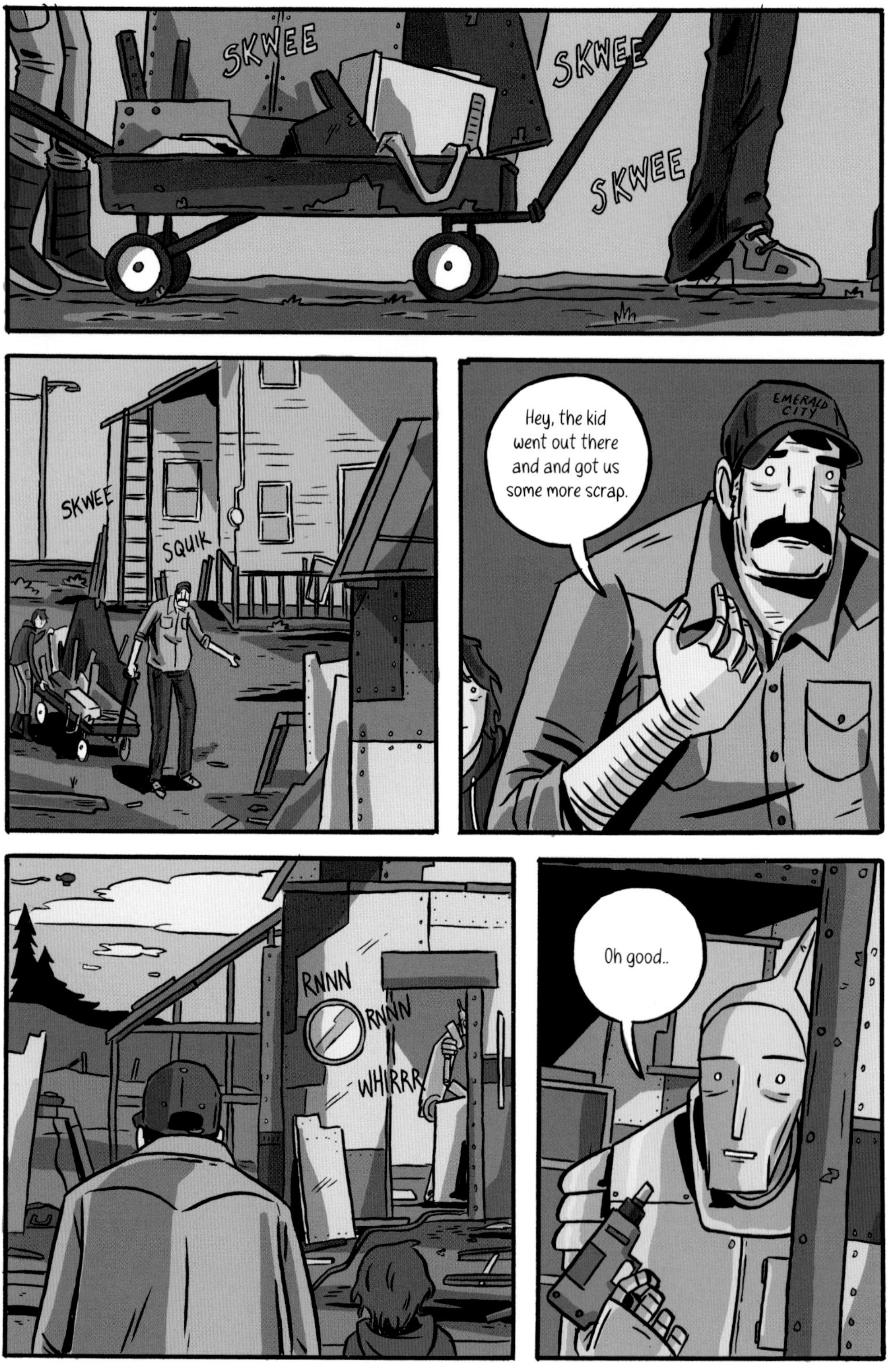
SKWEE
SKWEE
SKWEE
SKWEE
SQUIK
Hey, the kid went out there and and got us some more scrap.
EMERALD CITY
RNNN
RNNN
WHIRRR
Oh good..

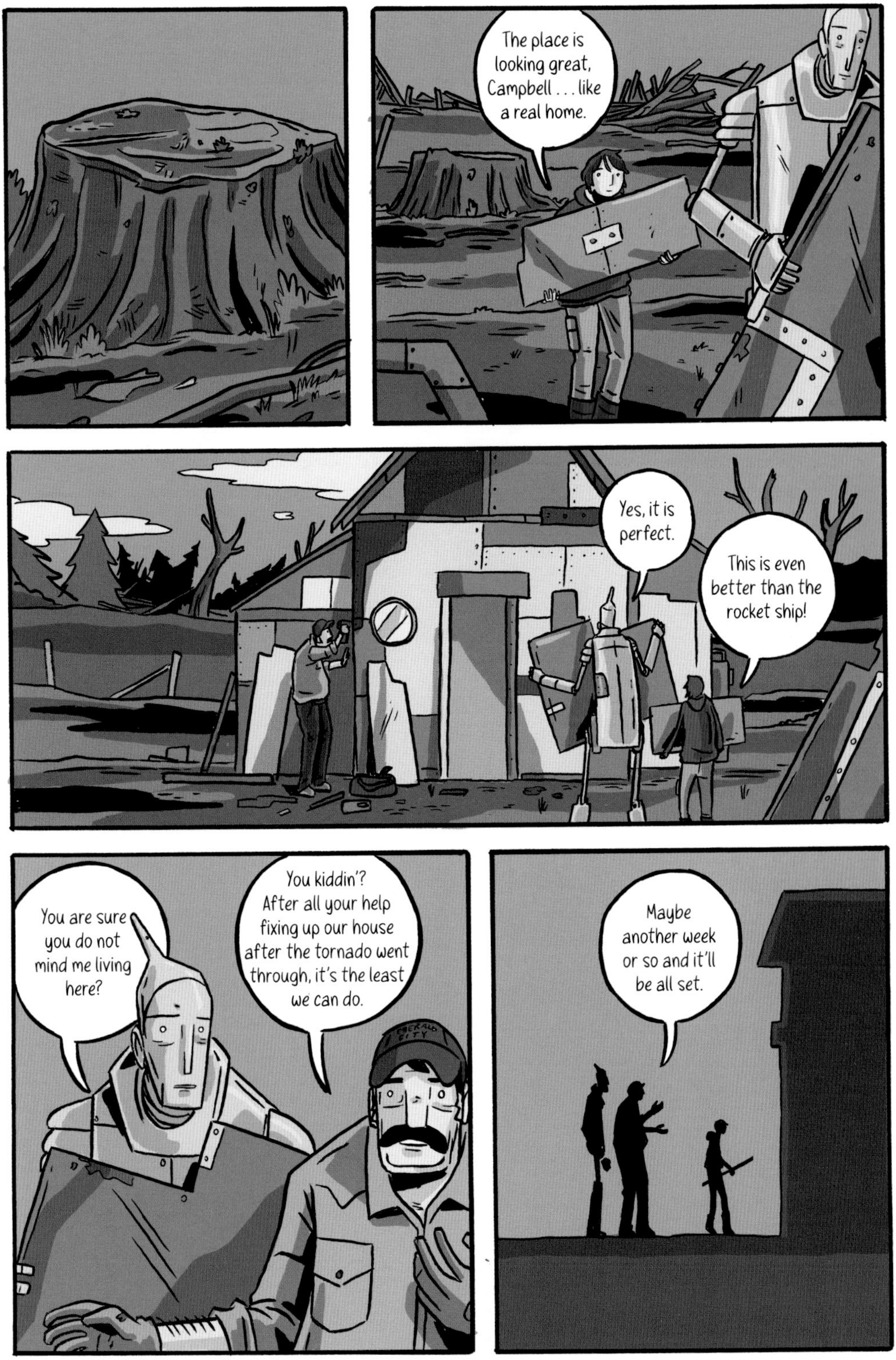
The place is looking great, Campbell . . . like a real home.
Yes, it is perfect.
This is even better than the rocket ship!
You are sure you do not mind me living here?
You kiddin'? After all your help fixing up our house after the tornado went through, it's the least we can do.
Maybe another week or so and it'll be all set.

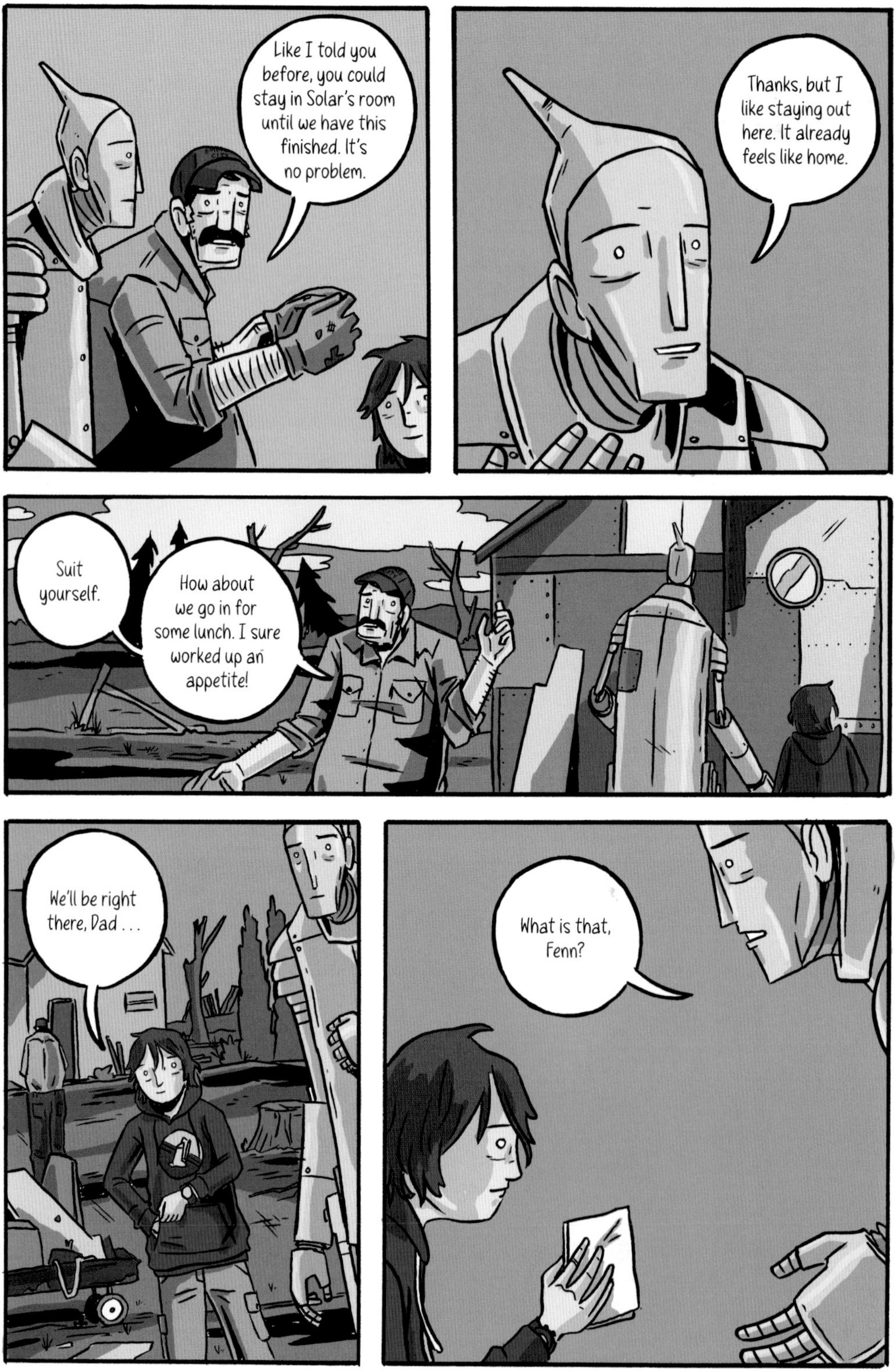
Like I told you before, you could stay in Solar's room until we have this finished. It's no problem.
Thanks, but I like staying out here. It already feels like home.
Suit yourself.
How about we go in for some lunch. I sure worked up an appetite!
We'll be right there, Dad . . .
What is that, Fenn?

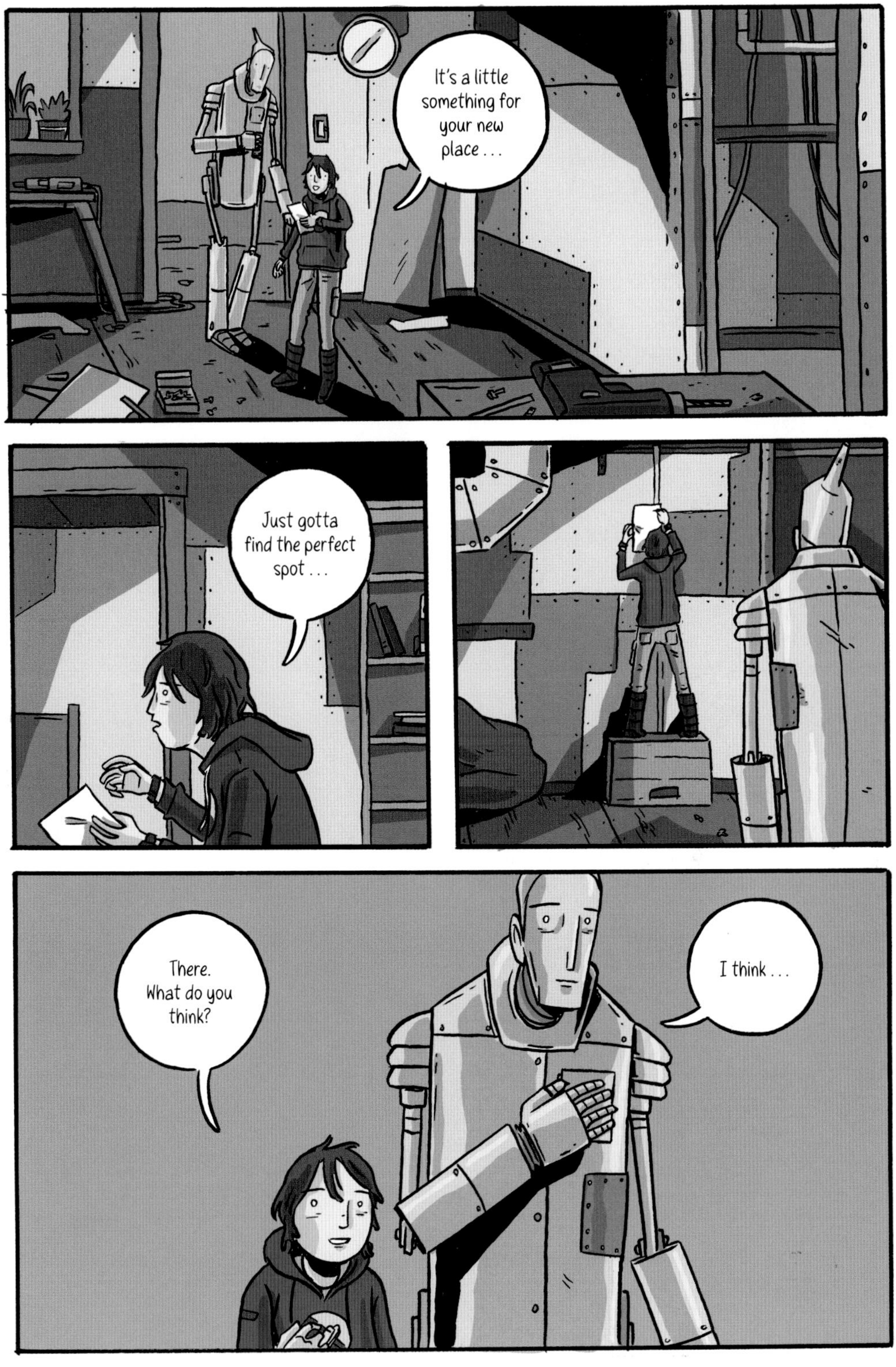
It's a little something for your new place . . .
Just gotta find the perfect spot . . .
There. What do you think?
I think . . .

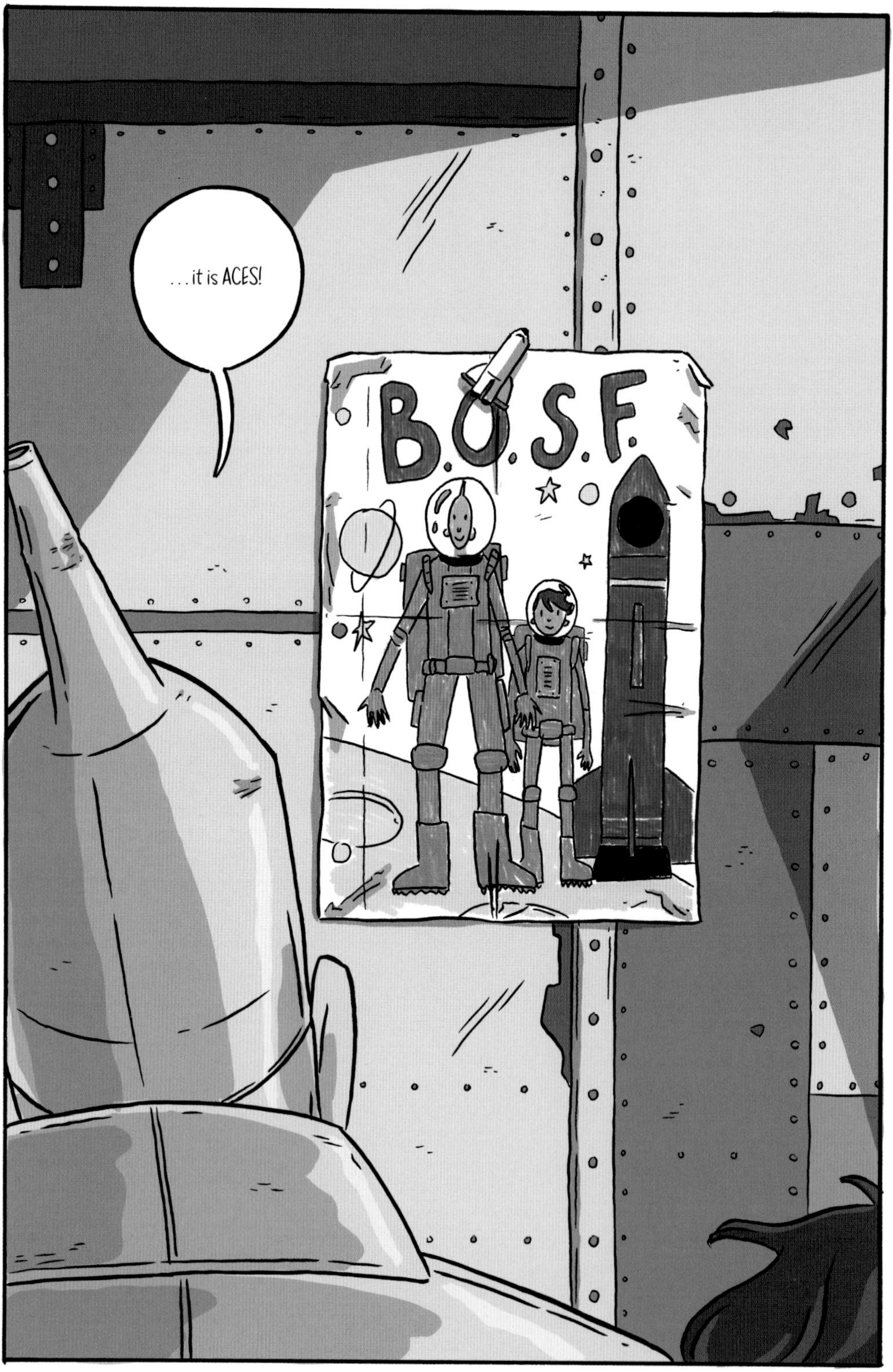
. . . it is ACES!
B.O.S.F

The End

Acknowledgments

First and foremost, a huge thank you goes out to my wife, Kate. Having your endless support throughout the making of this book (and in life) cannot be overstated. You gave me the much-needed nudges and much-needed time to keep this ball rolling. Without you, I'd be like a Tin Man without a heart. I never would have written such a story if not for my kids, Ella and Lincoln. I draw inspiration from you both every day and hope that, just like Solar and Fenn, you stay friends forever.

I owe a great deal to the amazing team at Abrams. Thank you to my excellent editor, Charlotte, for your story insights and direction. To my book designer, Andy, for all your helpful design and coloring advice. And to Charlie, for seeing something in *Tin Man* from the beginning.

Thank you to my agent, Mark, and the folks at Trident Media Group, for finding *Tin Man* such a wonderful home.

Of course, I must give a nod to L. Frank Baum, for there would be no *Tin Man* without the magnificent world that he created.

And a big thank you goes to you, dear reader, for picking up this book and giving Campbell, the Tin Woodsman, a place on your bookshelf, and, perhaps, a place in your heart.

To Ella and Lincoln

Library of Congress Cataloging Number
for the hardcover edition: 2021941599

Hardcover ISBN 978-1-4197-5104-2
Paperback ISBN 978-1-4197-5105-9

Printed and bound in China
10 9 8 7 6 5 4 3 2 1

Amulet Books are available at special discounts when
purchased in quantity for premiums and promotions as
well as fundraising or educational use. Special editions
can also be created to specification. For details, contact
specialsales@abramsbooks.com or the address below.

Amulet Books® is a registered trademark
of Harry N. Abrams, Inc.

ABRAMS The Art of Books
195 Broadway, New York, NY 10007
abramsbooks.com